THE FLIRT

Born in Pittsburgh, Kathleen Tessaro is the author of two previous novels, *Elegance* and *Innocence*, which became bestsellers in both hardback and paperback. She lives in London with her son.

Visit www.AuthorTracker.co.uk for exclusive updates on Kathleen Tessaro.

Praise for Kathleen Tessaro's previous bestsellers:

'More heart than you'll ever find on a catwalk . . . written with élan and panache.'   *Daily Mail*

'It's friendship, not elegance, that proves Louise's real saviour, and the friendships that develop through the book are drawn carefully and with insight.'   *Independent*

'A perfect pick-me-up.'   *Cosmopolitan*

'It's surprising that this is Kathleen Tessaro's first novel as her style shows the confidence and ease of a more seasoned writer. A charming, entertaining novel.'   *Punch*

D0268958

Also by Kathleen Tessaro

Elegance

Innocence

KATHLEEN TESSARO

THE FLIRT

HARPER

This novel is entirely a work of fiction.
The names, characters and incidents portrayed in it are
the work of the author's imagination. Any resemblance to
actual persons, living or dead, events or localities is
entirely coincidental.

Harper
An imprint of HarperCollins*Publishers*
77–85 Fulham Palace Road,
Hammersmith, London W6 8JB

www.harpercollins.co.uk

A Paperback Original 2008
1
Copyright © Kathleen Tessaro 2008

The author asserts the moral right to
be identified as the author of this work

A catalogue record for this book
is available from the British Library

ISBN-13: 978 0 00 721538 6

Set in Bembo by Palimpsest Book Production Limited,
Grangemouth, Stirlingshire

Printed and bound in Great Britain by
Clays Ltd, St Ives plc

This book is proudly printed on paper which contains wood
from well-managed forests, certified in accordance with
the rules of the Forest Stewardship Council.
For more information about FSC,
please visit www.fsc-uk.org

Mixed Sources
Product group from well-managed
forests and other controlled sources
www.fsc.org Cert no. SW-COC-1806
© 1996 Forest Stewardship Council
FSC

Acknowledgements

I'd like to thank Lynne Drew, Claire Bord, Carrie Feron and Maxine Hitchcock at HarperCollins and Jonny Geller at Curtis Brown for their unparalleled editing, guidance and support.

I'd also like to thank Jill Robinson, Debra Susman, Kate Morris, Gillian Greenwood, Liza Campbell, Juliet Nicholson, Bernadette Hoffman and Stephen Harris for sharing their considerable talent, experience and hope with me. Thank you for generously allowing me to steal all your best ideas.

Finally, I owe a huge debt of gratitude to my friends Dr Matthew Knight, Dr Nora Whitehouse Brennan, Annabel Giles, Frances Geary, Jennifer Ward, Bob and Ragni Trotta, Karen Tippet, Keely Deller, Hannah Deller, Trisha Valaydon, Margie Dane and my family, Edward, Anne, Michael and Patrick Tessaro and Martha Nelson. Your actions speak so much more eloquently of love than my words.

La Vie Bohème

The ad appeared in the *Stage* in the second week of September, when the Edinburgh Festival was officially over and real life made its unpleasant appearance again in the collective consciousness of the large number of unemployed young actors who populate the London area.

It read:

> *Unique situation available for an attractive, well-mannered, morally flexible young man. Hours irregular. Pay generous. Discretion a must.*
>
> *Please send photo and brief romantic history to:*
> *Valentine Charles*
> *111 Half Moon Street*
> *Mayfair, London*

Hughie Armstrong Venables-Smythe was sitting at his usual table, next to the window in Jack's Café, armed with a pen he'd nicked from the waitress, a strong cup of builder's tea and his mobile phone, which was running out of credit. Outside, the sun was radiant, the air sharp with a brisk autumn breeze. Elderly shoppers, dragging battered tartan trolleys, paused to examine the merits of the half-price bleach in pink plastic baskets outside the Everything For a Pound shop on Kilburn High Road. Others hurled themselves into bargaining sessions with the red-faced Irish butcher, his bacon suspiciously reasonable.

Here, Hughie was among his people; living the front-line, hand-to-mouth existence of a jobbing actor in NW6, still quite a rough neighbourhood according to his mother, despite the recent boom in house prices.

Spotting the ad, he circled it and leant back, satisfied. In his trade, buying the *Stage* and circling ads was considered an entire day's work. He lit a fresh cigarette to celebrate.

He'd only just started smoking; Marlboro Lights. It was a disgusting habit. He'd picked it up from his girlfriend Leticia, who was full of the most delightfully disgusting habits known to man, of which smoking was easily the most socially acceptable. At twenty-three, it made him feel sophisticated. But then Hughie needed all the help he could get, especially as Leticia was a great deal older than him and more sophisticated than he was ever likely to be. Although they'd only been (he was thinking of calling it 'going out'. But was it really going out if in fact you never went anywhere or did anything but just met several times a week in strange, dark places to have wild, wordless, pornographic sex? Probably not. The proper social heading was more likely to be 'seeing one another', which they'd only been doing for about two weeks), Hughie was already violently in love.

Ah, Leticia!

What was not to love?

Everything about her was perfect – from her glossy, black bob, doe-like brown eyes and soft, pink Cupid's bow lips, to the way she screamed, 'Spank harder, you horny little bastard!' in the alleyway behind the bespoke lingerie shop she ran in Belgravia.

Closing his eyes, he silently thanked the Lord above, as he did many times a day now, for the particular good fortune that forced him to sit down next to her on that crowded number 12 bus. From the first moment he felt her delicate hand creeping up his inner thigh as they passed Marble Arch to the hasty exit they both made at Piccadilly Circus, he'd known that the course of his life was changed for ever. Until that day, God had been little more than a vague concept but afterwards, Hughie concluded that no other force in the universe could've so perfectly answered all of his prayers.

Then, taking another drag, he frowned.

Leticia was a real woman, not some fluffy student. Deliciously perverse, she was also popular, ruthless and easily bored. How was he going to keep her? Love alone was not enough. A diet of non-stop delights and amusements was needed to sweep her off her feet.

Having no money was neither delightful nor amusing.

This was the torment he'd been warned about in drama

school: the very crux of *La Vie Bohème*. Here he was, a struggling young actor caught in the maelstrom of artistic integrity versus commercial demands. He imagined an audience observing his silent heroism and, with a gallant gesture, swept his mop of ash-blond hair back from his handsome face.

In fact, everyone he met expected him to be employed. How few people understood the fragile relationship between working in the acting profession and actually being paid!

Hughie took another drag.

Whatever happened to art for art's sake?

Hughie's mother and sister, Clara, went on endlessly about how was he going to live, to eat, to be a useful member of society, blah, blah, blah. But they were missing the point. And not for the first time, Hughie felt the familiar, frustrating weight of being a Venables-Smythe.

There was a time when being a Venables-Smythe was a destiny; a passport into the world of the English upper classes. However, by the time Hughie was born into the once-illustrious clan, all that was left to inherit was the name, posh accent and a mildly traumatizing public-school education. His grandfather had sold the family pile, priceless antiques and family portraits included, to an American hotel chain in 1977 for what had seemed an enormous amount of money at the time but in retrospect had been a bargain. Instead, he'd bought a badly converted flat in Chelsea, invested heavily in Betamax, and funded Hughie's father, Robert Armstrong Venables-Smythe, in his playboy lifestyle. His father, as attractive as

4

Hughie was now, had a taste for Ralph Lauren shirts, Gucci loafers, Italian cars and bubbly, big-breasted blondes. He met Hughie's mother, Rowena Compton Jakes, a nineteen-year-old, flat-chested brunette, shy to the point of being socially disabled, when she was working in the wedding-list department of Tiffany's. They were married two years later and Robert set up business as a Fulham estate agent. He knew nothing about the property market. He did, however, have a great deal of charm which he expended on long lunches at San Lorenzo with a series of young secretaries who called him Bobby.

When Hughie was five, his father disappeared in a mysterious deep-sea-fishing accident off the coast of Malta. His mother still claimed it was all a hoax but he never returned and his business went quietly bankrupt. This devastating blow signalled the beginning of Hard Times.

However, Hard Times give rise to great acts of heroism. And so it came to pass that Hughie's mother showed her true mettle. She painted the living room red, bought a few scatter cushions from Peter Jones and announced that she was now an interior designer of the Jocasta Innes variety. One stiff early-morning drink took the edge off her shyness. She maintained a veneer of social respectability by shopping at designer second-hand shops and, at tremendous personal sacrifice, sending her children to the best schools. Her single obsession was that they should gain not only the kind of financial security that had eluded both their father and their grandfather, but also launch themselves back into the bosom of their class.

And so, Hughie's older sister Clara diligently won a scholarship to study classics at Cambridge while Hughie, rejected from almost every institution of any note, enrolled in a third-rate drama school in King's Cross, where he set about studying his craft.

Every once in a while, Hughie tried to imagine his father's face. (His mother had systematically eliminated all his photographs.) What might he look like now?

Tucking the cigarette into the side of his mouth, Hughie took out the one remaining photo from his wallet. The faded Polaroid showed Hughie at three, holding his father's hand on a beach in Spain. Robert was bending towards him, his hand pressed into the small of Hughie's back. He was laughing, tanned, happy.

Hughie had studied the photograph for so many hours, over so many years, that it formed a memory where none existed. Sometimes he imagined he could still feel his father's reassuring touch, a firm hand guiding him through the unknown, towards a version of himself he would be proud of.

Hughie slipped the photo back into his empty wallet.

The Unknown: here it was again, looming before him.

He was just back from a three-week stint in Edinburgh performing in an improvised musical about homelessness called *Waste!* He couldn't sing much beyond 'Land of Hope and Glory' but he'd listened to enough Benjamin Britten during his Harrow education to pretend he was obsessed with atonal harmonies. Whenever he hit a sour note, he looked very serious and sang louder. Over time, the rest of the cast came to admire his musical daring. (After the late-night drinking sessions, he'd done a lot more atonal singing than even he'd intended.)

But now he was back in London, living on the sofa in Clara's front room, and money was officially a problem. Actually, Clara was a problem too.

Clara had taken her mother's advice: she worked in a large business PR firm in the City. She walked like a man in heels and wore navy-blue suits, hair in a limp, mousy bob – a look that might have been sexy in a Miss Moneypenny kind of way on anyone else but Clara. Her hours and ambition were such that Hughie hardly ever saw her but she left little yellow Post-it notes telling him what to do (or not, as the case might be). Sometimes, Hughie felt sure that she'd come home in the middle of the day to plaster a fresh supply on everything he'd ever touched. 'This is NOT an ashtray!' on the eighteenth-century porcelain china planter given to her by her fiancé Malcolm (a china specialist at Sotheby's who was so obviously gay to everyone else in the world but Clara). 'Put the seat DOWN!' on the loo lid, 'Buy your OWN MILK!' on the refrigerator and 'Don't forget your fucking KEYS again!' on the back of the door, just as he was about to go out (without his fucking keys). True, he'd only meant to stay a few days but she was being a cow about the whole thing. Nothing had changed between them since he was six and she ten, bossing him around all day like a shorter, fiercer mother, only she was considerably more sober than their mother and therefore more relentlessly eagle-eyed.

Stubbing out his cigarette, he hailed the waitress.

A tiny, auburn-haired girl came over and handed him the bill.

'You don't, by any chance, take Amex, do you?' Hughie smiled. (The Venables-Smythe smile was something to behold – two dazzling rows of even white teeth, punctuated by dimples and a pair of intensely blue eyes.)

'I, ah . . .'

'Look,' he peered at her name tag, 'the thing is, Rose, I'm a bit short of change. But I'm a regular – you've seen me. I'm here almost every day.'

'Yes, yes . . . that's true,' she admitted. 'But this is the third time in a week you've been short.'

'Listen.' He stood up. 'I'll tell you what, why don't you spot me for one more day and I promise, on my mother's grave, that tomorrow I'll come in and make it up to you.' He smiled wider. She blushed bright scarlet. 'So do we have a deal?'

'OK.'

Hughie landed a quick kiss on her cheek. 'You're a star, Rose! An absolute star!' He swung open the door.

'Wait a minute! What's your name?'

'Forgive me! Hughie.' He offered his hand. 'Hughie Armstrong Venables-Smythe. Now, don't give up on me, Rose, will you? I'll be in first thing in the morning, you have my word.' And tucking his copy of the *Stage* under his arm, he left.

Once outside, he picked up a rogue apple rolling just out of sight of the fruit seller on the corner, rubbed it clean on his jeans, took a bite and considered the ad as he strolled home.

Hours irregular. Pay generous. Both sounded just the ticket. But the moral flexibility excited him most. He was uncertain as to the existence of any moral substance in his nature to begin with. How did one know nowadays? What were the criteria? Apart from the most obvious guidelines (would you kill anyone? How do you feel about stealing from old people?), he felt curiously uninformed in this area. It was clear, though, that morally flexible was by far the sexier of the two options.

And Leticia would love him for it.

A Self-Made Woman

Leticia Vane jangled the set of keys in her hand and sauntered down Elizabeth Street. She was the kind of girl (and even nearing her mid-thirties, she still thought of herself as a girl) who was aware of how her body looked and the shapes it made when she moved. Even though there was no one about much before noon in this part of the world, she liked to think she was being watched and that people noticed in her a certain dangerous pleasure.

And indeed, Leticia Vane was in many ways her own finest creation. She'd taken what little rough material nature had allotted her and moulded, shaped, hacked away at it as a sculptor chips away at a hunk of marble.

Nothing remained from her previous life as Emily Ann Fink of Hampstead Garden Suburb. The uni-brow that God had seen fit to adorn her with was gone, plucked into two slim, expressive arches; the overbite long replaced; the dull, brown hair dyed a gleaming black that brought out the colour of her eyes. Her face was pleasing but, understanding that she was no

10

beauty, she'd taken a great deal of time over her figure. She ate once a day and smoked the rest of the time. Dying young was far preferable to dying fat. It had taken a lot of hard work to make Leticia Vane, the kind of work not a lot of people appreciated.

And of course there was the back story, too. One of two children of a chartered accountant and a depressed school-teacher wouldn't do. Leticia wanted something more fascinating. So she transformed her parents into diplomats, serving in faraway countries. She'd been raised in a series of exotic locations; learnt languages (she was far too polite to show them off in public); had affairs at a preternatural age; been doted upon but still suffered from a past too secret and too painful to reveal to anyone.

She'd always longed to be exclusive. Rare. And now she figured she probably had another ten years to really enjoy the fruits of her labours. However, the fragile nature of her accomplishments made them all the more dear.

And so she sauntered, just in case someone was looking out of the window, wondering what that fetching young woman was doing up at this time of day. And with a swagger, she twisted the keys in the lock of the tiny shop.

Bordello was a lingerie shop but it had no shelves, no long lines of silk nothings swinging on rails, no emaciated mannequins with stiff nipples adorned in lace thongs. In fact it looked more like a small, turn-of-the-century Parisian drawing room than a shop. The walls were papered with fine black-and-white stripes,

11

the Louis Quatorze *fauteuils* were covered in ivory raw silk; a rare, cobalt-blue chandelier sent beams of azure light darting around the room. Leticia offered a bespoke service. There were no samples. There were, however, yards and yards of the most exquisite aged silk and satin in the palest colours: champagne, dove grey, pearl and thumb-nail pink. Bolts of filmy organdies were piled into corners and there were baskets with drifts of lace – antique, handmade, tiny works of art she'd collected from all over the globe. On a round mahogany table in the centre of the room, her sketchbooks were piled high, full of her latest creations. There were no changing rooms, only a luxuriously appointed bathroom to the rear, complete with an antique slipper bath, next to a narrow workroom.

Leticia was selling a sexual dream in which each of her clients starred. So she created a stage setting of subtle erotic chic; just glamorous and sensual enough to stir the imaginations of the women she catered to.

And Leticia Vane didn't cater to just anyone. Clients had to be referred. Exclusivity wasn't a matter of money nowadays; everyone and anyone had money. In order to be desirable, you had to be unavailable. Celebrities were the kiss of death to any business; as they went out of fashion, so would you. And she didn't make anything for women who'd had breast implants. Leticia's objections were purely aesthetic. They simply ruined the balance of her creations. She prided herself on being able to lend a hand where nature had been careless or abrupt. Her nightdresses all had inbuilt bras which she fashioned from plaster moulds of her clients' breasts. Discrepancies in size and shape were all catered to and gently adjusted. By raking the insides of each cup, she made the breasts fall forward, spilling recklessly, yet never fully escaping, bound by tissue-thin layers of sheerest net.

She didn't make anything as vulgar as crotchless panties or cut-out bras, but she knew how to heighten the colouring, hand tinting the fabric of each design so that the nipples appeared pink and slightly swollen. And her famous French knickers were so silky and loose that they could easily be pushed to one side without ever completely removing them.

Leticia's greatest asset was that she understood men and sympathized with women. The difficulty with most lingerie was that it repelled the very thing it claimed to enhance. Not every man was thrilled to arrive home after a long day to find his wife trussed up in three hundred pounds' worth of bizarre, lurid corsetry – trying to act sexy in a get-up that had taken her a full half-hour to wriggle into. Both of them would be embarrassed by the effort of such a blatant overture; unsure of how to work various snaps and ties. Then there would be added pressure of having an unprecedented sexual experience that would warrant the expense. Leticia understood that when a woman went to such trouble, it was usually because her sex life had reached a crisis. But the very unfamiliarity of such a costume could make her feel ridiculous and, even worse, desperate. A deliberate performance always increases the possibility of sexual rejection.

Leticia firmly believed that quality was the result of quantity.

Good sex was simply a by-product of having a great deal of all sorts of sex; rough, slow, quick and to the point or dreamy and drawn out, random gropes, teasing touches, full-on oral feasts – all these things qualified as sex to her. And so, to facilitate an unconscious air of sexual susceptibility, she created heightened versions of everyday pieces; deceptively simple white nightdresses, only fashioned from such sheer material and cut so cleverly that they draped the body in a provocative, filmy gauze, accentuating the peek of nipples, hugging the curve of hips, lengthening legs; billowing beguilingly with each movement. Because they appeared so innocent and unassuming, they were undeniably erotic. Instead of shouting, 'Fuck me!' they whispered, 'Take me . . . see . . . I'm not even looking!' The cleverest bit was that, while a man couldn't help but be hypnotized by the erotic undertones, the idea of sex would be his. The pieces compelled a man to act, and made the woman feel languid. She could lie back and lure her husband into action. And a man who initiates sex always feels more virile than one who has it thrust upon him.

Leticia had been taught this invaluable insight along with the rest of her trade by her godfather, Leo. He'd been a West End theatrical costume designer. And like Leticia, he was entirely self-created. He smoked thin, black Russian cigarettes, probably had his nose done back in the sixties and wore his beautiful silver hair loose around his shoulders. His uniform was what he called 'an Audrey' – a black cashmere polo neck, black tailored trousers and soft, leather slippers he had specially made.

He laughed often and firmly refused to countenance any form of self-pity or pessimism.

He came from a different world – not just a theatrical one but from another age entirely – an age that had no qualms about artifice; that had no desire to appear natural, and understood that a little sleight of hand was nothing to be ashamed of. He'd been a dresser to Marlene Dietrich when she used to pin her scalp back under her wig; had sewn sweat guards into Julie Andrews's gowns in *My Fair Lady* and even adjusted the sleeves on Vivian Leigh's costumes so that no one could see her hands shaking after a bad night.

Leticia slipped off her jacket, hung it up on a hook behind the door and looked round with satisfaction. Leo was retired now but he adored the shop. The slipper bath had been his idea. (It shuddered violently if you turned on the taps but it looked exquisite.) He was the only other person who really appreciated her collection of lace or the rare quality of the bolts of beautiful fabric.

If it hadn't been for him, she might still be languishing in Hampstead Garden Suburb. He gave her a subscription to *Vogue* when she was eight. When she was ten, he presented Leticia with a little work table all her own in his studio. There she sat, making sketches, watching carefully as the greatest stage divas of the day were transformed from frightened, self-obsessed neurotics into creatures worthy of universal adoration. In her teens, he took her to the theatre, bought her her first cocktail in Kettner's, showed her how to pluck her eyebrows and move in a way that commanded attention. He taught her the difference between presence, which includes everyone in its warm glow, and attitude, which keeps the whole world at bay.

There was nothing Leo couldn't render magical. Nothing he couldn't fix.

She opened her appointment book and examined the names. A romance novelist, a duchess and a rich American woman from Savannah. She didn't like more than three appointments a day and nothing before 11 a.m. Early morning wasn't sexy; once you were out of bed and dressed, the weight of the day pressed too hard on everyone's conscience.

Her phone buzzed. She flicked it open. It was Leo.

'Angel, how are we this morning?' he purred, his voice tempered by thousands of cigarettes.

'Brilliant. Are you coming in today? Please say you're coming! I've got an order for a silk kimono I can't make drape properly for love nor money. The woman has a bust like a mountain range. I promise to buy you a long, boozy lunch if you can fix it.'

'Would love to but I can't. Feeling a bit rough this morning. Truth is I was up late last night playing strip poker with Juan. You remember Juan, don't you?'

'That male nurse from Brazil?' She riffled through the morning post. Another postcard from her parents in Israel. More brown envelopes. How boring. She tossed them unopened into the bin. 'Didn't you decide he was too young for you? Does he even speak English?'

'Don't be catty, darling. His English has come on a treat. Besides,' she could hear him lighting a fresh cigarette, 'we don't waste our time on conversation.'

'Please! I don't want to know all your secrets!'

'You know them all anyway.'

She smiled. 'I have one.'

'Really? What or rather who is it?'

'Now who's being catty? His name's Hughie and he's delicious!'

'How old?'

'Oh, I don't know . . . early twenties?'

She heard him exhale. 'You need a real man, Leticia. Not some boy.'

'This from you!' She closed the appointment book firmly. 'Real men don't exist. Or haven't you noticed? Besides, he's only a fling.'

'They have feelings, you know.'

'I doubt it. All men want is sex. Especially young men.'

'And what about you? What do you want?'

Her fingers ran over a particularly exquisite and costly bolt of French blue silk organdie. 'Who cares what I want? It's what I can have that matters.'

'Emily Ann . . .'

She winced. 'You know I hate that name; it's so impossibly ugly!'

'Emily,' he repeated firmly, 'I'm concerned. These flings are getting to be a habit with you.'

'And why not? We live in a disposable world. There's no point in investing yourself too heavily.'

'You're too young to be so cynical.'

'Oh, please!' She sighed. 'Let's not do serious today! I can't; I'm not in the mood. I just want to have some fun. And Hughie's fun.'

'He's also real.'

'What am I now, some corrupting influence? No lectures – not today.'

'I'm only saying that you've got to be careful.'

'Stop, Leo,' she warned.

He ignored her. 'You pretend to be tough but we both know you're not.'

'I have to go.'

'Darling, I love you and I don't want to see you hurt.'

'What? By Hughie?' she laughed. 'See, that's the whole point! He can't hurt me! And I can't hurt him. We have rules, Leo. It's strictly sex . . . nothing more.'

'I've got news for you, sunshine. Rules or no rules, you're not in control of your heart. No one is.'

'Listen, I'll call you later. I have heaps to do and if you're not coming round I'll have to try to sort out this kimono monstrosity by myself. Speak later? And no more hot Brazilians, understand?'

She clicked the phone shut, pressed her hand over her eyes. He was being so difficult.

And suddenly, it was back again; the dull ache, pressing hard.

It was an ache now, but for at least a year it had been a searing, slicing pain across her whole chest, like someone performing open-heart surgery without an anaesthetic. She couldn't eat, couldn't sleep . . .

Damn him! Why did he have to be so . . . so judgemental?

She took a deep breath.

It didn't matter. It was all over now. She was on her feet again, better than ever.

In her workshop, Leticia put the kettle on and lit a cigarette. There was time between the duchess and the novelist to have Hughie come round. And leaning her back against the counter, she inhaled deeply and closed her eyes.

Hughie was so tall, so young, so classically handsome. And so easy to control! There were no power struggles, no coy dating rituals or manipulations. She rang, he came, they fucked. And then they fucked some more.

It was a simple relationship and, in a way, beautiful. There was something different about Hughie: a freshness. No deep thoughts or dark moods interfered with his performance. Of course, he had a lot to learn; a diamond in the rough. But that was exciting. And the best part was, he was insane about her. It was only a fling, but in every relationship there was the one who adored and the one who was adored. She'd done the adoring and preferred by far when it was the other way round.

The kettle boiled. Spooning the loose leaves of Earl Grey tea carefully into a Tiffany blue pot, she poured in the hot water. The aroma of bergamot filled the room.

She stared out of the window into the small garden at the back.

Leo was wrong. No one could hurt her again; she wouldn't let them.

Giving the tea a quick stir, she poured herself a cup. These were the hours she liked best; the day glimmered before her like a golden promise, untouched by disappointment or frustration. And sitting down at the table, she placed her teacup on a small bench well away from her work, unfolded a tissue-paper parcel full of silk and deftly threaded her needle.

The morning sun warmed her back, outside birds sang. Leticia sipped her tea.

Few things were more fragile than antique lace or the human heart.

Then she heard something.

Persistent, irritating.

Coming from the bathroom.

A dripping sound.

The kind of sound, in fact, that signalled the urgent need for a plumber.

Tea for Table Five

The waitress at Jack's Café, Rose, paused by the window, watching as Hughie Armstrong Venables-Smythe sauntered away down the street through the crowds of people.

'Order up!' shouted Bert from the kitchen behind her.

'I said, order up!' he called again.

Rose turned and delivered the two fried eggs, sausage, beans and tomato to the man at table seven before clearing away Hughie's breakfast remains. Then she took £4.95 from her own pocket of tips and put it into the till.

'Rose! Tea for table five!' Bert shouted. 'What the hell's got into you today?'

'Nothing,' she said, pouring out the tea. 'Nothing at all.'

She took it over to Sam the plumber, a regular at table five. In his late thirties, Sam had a mop of dark unruly hair, now flecked with grey, wild pale green eyes and a sardonic smile. He'd inherited his father's floundering plumbing and heating business earlier that year; along with the same ready laugh and long, loping gait. He was poring over a catalogue of plastic U-bend pipes.

'Thanks.' He took a sip, frowning with concentration.

'God, Sam, don't you ever take a break?'

'What for?' he shrugged. 'It's my business now; no one's going to make it a success but me.'

'But U-bends at breakfast?' She shook her head. 'Your dad was always more relaxed.'

'Yeah, well, if my old man had put as much time into the business as he did into going to the pub, he might still be with us.' His voice was sharp.

Old Roy, Sam's dad, had lived in the same block of council flats as Rose; she'd known both of them for years. He'd been a larger-than-life character, equally popular with men and women; a man whose cheeky good humour seemed to exempt him from the normal rules of life. Over the years he and Sam, both stubborn characters, had spent a lot of time at logger-heads. Sam was ambitious and Old Roy was usually hungover. But now that he was gone, Rose detected an edginess to Sam; a cloud of uncharacteristic seriousness coloured his personality. Lately he only had time for one thing: his career.

'Sorry, Sam, I'm not thinking today.' She pushed a cloth absent-mindedly around the tabletop, knocking the sugar over. 'Oh, damn!'

He glanced up; clear eyes surrounded by a thick fringe of lashes. 'Off in your dream world again?'

'What are you talking about?'

'Well,' he put his mug down, 'he kissed you, didn't he, Red?' Sam was nothing if not observant.

22

'So what if he did?' She was blushing again. Turning, she pretended to be deeply engrossed in removing a coffee stain from another table. 'And don't call me Red. I'm too old for nicknames. I'm nearly twenty-two, not some child.'

'Yeah. Sure.'

Without looking round, she knew he was laughing.

'You like him,' Sam teased.

'Oh, I don't know,' Rose tried to sound blasé and sophisticated. Unfortunately, she was too excited to keep up the pretence for long. 'But I think he likes me. He's coming back tomorrow!'

'Did he pay his bill?'

'Well, he would've, only we don't take Amex.'

Sam rolled his eyes. 'Every time he comes in, you end up out of pocket.'

'He's just short of cash, that's all. A lot of people don't get paid till the end of the month.' She knotted her hair back in a ponytail at the nape of her neck. (Now that he was gone, she could put it up again.) 'I think he looks like Prince William.'

'Why don't you meet a nice normal guy?'

'And where would I find the time for that?' she asked, irritated. 'Remember, I have a child to feed. Who wants to go out with a single mother?'

'Oh, bollocks, Rose! You're only young! There will be plenty of guys. You know, real guys – with cash instead of promises.'

Rose made a face at him.

'Speaking of kids, how is Rory?' he asked.

She sighed. 'He bit another kid in nursery yesterday.'

'Well, all of them go through tricky patches when they start school.'

'You don't understand.' She gathered up all the ketchup dispensers and began refilling them. 'He bit the little boy who's allergic to nuts, wheat and milk; this kid hardly has anything to live for! And the day before that he headbutted the teacher. She had a lump on her forehead the size of an egg!'

'Well . . .' She'd obviously stretched his bachelor experience to the limit. 'I wouldn't worry about him. Now,' he shifted the subject back to more familiar ground, 'what are we going to do with you?'

'Me?' Rose wiped the shiny lids clean.

'Yes, you. You're a smart girl. Don't you think it's time you did something more than waitressing?'

She smiled wryly. 'Not all of us are business tycoons, Sam.'

He arched an eyebrow. 'What does that mean? Listen, I'll make a going concern of this business if it kills me. If you think I'm going to live and die like my dad in a council flat in Kilburn, you're wrong.'

'Hey!' She swatted him with her tea towel. 'What's wrong with that, I'd like to know?'

'What's wrong with what?'

They turned.

It was Ricki, Rose's cousin. Ricki worked as a landscape gardener for a company in Islington. With her cropped hair, tanned muscular frame and uniform of heavy work boots, a

24

fitted T-shirt and jeans slung low across her hipbones, showing off her firm, flat belly, she looked handsome rather than pretty. Every day she stopped in on her way to work for a takeaway coffee and toast. Hands thrust deep into her pockets she strolled over, grinning slyly at Sam.

'He's not banging on about conquering the world with his plunger again, is he?' She gave his shoulder a squeeze. 'How many times do we have to tell you? It's OK that you're insane and power crazy. We support you.'

'Thanks. I feel a lot better.'

'How's it going anyway?' She slid in across from him, picked up the catalogue. 'Wow. Fascinating. You know, you ought to get out more.'

'I know, I know,' he admitted, running his long fingers through his shaggy curls. 'But if I can get the business to turn a profit this year, then pretty soon I'll be able to expand, take on a few more guys. I mean, my old man left it in a real state. Everything was about flying by the seat of your pants with him. You want to know what his filing system was? A cardboard box shoved under the kitchen sink.'

Ricki stole a slice of toast from his plate. 'You could do with a bit more flying by the seat of your pants.'

'What's that supposed to mean?'

'It means,' she tore off a bite, 'that you're too bloody serious. When was the last time you went out?'

'You don't get it.'

Ricki looked at him. 'I do get it. You miss him.'

Sam shifted, stared out the window. 'Yeah. Well . . . actually,' he changed the subject, 'I was picking on Rose for a change.'

'Oh, yeah?' Ricki grabbed Rose's hand, pulled her down onto her knee. 'I'll take some of that action. So what are we picking on her for today?'

'Piss off!' Rose squirmed but Ricki was strong and held her fast.

'I'm thinking she can do better than Jack's Café, what do you think?'

'I agree. Two thousand per cent.'

'And that blond guy she likes gave her a kiss today!' Sam added.

'No way? Posh Pants?'

'Enough!' Rose managed to wriggle free. 'I don't need career or love advice from you two losers! Besides,' she straightened her apron imperiously, 'I've got plans.'

Sam and Ricki looked at each other. 'Ooooooooo-ooowwwww!'

'Like what?' Sam wanted to know.

'They're private,' Rose sniffed, heading back to the kitchen to get Ricki's coffee. 'But rest assured, it doesn't involve pouring you idiots cups of tea all day long!'

'Good. Glad to hear it,' Ricki called after her. She looked at Sam, shook her head. 'Fuck.'

'Yeah, that about sums it up,' he agreed. 'You OK?'

'Just tired,' Ricki yawned. 'And lonely. And tired of being lonely.'

Sam finished off his tea. 'So get a girlfriend.'

'Yeah, right. If it were that easy, even you would have one by now.'

'Hey, I'm not lonely!' he objected. 'I'm just too fascinating and busy and . . .'

'Old?'

'Yeah, old. You could always lower your standards.'

Ricki snorted. 'I will if you will.'

'Actually,' he considered, 'I'd rather be alone.'

'Me too.'

Rose came back with her order and, handing her a fiver, Ricki stood up. 'Well, I'd better get my skates on; I've got a new client today.' She kissed Rose on the cheek. 'Give me a ring if you need a hand with Rory this week, OK?'

'OK. Thanks.'

'And you,' Ricki turned to Sam, 'take care of yourself. Don't get too obsessed about work. Take it easy.'

'I'll take it easy when I've retired early to my holiday home in Tuscany.'

'Yeah, well, ciao, baby!'

Sam picked up the catalogue again.

Rose replaced the ketchup dispensers.

The breakfast rush was over.

Straightening a few chairs, Rose propped open the door. Fresh air rushed in. She closed her eyes; it felt cool and refreshing on her face.

Her luck was turning; she could feel it. Not only had the

man she'd had a crush on for two weeks finally noticed her but she also had a job interview; the first real interview of her life. And wasn't just any job; it was prestigious – for the position of junior assistant to the acting assistant household manager of a grand house in Belgravia.

Number 45 Chester Square.

Belgravia.

Even the name had poetry!

Last Saturday afternoon, she'd taken Rory there on the bus, just to make certain she knew where she was going. They'd stopped in front of number 45, with its tiers of neat window boxes and round bay trees bordering the front door. The brass knocker in the shape of a lion's head gleamed against the lustrous black paint. The windows sparkled in the sun. Everything was even, balanced; pleasing to the eye.

Nothing bad could ever happen in a house as beautiful as this. A longing filled Rose's chest. She wanted to have her own front-door key. She'd step inside and find a world marked by ease and elegance, a world completely removed from the one she inhabited now.

Perched behind the till, Rose took out a copy of *Hello!* magazine, losing herself in the glossy pages of celebrity photos.

The café was peaceful; quiet.

Then Sam's phone rang.

'Yes? Yes, that's right. A drip? What kind of drip? Oh. A gush, eh? Yeah, well,' he checked his watch, 'I could come by now but I may not be able to fix the whole thing today.' He collected his things. 'What's the address?'

A pack of off-duty dustmen piled through the door. Sam pushed past them, waving to Rose as he went.

Rose nodded back.

In a few short days, life was bound to become very interesting indeed. But until then, there were tables to serve.

45 Chester Square

Olivia Elizabeth Annabelle Bourgalt du Coudray sat in the gold-and-blue breakfast room of number 45 Chester Square, twisting the enormous diamond eternity ring round on her finger, waiting for her husband's wrath to begin.

She'd made the mistake of getting up in the night, waking her husband. So he'd spent the entire night tossing round as violently as he could, whipping the sheets on and then kicking them off again, pulling at the pillow and sighing in frustration. And now, sick with nerves, Olivia sat holding her cup of coffee, knowing that as soon as he came down he'd lecture her and accuse her of keeping him up.

Her husband, Arnaud, liked to get angry. Along with Cuban cigars, and being recognized in public, it was one of his favourite things. There was nothing like a good rant to start the day off; his eyes lit up and his skin glowed. It didn't matter that he owned half of the world's tennis-ball factories or that his family wealth was such that he was regarded as a political figure in France (his views were petitioned on everything from the future of the European Union to cheese production). Even billionaires could have their peace destroyed by an insomniac wife.

As one of six daughters of the famous Boston Van der Lydens, Olivia had spent her youth gliding between New York, the Hamptons and the French Riviera, lingering in Boston only so long as it took to scrape together a degree in Art History. She'd been privileged, emulated; photographed regularly for *Vogue* and *Harper's Bazaar*. When Arnaud began his rigorous courtship of her, the American press greeted it as a union between two shining stars in the international social firmament. But here in England she was virtually invisible. And in Paris with Arnaud's family, she felt positively gauche. It didn't help that Arnaud's mother, the fearsome Comtesse Honorée Bourgalt du Coudray, followed her around her own wedding reception at the Paris Opéra correcting her French and apologizing for the state of her new daughter-in-law's hair.

Olivia glanced up, catching sight of her reflection in the oval mirror that hung across the room. She possessed the wholesome American glamour that inspires Ralph Lauren and Calvin Klein; athletic good cheer coupled with classical features. Her blonde hair was thick and even, her blue eyes large, her cheekbones high, but, as she'd heard her mother-in-law declare loudly one evening to Arnaud, 'She's unremarkable, bland, no cachet.' Then she'd uttered the damning verdict that had obsessed Olivia ever since. 'Why choose fromage frais when you could easily afford camembert?'

Even now, the spectre of her mother-in-law haunted her; a constant front-row critic in her head.

Bland. Unremarkable. The Comtesse had only articulated what she had suspected all along: she was a fraud; a pale imitation of a person with no real talents or original thoughts, no tangible purpose in life. Her beauty and breeding had been sufficient for so many years. And now that she was forty, even those were fading.

Olivia was Arnaud's second wife. By the time she married him, he already had two grown-up children, a huge social network spanning several continents, a daunting diary of engagements, houses all over the world, a variety of businesses, and armies of staff. He also had a reputation as an incurable playboy. At the time, she'd been foolish enough to think she could influence him. But after ten years of marriage, the opposite had happened.

And she'd failed in the one role nature might have provided.

No wonder Arnaud had grown so indifferent.

She sipped her coffee.

It was cold.

He had always been difficult, dictatorial. But before, she'd occupied a privileged position in his psyche; she was the prized object, perfect, unassailable.

Last year changed all that.

She'd wanted children so badly, for so long. Then she finally discovered she was pregnant. No longer clinging, limpet-like to Arnaud's life, she developed poise and sureness. Best of all it endowed her husband with the one thing money couldn't buy. He was young again, about to be a father; bursting with unassailable masculinity. Hand over her growing bump, he ferried her around London with pride. Never before had they been so close. Together they'd chosen nursery furniture, selected schools, debated names.

Then at eighteen weeks, she woke in the middle of the night. There was blood, sticky and warm, between her legs and pain, like a tightening fist, gripping her torso.

Arnaud was out of the country. She'd gone alone to the hospital. The delivery was long, painful.

She never saw her child; never held it.

Arnaud refused to mention the miscarriage. Instead, he bought her the eternity ring: flawless; gleaming; hideously expensive.

Night-time haunted her ever since.

So Olivia sat, holding the cold coffee in the beautifully decorated Regency-inspired gold-and-blue breakfast room of Chester Square. Behind her, on the mantelpiece, the ghastly ormolu clock the Comtesse had given them as a wedding present ticked loudly.

Fifteen minutes later Arnaud descended. At sixty-two, he was still tanned and trim; he was an avid tennis player and kept up to three yachts moored in Monte Carlo, depending on his mood. His black hair was thinning. He had it trimmed each morning by his valet so that it fell over any balding patches. He shook his head now, it tumbled into place.

33

Olivia ran her fingers over her hair; there was the familiar fear of being less than satisfactorily groomed in his presence.

Gaunt, the butler, stalked in, delivering fresh coffee and toast with grim formality.

'Good morning, sir.'

Arnaud grunted.

Gaunt slunk away.

For a while Arnaud said nothing; tossed his toast aside, folded open the paper loudly . . .

Then, of course, she had to ask. 'How did you sleep?'

His black eyes narrowed. He put the paper down. 'How did I sleep? Let me ask you, how do you think I slept?'

'I don't know.'

'Badly! That's the answer: badly!'

'I'm sorry,' she faltered.

'Up and down! Up and down! What do you do all night?'

'I don't know. I'm sorry, Arnaud.'

'You need a pill! You need to go to the doctor and get a pill.'

'Yes.' She stared hard at her plate, at the black interlocking chain design that bordered its silvery white edges.

'I'll have my things moved into another room if this goes on.' He pushed away from the table. 'I have important things to attend to. Gaunt! Gaunt!'

'Yes, sir?' Gaunt appeared out of thin air.

'Get Mortimer on the phone for me! I promised Pollard supper at the Garrick tonight. We have to discuss marketing strategies.' He tossed his napkin down.

'Yes, sir.'

'I want the car out front in forty minutes.'

'Very good, sir.'

'Will you . . .' Olivia hesitated.

He stared at her. 'Yes? Will I what?'

She hated asking the question; her voice sounded small, plaintive. 'Will you be home tonight?'

'Sweetheart, what have I just said? I'm meeting Pollard at the Garrick tonight. Perhaps if you slept at night instead of wandering around like a cat I wouldn't have to repeat myself.'

He stalked away, taking the paper and his coffee with him. Halfway up the stairs, she could hear him ranting at Kipps, the valet, who'd placed his slippers on the wrong side of the bed. Eventually a door slammed.

In the silence that followed, Olivia was aware of countless pairs of unseen eyes upon her; witnesses to their growing domestic disharmony. The months that Arnaud had spent wooing her belonged to another lifetime.

His personality was so strong, so forceful; he always knew exactly what he wanted and what to do. Then he turned the full glare of his powerful attention on her. Her initial indifference spurred him into unprecedented romantic gestures. Fresh boxes of flowers were delivered to her each morning; gifts of diamond earrings, a sapphire ring, even a rare black pearl necklace, were sent from the finest jewellers. Once he bought her a Degas sketch she'd casually admired in a Bonham's catalogue. They'd travelled in his private jet to exotic locations all over the world where her every need was quickly catered for. She receded into the shadow of his larger-than-life persona. It was a relief to slot into a readymade life; where every decision was made for you.

But all that was gone now.

Slowly, she pushed her chair back.

Suddenly Gaunt was there again, picking up the napkin from the floor, folding it, holding the door open.

'May I get you anything, ma'am?'

His attentiveness almost felt like kindness. The prick of tears threatened. 'No,' she forced a smile. 'Breakfast was lovely. Just perfect. Thank you.'

She wandered out into the hallway. Hours stretched out before her, empty and unbearable.

'Begging your pardon . . .' Gaunt hovered like a dark shadow in the doorway.

'Yes?'

'The gardener would like a word about the new water feature.'

'Oh. Of course.'

Olivia followed him outside.

It was a London garden: a small courtyard leading to a narrow patch of grass, augmented by neat rows of flower beds. A tiny fountain trickled away in one corner and there were three long, slender eucalyptus trees near the back wall for privacy.

A dark-haired young man was waiting with his back to her.

He turned as Olivia stepped forward into the sunlight; for

a moment its rays blinded her. But as her eyes adjusted, she realized that he was in fact a she; a tall, tanned young woman with dark, cropped hair. She was wearing a white T-shirt, her thumbs hooked into her pockets. Her dark eyes met Olivia's, lips parting into a slow smile.

'This is Ricki, the gardener,' Gaunt introduced them.

'Hi.' She offered a firm handshake. 'So, you want to get rid of this fountain, is that right?'

'Yes, it makes the most irritating dribbling sound.'

'Humm. It's easily done. Have you thought about what sound you want it to make?'

'You mean I can choose?'

'Yeah, water makes different sounds depending on the material the feature's made of, how high the drop is, the depth of pool underneath . . . it's up to you. Personally, I'd move it out of the corner, get something a bit more dramatic going, right here,' she indicated the centre of the lawn, 'right down the middle. Do you have any kids?'

'No,' Olivia replied sharply. 'Why?'

'Nothing. Only kids and water don't mix; it's dangerous.'

'Oh. Yes. Of course.'

'But since that's not a problem,' Ricki continued, 'we could do something fantastic. An aluminium gulley, maybe, running the full length of the lawn.' She strode into the centre. 'Water can be fed in from a tall black slate waterfall here at the back, against this wall. See, the aluminium catches the light, contrasts with the density of the slate. Really stunning! And in the summer when the grass is bright green, it's like a silver blade, cutting the lawn in two. Placed high enough it makes the most wonderful, rolling sound, you know, no burbling or babbling brook bullshit, but something strong, soothing . . . What do you think?'

The vision of a blade of water slicing across the lawn intrigued Olivia. And Ricki's enthusiasm was compelling. 'Oh, yes! That sounds beautiful! There's only one thing: my husband will hate it.'

Ricki laughed, shrugged her shoulders. 'So what?'

'You don't know my husband,' Olivia smiled wryly. 'It's safer if we go for something a little more traditional.'

'Let me guess, a seashell bird bath with a peeing cherub on top?'

'Yes, that sounds more like what he was expecting,' she admitted.

Ricki shook her head, looking at her hard with those large black eyes. 'Sometimes the most dangerous thing you can do is play it safe. We could do something really interesting here – something bold.'

To her surprise Olivia blushed. 'Well, yes, but . . .'

'Pardon me, madam.'

It was Gaunt again.

'Simon Grey from the Mount Street Gallery is waiting in the drawing room. He doesn't have an appointment but he says it's a matter of some urgency.'

'Of course.' She turned back to Ricki. 'I'm sorry, I must go.'

38

'So, it's peeing cherubs all round?'

'Yes. Yes, I'm afraid so. Lovely to meet you.'

Ricki tilted her head. 'And lovely to meet you.'

Heading back into the house, Olivia felt perplexed. Simon, here, at this hour? How strange.

Simon Grey was the curator of the Mount Street Gallery, which she generously helped fund for the promotion of young artists. At his urging, she'd recently become chairman. They were opening their biggest show ever in two weeks' time: The Next Generation, featuring the work of a controversial new performance artist named Roddy Prowl.

Art was one thing that ignited Olivia's whole being. She often regretted she had no ability herself. Not that she'd ever dared to take a drawing course. But when she first expressed a desire to paint at the age of nine, her parents steered her firmly towards the old masters.

'*This* is painting,' her mother explained, removing a bit of lint gingerly from her daughter's otherwise immaculate school uniform. 'So don't even try.'

'When a Van der Lyden attempts, a Van der Lyden succeeds!' her father boomed in his gin-soaked voice.

They suggested art history instead. 'So much more useful and infinitely less messy than dabbling with paint.'

Perhaps this is what inspired Olivia's appetite for the postmodern.

She pushed open the drawing-door door. 'Simon. Oh, dear! Simon?'

39

Normally fastidious and fearsomely arranged in the manner of only the truly visually gifted, Simon's state of disarray was shocking. His sleek dark hair was all on end, his trademark Paul Smith scarf askew; he paced the floor like a caged animal. In an instant, she knew something was terribly wrong.

'What's happened?'

'Olivia, it's nothing short of a disaster! Roddy Prowl's checked himself into rehab! He refuses to come back!' Tears filled his prodigiously lashed brown eyes; his long aquiline nose flared red at the end. 'We have no *enfant terrible*, Olivia! The entire show is ruined!'

Free Lunch or a Shag

Come and have your evil way with me.

When Hughie got the text message from Leticia, he was busy rifling through his sister Clara's things, looking for a stamp and already bordering on late for meeting his mother for lunch. He wanted to post his response to the ad in the *Stage* that morning, and luncheon was a standing date he and his mother had for the first Wednesday of every month at a small hotel in Victoria called the Goring. There the staff remembered Rowena Venables-Smythe and treated her like a society widow. Together they would feast on the enormous roasts, argue and gossip; his mother would try to force him into some sort of employment; Hughie would charm her and leave with whatever spare cash she had in her wallet. The meal itself was one of the highlights of Hughie's month; he rarely slept the night before for excitement – Scottish roast beef, fluffy Yorkshire pudding, piles of crispy potatoes drenched in gravy, all washed down with something Mum had chosen to impress the wine waiter. (Lunch with Mum was early enough in the day to be manageable. By supper, she was often a bit liquid for Hughie's taste.)

But now there was a rival invitation from Leticia. Visions of her long naked limbs, creamy white against the black velvet chaise longue, stretched out for his personal use made him swoon with lust.

Hughie found himself facing one of the most difficult dilemmas of a young man's life: free lunch or a shag?

He tipped out one of Clara's handbags, found a book of stamps at the bottom and took one. Then he pulled a jumper over his head and bounded out the door – ignoring Clara's Post-it about not forgetting his keys.

Of course, it might just be possible to have the best of both these offers. Leticia's shop was only a few blocks from the Goring. An enterprising young man like Hughie might find himself fucked, fed and funded by tea time.

All it would take was a bit of finessing.

Hughie shoved his letter into a postbox and flagged down a passing cab. 'Hey, I say, you don't take Amex, do you?'

'Fuck off,' suggested the cabby, driving away.

Hughie ran to catch the bus, dodging traffic to cross the road in time.

'Single to Victoria,' he panted to the driver.

'Two pounds.'

'Oh.' Hughie pulled out a few loose coins from his pockets. 'As much as that?'

An old man pushed past him and a woman with a pram.

'What's that? Seventy? Seventy-three, seventy-four . . .'

The driver glared at him. 'Have you got it or haven't you?'

'I'll spot you.'

Hughie turned. It was Malcolm, Clara's fiancé.

'That's very good of you, Malc.'

'Think nothing of it! Glad to help!'

Hughie climbed to the top deck and Malcolm struggled up the steps after him.

Malcolm was pretty much the same height and build as Hughie only his centre of gravity resided in his bottom, pulling at him like an undertow. (In prep school he was known as 'Girlie-Arse Gritton'.) As for his features, everything was just a bit too much; his lips were too thick and red, his nose too long, his eyes bugged out and were framed by strawberry-blond lashes, matching the pinky blond mane on his head. Then, too, he smelt disturbingly of violets.

He threw himself down next to Hughie, or rather almost on top of him, the seat being too snug for grown men.

'Thanks for paying my fare.'

'Think nothing of it! What are friends for, right? We are friends, you and I?' Malcolm looked at him eagerly, blinking his bug eyes.

Hughie hesitated. This wasn't entirely accurate. If he hadn't been engaged to his sister, Hughie would've preferred to avoid Malcolm. But a man down on his luck couldn't afford to be pedantic.

'Sure,' Hughie smiled.

'Good stuff! Very good stuff. Oh, God, Hughie! I can't tell you how difficult things are for me at the moment!'

'Really?' Hughie forced a window open. (The violet water was particularly strong today.)

'Yes! I need a break. Maybe a drink with some friends.' He stared at Hughie, who was busy eyeing up an Aston Martin that growled into view.

'Good plan,' Hughie agreed, wondering if the driver of the Aston was under or over thirty (these questions being of significance to young men who hadn't yet made their first million).

'I was hoping you'd say that!'

'I can always be counted on to endorse a drink.'

'So, what time would you like to meet?'

'For what?'

Malcolm peered at him with an anxious smile. 'Drinks, silly! You said you were my friend.'

'Yes, yes. But that's different from . . . I mean, it's not the same as having one's own friends.'

Malcolm straightened. 'For God's sake, Hughie, I'm engaged to your sister!'

'Yes, I know. She's a lovely girl, don't you think?'

Malcolm winced, as if retreating from an unseen belt across the jaw. 'Yes, a lovely girl.'

Hughie had an idea. 'Maybe she'd like to come along?'

'Perhaps . . .' Malcolm agreed, slowly. 'Then again, there's also nothing to prevent us from having a quiet drink on our own.'

'I just don't think I've got the time, Malc.' Hughie's phone rang. 'Excuse me,' he said, grateful for the interruption.

It was his mother.

'Hello, Mum.'

'Yes, a large gin and tonic, please,' she was saying to the waiter. 'Oh. Hello, darling, I'm here a little early. How long will you be?'

'I'm on my way. What time is it, anyway?'

'Quarter to. How close are you? Shall I order you something to drink?'

'I'm, uh, somewhere on the Edgware Road.'

'That's miles away, Hughie! We're meant to be meeting at one!'

'Like I said, Mum, I'm on my way. Traffic's bad.'

'This is London, Hughie. Traffic is always bad. A little forward planning wouldn't go amiss! Really!'

She rang off before he could reply.

(It was going to be a real trick getting any cash out of her today.)

'You're in a bit of a pickle,' Malcolm observed.

'Oh, you know what they're like.'

His phone rang again.

'Where are you?' Leticia purred.

'Almost there, darling. Just coming up to Marble Arch.'

'Marble Arch! Are you in a cab?'

'No, I'm on the bus, angel.'

'How quaint!' she laughed. 'Is this your way of telling me you don't fancy me any more? Taking public transport?'

'No, no! I fancy you like mad!'

'Then show me. By the way, I'm wearing nothing but double cream.'

She made a low, thoroughly filthy growl before hanging up.

'Now, there's a place I know of in Soho where we could meet.' Malcolm was jotting down the address. 'Most amusing. Members only . . .'

'To be honest, I don't think I can, Malc.'

'Oh. Really.'

'I've got a hell of a lot on . . .'

'I see.'

'Tickets, please!'

Swaying in front of them was a ticket inspector, pad at the ready.

Hughie prodded Malcolm. 'You've got my ticket.'

'Have I?' Malcolm raised an eyebrow. 'You know, I've got a hell of a lot on, Hughie. I'm not sure I can remember where I put it. Perhaps if I had something to look forward to,' he sighed, '. . . a drinks engagement perhaps, I might be able to recall what I did with it.'

'Tickets please, gentlemen!'

Malcolm produced his bus pass with a flourish. 'Here's mine!' He smiled sweetly at Hughie. 'And you?'

Hughie wished, not for the first time, that his sister would find herself a different beau.

'You do have a ticket, young man? There's a fine if you

46

haven't.' The inspector tapped his pad. 'Quite a considerable fine.'

Malcolm shrugged. 'Oh, dear!'

Hughie was just about to give up when there was a gentle tap on his shoulder.

'Excuse me.'

He twisted round to find a dashing man in his fifties behind him. He wasn't the sort of man you'd expect to find on the top deck of a bus. Exquisitely dressed in a tailored grey wool suit and gold silk tie, he radiated authority, ease and polish. His hair was impeccable, nails trimmed, his skin had the soft golden glow of tan. But it was his eyes that were so arresting. They were a rare intensity of blue, not unlike Hughie's own.

'I believe you dropped this,' he smiled, holding out a ticket.

Hughie hesitated, then took it. 'Thank you.'

The man stood up. 'My pleasure.'

Then he clasped the hand of the ticket inspector and shook it warmly. 'I just want to say I think you're doing an excellent job. I work at Head Office and rarely have I seen a servant of the people as devoted and diligent as yourself. It makes me proud, my good man! Proud to be part of this great public transport system, and I must say, proud to be British!' He looked to Hughie. 'Don't you agree?'

'Absolutely!'

The ticket inspector blushed. 'I don't know what to say! It's so nice to be appreciated for a change. The number of people who abuse you, just for doing your job!'

The man nodded and patted him on the shoulder. 'You're a brave soldier.'

'You have to be!'

'I'll tell you what,' said the man, taking out his mobile. 'I'm putting in a call to Head Office right now and I'd like to mention you by name.'

'Really? Do you mean it? It's Paul, sir. Paul Pullerton.'

'Mr Pullerton, you're a credit to your profession! I'm dialling right now. Keep up the good work!' he called as he headed down the steps and off the bus.

'Now there's a gentleman!' the inspector declared to anyone who would listen. 'Last of a dying breed!'

'He didn't have to show his ticket!' Malcolm pointed out.

But the inspector ignored him. 'A dying breed,' he repeated and moved down the aisle.

Hughie looked out of the window. The man had disappeared.

Surely he'd given him his ticket. But why had he bothered to save a complete stranger?

Halfway down Park Lane, the bus shuddered violently. Clouds of black smoke billowed from its engine. The driver pulled over and rang the bell. 'Everyone off! Everyone off the bus!'

Hughie climbed off and managed to lose Malcolm in the outraged throng of pensioners and pushchairs. Traffic had ground to a halt.

There was nothing for it. So he ran down Park Lane.

At Hyde Park Corner, his phone rang again.

'I'm ordering without you,' his mother said. 'You forget that not everyone is unemployed and can laze about all day like you.'

'Mum . . . I can explain . . .'

'You have so little respect for other people. Time is more than money, Hughie, it's the stuff of life. You are wasting my life! Why are you panting? Is something wrong with you? Are you ill? How is it that any child of mine could be so badly brought up as to think . . .'

Another call was coming through. It was Leticia.

'After all the money I've spent trying to give you the best possible start – yes, I'll have the lamb please and a bottle of Château Margaux . . .'

'Sorry, Mum . . .'

'Hughie, don't interrupt! What have I just been telling you about respect?'

'Mum, if you could just hold a minute . . .'

'Hold! I will certainly not hold!'

Leticia rang off.

'My God, Hughie, you really take the biscuit!'

'Mum! This is a very important call!'

He put his mother on hold and rang Leticia.

'The Vane home for very, very wayward women,' she answered.

Then Hughie's credit ran out and the line went dead.

By the time he arrived at Leticia's shop, her next client was already there. He rang the bell anyway.

'Can't you read the sign?' she said, opening the door. 'No soliciting.'

He pushed his hair, damp from all the running, back from his face. 'I'm here to pick up the samples, Miss Vane. I'm so sorry I'm late.'

'And what samples might those be?'

'The ones for Mr . . . Mr . . . Mr Licktitslowly.'

'Mr Licktitslowly,' she repeated.

'That's right, Mr Licktitslowly and the Reverend Hardascanbee.'

She sighed. 'Those samples have been put away. I don't have time to get them out now.'

Hughie leant in. 'I'm afraid the Reverend in particular is most insistent.'

She smiled, brushing her fingers softly against his thigh. He stiffened. 'Tell the good Reverend Hardascanbee that another time, I'll personally ensure he samples everything.'

She shut the door.

Hughie waited a moment for his erection to go down, then bolted across to the Goring. He was just in time to see his mother climbing unsteadily into a cab and it pulling away.

'Bugger!'

By now, breakfast had worn off. He went into the Goring anyway, lifting a copy of *The Times* from the front desk as he passed. There was no point attempting the dining room. And the bar was heaving. Instead, he squeezed into the lounge which was full of people lunching on sandwiches. He scanned the busy room until he found a table where a middle-aged couple were just paying the bill.

'I'm sorry to disturb you.' He flashed his most charming grin. 'It's so crowded, is this seat taken?'

Hughie's Harrow education was useful for the accent alone.

'Oh! No, please!' the man gestured to the spare chair. 'We were about to leave anyway.'

'That's very good of you. Here.' Hughie held out the woman's coat for her.

'Thank you,' she smiled.

'No, thank you!' Hughie waved as they made their way towards the door.

Then he settled down, folded out his paper and disappeared into the general throng. The woman had left half her crab-and-avocado sandwich and most of her crisps. There was a small bowl of olives and even a bit of wine left in the bottle. He'd chosen well.

Wiping the lipstick off the woman's glass, he poured out the rest of the wine. Not a bad year, he thought, settling back.

At least the letter was off, winging its way across London. He was in with a chance. Today, he was scrambling for spare change but tomorrow? Who knows? He popped a crisp into his mouth. After all, it was difficult to keep a Venables-Smythe down.

He made a note of the time on the clock by the front

door, then turned to the sports page and checked the cricket score.

Sooner or later, Leticia's client would leave.

And sooner or later, the Reverend Hardascanbee would have his evil way.

Armenian Plumbers

Leticia closed the door.

Nothing was going to plan today. Hughie was late, the romance novelist turned out to be four foot seven, a size twenty, and obsessed with the colour pink and now she'd have to measure her in the workroom because the plumber was poking about in the bathroom, trying to locate the mysterious leak. He was hammering on something, making the most God-awful noise.

She checked the tea things she'd laid out earlier, running her fingers over the exquisite china cups and saucers. Thin, tangy lemon biscuits, smoky Assam tea, fine white sugar, milk, all neatly arranged on the large silver tray. Turning on a CD of Handel arias, she tried to look serene and composed, taking it back into the main room. 'Please forgive me!'

The novelist beamed up at her, dressed in a pair of too-tight jeans and a waxed Barbour jacket, smelling of wet dogs and hand lotion. 'No problem at all!'

'So,' Leticia poured a little tea in a cup, checking the colour, 'you want something with puffball sleeves, is that right? And a train? Are you sure?'

She nodded eagerly. 'Do you think you can do it?'

'Well.' How to break the news to her? 'It's not what I would recommend. Why don't we go for something more . . . streamlined . . . more sophisticated?'

The woman's face fell. Leticia was clearly demolishing a childhood dream.

'Milk and sugar? That's not to say it won't be gorgeous,' she added temptingly.

'Excuse me.'

It was the plumber, standing in the doorway, wiping his hands on an old rag. These people had no sense of timing.

'May I have a word?'

'Pardon me.' She eased the novelist into a chair, piling a stack of sketchbooks onto her lap and popping a biscuit in her hand. 'Have a look through some of these. It will give you some fresh ideas. I won't be a minute.'

She followed him into the bathroom. 'Yes? So what exactly is wrong?'

'How long ago did you have this put in?'

'Three years ago. Why?'

'And who did it?'

'Freelance guys. Armenians. Friends of my godfather's.' ('Friends' was a euphemism.)

'So not a proper outfit, is that right?'

She didn't like all these questions. 'Well, no. Not as such.

54

Why?' She folded her arms across her chest. 'What has that got to do with anything?'

Sam sighed. 'I didn't think it could be done by a legitimate company. Not by the quality of the work. But I wondered for your sake. Then you might have some legal recourse.'

The word 'legal' sounded ominous.

'See this,' he continued, pointing to the pipes that fed into the freestanding bath. 'Underneath the floorboards there are places where they've been held together with chewing gum and electrical tape. These pipes aren't even the same width. You've got a well of water underneath there that's rotting the wood. I'm surprised you couldn't smell it.'

The Armenians had done it at the most amazing price. And so quickly too.

She ran her hand over her eyes. 'Can you fix it?'

He shook his head. 'I can fix it but it means tearing up these floorboards, maybe even starting from scratch.'

'And how expensive will that be?'

'Hard to say. Twelve hundred?'

'No!'

'You can get a second opinion. I mean, another quote. But don't use it for a couple days. It needs to dry out.' He began packing up his bag. 'If you want me to do the work, I can fit you in, but you need to let me know quickly. Here,' he took a card out of his back pocket. 'Let me know what you decide.'

'Thanks,' she said grimly, leading him through the workshop and opening the back door.

'By the way,' he stopped on the threshold, looking around, 'what is it you actually do here?'

'I design bespoke lingerie.'

'You're kidding!' he laughed.

Leticia straightened. 'What's so funny about that?'

'Nothing. Hey, any chance of coming to a fashion show?'

'Thank you for coming by,' she said briskly, shutting the door.

Twelve hundred for pipes! Of all the things to have to spend money on! Then she thought of her ever-climbing overdraft. It was all so depressing.

She tossed the card down on the counter, adjusted the music and went back to her client.

This really wasn't her sphere; she was an artist, after all.

The King of the Tennis Ball

Arnaud Bourgalt du Coudray was the king of the tennis ball. Anyone who ever thought about tennis balls (and there were those who did), couldn't help but consider the du Coudray Imperial, with its bold mandarın-yellow felt and exceptionally springy rubber core, as everything a tennis ball should and could be.

But the du Coudray Imperial had been Arnaud's father's accomplishment. (Actually, it had taken two generations to perfect — one for the felt and another for the springy core.) By the time Arnaud was born, the Imperial was the established tennis ball of champions. And so throughout Arnaud's privileged life, his mother had followed him around, first when he was too small to get away from her and later, when he was too guilty to try, drilling into him that he would never match his father's success as a son, a human being or a producer of world-class tennis balls. He might as well give up right now. Which would, of course, be disgustingly lazy.

But Arnaud did not give up. It is a credit to his sheer

stubbornness that every year he embarked upon a new scheme to make his mark on du Coudray Industries and increase the already ludicrously large family fortunes.

And year after year, under the cynical eye of Arnaud's mother, his schemes failed.

There was the rubber tennis dress that never needed to be washed. The coaching racquet that hurled abuse every time a player missed a shot. And the legendary Tennis Caddy, a remote-controlled tennis bag on wheels which premiered at Wimbledon, famously reaching speeds of up to sixty miles an hour. Unfortunately, these were recorded during the men's finals when one rogue version terrorized a slow-moving ball boy on national television.

But now at long last, Arnaud's hour had come. The Nemesis All-Pro Sport 2000 tennis shoe was a marvel of engineering, a triumph of fashion design, and a veritable orgasm of shiny lurex, flashing lights and gravity-defying rubber springs. And with Men's Top Seed Ivaldos Ivaldovaldovich flying in from Croatia to launch it in a special ceremony in Hyde Park, it was certain to fly off the shelves despite its £299 price tag.

Standing in the middle of the vast sporting goods department of Harrods, Arnaud eyed up the competition. This time he had cracked it. None of them – Nike, Reebok, Puma – were a patch on his creation, he noted, smiling with satisfaction. Amateurs, all.

Behind him Jack Pollard, his marketing director, was

negotiating an exclusive display with the buyer; gesturing wildly, virtually battering the poor woman into submission with his enthusiasm. But Arnaud, restless, excused himself, wandering alone through the maze of exercise bikes, yoga mats, rowing machines – an endless parade of products aimed at the preservation of youth. How depressing. There was some woman in her fifties trying to balance on a ski machine. 'It's too late!' he wanted to shout at her. 'Give up!'

Rounding a corner, he came face to face with an older man. The man barred his way, glaring at him. What an old shit, Arnaud thought. He was about to say something when he realized with horror that it was a mirror.

Those were his lined features, his thinning hair, his sagging shoulders. For a moment, he thought he might be sick. Then he turned anxiously to see if anyone else had witnessed his discovery.

He was alone.

Backing away from the mirror, he averted his eyes, moving quickly into another section. Rage, unholy and mountainous, boiled up inside him. The events of the past year had clearly ruined him, draining away his mental, emotional and physical well-being. And he thought of Olivia, of how she had failed him. If only she were a proper, functioning woman, things would be different!

For it is true to say that, while Arnaud hated himself, he despised Olivia even more.

He kept walking, barely noticing where he was going.

Of course he could have plastic surgery but then everyone would know; his insecurity would be revealed for the entire world to see. Besides, it was pathetic; one of his oldest friends, Fabrice, had succumbed and now he looked positively bizarre – tight bits here, saggy bits there – his facial expression was one of permanent surprise. It was impossible to hold a conversation with him without being offended.

It wasn't a dignified solution. Was there a dignified solution? More and more, Arnaud began to think not.

He turned a corner into the ski department.

He hated life; hated everything about ageing and being old. If only he could begin again.

That's when he saw her.

She was trying on a fur-lined Prada ski jacket, pouting and posing in front of the mirror. Almost six foot tall, with long black hair, a round face and enormous brown eyes, she radiated a languid, almost bored sexuality. Her jeans were skintight, emphasizing to great effect her model's figure. She couldn't be more than twenty-four.

Arnaud was mesmerized.

'I don't know,' she sighed, speaking in a thick Russian accent. 'Is so expensive!'

'And yet,' pointed out the sales assistant eagerly, 'it will never go out of fashion. It's an investment piece.'

'Everything goes out of fashion!' she snorted, turning again to examine her lovely profile with the hood on. 'Nothing lasts in this world! Nothing.'

Then she caught Arnaud's eye. In an instant, she recognized him and determined to seize her chance.

'Isn't that right?' she challenged, fixing him with a sultry stare, full of pornographic promise. Then, just as quickly, she removed it.

(Hot, cold, scalding, freezing; here was a girl who knew how to hook a man.)

Arnaud couldn't believe his luck. This sexy young woman wanted him! In a few seconds she'd managed to obliterate months of self-doubt.

He'd obviously been oversensitive about the business with the mirror.

Leaning back casually against the counter, he dug his hands deep in his pockets, grinning. When he was younger, he'd possessed a pair of captivating dimples; he did his best to flash them now. 'I think you're too cynical.'

'No. I'm a realist. So. What do you think?' She licked her lips, slowly zipping up the front. 'I want a man's opinion.'

He held her gaze. 'I think that you are too beautiful not to have exactly what you want.'

She laughed, tossing her mane of black hair over her shoulder. (Here's what I look like in the throes of passion, she signalled.) 'Easy to say, but hard to do!'

He had a vision of her, writhing above him, dark hair across her bare chest.

Out came his wallet. 'Allow me.'

Her eyes widened.

'On one condition, of course,' he handed his credit card to the stunned assistant, 'you must allow me to drive you home.'

A Stranger at the Garrick Club

Jonathan Mortimer Esq. of the solicitors Hawes and Dawson, paused at the bottom of the stairs and rubbed his eyes.

It was late.

He'd struggled through another supper with his most important client, Arnaud Bourgalt du Coudray and one of his yes men, Jack Pollard, securing a private dining room at the Garrick Club at short notice. Arnaud had insisted on bringing some Russian escort along. What should've been an hour or two at most discussing yet another merger, dragged into three while they groped and pawed one another. It was so tedious; rich people were like toddlers with their constant demands for attention.

Now all he wanted to do was go home. But the thought of climbing the stairs, his wife Amy's back turned pointedly towards him as he got into bed, made him hesitate.

Why was being married so bloody difficult?

They'd had yet another argument this morning. He couldn't even remember what set it off – only that it had escalated into dangerous territory too quickly. There was only one scene they played out nowadays. He was unsure exactly what it was about, only that it was bitter and full of tension.

So instead he wandered back into the bar of the Garrick Club and, slumped into one of the decrepit leather armchairs, began working away on his fourth Scotch.

All around him the comforting noises of men acting like men lulled him, tugging away at the frazzled threadbare edges of his soul. That was what gentlemen's clubs were for; a last refuge from any form of female-ridden reality.

Swallowing a thick, amber shot in one, he reflected on the state of his life. If he'd bought it in a shop, he'd demand a refund immediately; it was clearly not as advertised.

And it was all Amy's fault.

He remembered the plans they'd made, when there were only two of them, tucked into bed in his Chelsea bachelor pad; the picture Amy painted of a large, comfortable family house filled with song and laughter, like *The Sound of Music*; the discreet, grateful army of cheerful nannies, demure cleaners, and cheeky au pairs serving delicious meals round the dining table where adults and children would share a quiet hour of civilized conversation . . .

Then he thought of the mouldly Marmite sandwich and Stickle Bricks he'd discovered wedged into his briefcase this morning by one of the boys. Of the pokey, overpriced house they were all crammed into in the less fashionable environs of South London. Of the sullen Spanish au pair who regularly ate all the ice cream.

This was not that vision.

You only had to look at Amy and she conceived again. Three children under nine and now another one on the way! Of course he loved the children. That wasn't the issue. The real crime was Amy's. She'd abandoned him; the delicate, devoted woman he'd married had evaporated early on in the first pregnancy. Overnight she'd been replaced by a wisecracking, middle-aged Shakespearean wet nurse, complete with the matching body of cartoon proportions.

He'd been left to fend for himself; relegated to a marginalized authority figure, endured for his only useful quality – his ability to fund this extravaganza.

It was unfair.

And he was lonely.

He tried to focus on his watch.

Just time for one more drink.

The bar was still quite full, despite the late hour. Jonathan was having trouble attracting the waiter's attention. He stood up, legs unsteady. Lurching forward, he tumbled straight into a fellow member reading a copy of the *Financial Times*.

'Terribly sorry!' he gushed, trying to rebalance himself, smooth his tie down and uncrumple the man's paper all at once, all unsuccessfully.

The gentleman smiled, brushing off his exquisitely cut Savile

Row suit with quick strokes. He led Jonathan back to his own chair, where he collapsed gratefully.

'Really, I can't apologize enough.' Jonathan's cheeks were flushed from embarrassment and effort. 'Stupid of me. Clumsy. I'm really terribly, terribly sorry . . .' His voice faded. It was all turning into a nightmare. The porter would end up calling him a cab and Amy would have a field day. Consequences stretched out before him, predictable and unavoidable.

He sighed.

The man tilted his silver head to one side, then sat down next to Jonathan and crossed his legs. 'I hope you'll forgive me, but it seems to me as if you have a great deal on your mind.'

Jonathan looked up into his still, grey eyes. They were so calm, so friendly, so non-judgemental.

'Yes,' he nodded. 'Yes. You see, I do. I really do.'

The man smiled. 'It's very difficult sometimes. No one really understands.'

Jonathan leant forward eagerly, clutching his empty glass. 'Yes, that's true!' he agreed.

'Just because we're . . .' the stranger paused, 'men of the world, shall we say? Everyone assumes we can handle things on our own.' He raised his arm and almost instantly a waiter appeared. 'May I buy you a drink?'

And in that moment, there seemed to be more kindness than Jonathan had felt in a long time. 'Thank you,' he said gratefully. 'Thank you very much!'

66

The waiter took their order, moving soundlessly away, and Jonathan settled back into his chair. Almost unconsciously, he checked his watch and frowned.

'Late?' the stranger ventured.

Jonathan laughed stiffly. 'Not yet. No, no. Not yet.' He was aware of how henpecked he sounded. 'You see, my wife's pregnant. Again. Doesn't like to be alone in the house at night,' he lied.

'Ah! Married life!' The man smiled knowingly.

Jonathan felt the stiffness in his shoulders relax; he smiled too. 'It should come with a warning, shouldn't it? Like they put on packets of cigarettes: marriage kills!' He felt instantly guilty. 'Or at least, all the best bits die . . . the sex for starters!' This time his laugh sounded hollow and forced.

The waiter returned and, armed with a fresh glass of Scotch, Jonathan rallied. 'I mean, everyone has bad patches, right?'

The man was still.

'It's just, my wife has been pregnant for so long! One kid after another . . . It changes a girl. She's not the same,' he added, staring into his glass.

'Yes, everything changes,' the man agreed, gently.

It was a simple enough comment, but the man's voice had a wistful quality. In his drunkenness, Jonathan imagined this stranger understood, with greater subtlety, a whole range of experience none of his other married friends would admit.

'Thing is,' Jonathan leant in closer, lowering his voice, 'I don't actually fancy her any more!'

There. At last, he'd said it out loud. To a complete stranger, but perhaps that was for the best. He felt a mixture of relief and panic. 'I mean, I love her. Of course I love her . . .'

Did he?

Was it love or just habit that kept them together now? A sharp burning sensation filled his chest; the question was too painful even to contemplate.

'Yes,' the stranger tilted his head thoughtfully to one side. 'You see, my view of marriage is that it's an extremely delicate thing. Resilient, yes. But more like a finely made Swiss watch than, say, a huge, muddy piece of farm equipment. Sometimes, when it's all come to a grinding halt, what's really required is a little fine tuning rather than a large, clumsy repair job.' As he spoke, the man re-crossed his legs. Jonathan was aware of the glossy black sheen of his handmade shoes and the way his dark navy silk socks matched the shade of his pinstripe suit perfectly. Elegant silver cufflinks flashed as he drew his elbows up, pressing the tips of his long fingers against one another. 'From what you've said, it's possible that both sides are feeling neglected, perhaps a little unappreciated. Does that sound like an accurate appraisal to you?'

He made it sound so light, so normal.

Jonathan nodded. 'Yes, I suppose so.'

'These situations can so easily get out of hand. Snowball, so to speak. But,' he held his finger up promisingly, 'if one of you were to make an effort, the whole thing could easily be reversed, don't you think?'

Jonathan imagined a large snowball barrelling towards him, then suddenly swerving, heading in the opposite direction, growing smaller and smaller until it disappeared.

'Perhaps . . .'

The man sensed his hesitation. 'But when a dynamic has been allowed to grow unchecked for so long, one doesn't always have the emotional resources to make the effort required,' he concluded.

'That's right!' Jonathan had never heard anyone describe his particular malaise so succinctly or accurately.

'Yes, yes, of course!' the man nodded. 'I've seen it a thousand times!'

'Have you?' Jonathan leant forward.

'Absolutely! Don't despair. This whole difficult chapter of your marriage can be behind you in a week,' the man assured him breezily. 'In place of a distant, sullen wife who's given up on herself, you can have a delightful, confident creature – without the time, expense or distress of resorting to long-drawn-out discussions where intimate details are dragged out in front of third parties.'

'Really? But what's to be done?'

The man took something out of his breast pocket; a thin silver card holder. And moving with no particular speed or urgency, he removed a card and handed it to Jonathan. 'I might be able to help you.'

The card read:

Valentine Charles.
Procurer of Rare Domestic Services.
Satisfaction Absolutely Guaranteed.

111 Half Moon Street

Two days after the advertisement appeared in the *Stage*, 111 Half Moon Street was inundated with responses and the postman had to ring the bell because all the thick envelopes wouldn't fit through the letter box.

Valentine Charles couldn't quite decide if he enjoyed this bit of the proceedings; it was time consuming and exhausting sifting through all the letters, but also thrilling when one happened upon that rare gem. This morning, the deluge had been particularly heavy and as he sat there, in his cashmere dressing gown, with his morning coffee, he looked upon the pile with satisfaction. In there, somewhere, was a budding new apprentice and an answer to the staff difficulties that had plagued him for the past months.

He considered diving straight in but then dismissed the idea. He was a creature of habit and married to the inflexible, set routine of his daily life. One of the pleasures of living by your-self is the privilege of being able to practise, day after day, in whatever order you wish, the rituals that define your tastes and aspirations without any threat of disruption. And at fifty-eight, Valentine was deeply grateful for his solitude.

He had loved, a few times briefly but only once seriously. The love wasn't returned and so he made peace with all the aspects of single life that many people find so abhorrent. Now he valued them above all else. Over time he'd mutated from a lonely, watchful person into a completely self-sufficient one, treating himself with the same affection a lover would. The older he was the more he realized that few people were given the time and means to be as completely indulged as he was. He hadn't had to accommodate another human being on any matter of significance for years. He was entirely, unapologetically selfish and grateful for the opportunity to be so. Now, when he thought of the woman who broke his heart (which was rare), he viewed it as a narrow escape.

No, he'd finish his coffee, glance at the crossword, then have his bath. And while he was dressing, his assistant, Flick, would arrive.

Flick had been sent from an agency twelve years ago. She'd turned up, a rather dour middle-aged Irish woman in a beige Marks and Spencer twinset, shortly after her husband died. Her full name was Mary Margaret Flickering, but Valentine had christened her Flick early on. At first she was horrified. But gradually, Mary Margaret Flickering began to fade and Flick took hold. The beige twinset disappeared; her actions became sharper, her tone confident and Valentine learnt the power of re-framing someone. Flick was more daring and resilient than

Mary Margaret Flickering had ever been. And she was funnier too. Now she was invaluable to him.

Half Moon Street wasn't a traditional office. It was an old-fashioned bachelor pad. It had last been refurbished in the late fifties and still had some of the plumbing features from the thirties that are so popular now. There was a large reception room, a tiny office, a single bedroom and the kind of kitchen only a man would find adequate. It was furnished like a set from *Brideshead Revisited*; a look of luxurious, old moneyed antiques shoved into students' quarters.

There had been a time when Valentine had toyed with the idea of having a separate office but in truth he enjoyed having Flick about. She provided just the right touch of domesticity to his life. He liked the fact that he could emerge from his bedroom to find her rifling through the post; more often than not she'd make some small adjustment to his tie in the same casual way a wife would. It was all the intimacy he required without any of the emotional turmoil.

After she arrived, he took a brisk morning walk around St James's Park, then popped into Fortnum's to pick up something for lunch (at the moment, they were both fond of *campagne* bread, foie gras and fresh figs). Then he returned, settling down to review all the applications that she'd opened and sorted, removing the most blatantly hideous.

There were only two that were of interest. One was a darkly sensual young man from Wales and the other, a blond public-school boy from North-West London. The Welshman's romantic résumé was quite shockingly graphic; he obviously thought the position was for some sort of gigolo and wanted to show that he'd received adequate technical training. But the school boy's was endearingly brief; he'd lost his virginity to a friend of his sister's, dated a few girls, fell in love with the student in drama school who played Juliet to his Romeo only to discover that when the production was over, the feeling faded. And now he was involved with an older woman.

Valentine examined the photo carefully. For all his Merchant Ivory good looks, the boy had the feel of a blank sheet of paper; a kind of wide-eyed optimism emanated from him that was the hallmark of either an idiot or a saint. Next to him, the young Welshman seemed positively louche.

Valentine held the picture up triumphantly. 'Flick, can you see it? Isn't it amazing? I haven't seen a specimen like it in years!'

She leant back in her chair and narrowed her eyes. After a moment, she nodded. 'Yes, I do! It's remarkable! Like looking into a void!'

'A completely unformed character!' he agreed. 'Perfect! Would you be so kind, Flick, as to give Mr Hughie Armstrong Venables-Smythe a call? If he's half as malleable in real life as he is on paper, then I do believe our search is over.'

A Subtle Twist of Fate

Rose stood awkwardly in front of a table massed with silver-ware. Her interview wasn't going well. It began over an hour ago when Mr Gaunt, the butler, interrogated her about her slender CV. Then he moved on to what he referred to as 'the practical exercises'. They'd just established that she knew nothing about the proper care of silver and now were involved in a guessing game with various bits of cutlery. The suit she'd borrowed from her friend Sheri was too big in most places and too tight in others. And it itched. But she didn't dare scratch in front of Mr Gaunt.

Gaunt, in turn, had never recovered from the considerable impression that the television series *Upstairs, Downstairs* had made on him in the seventies. It was an era when he'd struggled with his identity and the result was a curious devotion to archaic class distinctions along with a violent obsession with Jean Marsh. Power plays that might have resolved themselves quite harm-lessly in the more traditional sado-masochistic club circuit thus oozed out into his professional life with alarming regularity.

75

Poor Rose watched in dread as his gloved hand moved towards another exotic utensil.

'And this, Miss Moriarty?' He held up a narrow, curved piece with three long prongs.

It was agony.

She hesitated. 'Another fork?'

He sighed, making a mark in his notebook next to all the other marks, before replacing it with the rest. 'It is a lobster trident, Miss Moriarty. Extremely rare. At a push it may also be used to serve crab. But only at a push.'

'Oh.'

She'd tried being funny about her mistakes in the beginning but that was a long while ago now and there weren't that many amusing things to say about cutlery.

'This is the last one,' he informed her, making his final selection.

She nearly laughed with relief. 'A dessert spoon!' she cried triumphantly.

Gaunt's silence was withering.

'It is a serving spoon,' he said at last. 'And a particularly large one at that.'

Rose watched as he made a final, devastating mark, then closed the notebook.

'I'm afraid, Miss Moriarty, that your dinner-service knowledge leaves something to be desired.'

Her golden life-changing opportunity was slipping through her fingers.

'Yes, but I could learn about that. You know, get a book from the library or something.'

'The position of junior assistant to the acting assistant household manager is one of extreme delicacy and discretion. The circles in which the Bourgalt du Coudrays move are filled with aristocracy, politicians, famous actors and actresses, well-known figures from the art world, musicians . . .'

'Yes,' Rose cut in eagerly, 'I know all about them! Ask me some questions!' An avid reader of *Hello!* magazine, here was one test she was bound to pass with flying colours.

'My point,' Gaunt went on, glaring at her, 'is that these are people who are used to a certain level of service and with whom mistakes must simply not be made. Under any circumstance. In addition, Mr Bourgalt du Coudray is a gentleman of very little patience. If he asks for a lobster trident, my girl, and you send him a dessert spoon, you'll be in no small amount of trouble.'

'Oh,' said Rose again.

It was all proving a great deal more difficult than she had imagined.

He walked out into the front hallway and she followed him, giving her left thigh a quick scratch while she had the chance.

'Language is of the utmost importance.'

'I hardly ever swear!'

'I'm not referring merely to foul language, Miss Moriarty.' He flung open the double doors of one of the largest, most ornately furnished and beautiful rooms she'd ever seen in her life. 'What would you call this room?'

77

It was the room closest to the door, she calculated. 'The front room?'

'The drawing room,' he corrected her. 'This is my point exactly. You need to use the proper language, not only because directions become confused but because language sets the tone, to guests as well as one's employers. No one wants to work in a house where the tone is lax. "Madame, Mr So and So is waiting in the drawing room." It reminds them of who they are and what they are about. When you're gone they may roll around and grunt like pigs, for all you care. But it's the tone of the household and the quality of the staff that make a situation civilized. To lower the tone is to degrade yourself, Miss Moriarty.'

He handed her a small stack of note cards and a pencil. 'For your last exercise I would like you to write down the proper name of everything you see in this room. I will be back in fifteen minutes to check your progress. And remember, good penmanship is also a consideration.'

He closed the doors.

Rose looked round.

There was an awful lot of stuff.

She started with basics.

'Settee,' she wrote and placed the card carefully in the middle of the velvet Knowle sofa. 'Pouff,' she labelled the matching ottoman. On either side stood a pair of large salon chairs with elaborate claw arms, painted with gold leaf. They reminded her of the ones Posh and Becks used at their wedding. 'His and Hers Thrones,' she wrote neatly.

Now, there must be a television somewhere. No one had a settee without a television. She scanned the room. Wait a minute . . . it must be behind one of the wall panels! She smiled. Very clever! A lot of people were probably fooled by that one. 'Television,' she wrote, being careful to use the full and correct name rather than just TV. Licking the back of the card, she stuck it to the wall.

The marble-topped Empire commode had bottles of liquor and glasses on it: 'Home bar,' she inscribed. And these bookshelves were filled with fake books; she tried to pull one out but they were all glued together. Why would anyone bother to do that? They must have something to hide. It was probably a secret panel, the kind which when you pressed, led to another room. 'Secret Panel!' she wrote boldly, adding an exclamation point to show that she too had been amused.

Six Holbein self-portraits fell under the heading of 'A Few of the Apostles' (she wondered that they hadn't bothered to buy the rest) and the unfinished Degas sketch was labelled 'Picture of a girl with no legs'. The chaise longue was cast as a 'Broken Settee', the Ming Dynasty vases as 'Sweet Jars' and the elephant foot's table as 'a badly burnt stump'. (There was no accounting for taste.)

Next she turned her attention to the priceless collection of Dresden china figurines massed on the mantelpiece. There were a couple of words one was meant to use for things like this. Rose had heard her father, who ran a junk shop, use them. And she dearly wanted to impress Mr Gaunt with her expertise.

It wasn't 'bits and bobs', but it was something like that . . . ah!

'Nick Naxs,' she wrote quickly.

And to the assortment of tiny seventeenth-century *cloisonné* snuffboxes, she gave the other specialist heading of 'Brick a Brack'.

But then Rose wavered.

This was the trouble with getting clever, there was always something to catch you out.

Surely the chief differentiating feature between a knick-knack and bric-a-brac was the size of the object.

But which was larger?

Her confidence faltered. There were only a few minutes left and still so many things to label.

Rose's concentration began to fray.

'Faded old rug,' she jotted, dropping the card on the Aubusson. 'Half a table' landed on the *demi-lune* console, and 'Fun House Mirrer' on the large Georgian convex looking glass above the mantel.

But still the larger question wrangled: which was bigger? A knick-knack or bric-a-brac?

Two minutes left. Rose began to panic. 'Picture Book Bible' on the large edition of *Les Très Riches Heures de Jean Duc de Berry*. She frowned. 'Dirty Pictures,' she scribbled disdainfully on the signed Helmut Newton photography book. (You'd think he'd have the decency to at least hide them!)

Only one more minute!

Should she switch them?

Her throat constricted, heart raced. All her past failures and missed opportunities distilled into this single task. What was the use anyway? She'd failed the cutlery test. And the one about the silver. Her entire life was one big stupid mistake after another!

And, in the shadow of this sudden, crushing depression, Rose's standards began to slip.

'Another fucking chair' on the Victorian reading chair, 'Two ugly pillow biters' on the portraits of Arnaud's great-great-grandfather and uncle, 'A bunch of total strangers' on the cluster of silver-framed family photographs on the piano. And on top of the Steinway, in capital letters, 'I'LL BET NO ONE EVEN PLAYS!'

And so on it went.

Until Mrs Bourgalt du Coudray herself walked in, followed by Simon Grey.

Now, as is often the way in large households, a great many things were all going on at the same time. So, while Gaunt was busy vetting young hopefuls for the position of junior assistant to the acting assistant household manager, somewhere on a floor above him Simon Grey and Olivia were conducting their own fevered interviews for a replacement for Roddy Prowl. They had scoured the art schools of London for someone daring, original and preferably offensive to take Roddy's place and were promised that several candidates would appear at 45 Chester

Square before the day was out. Indeed, in bedsitting rooms all across London, young artists were gathering together portfolios, throwing on clothes, and gulping down vast amounts of coffee in an attempt to sober up in time to make an impression on this powerful duo.

But they needn't have bothered.

Because fate had another thing in mind.

Olivia flung open the drawing-room doors.

Her head throbbed from worry and nerves. Never had she imagined that agreeing to become chairman of the gallery would involve so much hands-on interaction. Now all of a sudden they were in crisis and Simon was looking to her, of all people, for help. Already they'd seen dozens of portfolios, none suitable. Hope waned. They would never be able to find a worthy replacement in time.

It was time to face facts.

'The thing is, Simon,' she explained, 'we need an original statement, not just a worthy candidate but an exceptional one, with something daring to say. But the chances of us finding an artist of that calibre at such short notice . . .'

She stopped. Something above the mantelpiece caught her eye.

'Fun House Mirrer,' a small note card read, written in careful, childish writing. Lower down, by the china figurines, was another.

'Nick Naxs.'

And on top of the collection of snuffboxes, 'Brick a Brack.'

She turned round.

Little cards were everywhere!

'Sette.'

'Pouff.'

'Half a table.'

'My God!' Simon gasped. 'Your home has been vandalized! Shall I call the police?'

Olivia didn't answer.

She was staring at the photographs in the silver frames.

'A bunch of total strangers,' it said.

A bunch of total strangers!

Who could've done such a thing?

What did it mean?

Still, she couldn't escape the bizarre feeling that she was seeing her relations clearly for the first time.

'Another fucking chair . . .' she murmured, reading the cards out loud. 'Secret Panel?' The breath caught in her chest. 'His and Hers Thrones!'

How ghastly!

How intrusive!

How accurate!

Simon was right: it was vandalism. But it was also something more.

Here was the room, just as she'd left it except for the mysterious cards. Nothing had really changed. And yet suddenly her perspective was irrevocably altered. It was offensive, shocking; subtle.

Simon tried unsuccessfully to suppress a laugh. 'Look at this one!' He pointed to the Helmut Newton. 'That's hysterical!'

'I've always hated that book.'

'Really?' He leafed through it surreptitiously. 'I think it's kind of sexy.'

Olivia gripped his arm. 'This is extraordinary!'

'Yes. The spelling is atrocious and the handwriting!'

'You said Mona was sending someone?'

'Yes . . .'

'Do you think?'

His eyes widened. 'No!'

'What else could it be?'

'An installation! My God! How remarkable! The absurdity – like Dadaism!'

'I've never encountered anything like it,' she agreed.

A small figure was slumped in a corner.

'My God, the artist,' Olivia pointed. 'She's so young!'

They approached.

'Hello!' Olivia smiled brightly.

The girl nodded.

'What do you call this piece?'

'I'm sorry?'

'The name of this piece,' Simon spoke slowly, clearly. 'Does it have a name?'

A large tear rolled down the girl's cheek. 'I just don't see . . . I mean, what's the point in carrying on?'

Her words cut through Olivia like a blade.

'"What's the Point in Carrying On",' she repeated.

Only a few times in her life had anything struck her so forcibly. A terrible feeling of transparency flooded her.

Here it all was; the world she struggled to create, her public face in all its desperate grandeur and ostentatiousness. How could this stranger, little more than a teenager, really, have guessed so accurately at the emptiness beneath the surface?

What was the point indeed?

Olivia crouched down next to the girl. 'I can't tell you how much I admire what you've done.'

The girl blinked.

'Look, Simon, at the detail! I mean, even the suit she's wearing!'

'Yes, dreadful! What's your name?'

'Rose.' She struggled to her feet. 'Rose Moriarty.'

'Oh, dear. Do you have another one? Names in this business are important, you see.'

'Sometimes people call me Red.'

'That's good!'

'But I don't like it,' she added.

'Never mind. Red Moriarty!' He turned to Olivia. 'How's this? "Subversion has a new name: Red Moriarty"!'

'Brilliant!'

'Does this mean I'm hired?' the girl asked.

But Olivia didn't hear. This remarkable young woman had taken the very lack of substance in her life and elevated it to the status of art.

For the first time in a long time, she felt energized.

'No one is to touch this room! Simon, get Mona Freestyle on the phone! I want this whole piece transferred to the gallery immediately. You're a very clever girl.'

'Really?'

'Incredibly talented!'

'At what?'

Olivia and Simon exchanged a look.

'And witty!' Simon laughed. 'Where did you train?'

'Train? I left school when I was fifteen. You see, I have a little boy.'

'A child? But you can't be more than twelve yourself!'

'I'm twenty-two. Well, almost. Next month.'

'And your background?' Simon demanded. 'Where were you born? Where do you live? What are your family like?'

'I'm from Kilburn. My dad owns a junk shop. My mother left when I was ten. I live in a council flat on an estate near Queens Park.'

He could hardly contain himself. 'How perfectly Tracey!'

Olivia gestured for her to sit. 'And your love of conceptual art . . . where does it come from?'

'Art?' The girl tugged at the ugly suit. 'I can't even draw.'

'Nobody draws any more!' Simon assured her. 'I couldn't sell a drawing if my life depended on it!'

'An utterly raw talent,' Olivia shook her head in amazement.

'You're right,' Simon nodded. 'God has answered all our

prayers! Here is the *enfant terrible* we've been looking for! Even more *enfant* than Roddy and infinitely more *terrible*!'

Meanwhile, downstairs, one of the artists that Mona Freestyle of the Slade had recommended, a lanky young man with a large nose and beady eyes who specialized in preserving human remains in aspic, was being interviewed by Gaunt. He'd done quite well on the silver-polishing exercise and acquitted himself admirably during the cutlery identification. (The lobster trident was no stranger to him.)

Unfortunately, he didn't have the opportunity to attempt the final exercise, as Simon Grey had the drawing room cordoned off and everything removed to the gallery later that afternoon. But Gaunt decided to hire him regardless. The quality of his sneer was first rate; he possessed a natural sense of superiority which couldn't be taught. And if truth be told, there was something of Jean Marsh in the way he moved.

So perhaps England lost yet another great artist in the making to the service industry.

Then again, perhaps not.

The Interview

Hughie was sitting in a warm patch of sunlight on a bench in Green Park, with ten minutes to go before his appointment. He felt stiff and uncomfortable wearing the dark wool suit he'd borrowed from Malcolm. But at least it didn't smell like violet water.

Perhaps it had been a mistake allowing Clara to dress him. But when she heard he finally had a job interview, she wouldn't leave him alone. Her trademark yellow Post-its began to appear offering advice instead of warnings: 'Make eye contact and smile! But not like an IDIOT!' 'Don't eat anything smelly the day before.' 'Remember to shave!' As the week wore on they grew increasingly more like American life-coaching slogans: 'You can do this!' 'This job already belongs to YOU! All you have to do is reach out and GRAB IT!' 'Failure is for LOSERS!' Hughie had begun to miss the Post-its that only required him not to forget his fucking keys.

He looked around at the people strolling past and the ones

lolling, reading papers or dozing on the grass. And he wondered if any of them might be the person he was waiting for.

It was unusual to hold a job interview on a park bench. It was one of the things he'd kept secret from Clara and her endless grilling. But then, he was an actor and used to strange impromptu arrangements. Besides, any job that required discretion coupled with a romantic history was bound to be a bit unorthodox.

He checked the time again on his mobile phone. Any minute now, the man he spoke to would be here.

Then a red-headed woman sat down next to him, unfolded a newspaper and began to read. Hughie felt a bit anxious. This was the difficulty of using public spaces; namely the public. Should he ask her to sit somewhere else? Or perhaps he should just wait until the man arrived and take it from there?

Suddenly his phone buzzed. A text appeared.

The message read, *Flirt with the woman next to you. Your interview has begun.*

Hughie blinked.

Flirt?

He read the message again.

Then he peered across at the woman reading her paper. She was about fifty-five, sensibly dressed; she looked like one of his mother's friends. Definitely not the sort of woman he'd ever flirt with. Not that he was much of a flirt in the first place. His normal opening gambit was something along the lines of, 'Hey.' And occasionally, he'd add, 'Nice shoes.'

Just on the off chance, he glanced down. She was wearing a pair of flat, black loafers, what his mother called a 'driving shoe'. He knew that because they were her favourite footwear. The originals were from Todd's but his mother bought them in bulk from Marks and Spencer's in a variety of garish colours. An involuntary shiver shot up his spine. How could he flirt with a woman who dressed like his mother?

His phone buzzed again.

A second message popped up.

There's a time limit.

Hughie slipped his phone into his pocket. Was he being filmed? Was this some sort of reality television show? Whatever it was, there were clearly two choices: to play along or to stand up and walk away.

Well, he was here now, up and dressed. And anyway, he'd get an earful from Clara if he just wandered off. He stole another glance. She wasn't such a bad old bird. Her eyes were quite friendly and at least she didn't have any disfiguring facial features – moles, moustache, or the like.

Still, he didn't know quite how to get going. Lust or alcohol had always fuelled his previous conquests. He tried smiling at her, but she wasn't paying attention. An opening was required. Something sexy.

The woman was checking her watch, folding up her paper, pushing it back into her bag . . .

Then something caught Hughie's eye.

'God! Excuse me . . . is that the cricket score?'

The woman looked up at him. 'Pardon me?'

'I'm sorry.' He grinned. 'I'm rude, I know. It's just,' he gestured to her paper, 'that can't be the cricket score! I mean, this is still England, isn't it? I am awake, aren't I? When was the last time you saw a score like that?'

The woman unfolded the paper again from her bag and laughed. 'I don't know. It's not a sport I follow.'

'May I? Nice shoes, by the way.'

'Oh! Thank you. Of course you may.' She offered him the paper and he took it, his fingers brushing lightly against hers.

'Shane Warne! God, those figures are insane! I reckon he's made a pact with the devil. So you don't do cricket? What do you follow? Wait,' he held up his hand, 'let me guess! Football! Beckham's latest haircut, tattoo, fashion statement!'

'God, no!' she laughed again. 'No, not my cup of tea, at all.'

'Rugby then. Large men in tight shorts.'

'Not rough enough.'

'Tennis.'

She wrinkled her nose.

'Golf!'

She pretended to yawn.

'Championship Tibetan goat hurling!'

'Only the Tibetans know how to really hurl a goat,' she sighed wistfully.

'You've obviously never seen the Spanish have a go.'

She laughed.

He felt his nerves steadying.

Actually, she was easy to talk to; much easier than many girls he really fancied. And she had lovely eyes; a mixture of green and grey. When he concentrated on them, she could've been any age at all. Then it occurred to him that all he was doing was acting – just playing a part.

And he started to really enjoy himself.

'OK, OK.' He frowned in mock concentration. 'Horse racing!'

Her eyes flickered.

'You cheeky devil! You play the horses! I know I'm right!'

Suddenly she was giggling. It was a delightful noise; unrestrained and girlish. 'Only occasionally,' she admitted. 'I'm Irish,' she added. 'I was raised with it!'

'Raised with it, my arse!' He tapped her knee with the rolled-up paper. 'You're a thrill junkie! Don't deny it! Look at how your eyes light up!'

And they had. Years seemed to have dropped from her; her face was glowing as she laughed again. 'Everyone has a vice or two,' she said, looking away coyly.

'Thank God!' He leant in. 'I have a confession.'

'What?' She tilted towards him.

'The truth is, I'm not really into cricket either.'

Her eyes widened. 'You're not one of those dreadful cricket frauds I've been reading about, are you? Pretending to know how the game's played, babbling on about wickets and overs, parading around with picnic hampers filled with nothing but bunched-up old newspaper.'

'Named and shamed!' Hughie hung his head. 'Don't hate me! It's just, how else was I going to get the chance?'

'The chance at what?'

He had intended to lock her with an intense, sexy stare but then something happened that surprised Hughie; something that had only happened a few times in his acting career, when he was completely lost in the role. A strange rush of feeling flooded through him. His cheeks burned. 'The chance to talk to you.'

For a moment, she said nothing. A delicate thread of intimacy wrapped itself around them.

'Why would you want to do that?' she asked quietly.

His blue eyes caught hers and he blushed even harder. 'It's just, well . . .' he fumbled, 'it doesn't happen very often. I mean . . . It's not every day someone like you just . . . appears . . . out of nowhere . . .'

'Someone like me?'

'Yes, someone so . . . lovely. You have a certain way about you. I really like talking to you.' He was aware, even as he spoke, that it was true.

For a moment, it looked as though she might say something. But then an odd expression clouded her face.

It wasn't quite the effect he was going for.

'I didn't mean to offend you,' he apologized.

She shook her head. 'No.' Then she was silent.

Fuck, he thought. I've buggered it up.

Shrugging his shoulders, he pushed his hand through his

mop of blond hair and gave her one last smile. 'Can't blame a guy for trying, can you?'

But she just blinked.

He stood, handed her back the paper.

Oh, well, he thought, as he ambled up towards the tube entrance. That's fucked.

Maybe there's a job going at HMV or something.

Flick sat very still, for a long time, on the bench in Green Park. It had been a beautiful early-autumn day, and now it was just beginning to fade, mellowing into that time of evening when the light drains from the sky. The people around her were moving slowly, enjoying the last of the hazy warmth.

But Flick sat frozen.

She felt unusual, disorientated, flustered even. And she wasn't the kind of woman who was accustomed to feeling flustered. After all, she'd been through this process a hundred times over the past twelve years. Normally these auditions were either excruciating or comical. But today was different. This young man had stirred something inside her; something she'd almost forgotten existed. He'd managed to disturb her entire equilibrium in a way that left her feeling exposed, vulnerable but at the same time exhilarated.

Valentine walked down from Piccadilly and sat next to her. He handed her a takeaway coffee. 'Well . . . ?'

This is where the two of them would usually dissect the

whole adventure and more likely than not, have a good laugh. Instead, she frowned.

Hughie had reminded her of someone.

'Flick . . .'

A memory floated to the surface, of another young man, different in physical type from Hughie but similar in his eagerness and enthusiasm.

It had been years since she'd thought about the way he'd looked at her, the way he'd struggled to make conversation the first time they'd met. His desire to be with her had been palpable; a solid, physical force she'd found irresistible. And she'd yielded, almost immediately. Her face flushed from the recollection.

'Flick!' Patience was not one of Valentine's virtues. 'What's come over you?'

She forced her eyes to focus on Valentine's face and suddenly it dawned on her, what had happened.

'I've been seduced!' she said. 'That little shit has just charmed the pants off me!'

Valentine's mouth curled up at the corners as he slowly stirred his tea. 'You don't say.'

Shaking her head, she sipped her coffee. But it was too hot; too sweet and strong. She put it down again. 'He's really very handsome,' she added, 'much handsomer in real life. I didn't expect him to be so tall. And then there's the smell of him . . . none of that dreadful thick cologne but a kind of clean, soapy freshness.'

Valentine laughed. 'Mary Margaret Flickering, I do believe you're smitten!'

She tossed him a look. 'You wouldn't understand. There was nothing at all forced about it, or smarmy. My God, he even blushed! So sweet! So terribly, terribly sweet . . .'

'Ah,' Valentine arched an eyebrow, 'but do we need sweet?'

She thought a moment.

'Yes,' she decided firmly. 'We need something unrehearsed, raw, a bit awkward. Not prepackaged or particularly sophisticated . . .' Standing up, she pulled her mackintosh around her. 'We need something fresh, Valentine.'

'Where are you going?' He rose too, affronted. He wasn't used to being taken for granted; normally just the fact that he was present was reason enough to warrant her undivided attention.

But instead, she handed him back the takeaway coffee, as if he were a bus boy.

'I'm going for a walk.' Her voice was dreamy, faraway. 'If you don't mind, I'd like to be alone for a little while.'

He'd never seen her so distracted. He watched as she made her way down the hill, through the avenue of plane trees towards St James's, until he felt a bit poignant and ridiculous and decided enough was enough, this wasn't an old film and he could really do with a drink.

As Flick strolled along, dry leaves, bereft of colour, crunched underneath her feet. Her thoughts were drawn again to the past and her gauche young lover – of the way he used to look at her. He was the first person who'd made her feel intoxicated; completely alive and powerful. At the time, she imagined that feeling would be hers for ever.

What a shock it had been when she began to grow invisible to men and they no longer registered her. How humiliating to discover time had abducted her favourite version of herself and replaced it with a saggy middle-aged woman instead.

Then she thought of Hughie Venables-Smythe's amazing, clear blue eyes. Even now, she could still feel them gazing into hers, taking her in; seeing her.

And she smiled.

It was autumn. The leaves had begun to fall.

And she was still lovely, after all.

The Rules

Hughie rang the bell of Leticia's shop later that evening.

'I've never seen you in a suit,' she said, as she unlocked the
door and let him in.

He smiled.

They hadn't seen one another in days. And now a delightful
frisson sparked between them, a certain shyness that made him
feel as if they were starting all over again. She looked perfect
tonight; all soft and so young in a simple pink silk dress. And
he was struck again by how much he'd missed her. The room
was dimly, sensuously lit and a breeze lightly ruffled the sheer
curtains of the open window.

'I had an interview,' he explained, catching her about the
waist and pulling her to him. 'But seeing as we're all dressed
up, why don't I take you to dinner?'

Her body yielded against his. And, nuzzling into his neck,
she traced her fingers lightly over his torso. 'Fuck me first,
darling. You know I hate sex on a full stomach.'

He sighed.

It had been a long, weird day. Sometimes he wished he could just take her out on a date like any normal girl.

But, as her hand slipped down the front of his trousers, he reconsidered. 'Oh, all right then.'

'Your suit makes you look so distinguished.' There was a gleam in her eye. 'Like a big, powerful businessman.'

Forcing him backwards, she toppled him into one of the chairs. She shimmied a little and the silk dress shifted, slowly working its way down her naked shoulders. Brushing her mouth against his, she climbed on top of him and the dress fell to her waist. 'I'm so sorry, sir,' she whispered, her lips caressing his neck. 'It seems I've forgotten to type those letters you wanted.' He tried to pull her closer but she continued to work her way down. 'I'm a very bad secretary.' She deftly unzipped his fly. 'But perhaps I can make it up to you.'

Hughie closed his eyes.

Her mouth was so warm, soft, wet . . .

Amidst the usual parade of pornographic images, his day began filtering through his mind. The woman on the bench, cricket scores, yellow Post-its screaming, 'You Can Do It!' Suddenly he felt tired and unexpectedly emotional. Loneliness threatened, of the variety he'd remembered as a schoolboy, dumped at the train station with his trunk and his uniform at the beginning of each new term.

Opening his eyes, he focused on Leticia's breasts, their nipples stiff and pink, bobbing up and down between his thighs. Her lips were slightly swollen, her eyes half-closed with pleasure;

she was doing something wonderful – stroking gently, her tongue everywhere. But, still, it was hard to concentrate. And he hated to disappoint her.

Taking her face in his hands, he stopped her. She looked up, surprised.

Hughie stood up. 'If you've forgotten to type those letters, you're in real trouble, Miss . . . Miss . . .'

She blinked at him. 'Miss Love to Suck Your Cock?'

'Well, be that as it may, I'm afraid this is a very serious matter.' He shoved a pile of sketchbooks off the large mahogany table and they scattered across the room. 'Pull down your knickers, Miss Love to Suck Your Cock. I'm going to have to spank you.'

'I'm not wearing any knickers, sir,' she giggled.

'How convenient.'

He forced her over the round table and pushed what remained of the dress to one side. Her buttocks were round and white. As he lifted his hand, he caught sight of her face in the floor-to-ceiling mirror opposite. Hair tousled, lips parted in anticipation – he knew he was on to something. 'I'm warning you, Miss Love to Suck Your Cock, if your bottom becomes too red, I may be forced to take you from behind.'

She squealed.

'Or some other ghastliness,' he added.

'Oh yes, more ghastliness!'

His hand landed roughly on her cool cheeks.

'Oh, sir!'

'Be quiet, Miss Love to Suck Your Cock!'

'But, sir!'

He spanked her again. A red welt formed.

'Oh, sir! I've also broken the typewriter, sir! And killed all the office plants!'

'You're a dreadful secretary!'

He spanked her again.

'Yes, yes! I'm just awful!'

Hughie turned her over roughly and pinned her to the table. 'What is it you want, Miss Love to Suck Your Cock?'

'I want to be used!' She arched her back, pressing herself against him. 'I want to be used and taken and satisfied and then used again!'

'By whom?' Hughie persisted.

Her eyes widened. She'd never imagined he could be so forceful.

She liked it.

'By you! Only by you!'

And so, Hughie watched himself in the mirror as he performed an act of utter ghastliness upon the enraptured Leticia. As her body shuddered beneath his, he gently pushed a strand of hair back from her cheek.

Perhaps they might wander down to that tiny restaurant in Pimlico and have Chinese food afterwards.

And maybe, he thought, just maybe, she'd let him hold her hand as they walked home.

★ ★ ★

It wasn't until later, when they were feasting on duck pancakes and jasmine tea, that the text came through.

The job is yours. Welcome to the firm.

Hughie walked Leticia home in glowing twilight. He wanted to be close to her. But each time he reached out to take her hand she deftly moved it away, swinging her handbag coyly. Finally, they stopped in front of the tall, terraced house where she owned a flat on the second floor, overlooking a leafy garden square.

'So,' he said.

'So,' she smiled up at him, tracing her fingers lightly along the lapel of Malcolm's suit.

'This is where we say goodnight. Unless, of course, you change your mind and invite me up,' he grinned hopefully.

'You know the Rules, Hughie.'

'Ah, yes. The Rules.'

'No point being sarcastic; they're there for a reason.'

His hand travelled into the small of her back, pressed her close. 'No emotional attachments, no gifts, no staying over, no sweet sentiments . . .'

'And no nasty surprises!' she concluded. 'The Rules keep us safe, Hughie. You don't think for one moment we'd be having this much fun if we were a couple, do you?'

'Hummm,' he buried his face into the curve of her long neck. 'I wonder . . .'

She pushed him away. 'You're not in danger, are you?'

She looked at him hard. 'Remember, if you're falling in love . . .'

'Only I'm not!'

'Swear?'

He went down on one knee. 'I prostrate myself before you in indifference!' Then, while he was down there, he tucked his head under her skirt. 'Ahh! Here's a bit I missed!' His lips moved up her inner thigh.

'Hughie! We're in the middle of the street! Oh!' she swooned, gripping the iron railings. 'Oh, yes!'

He poked his head out. 'Of course, we could go upstairs . . .'

'That would be against the Rules!'

'Yes! But it would feel so wrong, wouldn't it?' Standing, he pulled her close. 'It would be so incredibly . . . bad!'

She couldn't resist. He really was a terrific playmate. 'Oh, here!' Giggling, she dragged him across the street, into the garden square, behind a hedge. 'Only I'm warning you . . .'

He kissed her hard.

They tumbled onto the sweet-smelling grass. He looked into her beautiful dark eyes, hair tousled, lips parted.

'I don't love you,' he whispered.

Her arms wrapped round his neck. 'You say the sweetest things!'

Professional Massagers of the Female Ego

Two days later, Hughie found himself sitting on the same bench in Green Park, waiting for the man called Valentine. It was no name for a guy, that was for sure. He was wearing the same borrowed suit. (Already Malcolm was demanding that he have it professionally dry-cleaned.) The sunny day was almost identical to the one earlier on in the week and the whole experience was coloured by a strong sense of déjà vu. Hughie found himself scanning the figures in the distance; not searching for this unfortunately named man but for his red-headed woman instead. He was strangely disappointed when Valentine finally did appear.

'You're Hughie,' Valentine announced, stopping in front of him and holding out a hand.

'Yes,' Hughie stood and shook it. It struck him as an odd way to begin the conversation.

'Pleased to meet you. I'm Valentine Charles. What do you say we go get a drink in Shepherd's Market?'

'Sure,' Hughie smiled.

Any job where your employer buys you a drink on the first day has to be good.

They crossed the street and Valentine led him up a narrow alleyway. At the top, Shepherd's Market emptied onto a tiny square and in one corner there was a pub called the Adam and Eve. The sign had a picture of a man and woman divided by an apple. They stepped inside and as Hughie's eyes adjusted to the hazy darkness of the half-empty bar, he recognized a familiar face. She was sitting at a table in the corner, sipping a glass of white wine.

'It's you!' Hughie was surprised by how pleased he was to see her.

She smiled.

'Allow me to introduce my assistant, Mrs Flickering. Flick for short.'

She gestured to a chair. 'Take a seat, Hughie.'

'What will you have?' Valentine asked.

'Oh, I don't know . . .' Surely this was a test; the right answer was probably to order a soft drink.

'I'm having Scotch but that's probably a bit old for you. A pint of something?'

Hughie relaxed. 'Yes, please.'

Valentine went to the bar. They were alone.

'I didn't think I'd ever see you again,' he said softly.

Flick traced her fingers along the edge of her glass. 'And yet, here we are. Life's a funny old business, isn't it?'

'I'll say.' He shifted, unsure of how to continue. 'The other day in the park . . . what happened . . .'

She stopped him. 'Don't worry. I don't take it personally. All part of the interview process, Hughie. I've been through it a hundred times.'

'I see.' He looked crestfallen.

'Why so serious?' she laughed. 'Surely you're relieved!'

He let out a sigh. 'But how many times do you meet a stranger you can talk to?' The directness of his gaze was unnerving. 'That you really want to talk to?'

'Well, yes, but the thing is . . .' He had a knack for creating instant intimacy; disorientating her with his artlessness. She'd never encountered anything quite like it.

Valentine came back with the drinks and sat down.

'Cheers, Mr Venables-Smythe!' They raised their glasses. 'Congratulations on your appointment!'

'Thank you!' Hughie beamed.

They beamed back.

'So,' he ventured, 'what is it exactly that we do?'

Valentine looked at him closely. 'You've received one of the greatest honours of your life. You've been chosen; hand-selected to join one of the oldest and most secret professions in the world.'

Hughie felt uneasy. 'Not . . . the Oldest Profession?'

'Hardly!' Valentine bristled, offended. 'We are professional massagers of the female ego. We notice, flatter, attend to the delicate matter of romantic yearnings, that despite science and technology and sexual revolutions of all descriptions, still linger, languishing, in the human soul.

'In short,' Flick cut in, 'we flirt'.

'And we are master craftsmen at our vocation,' Valentine added proudly.

'You mean we pick up women?'

'Rule number one,' Flick outlined, 'you absolutely, categorically do not pick up women.'

'Not under any circumstances. We flirt, Hughie, make women feel good about being alive. We notice them. Smile. Talk a little. Pay them some attention.'

'And then leave,' Flick added. 'Rule number two: always know your exit.'

Things were looking up. He wasn't going to be a rent boy after all.

Still, his new profession wasn't entirely clear.

Valentine sensed his confusion. 'Let me start at the beginning. Imagine,' he made a bold, theatrical gesture with his hands, 'one day a lonely, dejected woman is waiting for a tube train or queuing in a shop when suddenly she's aware that a well-dressed, handsome young man is looking at her. Perhaps she turns away, pretends not to notice. But he's unable to stop staring. She grows flushed, excited. And at last, just as she's about to leave, he stops her. And stammering shyly, pays her a kind, warm compliment. "I just had to say, what lovely blue eyes you have . . ." and so on. To us, it's nothing. But to her, a perfect stranger would have been struck by her charm and beauty — a charm and beauty that she'd imagined she'd all but lost.'

'So, where do we find these women?' Hughie asked, taking another drink.

'That's Valentine's area of expertise,' Flick explained. 'He has connections all over the world. He's the one who manages the enquiries. We have a great many repeat customers. The same husbands have been coming to us for years.'

'Husbands!' Hughie choked on his lager.

Flick thumped him on the back. 'Yes, that can be a bit of a shock.'

'Let's face facts, shall we?' Valentine proposed. 'Nowadays, the only thing that keeps a marriage together is the intervention of strangers. Normally those strangers are likely to be an army of counsellors and therapists. But we can achieve tremendous results from a few well-timed words. Everyone, no matter how old they are or how long they've been married, needs someone who sees them as an object worthy of desire. It's just that one's spouse isn't always likely to provide it.'

'The key point is,' Flick explained, 'we break the cycle. A woman who's been flirting is an entirely different creature from one who feels rejected and unappreciated. Instantly, the dynamic shifts, and with a little effort on the husband's part, the rough patch is over.

'You see, said wife,' Valentine continued, 'otherwise known as the Mark, will be having a highly charged clandestine experience. A completely harmless, entirely manufactured experience, but a thrilling one nevertheless. And the most natural response in the world will be to treat her husband with extra care and affection to mask her little secret.' His eyes sparkled in the dim light. '*Et voilà*! Domestic harmony is once more restored.'

'But . . . but that's dishonest!'

Valentine tilted his head to one side. 'Is perfume dishonest?'

'What?'

'We don't naturally smell like crushed rose petals and jasmine, do we? And yet who would begrudge us a little harmless artifice? Honesty is only of value to doctors or lawyers. But in marriage, it can be fatal.

Of course, we don't always do married women,' Flick took a sip of her wine.

'Widows, divorcees, virgins, long-term singles . . .' Valentine reeled off.

'Yes, I see,' Hughie said, not really seeing at all. The very scope of it all was overwhelming.

'Don't worry,' Flick smiled. 'It can be a bit much to get your head round at first. But pretty soon it will all be second nature.'

Just then Hughie became aware that three of the most handsome men he'd ever seen were making their way across the pub towards them.

'Here are the boys.' Valentine turned to to greet them. 'I want you to meet the rest of the team.'

As they approached, Hughie recognized the man from the bus. 'Good God!'

'Well, fancy that!' the man countered, with a smile.

'You know each other?' Valentine sounded irritated.

'No,' the man said, 'not exactly. My name's Henry,' he held out his hand. 'Henry Montifore.'

Hughie shook it. 'I can't tell you what a spot I was in! I really owe you one. We met on a bus,' he explained to the others. 'I didn't have a ticket or rather I had one but couldn't get at it and there was an inspector . . .'

Henry laughed. 'Think nothing of it. Only I'd avoid that young man in future if I were you. Oh, and let me introduce you to Marco and Jez,' he indicated the two men next to him: a slim, roughly handsome Italian, with long dark hair, green eyes, and the smile of a wicked cherub; and to his left, a tall, muscular black man, who showed off his Olympian physique in a simple white T-shirt and jeans. He had the classical chis-elled features of a Greek statue, crowned by a close crop of white-blond hair.

'Welcome aboard!' Henry added.

They were all smiling, patting him on the back, laughing. A fresh pint appeared before him and Hughie experienced the rare and pleasant feeling that he'd arrived.

He wasn't exactly sure where he'd arrived or for how long. But he determined to enjoy it while it lasted.

110

La Dame aux Camélias

Leticia pressed the buzzer of Leo's flat and readjusted the shopping bags she was carrying. She'd lugged them all the way from Goodge Street in heels.

No reply. She rang again, looking around at the enviable location. Leo lived in a small Edwardian mansion block tucked away in a narrow alley across from Covent Garden Opera House. He'd had the tremendous luck and insight to buy it back in the late seventies when living in town was still a novel idea. Now the flats above and below his were gutted, turned into sleek, loft-style apartments, and prices had soared. His, however, was still firmly rooted in all the mod cons of 1982. She teased him that if he hung on to it long enough, perhaps the avocado bathroom suite might actually come back into fashion.

'Yes?'

'I'm here!'

The door clicked open and she struggled up the three flights of stairs. Leo was standing in the doorway wearing a red silk dressing gown worthy of Noel Coward; cigarette in one hand, coffee cup in the other.

'At last!' he grinned.

'What do you mean at last!' She walked past him into the kitchen, dumping the bags onto the table. 'I trot all over town doing your grocery shopping and that's all the thanks I get?' She planted a kiss on his cheek, then frowned. 'You've lost weight, old man. You can't afford to lose weight. This cold is taking its toll on you, which isn't surprising. How long have you had it? Almost a month?' She began unpacking the food. 'Let's get you something to eat.'

'Actually, I think I look rather well,' he said, striking a pose. 'I tried a pair of trousers on the other day I haven't been able to wear since 1983. They looked fabulous! Perry Ellis grey flannel with pleats like you wouldn't believe! Of course you won't remember Perry Ellis; you're too young.' He sat down. 'Did you get the fish fingers? And the pickles?'

'Yes. Since when do you eat fish fingers? Or pickles?' She opened the fridge. 'Tell me straight, are you pregnant?'

He laughed. 'Not this month. Juan likes them. He thinks they're exotic. They don't have fish fingers in Brazil. But the sweet things are all for me. Ahh! You genius!' He pulled out a tub of Belgian chocolate ice cream. 'Pass me a spoon, will you? It's at the ideal level of softness!'

She searched the draining board and handed him a teaspoon.

He took a bite. 'Heaven! There go those Perry Ellis trousers for another twenty years!'

'Juan, eh?' Leticia shook her head. 'You do realize you're seventy? Thirty-five-year-old male nurses are dangerous for your health. Or has no one told you?'

'Stay near the young and a little rubs off. Are you staying for lunch?'

'What are we having? Pickles and fish fingers?'

'Well, I'm having ice cream. But we could ring Bartolli's around the corner and pick up an order of minestrone if you like. Or spaghetti.'

Leticia filled the sugar bowl. 'That's OK. It's a little late for lunch; it's gone three. God, Leo, when was the last time this floor was washed? That's not like you.' She peeled off her coat, throwing it on top of the radiator. 'Where do you keep a bucket and some bleach?'

'Under the sink, O She of the Hardened Heart.' He spooned in another mouthful of chocolate ice cream. 'I adore Juan for his mind. Which reminds me, how is your young man?'

'Hughie?' Leticia filled the bucket with hot water and detergent. The smell of lemons filled the kitchen.

'Yes, Hughie.'

She smiled. 'Oh, he's all right.'

'You're blushing!'

'No, I'm not!'

'Yes, you are! Bright red!'

She pressed her hands to her cheeks. 'It's the steam from the water!'

'Steam, my arse!' Leo waved his spoon triumphantly. 'You like him!'

'Do not!'

'Do too, you great big nanna! All I have to do is mention the boy's name and you turn into a beetroot!' He began to cough, then to choke, clutching the side of the table.

Leticia thumped him on the back.

'Pardon me!' he gasped.

'Serves you right! Now out!' She ushered him into the living room, ice cream in hand. 'Feet up, on sofa while I scrub this floor, understand? And if that cough isn't better by tomorrow, I think we should call the doctor. You could have a chest infection.'

'Bollocks! This isn't the last act of *La Traviata*. You're changing the subject and you know it!'

'So what if I am?' She piled cushions at one end for him to lie down on and turned on the television. 'What do you want to watch?' She flicked through the channels. '*Richard and Judy*? *Through the Keyhole*?'

'Why are you so afraid to admit it?'

'Because there's nothing to admit. I have a system in place, Leo. Hughie's lovely; he's fresh, keen, delightful. But just like milk, men go off. Of course I like him; he's charming. But what I don't like is sour milk.' She checked the date setting on her wristwatch. 'I give him another two weeks, tops. Then I'm afraid he's going to have to go.'

She winked at Leo.

But Leo wasn't smiling back. 'This isn't a good look, darling.'

'Isn't it?' She pretended to concentrate on the television. 'What's this? Reruns of *ER*?'

He sat down, took her free hand. 'It wasn't your fault. It wasn't anybody's fault. You know that, don't you?'

'Let's not go there.'

'He was ill. That's all. Just terribly, terribly ill.'

She pulled her hand away. 'Enough. We're not going to discuss this again, understand?'

He shook his head. 'It breaks my heart to see you like this.'

'Like what? My God, Leo! I'm fine! Look at me! Running my own business, successful, cute young lover! I've got a life most women would kill for! Now, do you want to watch these sexy doctors, yes or no?'

He sighed, settling back onto the sofa. 'Absolutely not! The costumes – so dreadful! All those white lab coats!'

'Couldn't agree more. Oh, look! A showing of *The Red Shoes* on Channel Four. That looks like your scene.'

'Perfect.' He squinted at the television. 'God, I can't see a thing! Is that a car or a chorus girl?'

She passed him the remote. 'Where are your glasses?'

'In the bedroom. Do you mind, angel? I don't like Juan to see me wearing them.'

Leticia found his glasses on his bedside table, next to a row of unfamiliar prescription medicine bottles. She came back into the living room and handed them to him. 'I see you've already been to the doctor. What did he say?'

'Thank you, darling. Sorry, what was that?'

'The doctor. Have you seen him already?'

'Oh, yes. Juan made me go. Complete waste of time.'

'What did he say?'

'Bed rest, liquids, the usual malarkey.'

'I see. Well, then, you'd better rest. And I'll make you a cup of tea. After all, I need you back at the shop as soon as possible. That romance novelist wants a Barbie-pink Empire-line night-dress with purple trim.'

Leo winced. 'How revolting!'

'And she's a size twenty and only about four feet tall!'

'Fantastic! I can't wait to see what you come up with. Something with a bit of give, I hope.'

'Me? I'm counting on you!'

He smiled up at her. 'And I'm counting on you. I do love you. Do you know that?'

'I know.' She bent down and kissed his forehead. 'And me you.'

Leticia went back into the kitchen.

Leaning against the kitchen counter, she looked out of the window at the beautiful façade of the Opera House across the street.

The last time she'd been there was with him; *The Marriage of Figaro*, her favourite opera. All that wonderful music; all the couples neatly paired at the end.

It was a warm summer's evening; they'd sat in the stalls at great expense.

116

He'd been distant, distracted that night. He'd lost so much weight, though he still looked handsome in his white blazer, navy shirt.

She winced.

It was the details that devastated. The ice cream they'd shared at the interval; the wooden fan he'd bought her at the shop. He'd made such an effort. She thought it might signal a new beginning for them.

She couldn't have known that he was marking time, even then, sitting in the dark theatre, holding her hand; that he was just counting the days until the end.

Taking a dry mug from the draining board, she filled the kettle up, put in a fresh tea bag.

Real life goes on. Hearts are broken every second of every day. But real life marches on, regardless.

She'd survived. She thought she wouldn't. There had been days, weeks where she'd thought she'd go insane with grief and loss; the sheer senselessness of it all.

But she hadn't.

She'd limped until she could walk, walked until she could run and then run as hard and fast as she could ever since.

'And now I'm new and improved,' she reminded herself, pouring the boiled water into the mug, pressing the tea bag up against the side with a spoon.

The person who wasn't new and improved was Leo.

He was getting old. She tried to ignore it but lately every time she saw him, he seemed a little more fragile than the last time. And it frightened her. Glasses frightened her, medicine bottles frightened her, a dirty kitchen floor frightened her. And there was nothing she could do about it which frightened her most of all.

What was that sound?

She looked down.

Her hands were shaking; the teaspoon rattling against the side of the mug.

Tossing the spoon into the sink, she pressed her palms together. 'Stop it!' she said out loud. 'Just stop!'

'What?' Leo called from the other room. 'Did you want me?'

Leticia took a deep breath. 'No. It's nothing,' she called back.

It's nothing, she repeated in her head. It's over. All over now.

Leo was right, this wasn't *La Traviata*. All she had to do was brew the tea, wash the floor, make the fat woman her nightdress.

Then she stopped.

What about Hughie? Was Leo right? Was she allowing herself to care about some boy who would no doubt leave her too? That was the last thing she needed. She couldn't risk falling apart over some kid.

She took the tea in to Leo, put it gently down on the table next to him.

He smiled up at her.

She smiled back.

I can't lose him, she thought, suddenly terrified. Please, God, not him.

'You OK?' he asked.

'Fine,' she nodded. 'Just fine.'

Heading back into the kitchen, she stacked the chairs on top of the table and took off her shoes. Then she rolled up the sleeves of her impeccable white silk blouse, took the bucket of scalding water and got down on her hands and knees.

Leticia scrubbed.

She scrubbed until the floor was spotless, until her hands were red and sore, until her shoulders ached.

And then she scrubbed harder, until her mind went numb.

High Tea at Claridge's

Later that afternoon, Hughie sat in Valentine's flat in Half Moon Street.

'Well,' Valentine settled into a large leather chair near the fireplace. 'My question to you, Mr Venables-Smythe, is, are you game?'

'Yes, sir. I think I am.'

'Good. You have a great deal to learn, young man, and very little time in which to learn it. It takes time to build up a repertoire, but I'm afraid current demand means you're just going to have to do the best you can. Henry will look after you. Listen and follow every instruction without fail. We're going to spend a considerable amount of money remodelling you. You need a haircut, a decent suit, a pair of proper shoes and a good watch. Here.' He stood up and took an ebony box down from the mantel. Opening it, he selected a gold Rolex from a long row of five or six and threw it across to him. 'Never underestimate details. Women notice them immediately.'

Hughie slipped the watch around his wrist. It was heavy,

gleaming, the kind of fuck-off piece of kit which instantly reminded him of his father. 'That's very generous of you!'

'Not that generous.' Valentine pushed a button on his desk and the doors of the cabinet behind him slid away to reveal a large screen. 'There's a tracking device in it.' He pressed another button and the screen flared to life, a mass of glowing points against the backdrop of a London street map. 'I like to know what my boys are up to at all times.'

'I see.' He felt like James Bond, part of a secret, underground organization.

Valentine pushed a state-of-the-art customized PDA across the desk to Hughie. 'Keep this charged at all times. It's a phone, Internet access and most importantly sat nav. You'd be surprised how many marks wander off course.'

Hughie turned it on. 'Brilliant!'

'Do you smoke?'

Hughie tried to sound responsible and grave. 'I've every intention of giving up.'

'Well, don't.' Valentine tossed a silver lighter across to Hughie. 'Yes, it's a lighter but it's also a highly effective listening device. Not absolutely essential but occasionally quite useful. And before you go, I need all your measurements. Leave them with Flick. Now down to the nitty-gritty. Your rate of pay will be £1,000 per hit. Aborted or imperfect missions will not be paid. For tax reasons, you need to file your own return and will be known as a personal consultant. And one final point, your entire career with this organization depends on your unconditional discretion.

No one must know what you do or who your clients are. A single leak could fatally compromise the security of this enterprise. From now on, as far as your friends and family are concerned, you've got a job making corporate training videos. Failure to comply with the terms of your confidentiality agreement will result in immediate dismissal. Do you have any questions?'

Hughie stared in wonder at the mass of top-of-the-range gear he'd suddenly acquired. 'So, you're saying that all I have to do is chat to these women and I'll be paid £1,000 a go?'

It was more money than he was used to making in a year.

Valentine pressed the tips of his fingers together under his chin. 'There's a lot more to a successful flirt than that.'

'Why did you choose me? I mean, I thought I hadn't done very well in my interview. It's not as if I'm some great ladies' man.'

Valentine regarded him closely. 'Contrary to what you might imagine, ladies' men do not make great flirts; their egos demand too much attention. A successful flirt is an entirely different experience than scoring with women. We don't collect phone numbers or chalk up sexual conquests. In fact, it's not about you at all. It's far more subtle. And the real art of flirting is dependent upon an unselfconsciousness with women that allows you to put them at the centre of your attention. You have that quality, Hughie. You're a natural. And I can tell you from many years' experience, it's extremely rare.'

Sandwiched firmly between his mother and Clara, Hughie

had spent his whole life surrounded by women. He'd also spent a terrific amount of time trying to figure out how to soothe, calm and flatter them – to quiet whatever storms were raging inside them, splashing out onto the comparatively uncomplicated surface of his life. They'd bullied him, spoilt him, taken him in hand and then dropped him; but the feeling of women, the act of sitting and listening to them, of being their confidant, was second nature. He was relieved that he didn't have to pretend to be a playboy or a lover.

'I think I can do this,' he said slowly. 'I think this might be something I can do.'

Valentine smiled. 'I think so too. Now, are you ready to begin your training?'

As if on cue, Henry appeared in the doorway, so handsome, flawlessly dressed, emanating smooth elegance.

I want to be like that, he thought. Leticia would love that. And another echo of his father resounded somewhere in his chest.

'Oh, there is one thing I failed to mention,' Valentine said, standing. 'You must be single.'

'Oh. Really?' To his surprise, Hughie felt the bottom of his stomach disappear.

'This isn't a profession that sits happily next to long-term relationships. Girlfriends, partners, wives are all strictly off limits. A little jealousy can destroy the entire set-up. We've tried in the past; invariably it's a disaster. Even the most self-possessed woman finds the idea of her man flirting with hundreds of women every month trying. Of course, we don't expect you to be celibate. Have sex to your heart's content. All we ask is that you confine yourself to sex and only sex. One-night stands, preferably. Anything more meaningful is forbidden.'

'Oh.'

Valentine's eyes narrowed. 'You're single, aren't you?'

'Sure,' Hughie nodded.

'Good. Make sure it stays that way.'

Hughie stood up, caught Henry's eye. For a moment he thought his face betrayed him. But, of course, that was stupid; what was there to betray?

Henry put an arm around his shoulder.

'Come on,' he said. 'Let's go for a walk.'

'Where do you live?' Henry was walking just ahead of him, through the back streets of Mayfair. The air around them was cooling, the sky dimming to a light grey. Street lamps began to flicker as they strolled into Mount Street Gardens.

'Kilburn.' Hughie took out his cigarettes. 'Want one?'

'Thank you.' Henry stopped and they both lit up. The dry, earthy scent of autumn leaves and crisp evening air mingled pleasantly with the acrid smoke. Henry inhaled deeply and their pace slowed. Bells began to ring, announcing evensong at the church opposite.

'I'll walk you to the train or bus or whatever it is you take.'

He managed to make the idea of travelling home sound alien, even passé.

'Where do you live?' Hughie asked.

'I keep a room. In a hotel.'

Hughie had never heard of such a thing. 'A hotel?'

Henry smiled. 'It saves me having to cook. And they have an excellent laundry service.'

'Which one?'

'The Savoy.' Henry kicked his way lazily through a pile of fallen leaves. 'I'm particularly fond of the view of the river, especially at night.'

'Wow!' Hughie took another drag.

He pictured himself lying in bed, ringing down for room service every morning: a full English breakfast, large pot of tea and a morning paper. They probably even had phones in the bathtub and little bottles with shampoo and free soap. Imagine never having to make a bed (not that he did now) or boil a kettle!

'Do the maids still wear those uniforms? You know, the ones with the little aprons and white hats?'

'They do indeed,' Henry grinned.

Hughie entertained a vision of Leticia wearing just such a uniform, bending over to make the bed.

Could there be anything more glamorous than living in a hotel?

They crossed into Grosvenor Square. The sky above was streaked with pink and orange, glowing like the embers of their cigarettes.

'So, your girlfriend . . . what's her name?' Henry asked.

'My what?'

Henry looked at him sideways. 'Your girlfriend,' he repeated.

Hughie considered lying to him, then gave up the idea as being too labour intensive in the long run. 'Leticia. Only she's not my girlfriend. It's a bit looser than that. Actually, a great deal looser.'

'Right,' Henry nodded. 'Been together long?'

'A few weeks . . . maybe a little longer. But honestly, all we do is fuck. She won't even let me stay over.'

'Yes.' Henry seemed unconvinced. 'So you don't care about her.'

'Well, I mean, she's great. Wild, sexy, beautiful . . .'

'Uh hum.' Henry shook his head.

'But it's not like I'm in love with her!'

'Really.'

'Really!'

Henry stopped, turned to face him. 'I'll bet she gives good head.'

Hughie's eyes widened. 'What did you just say?'

'I said,' Henry rocked back on his heels, hands in pockets, 'that I'll bet she gives good head.'

'Well,' Hughie bristled, 'I honestly don't see that that's any of your business and quite frankly, I take offence at the question!'

'Ah-ha!' Henry pointed at him triumphantly. 'You see! You do care! No feelings, my arse! You, sir, are in grave danger of being in love!'

Hughie was stunned. 'Really?'

'Absolutely. You're teetering, Smythe. Dangling dangerously on the edge.'

An emotional precipice suddenly gaped before him. 'Oh, God! Are you sure?'

'I can tell, just by looking at you, you're a romantic. And a romantic around love is like an alcoholic bartender – simply can't be trusted. Put her down, Smythe. Walk away right now.'

'Are you sure? I mean, seems a bit . . . rough.'

'See! You're dragging your feet! Very bad sign.' He shook his head. 'Best give her up, old man, if you want the job. Valentine's very strict on this point and not without good reason.'

'But you don't understand! It's the perfect set-up; she doesn't even believe in love! Ours is a strictly physical affair.'

'And yet . . .' Henry paused, looking at Hughie closely, 'I hear she's as hot and horny as a racehorse after the Derby!'

'Good God, man! Do you want to be punched?'

'See! Inability to tolerate locker-room banter is a dead give-away. Only with the woman we care about, is that sort of talk offensive.'

'Oh, God!' It was true. Henry was right. Hughie hadn't noticed it before, but somehow, when he wasn't paying attention (which could've been any time), he'd apparently crossed an invisible line. How could he have fallen so far without even noticing it? It wasn't like him. Normally he only realized he was in love when the girl he was seeing told him so. There was usually a moment, and an awkward one at that, when they'd gaze up at him, bat their lashes, look all soft and melting. 'You do love me, don't you?' they'd murmur.

And a bloke had to say yes. Anything else was just rude. Besides, if you didn't, they'd batter it out of you anyway.

'What about you? Do you mean to say you haven't had a girlfriend this whole time?'

Henry's gaze was far off, on some distant landmark. 'I loved a girl. Once,' he added wistfully.

'What happened?'

But Henry didn't answer.

Instead he patted Hughie on the back. 'Some day you'll understand. See, being a flirt is a vocation. A calling. We flirt, young Smythe, because others cannot. And we have the ability to foster love only because we're above it ourselves. But like all true vocations, it involves sacrifice and discipline.'

It sounded so noble. Hughie had never had a purpose in life. Henry's words seeped through to his very core. Could it be that he was destined for a higher calling?

They walked on.

After a while Hughie asked, 'So. How do you do it? What's the trick?'

'Do what?' Henry paused to let a woman thunder past in her high heels, swinging her handbag violently to and fro like a weapon.

'Flirt.'

'The thing about flirting is not to think of it as flirting. The minute you do, it becomes contrived and false. The trick, if there is a trick, is just about noticing. Paying attention. What you say is secondary. And forget poetry. Simple things are best. Specific is good; it shows you're really paying attention: "I've never seen such green eyes," but not, "Your eyes are like two shining emeralds." Women don't want to be endlessly flattered. They want to feel as if you find it a pleasure to be with them.'

'OK,' Hughie's brow knit. 'So to flirt you try not to flirt but pay attention instead.'

'There are three stages to any successful flirt; observing, making contact and re-framing . . . taking who they think they are and shaking it up a little. The matron wants to be told she's sexy or avant-garde. The new mother wants to be told she's handling it all seamlessly and hasn't changed. The sophisticate wants to be told she's delightfully unaffected, even charming. Your job is to see beyond the surface.'

'And how do you do that?'

'You're keen!' Henry laughed. 'All right, then. The easiest way is to show you.' And he led Hughie down Brook Street and into the grand lobby of Claridge's Hotel.

They sat at one of the small round tables in the foyer, buzzing with the sudden rush of early-evening activity that tourists generate upon arriving back from a long day's sightseeing. A string quartet was playing Mozart and the exotic ritual of high tea was just drawing to a close; hotels being the only place left where it was enacted in its entirety, like small historical dramas for people who had only read about it in books. Henry ordered them both a drink and then sat back, surveying the scene around him.

'There,' he said presently, pointing to a woman sitting with two young children at a table well away from the other guests. 'What can you tell me about her?'

Hughie looked across the foyer. The woman was about forty-two, with dark shoulder-length hair, wearing a pair of tailored trousers and a stiff white shirt. Her hands were covered in rings; gold bracelets dangled from her wrists, a thick gold chain around her neck and a pair of matching, large earrings. Her face was carefully made up, too heavily for Hughie's taste. She sat listlessly while the little girl and boy ducked in and around the table, arguing over a small electronic Game Boy. The table was set for high tea but, although the children's plates bore the remains of half-eaten cakes, the woman's was empty. A cup of black tea sat cooling in front of her and a pile of shopping bags from exclusive designer boutiques was stacked at her feet. The children, who were maybe five and seven, were dressed like two Ralph Lauren models, in pristine, almost Victorian children's clothes. As the argument over the Game Boy became more animated, she winced and whispered some-thing to them Hughie couldn't hear. They looked up at her anxiously. Then the girl berated the boy, gave her brother a shove, and they both settled back sullenly into their seats.

'Well, she's married . . .' Hughie began. 'She's got two chil-dren. She must be rich; she's done a lot of shopping . . .'

'How do you think she feels?' Henry pressed.

Hughie narrowed his eyes. 'Tired?'

Henry took another sip of his whisky and soda. 'Is that all?'

'I don't know. Hungry?'

'I'd say starving. But not just for food.' He leant forward. 'First off, she's American. Probably from somewhere provincial, like the Midwest; definitely not from New York or LA. That's why the children are dressed like extras from *Mary Poppins* and her make-up is ten, no, more like fifteen years, behind the times.'

Hughie was amazed. 'How can you tell?'

'You get a feel for these things. It's easy to tell she's not European; there's nothing at all natural about her.'

'Oh.'

'Secondly,' he continued, 'she's married a wealthy man but doesn't have a job of her own. It's unlikely the money is hers. Independently wealthy women don't spend money in such an obvious way. They buy things, of course. But what you see here is revenge shopping. She's spending her husband's money, piling up as many bags as she can in order to take what she can from him.'

'She could have a job,' Hughie felt a sudden desire to defend her against Henry's razor-sharp evaluation.

'See how her hair doesn't move with her head? That's because it's been blow-dried every other day. Working women don't have time for that, or for the freshly manicured nails.'

'I see.' Hughie felt suitably chastened.

'She's bored, depressed and, if I'm not mistaken, hasn't even

131

seen her husband recently let alone had any romantic attention from him.' He leant forward. 'See how she's wearing half
of the Bulgari collection? A sure sign of low self-esteem. Too
much jewellery, too much make-up; these things are like armour
for women. She obviously thinks she has something to hide.
So, what does she need?'

Hughie smiled wanly. 'A good therapist?'

Henry sighed. 'From you.'

Hughie looked at her again. A waiter tried to clear the plates
and she snapped at him, like a small dog whose tail had been
stepped upon. The young man retreated and for a while she
just sat, her fingers pressed over her eyes.

Something about her reminded him of his own mother, of
the overwhelming sense of failure that seemed to follow her
about like a cloud when he was small.

'She needs to be told she's good at something,' Hughie said
quietly.

Henry smiled. 'That's good. Very good. How do you think
you might do that?'

Hughie took another gulp of his drink.

This was the best job he'd had in his entire life. But he was
hopelessly out of his depth.

The little boy looked up and caught his eye. And before he
knew quite what he was doing, Hughie stuck his tongue out
at him.

The boy giggled.

Hughie pretended to ignore him and then glanced over

again. This time the boy made a face and his sister squealed in delight.

Very slowly the dark-haired woman turned round.

'I'm sorry,' she said, in a soft drawl. 'Are my children disturbing you?'

Hughie thought he caught a thin thread of fear in her voice. 'No, not at all,' he smiled. 'Except for that one,' he added, winking at the little boy. The child giggled again, squirming in his seat with glee.

'Oh, he's a terror!' his mother agreed. And as she smiled, her eyes settled upon her son's face. There was unmistakable tenderness in her expression.

She loves him, Hughie thought. Henry's right: she's just not that fond of herself.

'Are you in town long?' Henry asked, leaning in.

'No, we go to Paris tomorrow and then Rome. I wanted the children to see Europe.' She sounded wistful. 'You know, Americans abroad,' she added, almost apologetically.

'Ah! A Grand Tour!' Henry grinned. 'There's nothing like it!'

'A Grand Tour?'

The little boy had wriggled off the chair and moved as close to Hughie as he dared, waiting for him to do something naughty.

Hughie stuck a sugar cube up his nose.

'Oh, yes! An age-old English tradition; the invaluable education that comes from immersing yourself in the very bosom of Western civilization; inundating the youthful sensibility with the rich history and extraordinary aesthetics of the great cities of Europe ... It's the stuff of Henry James and Edith Wharton ... of Fielding ...'

Her eyes lit up. 'I read Edith Wharton once! *Ethan Frome*. But I don't think anyone went to Paris. It was all about these invalids on a sled.'

'Yes, well ...'

'But I like the idea of a Grand Tour,' she said quickly. 'I hadn't thought of it that way.'

'It's a noble tradition,' Henry assured her. 'Are you travelling alone?'

'Well,' her face clouded, 'my husband was going to come but he was detained in Chicago. And New York. Business, you see. But Daddy may join us in Rome, isn't that right?' she said brightly. The children nodded obediently. 'On our Grand Tour,' she added, smiling at Henry.

Henry leant back. 'You know, I admire you.'

'Me?' She laughed incredulously. Her daughter wrapped herself protectively around her mother's chair.

'It's quite an unusual thing for small children to be given the chance to have such an adventure. Imagine,' his voice lowered, gentle and intimate, 'wandering around the great capitals of Europe with a lovely, determined young mother leading the way ... mothers, especially, have the knack of making almost anything fun.'

She stared at Henry.

This was clearly not the scenario she had been living.

Hughie took the sugar cube out of his nose. 'Not a lot of parents would do what you're doing. Especially on their own.'

'That's true,' Henry agreed. 'You have spirit.'

'It's funny,' she paused, registering their words, 'I've never thought of it quite that way. Of course, I hadn't intended to do it on my own . . .'

'It's an opportunity!' Henry insisted. 'A wonderful, rare chance to be alone with you that your children will remember for the rest of their lives.'

The little boy had shoved sugar cubes in both his nostrils and was making faces at Hughie. Hughie grabbed him and tickled him until they fell out.

'Do you really think so?' she murmured.

'Without fail!' Henry pushed back his chair and stood up. 'Well, we were just admiring this lovely family portrait. I wish you luck in your travels. May I make one last suggestion?'

'Please.'

He clapped Hughie on the back. 'When I took my son here to Paris for the first time, some fifteen years ago now . . .' he gazed adoringly down at Hughie. 'Can that be true? Was it really as long ago as that?'

Hughie blinked up at him.

'Seems like yesterday,' Henry sighed, ruffling his hair. 'Anyway, we didn't bother with things like the Louvre or Notre Dame. We just explored. There's a wonderful merry-go-round in Les Tuileries and Les Deux Magots make a marvellous hot choco-late. And now of course he speaks impeccable French.'

'Really?'

They both turned to Hughie.

'*La voiture est rouge*,' Hughie observed sagely. '*Charles ressemble á un sange. Où est la bibliothèque?*'

The woman giggled nervously. 'Did he say Charles looks like a monkey?'

'He's mentally ill,' Henry explained. 'But his pronunciation is impeccable.'

Out on the pavement, Henry clapped Hughie on the back. 'See, that wasn't so bad, was it? And all we did was observe, make contact and re-frame her experience a little. Easy as pie.'

'Easy as pie,' Hughie repeated. 'Only . . .'

'Only what?'

'Only, it doesn't quite seem enough.'

'Really?' Hughie frowned. 'What more is there?'

'I don't know . . . some grand gesture . . . something she won't forget.'

Henry thought a moment. 'You're right! No point settling for half-measures. Let's push the old girl right over the edge, shall we?'

'Yes, let's!'

'Wait here.' Henry ducked back into the hotel.

Hughie shoved his hands deep into his pockets to look nonchalant. But his heart was thumping against his ribcage, adrenalin surging through his veins. Taxis pulled up, disgorging well-dressed passengers. Hughie was conscious of trying to look a part, and at the same time, feeling a fraud. He grinned, at no one in particular, nodded to the doorman who moved away.

Then, quite suddenly, he was giggling. He tried to control it. His shoulders shuddered and his eyes watered. The doorman stared straight ahead. And Hughie was reminded of the kind of hysterical relief of performing a ridiculous schoolboy dare.

When Henry came back, it was all Hughie could do to pull himself together and wipe the tears from his cheeks.

'Travis, Taylor! Come on!'

She stood, gathering the handles of all her shopping bags together; the pile of gold bracelets falling forward on her wrists. 'Children! Please!'

Taylor and Travis danced around her as they made their way across the lobby and into the lift. As the doors opened again on the fifth floor, they spilt out, racing each other down the long corridor. Rummaging in her handbag, she pulled out the credit-card-shaped room key and swiped it, forcing the door of the suite open. The children bounced into the master bedroom and, giggling, flung themselves onto the bed.

'Mommy, look!' Taylor shouted, pointing to the dressing table.

'What is it?' She turned, let go of the packages; her handbag slid to the floor. 'Oh, my goodness!'

An exquisite bouquet of creamy white roses interspersed with fresh, fragrant stalks of eucalyptus, was massed in front of the dressing-table mirror. Buried deep within the blooms was a small card.

She took it out.

'Are they from Daddy?' Taylor pressed herself around her mother's leg. 'What does it say, Mommy?'

'No,' she said in wonder. 'They're not from Daddy.'

'Who are they from?'

'Yes, Mommy!' Travis jumped up and down excitedly. 'Who sent you flowers?'

Looking up, she caught sight of herself in the mirror and paused.

Then she smiled.

Grabbing Taylor's hands, she spun her round and round until they collapsed on top of the massive bed. Pillows went flying. Shrieks filled the air. Travis clambered eagerly on top of them and she pressed them both to her, these two tiny wriggling bodies, smelling of warmth and youth and cake. She tickled them, covering them in kisses, blowing raspberries on the backs of their necks until they squirmed with delight. The perfectly made bed crumpled and creased as she threw them into the soft pile of pillows, until one of them exploded, sending a cloud of white feathers shooting into the air, drifting slowly, weight-lessly to the ground. They were laughing so hard they never even noticed the tears she quickly brushed away.

A Brief History of the Professional Flirt
(A Small Digression)

Now, you are probably wondering why you've never heard of a professional flirt before and some of you, the more jaded and pessimistic, might even imagine I've made up the entire occupation, that no such position exists.

Well, you're wrong.

It was during the famously hot summer of 1911, when Valentine Charles's own great-grandmother, Mrs Rowland Vincent (Celia to her friends), found herself recently widowed and struggling to save the rather dreary ladies' hairdressing shop in St James that she and her first husband had established with their life's savings. Poor old Rowland Vincent had died of a sudden diabetic attack brought on by eating too many rose crèmes. (What the crèmes were doing in the house, considering his condition and extreme partiality to them, remains a mystery.)

The fortunes of the Vincents' small shop were floundering, headed for disaster, when Celia had the good luck to meet Valentine's grandfather – the very tall, wickedly handsome Nicholas Charles.

Twelve years her junior with no hairdressing experience (in fact, at twenty-six he'd already had a suspiciously long and varied career in domestic service that spanned stable boy to gentleman's valet), he was nevertheless remarkably popular with her clients, creating hairstyles based on the long plaits fashionable for horses in dressage. (Luckily for him, the Russian ballet was in town that summer performing *The Firebird* and the Russian peasant look, along with thick braids, was all the rage.)

Seizing upon the fervour for all things foreign, Nicholas took to calling himself Nicolai and then the Baron Carvolski which was, in the autumn of 1912, shortened to the Baron. His accent was a beguiling if challenging mixture of cockney, Prussian and a bit of Franglais thrown in for colour. His signature style was *La Vie en Rose*: long plaits woven into a kind of basket on top of the head, then filled with a combination of real and silk roses. A client had to keep her head very still. In spite of, or perhaps, because of the fact that very few ladies could pull off such a feat, the style became legendary.

However, the trait that rescued the tiny shop from ruin, raising it to the enviable position of the most exclusive in town, was his remarkable, even heroic ability to flirt with absolutely anyone. Celia Vincent watched in fascination (and no small amount of jealousy) as day after day, he wove a spell around each woman, practically hypnotizing them with compliments and subtle sexual innuendoes, tailoring his words precisely. He'd flash his perfect teeth and had mastered the daring, direct stare that was to become the trademark of the screen idol Valentino (many say he stole it from the Baron).

But it wasn't until the Baron was approached by a distraught duke that the professional flirt as we know it today was born. The hapless peer had been caught in flagrante with his mistress behind the library sofa at a country-house party. His wife, a sadly plain and introverted woman, was, he felt, taking it all a bit badly. The Baron's reputation to lift a woman's spirits was well established and the duke wondered if, for an additional fee, he might not lay it on a bit thick.

Nicolai kept his side of the bargain, not only flirting the depressed duchess into a much better humour but also managing to give her a genuinely flattering hairstyle at the same time. The couple reached a reconciliation and soon word spread of the Baron's amazing abilities. Shortly after, he was inundated by wealthy husbands of a certain class with 'special requests'.

The enterprising couple set about expanding their business. They were quick to realize they'd stumbled upon a previously untapped service industry. An ad was placed at the back of *The Times*, not dissimilar to the one that Hughie answered in the *Stage*, and two more gentlemen were hired and trained in the Baron's methods.

And so the business flourished.

During the Second World War, the shop was badly bombed

and Valentine's grandparents were surprised that even without the shop front, clients still came flooding in – many of them anxious soldiers posted overseas, desperate to be assured that their wives and girlfriends remained faithful. (This was when the Cyrano was born, but more about that later.)

Thus the business quietly thrived and was handed down from one generation to another, mutating as such things do to keep up with the times.

There has always been a Charles presiding over England's oldest, and for all I know, only established agency of flirts.

But now our digression is over. Those of you who still doubt the existence of the professional flirt and accuse me of writing fiction are gently reminded to keep an open mind. After all, can you really be certain you've never been on the receiving end of their services yourself?

The World's Most Exclusive Hairdresser

'Old Compton Street,' Olivia called, climbing into the back of a black cab. 'And hurry!'

Weaving in and out of traffic, the cab negotiated the congested curve of Hyde Park Corner and Olivia sank back into the seat.

She was late. It wasn't like her to be late. But suddenly life had become interesting; there was so much to organize, so many changes to be made now that Red Moriarty was part of the new show. Before she'd realized it, half the morning was gone. Now her best friend, her only friend, Mimsy Hollingford, would be furious.

Mimsy was waiting for Olivia at the Factory, the hottest new beauty salon in Soho. Although getting an appointment with the owner, Rolo Greeze, was next to impossible, Mimsy had arranged one for Olivia months ago as a birthday present.

'Now that you're forty,' she counselled, 'you'll need to revamp your style. And Rolo is the most exclusive hairdresser in the world. He has clients in Rome, Paris, New York; he flies out once a month. Did I tell you he dyes Gordon Ramsay's roots?'

'But I like my style.'

'Yes, of course. But really,' Mimsy shot her one of those looks; the one that signalled in no uncertain terms that she was not impressed, 'let's be practical now. All these troubles with Arnaud; typical. It's a midlife crisis. Nothing a good haircut can't sort out.'

Olivia didn't like to ask whose midlife crisis. But by now she was well used to Mimsy's methodology. According to her there was no problem in life which couldn't be solved using sheer willpower and a platinum credit card. Fifty-five now, the veteran of four husbands, countless affairs and numerous surgical procedures, she was fond of taking people in hand. They'd met at a fund raiser when Olivia first arrived in London eleven years ago. Mimsy had struck her as powerful, chic; confident with her emaciated figure and strong, feline features. Olivia had allowed herself to become Mimsy's new project, not fully realizing Mimsy liked to revamp indefinitely.

'Forty is a milestone,' she'd continued. 'You need to rethink everything. Time to get the needles out, book a surgeon, hire a full-time Pilates instructor and a macrobiotic cook. And, let's face it, in the bedroom, you've got to work, work, work! You can slack off when you're sixty but this is the crunch period. Forty is when most women start to give up. What they really should be doing is upping their game. No more lying back and thinking of England. From now on, oral sex is always on the menu; if you can't give a good blow job, you'd better learn. To tell the truth,' she leant in, 'it saves so much time. Fifteen minutes and you can get back to watching telly. Oh, and make an appointment at Bordello. I have a dozen pieces from her – worth every penny. Arnaud should never see you wearing anything that isn't sexy or gorgeous. Lord knows, as soon as you take it off, he'll have to start using his imagination, so help him out a bit!'

The cab dipped into the narrow labyrinth of one-way Soho streets. Outside the window, the bold pink neon signs of sex shops blinked, cheek by jowl with bijou patisseries, oyster bars and coffee houses. A rainbow display of wildly coloured fishnet tights on naked mannequins graced the window of a whole-sale fashion outlet across from the West End production of *Mary Poppins*. Film production companies, ad agencies, sushi bars, Chinese herbalists; bicycle couriers veered dangerously onto the pavement, terrorizing slow-moving clots of disorientated tourists; a homeless man and his dog camped in front of the Ivy playing show tunes on a harmonica . . . all life spilt out, raw, unchecked, vibrant. Olivia soaked up the unfamiliar, louche atmosphere.

Mimsy had her heart in the right place, she reminded herself, staring at a young woman with a shaved head, washing down the windows of a venue called the Pussy Cat Club. For her, marriage was a full-time profession, a never-ending game of chess with houses, holidays, even children as rather useful pawns.

Men were to be outwitted, manipulated, cajoled. And Olivia had taken a lot of Mimsy's advice; she wanted to make her marriage work and hated how dramatically it had changed recently. But the military approach to relationships was still daunting. Buried deep in her heart, Olivia had a vague dream of reaching a place with Arnaud where the pretence would fall away and the constant forward planning become obsolete.

The bald girl tossed a bucket of soapy water across the front doorstep.

But she would never dare share that with Mimsy.

Just as she predicted, Mimsy was pacing the floor of the waiting area when she arrived. The whole place was done out like an industrial manufacturing plant with cold stone floors, sheet-metal counters, large black dentist-style chairs and huge communal wash basins like giant stone troughs. A soundtrack of Patty Smith blared 'Because the Night' and nubile young men in tight black over-alls balancing trays of cold drinks were everywhere.

'My God!' Mimsy threw her hands up. 'What are you wearing? And what took you so long?'

Olivia looked down at her jeans, cashmere cardigan and ballet pumps. 'What I always wear to the hairdressers. I'm sorry I'm late . . .'

'How is he going to be able to create a new look for you if you don't give him some inspiration!' she interrupted, peeling off an unstructured Chanel jacket and thrusting it at her. 'You look like you're about to do the school run, for Christ's sake!' Then she stopped. 'Oh, sorry, Olivia! Really, I am!'

'It's OK,' Olivia lied, taking the jacket. It reeked of Venom; a hangover from Mimsy's heyday in the eighties. And the couture piece wasn't anything she'd ever buy. Still, Mimsy had gone to a lot of trouble. Dutifully she slipped it on. 'Am I too late?'

'Well,' Mimsy readjusted the collar of her blouse in the mirror, 'he's running an hour behind. But that's not the point!'

'What is the point?' Olivia laughed, relieved.

Mimsy shook her head. 'The point is, you're not taking this seriously. And I'm telling you, God is in the details, darling. Everything flows from the head down. Besides, this man's a genius. He works miracles. He's the most exclusive hairdresser in the world!'

'Rolo is ready for you,' the receptionist informed them coolly, sashaying down a long grey corridor.

They followed her through the brigades of stylists, blow-drying, cutting, gluing on extensions, to a small raised platform in the centre of the salon. There, in a mirrored alcove, stood Rolo Greeze; all four foot nine of him. Like a dark dwarf he oiled up to them, smoothing down his goatee. Two terrified assistants stood at the ready on either side.

'Ah!' Arms spread wide, he embraced Olivia, as if they'd known each other for years. 'Sit down, sit down! NOW! Let me see!' And he began flipping her hair about. 'See this?' he positioned his hands at her jawline. 'Your hair must never be longer than this, right?'

'Then I won't be able to put it up.'

147

'Putting up your hair is over! Ageing!' He shook his head, emphatic. 'This is it! Anything longer and it's completely wrong for your face! And I want layers; lots and lots of layers! Let me see your hands!' He grabbed one. 'Perfect! Lovely! What I'll do is cut a long fringe, something that hangs right here.' He indicated the middle of her nose. 'And then you'll have to push it out of your eyes using these wonderful hands of yours! It will be so young! So sexy!' he enthused. 'Everyone will see that gorgeous ring of yours!'

'Oh, yes!' Mimsy was entranced. 'That's a brilliant idea! Very rough and tumble!'

'I won't be able to see.'

'You don't have to!' He laughed. The assistants laughed. Mimsy laughed. 'Everyone will be looking at you! And when you want to see someone, it's like you come out from behind this veil of hair . . .'

'Yes, yes!' Mimsy nodded.

Olivia shifted. The dentist's chair was uncomfortable. 'But I don't want hair in my eyes. I can't stand it.'

Rolo went quiet. His lip curled.

The assistants looked nervously at one another.

'Really, darling.' His tone was flat, bored. 'You have to trust me. I know what I'm doing.'

'Yes, Olivia!' Mimsy berated her, aghast. 'I mean, that's why we came, isn't it? To get expert advice?'

But surely I'm the expert, Olivia thought.

Then the inevitable undertow of guilt kicked in. She was

wasting their time; it was what Mimsy wanted; what did she know about hairstyling, anyway?

They were staring at her; waiting.

Rolo checked his watch.

The passion of the morning ebbed away; a thick, numbing layer of hopelessness replaced it.

'Well, I suppose . . .'

Then her phone rang.

It was Simon, calling to confirm that exact position of the Knowle sofa.

Olivia excused herself and under the withering gaze of both Mimsy and Rolo, took the call. Midway through, an idea came to her.

'I'm so sorry,' she gushed, when she'd hung up. 'A crisis at the gallery!' Pulling off the Chanel jacket, she passed it back to Mimsy. 'I've got to go immediately, I'm afraid. It can't be helped.'

Rolo regarded her sourly. 'There's a cancellation fee for my time.'

'Of course!'

'But . . . but what gallery?' Mimsy stammered. 'You can't just leave a hair appointment! We're about to transform your life!'

'They need me,' Olivia said simply. 'But why don't you take my slot? After all, you deserve it.' She eased Mimsy towards the chair. 'I can't wait to see how it looks!'

Sensing a far more lucrative client, Rolo sprang to life,

yanking bits here, flipping bits there. Mimsy was lulled into a trance by the authority of his voice and her own glorious reflection. (Rolo had invested in incredible rose-tinted lighting that instantly took years off everyone.)

'I'll ring you later!'

Olivia made a dash for the door.

As little as a week ago this appointment had been the highlight of her month; the lynchpin in her campaign to win back Arnaud's affections. And yet here she was, heading out onto the gloriously filthy streets of Soho unaltered; grateful to have escaped.

The gallery beckoned. There was that sofa to sort out, final adjustments to be made to the guest list and her very own protégée, Red Moriarty, to guide and promote. The girl was remarkable; both she and Simon were on tenterhooks to see what she would produce next. Already they'd reserved a space for it in the show.

Best of all, the spark of excitement was back, undimmed. And, stopping on impulse to buy a pair of electric-blue fishnets from the fashion wholesale shop (the colour was amazing even if she could never wear them) and a freshly baked croissant from Patisserie Valerie, Olivia took her time, wandering through an invigorating, strange, altogether darker part of London before returning to Mayfair.

Another Moriarty Original

Rose was standing in front of Moriarty's Second-Hand Furniture Emporium on Kilburn Lane, waiting for her father. He was late. He'd been late all her life. Mick Moriarty was famous throughout London for both his ability to find whatever you were looking for and not showing up on time. He'd get things wrong by days rather than minutes. Knowing this, Rose had rung him twice this morning. But still, Mick was nowhere to be found; the shop was closed and his mobile mysteriously unavailable. Luckily, Rory had fallen asleep in his pushchair on the way over. She gently rolled him back and forth. At least he wasn't awake, screaming and wriggling, wanting to get out.

Her father said he had something for her and Rose couldn't afford to turn him down. It was sweet, really, the way he earmarked various bits of furniture for her. But she didn't have all day to loiter about; she was due at the gallery this afternoon for a meeting with Olivia and Simon – a meeting she was dreading.

She checked her watch again. Now she was going to be late too.

Her dad was a law unto himself. He was a good father, so long as you didn't actually need him for anything. There'd been a time, when she was very small, when he'd been different. Normal almost. Mick Moriarty had always liked to fix things. But after her mother had left, what had been a hobby became not only a profession but a mania. He became obsessed with what everyone else thought of as just junk. He only had to clean it, repair it, redeem it and send it out into the world again; maybe it wasn't quite as good as new, but better than it had been. There was something in his zeal that Rose recognized; a way of making sense of the one event of his life he'd never managed to recover from.

Finally, just as she was on the verge of leaving, Mick rattled up in the battered white Transit van that had been the result of one of his earliest negotiations.

'Dad!'

'I know! I know! But you'll never believe it!' Hopping out, he flung open the back doors of the van. 'Just look at this!' He pointed to what looked like a pile of old kitchen units, in a strange turquoise colour. 'Flung into a skip! As if it were junk! Isn't that incredible!'

'It is junk, Dad.'

'You must be mad! Look! They're original fifties units; I can get three grand for them if I take them over to Islington. Get in the van.'

'Why?'

'We're going to Islington.'

'I don't want to go to Islington. I only came because you said you had something for me!'

'Yeah, that's right. You'll love it. Can you put Rory on your lap?'

'You're not listening to me! We're not going anywhere! As a matter of fact, I was hoping you'd look after Rory for me – I've got a big meeting and I have to get to Mayfair . . .'

Mick was already lifting the sleeping Rory out of his chair. 'I'll drive you, luv. Get in. God, he's heavy!' He gave him a cuddle, smoothing his hair down. Rory, exhausted from hours spent racing around the park chasing dogs and collecting used ice-cream sticks, wasn't waking up for anyone or anything. He flopped over Mick's shoulder, a solid, dead weight. 'Get in!'

'Mayfair's nowhere near Islington and I don't want you hauling him from shop to shop, Dad. He'll go mad.'

'Oh no, I can't take him, angel. Not till later, anyway. But I'll get you to Mayfair, no problem. Haven't had a look around there for years. They've got nice digs in Mayfair.'

Rose thought she would scream. He was impossible. But still she found herself climbing into the front seat and taking Rory, strapping the seat belt across the both of them, burying her nose in his hair. The only way to deal with her father was to go along for the ride.

She watched in the rear-view mirror as he folded the

pushchair up, putting it into the back along with the entire fifties kitchen and Lord knows what else. Slight, with thick dark hair and blue eyes, he was still an attractive man; handsome even in his funny white boiler suit. She'd never got to the bottom of the boiler suit – one day it appeared and suddenly it became part of his professional identity. Like a doctor in a white lab coat, he insisted upon wearing it every day, never visiting a client without it. Considering that most of his clients were willing to sell their own furniture to pay their debts, this delicacy struck her as particularly funny.

Climbing in next to her, he started the engine. 'So what's this meeting then?'

'It's to do with my new job.'

'Which is?' He pulled out, nearly slamming into a red Fiat. He thrust his head out the window. 'Wanker!'

Rose had avoided telling her father the details of her new profession, mostly because she wasn't sure if she could explain how she'd entered it and because she was absolutely certain she couldn't tell him what it entailed. 'Well, Dad, I'm an artist.'

Mick laughed. 'Really? You? But you can't even draw, can you?'

'Honestly, Dad! No one draws any more. Everyone knows that!'

'So what do you do? And I'm warning you right now, if it involves taking your clothes off, you're in big trouble!'

'I'm a contemporary artist. It's all about defamiliarization.'

'And what's that when it's at home?' Mick leant on his horn. 'Pick a lane, pal!'

Simon had spent the best part of an afternoon trying to explain it to her. At the time she'd been tempted to write notes on the back of her hand. But in the end she settled for memorizing a few key phrases. 'It's when you take familiar objects and put them in a different context so that the viewer is forced to see them in a new way.'

'Right.' Mick ducked into a bus lane, speeding past a long line of traffic. 'So, like if I put a cheese grater into, I don't know, the Albert Hall, suddenly it's art?'

He was trying to make her feel stupid.

It was working.

'Could be,' she said sullenly.

'What do you mean, could be? Either it is or it isn't!'

'Well, it all depends on who you are, Dad. It's not just about the art — it's about the artist. I mean, if Picasso draws on a napkin at dinner it's definitely art but if Rory has a go, it's just a ruined napkin, see?'

'So how did you get to be so special?'

This was the nagging question that had disturbed her ever since that fateful day in Chester Square. She'd gone over it again and again in her mind. Why was everyone so excited? Could it have been her handwriting? Or the way she'd balanced the cards? The worst part was, now they were all expecting her to do it again. The opening of the exhibition was looming and she had nothing else to offer them. And deep in her heart,

Rose had to agree with her father on the cheese-grater-in-the-Albert-Hall affair: at the end of the day, it was still a cheese grater to her.

'I don't know. Actually, Dad,' she confided, 'I'm in a bit of a pickle.'

Mick turned. 'Do they want money? Never do anything where you have to give money up front to get started.'

'No, Dad, it's not that. It's just I've done this thing, this installation . . .'

'Did you follow the instructions?'

'No, that's what they call the art, they call it an installation. I'm supposed to have another one for today and . . .' she hugged Rory closer for courage, 'and I can't do it, Dad! I don't know how.'

'Well,' he nipped down a one-way street, 'how did you do the first one?'

'It was an accident really. And I've tried coming up with another idea but it's . . . it's so hard, Dad! I'm completely stuck!'

While Rory was at nursery, Rose had spent the best part of the morning trying to be inspired.

She sat at the kitchen table.

And thought.

Hard.

About art.

Nothing came.

She made a cup of tea instead.

Drinking it, she concentrated on her favourite paintings. There was one her aunt had in her living room of a hay cart next to a river. That was nice. Peaceful. Maybe a bit too brown for her liking. Then she remembered nature was meant to be inspiring.

So she spent a long time staring out of the window of her flat at the small patch of scraggly lawn in between the council blocks. She never let Rory play on it because the man down-stairs took his bulldog there. All she saw was filth.

She concentrated harder.

But still, it was all dog poo to her.

Finally she tried her hand at drawing. Simon Grey claimed it didn't matter. He'd reeled off the names of half a dozen supposedly well-known artists who couldn't scribble a circle let alone render a reasonable likeness. But Rose didn't believe him. First she tried to draw Rory. After all, she was with him all day long; she ought to know what he looked like. But he came out all stiff and round, and his eyes too close together. He looked like an angry stuffed toy.

She might have more luck with Victoria Beckham. Opening a copy of *Hello!*, she chose a photograph of her standing outside the Ritz in Paris in an evening dress. That went a bit better. But still her head was far too big, the dress too long; she looked like a mermaid, except Rose got stuck on the feet and had to draw them both in side view. This gave it an Egyptian feel.

The whole morning was depressing. Rose felt inadequate,

irritable and small. The more she tried to think of something original or interesting, the duller and more mundane she felt.

'Well, can't help you there, luv. Why don't you get a proper job?' her father suggested. 'Be a hairdresser or something. People always need their hair cut.'

Rose's father had been trying to get her to be a hairdresser since she was three. 'Dad, I don't want to be a hairdresser! I've never wanted to be a hairdresser! Just because Mum wanted to be a bloody hair—'

'Oi!' he interrupted. 'Don't speak ill of the dead!'

'She's not dead, Dad. She lives in Brighton.'

'Same difference.' He ran through a red light. 'Anyway, you'll have to own up sooner or later. If you haven't got the gift, then that's that. Nothing to be ashamed of. Not everyone's a Damien Hirst, after all.'

Rose stared at him in amazement. 'How do you know about Damien Hirst?'

Mick laughed, pulling into Brook Street. 'You could always put a cheese grater in the Albert Hall, kid! Just remember, I want a little credit on that one! Now, where is this place?'

Rose sighed. He wasn't taking her seriously.

Then again, why would he?

It was so typical of her life; just when she thought she was going to get somewhere, be somebody, she fucked it all up. Always. It was like that at school when she was doing so well, studying for O levels, and then fell in love with Rory's dad, a DJ at a big club in the West End. For three whole weeks they were mad about each other; she actually thought he was going to propose. But the next thing she knew, she was pregnant, her father furious, and he'd buggered off to hit the club circuit in Ibiza with some girl named Doreen. There was no point continuing with her studies; her fate was sealed.

In school they'd studied *Hamlet*; the teacher banged on and on about him having a fatal flaw. That was her all over. No matter what she did, how hard she tried to alter her destiny, her default setting was failure. And now here she was again; she would have to explain to Simon and Olivia that her worst fears were true: she wasn't a natural talent, only a fraud. And her budding career as an artist would be over before it had even begun.

A few minutes later, Mick parked on a double-yellow line in front of the gallery, jumped out and opened the back of the van. Rory woke up crying and as Rose tried to soothe him, she spotted a parking warden heading their way.

'Dad! Dad!' she hissed.

Mick poked his head out. 'Shit! I just want you to have a look at this chair, luv. Wait a minute.' He ducked back inside the van and Rose could hear him struggling with something.

Simon ran out. 'There's no stopping here! Oh, Red!' he greeted her in surprise. 'Please say this is your latest piece! After all, we're opening soon!'

'I'm so sorry,' she stammered. 'I . . . I know you've been so supportive and I so badly wanted to be an artist but I have to tell you, I can't do it! I . . .'

159

The parking warden was upon them. 'What's going on here?'

'Unloading!' Mick shouted, struggling to unearth a particularly ugly brown velour armchair from the back of the van. 'Won't be a moment.'

Simon stared at it. 'What is it?' He gingerly picked up the yellowed lace doily from the headrest.

But Rose recognized it immediately. It had belonged to her father's neighbour, Mrs Henderson. She'd been a sweet old lady, like a grandmother to Rose. Unfortunately, she'd passed away two weeks ago.

'Oh no!' she murmured, her eyes filling with tears. It had been a tense morning and now just seeing it made her feel emotional. 'No, no, Dad!' she whispered. 'Put it away! I can't even look at it!'

'But wait!' Mick insisted, bending down to demonstrate the reclining feature; he pressed a lever on the side and a faded footrest shot up, nearly knocking Rory over. 'It's a beauty, Rose! It was broken but I fixed it. Another Moriarty original!'

Simon's eyes lit up. 'A Moriarty original? Rose! At last! I knew you'd come through!'

Rose shook her head. 'You don't understand,' she said to Simon.

'Oh, yes,' Simon smoothed the doily back in place. 'I think I do.'

'But Mrs Henderson died in this chair!'

'My God! That's powerful!' Backing away, he stared at Mrs

Henderson's recliner in awe. 'An entire tale of life and death in a single chair! The . . . sheer . . . ordinariness of the whole thing is so moving!'

'What's he going on about?' Mick wanted to know.

Rose ignored him. She grabbed Simon's arm. 'You don't understand! It's junk, Simon! Nothing but old junk!'

'It's always the same!' He squeezed her hand. 'Everyone thinks their work is junk when they deliver it. Nothing more than nerves!'

Rory was clambering all over it now. The parking warden reached for his pad and pen. 'Look here, there's no stopping any time . . .'

'Except,' Simon interrupted, 'when unloading valuable new pieces of art!' He plucked Rory off, handed him to Rose and picked the chair up. 'You have surpassed yourself, Red! I can't wait to show Olivia! Now, if you don't mind!'

He nodded imperiously to the parking warden, who, somewhat confused, held the door open while Simon pushed the chair inside.

Rose knew her father was staring at her but she found it hard to meet his gaze. After a while, he took Rory from her, turning him upside down until he giggled.

'So, I guess you'll take it,' he said, flinging Rory onto his shoulders.

Rose nodded. 'I guess I will.'

'Well, maybe Rory and I will go and have an ice cream, eh?'

'Ice cream!' Rory shouted, refreshed from his nap. 'Chocolate! Banilla! Ice cream!'

'What about Islington?'

'It'll be there tomorrow. Anyway, I think we need a break, eh, champ?'

Rory beamed up at him.

'Thanks, Dad.'

Rose gave Rory a kiss and watched as her dad strapped him into a booster seat. 'Drive carefully! Please!'

As they pulled away, the parking attendant smiled shyly. 'Would you mind?' he said, handing her the pad and pen.

'I'm sorry?'

'Your autograph! You're a famous artist, right?'

'Oh! Yeah, I suppose so.'

'You never know, it might be worth something!'

'You never know,' she agreed.

And then she signed 'Red Moriarty' across the page in a strange, firm hand. It glared back at her, full of sharp angles and unfamiliar shapes. She passed it back to him. He was looking at her in a different way, as if she were a completely new person from the one she had been ten minutes ago.

He walked back down the street, grinning proudly at the signed parking ticket.

Rose stood by herself on the steps of the Mount Street Gallery.

Maybe, she concluded, the whole art thing was like being a top model; you got loads of attention for doing nothing. And maybe, just like a naturally beautiful woman, she'd never be able to really see what everyone else saw or what the fuss was all about.

It was sad.

Still, there were probably worse things in life.

A Man's World

Hughie spent the next morning at Gieves and Hawkes being outfitted by Jez. They bought one suit off the peg and had another two ordered. Hughie had never had a suit tailored for him. It was amazing how natural it felt to have all these people fussing about him, kneeling at his feet, measuring and recording each detail of his anatomy as if it were vital state information.

Jez, dressed in jeans, a crisp white shirt and a creamy soft leather jacket, lounged in one of the deep armchairs, drinking tea and leafing through magazines. Just when he appeared to be disinterested, he'd bark out more instructions. 'No, get the lighter wool! I don't care what season it is! You'll be sweating like a pig from nerves most of the time. And there's no way you're wearing braces with anything! A plain waistline, gentlemen. More schoolboy than barrow boy, understand?'

Hughie was impressed; he watched as Jez deftly selected half a dozen daring shirt-and-tie combinations in about two minutes, and his views on socks were practically revolutionary.

'It's like this,' he explained to Hughie, 'it's no socks or knee socks.'

'Knee socks!' A radical suggestion indeed.

But Jez remained firm. 'It's all about a clean line. No ruched-up ankle socks with hairy legs poking out when you sit down.' He grabbed a sock and began pulling at it. 'See? A knee sock, made with cotton and a bit of Lycra, guarantees you a clean line at all times.'

'They won't fall down?'

'Fogal, man. You get them from Fogal.'

'But what about . . . I mean, I'll look stupid in them!'

Jez sighed. 'Shoes and socks off first. Then trousers. No one will ever know. And rethink those boxers. Baggy spoils the silhouette. We're talking classic Calvin Klein jocks from now on. It's all about the line, man. Line first, colour second.'

'How do you know all this?'

'I used to model.' Jez poured out another cup of tea.

'Really?' Hughie imagined Jez strutting down a runway or being photographed with three or four half-naked beauties draped around him. 'Why did you give it up? I mean, the girls, the locations . . .'

'It's toxic, man. And the travel doesn't suit me. You see, I have a lady in my life!' Eyes twinkling, he dug out his wallet, and handed Hughie a couple of photos. They were of an exquisite little girl, maybe four or five years old with light skin, a mop of curly dark hair and a pair of startling pale blue eyes.

'She's beautiful. What's her name?'

'Ella,' Jez said proudly. 'Her mother's Danish.'

Hughie passed the photos back. 'You're married?'

Jez's face clouded. 'Nah. She left me. Heidi was a model too. The most beautiful girl I'd ever seen. We met in Milan one season; we kept working the same designers. By the end of the week, that was it; I knew she was the one. But, well,' Jez stared at the ground, 'the truth was, I had a habit.'

'Oh, I see. Drugs?' Hughie asked softly.

Jez shook his head. 'Nah. I knit.'

'Pardon me?'

Jez narrowed his eyes. 'I like to knit, man. OK?'

'Sure.' Jez was a big guy. And fit. Not a man to be arguing with.

Jez looked across. 'You want to make something of it?'

'No. Not at all. Very noble sport. Well, not a sport, is it? Hobby.'

'Actually,' Jez straightened, 'it's a craft. A highly skilled craft at that.'

'I have no doubt.' Hughie crossed his legs. 'So, what are we talking about? Scarves, jumpers, the odd woolly hat?'

'You're doing it!' Jez pointed a finger in Hughie's face. 'Don't think I can't tell that you're doing it!'

'What? I'm not doing anything!'

'You're trying to wind me up, man! I can tell!'

'Honestly!' Hughie held up his hands. 'I'm curious, that's all! I mean, it's true – not many men knit. Not many women under the age of fifty-five knit, if we're honest. But so what? Am I

166

going to judge? Never! As a matter of fact, I'm willing to defend your right to knit. And I'd like to know exactly what it is that you get up to.'

'For real?'

'Absolutely.'

Jez considered. 'OK. Well, take this one,' he bent down, removing a piece he was working on from his bag. He passed it across. 'It's for Ella.'

It was a small pale blue cardigan, with the most intricate design of tiny dancing ballerinas along the hem, made from the softest stuff Hughie had ever touched.

'My God!' Hughie sat up. 'That's amazing!'

Jez smiled shyly. 'You're just saying that!'

'No, I'm serious! How do you make them so small?'

'The needles, man. They're a nightmare.'

'And these little dancers!'

'Yeah, yeah! Like, look at that one,' he leant forward, 'she's just about to jump, then she's jumping, now she's landed.'

'Amazing!'

'Ella's really into ballet.'

'And you made this by yourself?'

'Yeah. My own design too. I've been doing it for years. Being a model there's a lot of waiting backstage or on sets – make-up, hair, whatever. Some people do crosswords, sit on the phone. It's not like you can eat, right? And all the models are sixteen, seventeen, there's nothing to talk about. Then one day I met this make-up girl and she had this scarf she was working on and I thought, hey, I could do that. So I made her show me how. And I got hooked. I mean, you end up with something, you know? It's real. It lasts.'

'Absolutely. Jez, I'm impressed!'

'You like that? Here,' he pulled out a thick black portfolio. 'Have a look at these! I'm thinking of launching my own label.'

Hughie flipped through page after page of Jez's knitwear designs – a daring range, quite a bit of it photographed on Ella, who'd obviously inherited her parents' ability to strike a pose.

'My God! Put a bit of wool in your hands and it's clear you have something to say!' He passed it back. 'Seems a bit rough though, Heidi walking out.'

'Some people have to be the centre of attention. Beautiful women are often like that. They're used to being looked at and if you're not staring at them, they don't feel like they exist.' He smiled sadly at Hughie. 'If it wasn't the knitting, it would've been something else.'

Hughie tried to think of something profound to say.

Nothing came.

'After she left, I couldn't stand modelling. And I didn't want to leave Ella. Then I got drafted by Valentine one day, waiting at a bus stop. This work suits me.' Jez rubbed his eyes. 'Anyway, keeps me busy. I mean, I couldn't survive another relationship. All those feelings, man!'

The assistant brought their purchases. Jez stretched out his long legs and stood up.

'Come on, kid,' he patted Hughie on the back. 'I didn't

mean to bring you down. I've got my Ella. And that's all that matters. Now, you need a haircut. And then it's on to Nick's Smell Shop for some scent.'

'Nick's what?'

'Smell Shop. Now, don't get all arsey! Nick the Nose is the best in the business. You'll see.'

As they headed towards Trumper's for a haircut, Hughie looked across at Jez.

He had the profile of an Adonis, the body of an athlete, and the hobby of an eighty-seven-year-old woman.

The light changed. Jez strode on ahead.

But by gum, the man could knit!

Nick the Nose

Nick the Nose ran a flower shop in Islington Passage. His real name was Nicolai Verbronsky. From Warsaw, Poland, Nick was about five foot six, in his early sixties. He had a weakness for the classic shell suit, rustling around the narrow space like a plastic shopping bag caught in the wind. In today's ensemble of silver and metallic green, with his shock of red hair, he looked like an elderly evil nemesis to some second-rate comic-book hero. And true to Jez's word, there was a sign above that read, 'Nick's Smell Shop'.

Nick only sold flowers with scent. Banks of roses, buckets of freesias, baskets crammed with hyacinths, tuberose, verbena and lavender; delicate camellias and violets were stored in the cool darkness at the back of the shop; the perfume was overwhelming.

'It's a smell shop!' Nick enthused, when they arrived. 'Anything you want, I have it! As long as it smells good!'

Hughie looked round. 'My mother likes lilies.'

'Lilies!' Nick spat on the floor. 'I hate lilies! Anything except lilies! They are vulgar; for the dead! I hate them!'

'Look, Nick,' Jez intervened, 'we're actually here for something a bit more bespoke.'

Nick's eyes narrowed. 'Is that right?'

'We'll make it worth your while.'

'I don't know,' Nick shifted a pile of eucalyptus away from some bunches of sweet peas. 'I don't need to do that kind of thing any more. I've mixed my last scent! Things are good. I'm even expanding the business.'

'Yeah, well, that's what you tell me. But I don't see any gardenias, Nick. Business can't be that great. You used to be rolling in them in the good old days.'

'Gardenias,' Nick's voice softened and his eyes glazed over. 'The queens of flowers! It's true. I haven't smelt a gardenia in a long time.'

'Come on, Nick. Do the job right and you can fill the shop top to bottom with gardenias if you like!'

Nick weighed up the offer.

'I haven't done it in a long time,' he warned.

'You're the king! You'll never lose your touch! I'll never forget the first one you did for me,' Jez laughed. 'Remember, we actually had to tone it down because it was so potent! I couldn't move an inch without some woman accosting me!'

'All right! All right! Just this once!' Nick shut the shop door and turned the sign around to read 'Closed'. 'But I'm charging double,' he added, pushing them both towards a steep staircase at the back. 'Quick, before Ricki gets back.'

'Who's that?' Jez asked.

'My assistant. Does landscaping; a very talented gardener. She'll kill me if she knows I'm mixing scent on the side. You have no idea how it takes over your life. It's an obsession!'

Downstairs, past the piles of ribbons, wrapping paper and refrigerators filled with fresh blooms, there was a small, lopsided blue door. Nick pushed it open and turned on the light. As they stepped inside, Hughie could see it was a sort of laboratory, with a long wooden work table covered in test-tubes, bottles and Bunsen burners; its walls filled with narrow shelves upon which hundreds of tiny vials were stored in alphabetical order.

He scanned the rows. 'Amber, ground', 'Apple Peel: Green', 'Armpit: Female'. 'Baby hair: blond', 'Burnt matches', 'Butterscotch: cheap' . . . on and on they went.

'I see you've been stocking up,' Jez observed.

Nick sniffed. 'A man's got a right to keep his cabinets full if he wants to. Sit down, you two.' He pointed to a couple of stools. 'You great big louts take up all the air!'

Jez winked at Hughie, who balanced uneasily, clutching his packages. This was hardly what he'd imagined when Jez said they were going to get him some scent and he found it more than a little disconcerting to be in the hands of a man who collected baby hair.

First Nick scrubbed his hands with scalding water and a wire brush. It was painful to watch. Afterwards, he put on his glasses and asked Hughie to lean over. Then he buried his nose in the back of Hughie's neck (an event which traumatized Hughie for months afterwards) and inhaled.

172

'Ah! The boy eats almost entirely red meat! Has the digestion of an ox! Young, healthy, and very, very virile!' he smiled, tilting his chin down to peer over the top of his glasses. 'Hummm ... an interesting mix ... much more intriguing than I'd guessed!'

Then he began pulling down various vials, lining them up on the work top. 'Sand: Indian Ocean', 'Moss: Amazon', 'Black Earth: Yorkshire', 'Liquorice', 'Icing Sugar', 'Pomegranate', 'Pavement: Cleveland, Ohio', 'Pavement: Paris', 'Fresh Fig', 'Lime Flower', 'Old Cashmere Coat', 'Coffee Bean: Venice' . . .

He tutted slightly and put 'Coffee Bean: Venice' back, replacing it with 'Coffee Grounds: Brooklyn'.

Hughie was uncertain if he should be offended or not.

And then he began mixing.

Jez leant back. 'Mind if I smoke?'

Nick glared at him.

'Only joking!' Jez laughed. 'God, these divas! Hey, I'll bet you didn't know you were in the presence of the greatest perfume nose in history, did you? Nicolai the Nose Verbronsky! The toast of Paris, Moscow, New York, Rome! The undisputed king of the fragrance world for nearly thirty years.'

'So why are you selling flowers in Islington?' Hughie asked.

'Yes,' Nick measured out a single drop of 'Pavement: Paris' into a glass beaker. 'Yes, you might well wonder such a thing! I do!'

'Oh, how the mighty are fallen! Tell him, Nick. I'll bet he's too young to remember.'

Nick winced as if the memory pained him. But all the while he spoke, he continued mixing. 'It happened at the height of my powers. I was experimenting a lot with odours at the time.' He gave Hughie a look. 'I'm assuming you know the difference between a scent and an odour; an odour is stronger, unpleasant.'

Hughie nodded.

'Well, I was working for a certain house in Paris – this was in the early eighties. They were desperate for something revolutionary. Pass the "Sand", please.'

Jez obliged.

'And they happened upon my experiments. I wanted to see if you could take an essentially offensive smell and mix it in such a way that it would become irresistible. Well, they took one sniff and went insane!'

He stopped a moment, tilted the beaker on its side, poured half its contents down the drain, and continued.

'Of course, it was only a test; it wasn't meant to be quite so strong. But they stole it from me before it was ready. We argued and they kicked me out; disowned me.' Tears welled up in his grey eyes. Taking off his glasses, he dabbed them with a bit of paper towel.

'Hey, take it easy, man.' Jez patted him on the shoulder. 'It's over now.'

Nick shrugged him off. 'It was one of the worst perfume crimes in history! For nearly a decade every female on the face of the planet reeked of the stuff. It was overwhelming! Unbearable! A dark time. A very dark time!'

For a while he sat very still, staring at the table.

'You've heard of the perfume Venom,' Jez explained softly.

Hughie couldn't help himself. 'Oh, dear!'

'Yes, I'm responsible!' Nick turned on him. 'It was me, OK? And from that day on I vowed I'd never mix another perfume again!'

'But old habits die hard,' Jez said soothingly. 'And let's face it, you're still the best.'

'Yes,' Nick mixed in a touch of 'Pomegranate' and a drop of 'Lime Flower'. 'I'm still the best. It's a curse, really.' He spun the glass beaker between his fingers and handed the mixture to Hughie.

'Really?' Hughie stood up. 'Is that it?'

'Yes, that's it! What did you expect? A three-week gestation period?'

Hughie gingerly sniffed the beaker.

'Try it on! You won't be able to tell what it smells like from there.'

Hughie dipped a finger in, dabbed the scent on his wrist and inhaled.

It was the most extraordinary thing. It smelt warm, familiar; like him only more so.

Closing his eyes, he breathed in again. Instantly he was calmer, happier, more secure; a vision floated to the surface of his memory: a summer afternoon, napping in the sun, his head resting on his father's chest and the rhythmic sound of his heart-beat lulling him to sleep . . .

'Not bad, huh?' Nick laughed. 'Watch out! You'll fall in love with yourself! We should call it "Narcissus"!'

'I can't believe it!' Hughie said.

'Here, give us a go.' Jez grabbed his wrist and sniffed. 'Fuck me, that's good!'

Nick glowed with pride. 'Very few people can wear "Parisian Pavement". It has a far greater percentage of cigarette butts and bodily fluids than your average pavement. But on the right person, what a base!'

'But I don't get it. How can you mix all these disgusting things together and get something so, so,' Hughie pressed his wrist to his nose again, 'so amazing!'

Nick cocked his head to one side. 'This I will tell you for nothing: without exception it's always too much sweetness that kills a good perfume. There should be space between the different notes; gaps that only the imagination can fill. And just like in life, young man, it's the shit that adds depth. Now, to the real test.' He clapped his hands and a small King Charles spaniel came racing down the shop steps and into the room.

'Chanel here is a female. The feminine sense of smell is the most refined. Now,' he picked her up, 'if the dog bites you it's a bad brew. But if she doesn't, we're really on to something.'

Make Me a Willow Cabin at Your Gate

Arnaud Bourgalt du Coudray paused as he reached the bottom of the stairs. He was on his way out to supper. Again. He was taking Svetlana to George's and on to some club afterwards.

Automatically, he stopped to appraise himself in the mirror in the front hallway. How things had changed! A person might mistake me for forty-five, he thought, shaking his head so that his hair covered his bald patch, and flashing himself a strange little smile, parting the lips but keeping the upper half of the face completely immobile; a trick his mother had taught him for not getting wrinkles. (The fact that as an expression it failed to convey any warmth or good humour had escaped them both.)

Yes, in many ways, he considered, life couldn't be better.

Business was going amazingly well. In a couple of weeks when he launched the Nemesis All-Pro Sport 2000, he was certain to rise to the very pinnacle of the sporting goods industry.

He might even be nominated for the prestigious Silver Sock Award – the sporting industry's highest honour. In addition, he hadn't spoken to his mother in weeks. Normally she rang twice a day to vent her ill-will at him but she'd treated herself to a month-long spa break and they'd thoughtfully wired her jaw shut.

Best of all, there were no real obstacles to him seeing Svetlana. Here they were, trotting out for the third time this week. And he was guaranteed sex. (It took a couple of recreational drugs to work herself up to the task, but once high as a kite, she did a creditable impression of a sexually predatory creature possessed with lust and desire. One of the drawbacks of having been inconceivably wealthy all his life was that Arnaud was absolutely certain no one had ever slept with him for the sex alone.)

Still, a profound sense of unease stirred in the pit of his stomach.

Surely something was wrong, deeply wrong, if no one even cared where he was going or what he was doing? And he realized that the ingredient missing from this otherwise flawless existence was the presence of his beautiful, faithful, chronically unhappy wife.

Where was Olivia? Why was she no longer trailing after him in the mornings like a doomed wraith? In the almost eleven years that he'd known her, she'd never been so conspicuously absent from his life. He'd been threatening to move into one of the guest rooms every day this week – surely she should be frantic!

And, having done everything in his power to repel and degrade her for the past six months, Arnaud found himself outraged.

Was this part of some larger plan? Was she toying with him? Did she imagine he was like some schoolboy to be neglected and manipulated as she pleased?

'Gaunt!' he shouted, suddenly furious. 'GAUNT!'

Gaunt appeared from below stairs. 'Yes, sir?'

'Where is my wife?' He spat the words out, resenting them even as they left his lips.

'I believe, sir, she is still at the gallery. Shall I ring to confirm?'

The man was impertinent; laughing at him, he was certain.

'No.' Arnaud pushed his way past him, flinging the front door wide. 'I'll take care of it myself.'

When Arnaud arrived at the gallery, there were at least two dozen people milling about, unloading trucks, hanging canvases, repositioning video cameras, and shouting at each other. The artists were instantly recognizable as a small cluster of vagrants puffing away on cigarettes in a corner underneath the 'No Smoking' sign.

'Where is my wife?' Arnaud demanded of a scruffy young man.

'And, like, who are you?' the rogue challenged.

'I am . . .' Arnaud stopped himself. It was degrading to have to introduce himself. He cut straight to the point.

'Fuck off,' he said and stamped away, aware that they were laughing at him.

Arnaud loathed art. It had never bothered him much before he was married, but after Olivia became a devoted patroness, he came to despise it. He especially hated the word 'talent' and the way it was thrown about, landing on any and every sub-standard imbecile who took his wife's fancy. Michelangelo was talented. Leonardo da Vinci had ability. But Walter Fripp from Woking with his papier mâché mannequins dressed as sexually explicit Teletubbies had severe mental problems, not talent. He had tried on many occasions to explain this to his wife but she refused to see his point. She talked about vision and cultural references and metaphors for modern life until he wanted to shout. So he did. Educated women insisted on having ideas and opinions. His mother had enough opinions for all the women in the world. He didn't need any from his wife.

Then he spotted her, talking to that fop, Simon Grey.

Arnaud planted his feet where they were and bellowed. 'Olivia!'

Instantly everything stopped. All eyes turned.

'"Make me a willow cabin at your gate!"' Simon quoted under his breath.

Olivia looked round.

'Arnaud,' she smiled, crossing the floor with her hand extended, as if she were greeting a stranger. 'What are you doing here?'

Her lack of reaction disorientated him. She was meant to come running, with that familiar frightened look. Instead she took his arm and moved him firmly into a room covered with photographs of dustbins. And once she'd cordoned him off from the rest of society, she stopped, staring up at him expectantly with her large blue eyes.

Arnaud hadn't looked at his wife in a while. He didn't expect her to be so attractive. He was surprised by how young, how slim and compact she was. She was wearing a thin cotton eau-de-Nil Oxford shirt and a pair of mannish black linen trousers, a steel-blue cashmere pullover tied loosely around her waist. It was a casual, artless ensemble and yet oddly sexy. Her shirtsleeves were rolled up, exposing a taut forearm and tiny wrists. There was something about a woman's wrists, he noted; the way they tapered into the hands. He was particularly drawn to her long graceful fingers. Olivia's flitted towards her neck and his eyes followed. Her shirt was unbuttoned, her neck unadorned. Naturally his gaze wandered to the deep V below her throat where her cleavage began. He wondered if she was wearing a bra, almost hoping she wasn't. Something within him stirred.

How irritating to find her sexy! It disrupted his plans for the evening. There was a girl half her age preening and plucking herself into oblivion right now in anticipation of his arrival. Also it dulled his anger; he felt exposed, unarmed. Even more upsetting was her serenity.

'Well?' She crossed her arms in front of her chest so that her breasts sat firmly on top of them. Was she trying to drive him mad?

'I wanted to know . . . the thing is . . .' Having come all this

way, he was now at a loss. Feeling wrong-footed in any way
made him furious and, with the rush of feeling, he recovered
himself. 'What are you doing here?' he demanded.

'Working.'

'Working? Why?'

'What else am I to do?'

It was an oddly valid point.

'But it's late! What about supper?'

'Are you offering to take me out?' she countered.

He furrowed his brow in an attempt to look beleaguered
and put upon. 'You know I have to meet with Pollard this
evening,' he lied.

'Ah, yes,' she smiled, 'Pollard.'

'What's that supposed to mean?'

'It's meant to mean, "Ah, yes, Pollard."' He could feel her
concentration going; her eyes scanning the room. 'At any rate,
I'm not hungry. But thank you for thinking of me. Send Pollard
my very warmest regards.'

And she strolled away from him, back to where Simon was
overseeing the installation of a ten-foot-tall aluminium teddy
bear.

Arnaud knew that now was the time to leave; he'd made a
fool of himself and a speedy exit was required. But internally
he felt himself dig in for the long haul.

He followed her, glaring at Simon (who tried to shake his
hand) and sneering at the young artist who was nervously trying
to right his ridiculous creation.

'Pollard and I are involved with some very tricky negotiations,' he barked, to no one in particular.

Olivia made a small adjustment to the plinth and the teddy bear righted itself.

'Well done!' Simon patted her on the back.

'The Asian market is a nightmare!' Arnaud continued, trailing after Olivia as she walked into the next room. Suddenly he stopped. 'Wait a minute.' He had an odd feeling of déjà vu. 'This sofa looks like ours . . . My God! It is ours! This is our furniture!' He wheeled round. 'This is our drawing room!'

Olivia was waving to a tiny red-haired girl in the far corner.

'Yes,' she said matter-of-factly. 'Comes off rather well, doesn't it?'

'What?' he spluttered. 'Are you mad? What are we meant to sit on at home?'

She sighed. 'No one ever uses it, Arnaud. And here it's part of a work of art. I'd like you to meet the artist. Red Moriarty, this is my husband, Arnaud.'

He ignored the girl and pulled Olivia to one side. 'What's got into you? I will not have my private home life on show for every snot-nosed student to paw over!'

She shook him loose. 'It's going to be reviewed tonight, Arnaud. The art critic from *The Times* is coming for a sneak preview. Red Moriarty is going to be a household name, if I have anything to do with it. She's incredibly, uniquely talented!'

That word again! He rolled his eyes.

'Finally,' she continued, her voice strained with feeling, 'I've found something worthy of my energy and efforts. This is deeply important to me, Arnaud. And I will not have you destroying what you don't understand!'

'Don't understand? Don't understand! What do you think I am? An idiot?'

She was silent.

'Right!' he raged. 'That's it! I'm moving my things out tonight!'

No reaction.

'This is it!' He waved his phone in the air. 'I'm ringing Gaunt right now!'

'Fine.'

She marched away, heels echoing across the parquet floor, disappearing into the throng of activity in the main gallery. And Arnaud found himself stranded in the middle of his own drawing room which had washed up in Mayfair, complete with some strange girl in it.

He closed his eyes and clenched his fists in rage. Something worthy of her energy and efforts! What was he? Wasn't he completely worthy of her undivided attention and devotion? How dare she replace him with this ... this ... ridiculous show!

He rang Gaunt. 'I want you to move everything of mine out of my bedroom into one of the spare rooms, do you understand? And I mean absolutely everything!'

'Very good, sir.'

He clicked his phone shut. That would show her!

But instead of feeling back in control, terror took hold.

She was leaving him.

After all his years of devotion!

It wasn't fair! He was the victim here – of her unstable emotional condition.

He wanted her back; she belonged to him.

But it had to be on his terms. He wasn't prepared to be dictated to by anyone.

Arnaud paced the floor. He was damned if he was going to grovel!

If only he could catch her out; discover her in some compromising position. That was the surest way to gain the upper hand. Then *she* would have to beg for *his* forgiveness.

Trouble was, Olivia never did anything wrong. If only she could be tempted . . .

Frowning, he checked his watch. He was already late for Svetlana.

Once again, his wife was ruining his evening!

Wait. That was it!

It was so simple, he nearly laughed out loud with relief.

All he needed was some idiot to do his bidding; someone who couldn't afford to say no.

Taking out his mobile phone again, he sat down on his sofa, put his feet up on the ottoman and dialled.

Jonathan answered. Arnaud could hear the wail of various ill-tempered children in the background.

'Mr Bourgalt du Coudray! What a pleasant surprise!' Jonathan shouted above the din. He was panting now, as if he were jogging up a flight of steps; the wailing growing distant. 'What can I do for you, sir?'

'Seduce my wife, Mortimer.'

Jonathan stopped whatever aerobic activity he was doing. 'I'm sorry?'

'Seduce my wife. Hit on her. Pursue her.'

'I'm not sure I understand. You want me to—'

'I want you to make love to her,' Arnaud interrupted.

'But, sir, I don't know your wife. Besides, I happen to have one of my own.'

Arnaud laughed. 'And . . . ? You act as if you've never orchestrated an affair!'

'I haven't.'

'You English are such prudes! Listen, I haven't got time for this. It's really quite simple: all you have to do is woo her. It doesn't matter if she responds. In fact,' he considered smugly, 'I'm sure she won't. All I need is the evidence of a seduction. You're a clever man. It shouldn't be too difficult. Oh, and Mortimer?'

'Yes?'

'Don't even think of touching her or you'll live to regret it.'

He hung up.

Life was all about delegating.

Standing, he brushed off his trousers and left to pick up Svetlana.

Marriage was important, he reflected, as he climbed into the back of the huge black Range Rover waiting for him outside the gallery. It hurt him that Olivia was taking theirs for granted.

Settling back into the plush leather seat, he stared out of the darkened window.

Thank God at least one of them cared enough to do something about it.

Jonathan Mortimer sat stunned on the corner of his son Felix's bed. (He'd only made it as far as the children's bedrooms.)

What did he mean, seduce her?

How?

And more importantly why?

He'd only met Olivia Bourgalt du Coudray about three times; they were only barely acquainted. How was he meant to suddenly become her lover? He didn't have the energy to seduce his own wife, let alone someone else's! The man was insane!

Unfortunately, he was also his biggest client.

Arnaud had laughed at the fact that he'd never had an affair. Was he right? Was Jonathan nothing more than a prude?

He'd certainly never imagined himself as a ladies' man.

Pulling himself upright, stomach in, shoulders back, he regarded himself in the mirror hanging on the back of the door, cut out in the shape of a laughing giraffe.

His reflection blinked back at him.

Somewhere around forty, he'd developed the same shape as his father: long, spindly legs, a sloping, slightly apologetic stoop and a distinct absence of hair. His features, which had once been forceful and masculine, had softened – in much the same way that water wears away at stones in a brook – and now he seemed like a photograph that had faded in the sunlight; vague and unsure. The buttons of his tailor-made shirt strained over the width of stomach. Even it had lost its crispness.

I couldn't seduce a pensioner let alone a beautiful socialite, he thought, panicking.

His heart was palpitating. He grabbed Felix's favourite stuffed dog and curled up on top of his unmade Bob the Builder bed, staring at the dusty animal mobile dangling from the ceiling.

'I'm going to lose my job.' He pressed his eyes closed. 'I'm going to lose my job and we'll all end up penniless on the streets because of that fucking French fuck! Shit, shit, shit, shit, shit!'

'Daddy?'

He flicked an eye open.

His sons, Felix, six, and Angus, three, were standing at the bottom of the bed, looking at him.

'Yes?'

'Mummy wants to know if you have any money for the cleaner,' Felix said.

Jonathan dug out his wallet, struggling to extract the notes without actually standing up. Immediately he assumed his parent voice, the one he'd inherited from his father – exasperation mixed with a half-hearted attempt at authority. 'You cannot tell me a cleaner has been in this house today!'

Felix nodded. 'It's awful! She puts everything where we can't find it. It takes all afternoon to get it back to normal.'

'Here,' Jonathan sighed, handing Felix twenty pounds.

'Thanks, Daddy.'

'Why didn't she come herself?'

'Mummy's too fat to come upstairs.'

'I see.' That meant she was still sulking from their latest row.

'Only she's not fat,' Jonathan corrected him, 'she's pregnant.'

'I think, Daddy,' Felix explained gently, 'that maybe she's fat *and* pregnant. By the way,' he nodded in the direction of the dog, 'don't squash his head. He doesn't like it.'

'Yes, of course.' Jonathan readjusted the dog.

Felix trotted off and Angus remained, staring at Jonathan.

'Do you want to climb up?' Jonathan offered.

Angus shook his head. Then he bent over and picked something up from the floor.

'Daddy's,' he announced, handing him a small white card.

'Thank you, darling. Must have fallen from Daddy's wallet.' He glanced at it.

'*Valentine Charles*,' it read. '*Purveyor of Rare Domestic Services.*'

'That's it!' Jonathan sat up.

If there was one person who could solve this problem, it was bound to be the curious Valentine Charles!

Jonathan stood up. 'My boy, you're a genius!'

Angus grabbed his leg. 'Daddy sleep in my bed!'

'Daddy's got to make a phone call, darling.'

'No! Daddy sleep in my bed!' He began to cry.

So Jonathan Mortimer made one of the most important telephone calls of his career lying in his son's converted cot while Angus happily covered his daddy with all the stuffed toys he could find.

And while covered in toys, it occurred to Jonathan that if Mr Charles could sort out the bizarre, mystifying seduction of the Bourgalt du Coudray woman, he might be able to arrange something less dramatic but equally uplifting for his own wife, Amy.

The Cardinal Rule
(A Moment of Silence, Please, for Freddie)

Later that evening, they all assembled in Valentine's flat.

Thanks to Jez, Hughie had been transformed from a rather good-looking, shabby student to the very image of a sleek professional. With his new haircut, he looked taller, his aquiline features exquisitely refined. Jez had selected a very fine navy pinstripe suit which brought out the colour of his eyes, and a crisp blue cotton shirt worn open at the neck. Hands in pockets, the unselfconscious combination of youth, beauty and the excellent quality of the tailoring lent him a Gatsby-ish glamour. No longer a diamond in the rough, Hughie dazzled.

'Oh, yes!' Flick smiled when he walked in. 'Yes, that's the ticket! You could be the brightest young spark of a corporate enterprise!'

'Bravo!' Marco agreed, clapping his hands. 'You got rid of those boxer shorts, right?'

'Absolutely,' Jez said.

'Smith, you burn them, yes? They only come out again when you retire, get married and have children!'

'Smythe, Marco,' Flick corrected,

'Yes,' Marco waved his hand impatiently, 'whatever!'

Hughie could not believe his underwear had been such a hot topic of conversation.

'And the socks, old man?' Henry was standing near the fireplace, drinking a cup of tea.

'That boy's ankles are completely covered!' Jez assured him, throwing himself into one of the armchairs.

'Well, I think we can all agree, Jez, that you've done a sterling job.' Valentine was sitting at his desk, leaning back in the chair, the tips of his fingers pressed together under his chin. 'Now, Hughie,' he smiled slowly, 'the easy part is over. It's time for us to get to work.'

'Right.' Henry put his teacup down on the mantelpiece. 'Welcome to a crash course on the rudiments of the professional flirt. Lesson one: the all-important background check. Flick?'

Flick stood up. 'Valentine is in charge of the recruitment of new clients, managing existing clients and, of course, drafting in new staff. But the background information you need on each new mark will be provided by me. As soon as a client contacts us, I follow up with a long series of questions. I won't bore you with the details, but the end result is as complete a character portrait of the woman as I can manage.'

'Flick has an incredible talent in this area,' Valentine assured him. 'A knack for being able to read between the lines.'

'What husbands don't know about their own wives is a lot!' she smiled. 'Often they insist their wives are angry and sullen when obviously they're hurt and rejected or they have tastes that, with a little probing, I discover are theirs, not the wife's at all. Or sometimes, when I ask what their wife really wants from life or truly enjoys, they have absolutely no idea . . . either it's changed over the years or, in some extreme cases, they've never really bothered to find out in the first place.'

'It's no surprise that they're experiencing difficulties,' Valentine said.

'Then I have to play detective,' Flick continued. 'What magazines are on her bedside table? Does she look at any catalogues? What was the last meal she ordered in a restaurant? Who does she admire? What does her best friend do? By the end, hopefully I've got a clearer idea of what kind of flirt she needs, what she needs to hear, who would be the best man for the job, and what would be the ideal point of interception. And if possible, I like to have a look at them myself. It's amazing what you learn just watching someone go about their daily life for a few minutes. After I've drawn up my report, I make a few gentle suggestions to the client about how they might follow up on the service we provide; half the success of what we do depends on a husband making an effort to be more attentive as well. What you get from all this background research is a personality breakdown, a job brief, and a time and location for the flirt.'

'Sometimes,' Henry said, 'that window of time is quite

generous but sometimes, especially with working women, it can be a very narrow gap indeed.'

'Tube trains!' Jez shook his head ruefully. 'Wait till you have to do a train job!'

'Even a bus is better than the tube!' Marco agreed.

'With each brief, there'll be a suggested, well-established flirt,' Henry went on. 'For example, Casting Agent, Parking Meter, Interval Drinks or Shopping. Don't worry,' he smiled. 'We'll go over all those later. After you've been trained, there'll be a certain amount of creative leeway you can exercise, but in the beginning, there's so much to concentrate on, that it's best to stick quite rigorously to the script, so to speak.'

'And then,' Jez grinned, 'all you have to worry about are two things: how can I get to her—'

'And how can I get away from her!' Marco cut in.

'Always know your exit,' Henry stressed. 'Making contact is fairly easy . . . "Pardon me, my watch is slow, do you have the correct time?" Or, "Forgive me, I'm a little lost, I'm looking for Portman Square." But after you've made contact, flirted, got them all excited, making a clean getaway is imperative.'

'Remember,' Jez added gravely, 'not all our marks are married, some are single. You could get a Clinger.'

'A Clinger?'

'Ah! It's terrible!' Marco shuddered. 'The way they run down the street after you! Or follow you into the gents. One, she tried to get in the same cab! I had to pretend to suffer from . . . what is it? Falling asleep, you know?'

'Narcolepsy,' Flick volunteered.

'Oh, dear!' This was alarming.

'Normally I label the brief,' Flick interjected quickly, '"PC" for "Possible Clinger".'

'Still, any woman can become tricky,' Henry warned, 'and knowing your nearest exit, having your departing lines well rehearsed and moving quickly are your greatest safeguards against an emergency situation.'

'An emergency situation?'

'Remember, Hughie,' Valentine said, 'this is a highly improvised profession, full of huge unknown variables. The truth is, any flirt can go wrong at any time.'

'That's how we lost Freddie.'

'Freddie?'

No one had mentioned Freddie before.

'Freddie was a rare case,' Henry explained. 'It's highly unusual for an apprentice's training to go so . . . so extremely wrong.' His voice trailed off.

'Lost him?' Hughie felt a faint chill creeping up his limbs. 'How?'

Marco leant in. 'She was a Class A Clinger, Smith. Never, in all my years, have I ever seen anything like it!'

'Yeah, she had a kind of energy,' Jez recalled, 'a kind of rolling around on the floor, possessed look in her eyes . . . like someone plugged her into a light socket. But Freddie didn't clock she was mental – all he could see was that she was small and blonde.'

'Beware the Small Blonde Ones!' warned Marco. 'From the

first moment he spoke to her, you could just tell there was going to be trouble!'

'What happened to him?'

'He married her,' Valentine said sharply.

Silence.

Suddenly Hughie's shirt tightened around his neck, his skin prickled. A skull in the gardens of Arcadia.

'But . . . I mean, married!' He laughed hollowly. 'That's a bit extreme!'

'She was a Clinger, Hughie.' Valentine's face was devoid of any emotion. 'Never underestimate a Clinger.'

'She started crying,' Jez explained. 'A classic Clinger move. And of course Freddie made a mistake: a big mistake. He put his arm around her. We tried to intervene, tried to get him out of there . . . thing was, she was small but strong . . .'

'Never touch the mark!' Marco shouted. (The whole thing was clearly too much for him.) 'Never!'

'Which brings us to the cardinal rule of our profession,' Henry cut in, dragging the conversation back from the brink of hysteria. 'No physical contact, young Smythe. Crossing a physical boundary invites anarchy. From the moment poor Freddie gave the Clinger a hug, his defences began to deteriorate; before he knew it, he lost sight of his exit, then he was buying her a drink, trying to cheer her up. In an hour, he was lost to us for ever.'

Valentine stood. 'Distance, Hughie. The profession is a paradox – like being a physician. You must have compassion for them but you cannot help these women if you have no detachment. Remember that and you can have a wonderfully successful and lucrative career.'

'And you'll be shadowed for the first week or so,' Henry said. 'One of us will be with you every step of the way. Nothing can go wrong.'

Hughie swallowed, hard.

'Nothing,' Henry assured him, giving his shoulder a squeeze.

Still, the spectre of Freddie, the fresh-faced recruit who hadn't managed his escape, cast a shadow across the proceedings.

The phone rang. Flick answered it. 'The offices of Valentine Charles . . . yes . . . of course, sir, one moment please . . .' She put the call on hold. 'Mr Jonathan Mortimer on the line for you.'

Valentine took the phone.

'Class dismissed,' he said as Flick ushered them towards the door. 'Oh, Henry, a word please, when I'm done.'

Henry nodded.

The rest of them headed out to the street and said their goodbyes.

Hughie loitered.

After a while Henry came down. 'Are you waiting for me?'

'Sort of. Thought I might pick up a few more tips.'

Henry put an arm around his shoulders. 'Don't you think you've had enough for one day?'

They walked on through the narrow street.

'I don't know. It was kind of fun the other night, you know, at Claridge's. Didn't you think so?' He enjoyed having Henry show him things; working together as a team.

'You did very well.' Then he stopped, his face serious. 'The truth is, Hughie, Valentine has asked me to speak to you. We need your absolute assurance that you've finished with this girl of yours, Leticia.'

'Oh.' Hughie felt the walls closing in on him. 'Well, the thing is . . . I thought perhaps I should let her down gently.'

Henry shook his head. 'Not good enough, old man. It's got to be done. Otherwise you're out. Bit of a make-or-break situation, you see.'

'Yes. Yes.' Hughie stared at his shiny new shoes. 'I'm due to see her tonight. At the Victoria bus depot.'

'Really?'

'She's . . . you know,' Hughie flushed, 'fond of public places.'

'Oh. Yes,' Henry considered. 'I can see how she'd be a tough one to give up. What time are you due?'

Hughie checked his watch. 'Actually, I'm late!'

'Right.' Henry flagged down a cab, smiling grimly at Hughie. 'Best done quickly, son. Like chopping off a leg. Come on. And I'll get you good and pissed after.'

A Clean Break

Over the years Leticia had developed a strict protocol to deal with break-ups; she practised swift and humane methods, not unlike a kosher butcher.

First, break-ups needed to be staged in bland, neutral territory; ideally public places, where the chances for tantrums and tears were dramatically reduced. Car showrooms were good (men were always distracted there), as were shopping malls and hotel lobbies. Next, she rehearsed her speech, the one about them both being in different places and needing different things. Lack of blame was essential. Finally there was the costume. Unwashed hair, no make-up, a shabby tracksuit . . . he'd look at her and wonder why he'd bothered in the first place. These were the details that separated the men from the boys, ensuring a clean and painless closure.

The thing that most women wouldn't admit was that they didn't really want a clean break; they preferred to remain desirable, mysterious; in love with the idea of themselves as forties film stars, playing out tragic scenes in train stations. They enjoyed being tortured by their decision, filled with regrets; it provided the perfect excuse to act out their pain with drink, cigarettes and strange men, all of which were mother's milk to Leticia.

Drama: that was at the crux of the matter. Leticia prided herself on being above it.

And so, looking not at all like her normal self, Leticia arrived at Victoria bus depot and waited, sitting in her faded tracksuit on one of a row of blue plastic chairs anchored to the floor, before Hughie finally showed up.

She spotted him walking through the crowds of luggage-laden tourists. Her heart lifted. He looked different, still recognizably Hughie yet transformed. In fact, he'd never looked more handsome. He was carrying a bunch of shopping bags, wearing a new, expensive suit, and his hair was cut. Suddenly she wished she weren't drowning in a sea of faded grey poly mix. For a split second she considered making a hasty retreat. But it was only her pride, she reasoned. A bit of vanity rearing its head.

He didn't recognize her at first, so she waved.

He waved back. A sharp stab of longing cut across her chest.

'Courage, darling,' she told herself. Still, it was strange that she should need it; she'd never needed it before.

'I'm so sorry,' Hughie gushed as he approached and then he stopped, registering her curious ensemble. 'Are you all right?' he asked, sitting down. 'You look a bit . . . under the weather.'

'Hughie,' she began, 'I need to talk to you.'

'Oh, dear! You're not . . . you know . . . ?'

'Oh, no! No, no, no! Nothing like that!' His face relaxed. 'It's just we need to have a talk.'

'The six thirteen leaving for Brighton is now boarding at platform seven.'

A herd of gangly adolescents grabbed their bags and left, giving them a brief moment of privacy.

'OK.' He stared into her eyes. 'I'm really pleased to see you.'

'Really?'

'Yeah. I've missed you.'

It had been a long time since anyone had missed her. She shifted uncomfortably.

'The six twenty leaving for Winchester is now boarding at platform eleven. Passengers are reminded to keep their belongings with them at all times.'

'I think we should stop seeing each other.'

'I'm sorry?'

'It just isn't really working out, is it?'

Hughie stared at her.

Leo was right: he was so young, so terribly young.

'But why not? What's wrong with me?'

'Nothing. It's not you. It's not you at all. It's me, Hughie. It has to do with me.'

'But . . . but I don't get it. Have I done something wrong?'

'The six twenty bus to Reading is now leaving from platform four.'

More travellers lumbered past, dragging luggage, listless with heat and exhaustion. Leticia tried to swallow. Her mouth was dry, throat tight.

'Remember the Rules?'

'Yeah. But I haven't broken them.'

She stared down at the floor; at the space between her feet. 'I know. Like I said, it isn't you, it's me.'

'You mean you . . .' he concentrated, putting something together, 'you . . . like me?'

'I don't know. Maybe. Sort of. Anyway,' she snapped impatiently, 'it's not important. What's important is that we follow the Rules, Hughie. We need to protect ourselves.'

But Hughie wasn't concentrating. Everything had shifted. Bugger the job! Leticia loved him! She'd practically said as much.

'What do we need protection from? Especially if you like me and I like you, which, by the way, I do, you know,' he grinned. 'What could be better?'

'See!' she warned. 'This is how it begins! The whole thing is getting completely out of hand!'

'So what?' He embraced her, covering her face with kisses. 'Leticia, my darling!'

'OK, stop!' She pulled away. 'Stop right there! We're not doing a love scene, do you understand?'

'But why not? What have we got to lose?'

'Everything! You're too young to know. You don't understand now, but you will some day. Love doesn't fix anything, Hughie. In fact, it destroys more than it fixes. And when the dust has settled, it's just an afterthought. Lives still get ruined, people still leave, and life goes on and on and on. So the Rules matter, Hughie. They're the only thing that matters. Which is why this is over!' She stood up. To her horror there were tears running down her cheeks and people, stupid, fat tourists, staring at them.

He got up too. 'Someone's hurt you. You're frightened, that's all.' He wrapped his arms around her again. 'Don't be frightened.'

'I'm not frightened!' She pushed him away. 'It's the Rules, Hughie! Why can't you just accept that? We had an arrangement.'

'Leticia . . .'

'No! I have to go.' She grabbed her handbag from the blue plastic seat, brushed the tears away with the back of her hand. 'I'm sorry. Really I am.'

And before he could say anything more, she had pushed past the group of German backpackers who'd stopped to see how this scene would play out and rushed out the door.

What a disaster! What was wrong with her today?

She hadn't got very far when her phone rang.

Please God, don't let it be him! She focused on the number. It was safe; she didn't recognize it.

'Yes?' she answered, trying to pull herself together, sound normal. 'Who is this? I'm sorry. Juan? Juan who?'

Outside, Henry was waiting.

Hughie wandered out, dazed.

'What happened? Hughie?' Henry took his arm. 'What happened?'

'She broke up with me.'

'Congratulations!' Henry slapped him on the back. 'What a stroke of luck!'

Hughie stared at him, appalled. 'How can you say that?'

'Well, had to be done, didn't it?' Henry seemed surprised. 'Only this time, you got out of doing the dirty work. Brilliant!'

Hughie longed to tell him that Leticia loved him; that that was the reason why she'd dumped him. Longed to ask for his advice. But now the job was all he had left. He didn't want to lose that too. 'It's complicated. You don't understand. Actually, not even I understand.'

'Sure I do. Listen, the first forty-eight hours are the worst. The ego's taken a bit of a kicking. What you need is a constant supply of alcohol.' He took Hughie's arm. 'Come on. Let's get you something to drink.'

'No.' Hughie suddenly felt sick to his stomach. His whole world had been turned on its ear; he was suffering from emotional vertigo. 'I just want to be alone.'

'Bad idea. Let me take you home at least.'

'No.' Hughie shook him off. 'Please.'

Henry eyed him warily. 'No phone calls, old chap. That's the killer. Mustn't pick up the phone or before you know it you'll be back to square one with the whole damned thing!'

'Here.' Hughie handed him his mobile. 'Take it. I just want to be alone.'

Then he walked away, heading up towards the bus stop. There, he finally yielded to his nausea, throwing up in the rubbish bin and guaranteeing a seat to himself on the crowded bus ride home.

Poor kid! Henry shook his head, pocketing Hughie's phone.

An awful business, but had to be done.

He turned, lit a cigarette.

Ironic that he was the one sent to enforce Valentine's no-relationships rule.

Especially as he'd never managed to follow it himself.

Hughie sat on the top deck, thinking about Leticia.

Only true love could be so annihilating. Surely the pain alone was proof they weren't meant to be parted.

He sighed again and looked miserably out of the window.

If only there was a way to get her to take a chance; of persuading her to love him.

Eventually exhaustion overtook Hughie. It had been an overwhelming day and he'd understood only a bit of it. His eyes grew heavy and his breath slowed. Finally, he fell asleep on the top deck of the number 16 bus, missing not only his stop but the whole of Kilburn entirely.

The Ghost Chair

Without turning on the lights, Olivia walked into the empty house. It was late. The stifling, Indian summer day had faded into a warm, close evening. Light from the street lamps streamed in through the open windows. It was so hot. She was stiff and tired. Pushing a damp strand of long blonde hair back from her face, she kicked off her sandals, walking across the cool marble floor.

There was a note on the hall table.

Guest room appalling. Have checked into the Dorchester for foreseeable future.

Arnaud

It was in Gaunt's handwriting. Arnaud had obviously dictated it to him.

She crumbled the paper into a ball and let it drop to the floor.

She was exhausted, worn out from his scenes and tantrums. What did it matter who saw it now?

Climbing the stairs, she made her way to her room.

There was the bed, their bed; beautifully made with expensive linens, piled with elaborate needlepoint pillows. But true to his word, everything of Arnaud's was gone; his books and papers were no longer stacked on the bedside table, his dressing gown no longer hung on the back of the bedroom door.

Olivia opened the wardrobe; a rattle of empty hangers greeted her.

Nothing, not even a stray shoelace was left.

She looked round.

His absence was as tangible as his presence had been. The room felt not just empty but unexpectedly bereft.

There was something else . . .

Near the window, the old overstuffed armchair Arnaud loved was gone. There was a clear plastic Philippe Starck Ghost chair in its place. He'd obviously appropriated the other one, had this put in its place. Light and transparent; it seemed flimsy in comparison; insubstantial; a joke.

She sat down on the edge of the bed.

Clothes were one thing but furniture signalled something more permanent. Was this the beginning of a larger rift; first separate rooms then separate houses? Had things really progressed so far? Dread gnawed at her heart.

Dinner with Pollard.

How many times this week had he had dinner with Pollard?

And then she knew.

Getting up, she padded downstairs, a mounting sense of inevitability pulling her towards Arnaud's study.

The evidence was easy to find. There they were, in neat piles with the other household bills, waiting to be filed on his desk. He hadn't even bothered to hide them – receipts for jewellery she hadn't been given, the hotels she hadn't enjoyed, the restaurants she'd never been to. He'd simply assumed she was too stupid, too trusting even to look.

He was having an affair.

Olivia's knees gave way beneath her. She crumpled, cheek pressed against the cool wood floor.

Cut loose like a bit of flotsam; she floated, weightless and numb.

Night pressed in around her, airless, thick and black.

Juan was waiting for Leticia by the nurse's station. He was shorter than she'd remembered and looked older; conservatively dressed in a navy windbreaker and jeans. The vision of him as a flamboyant Brazilian wild child was instantly smashed.

'Where is he?'

'Near the window.' He took her arm, leading her onto the ward.

They stopped in front of the bed. Juan gently pulled back the curtain. Leo was asleep, a drip in his arm. Monitors beeped reassuringly but his breathing was laboured, skin pale and forehead damp. His legs looked like two sticks under the sheets.

'When did you find him?'

'This afternoon. He'd fallen. Luckily I had a set of keys. Usually, I check on him twice a day.'

'I see.'

He'd been his carer, not his lover. Leticia felt sobered, ashamed. Leo had needed a nurse and she hadn't even realized.

'I called an ambulance. He's got pneumonia and a bad kidney infection. They're giving him high doses of antibiotics.'

'But how? How did it come on so fast?'

'When the system is weak to begin with . . .' his voice trailed off.

'He was sick before? I mean really sick, not just a cold?'

Juan was silent.

'He was sick before,' she said again, remembering the prescription bottles.

'Yes. He has been unwell for a while.'

How could she not know?

She touched his hand. It was clammy. 'These blankets aren't warm enough. Look at how thin they are!'

'He has a fever. Too many and he will only kick them off.' He smiled. He had a nice smile. 'You know Leo.'

He offered her a chair. 'I'll get you a cup of tea. With sugar. You've had a shock.'

She watched as he headed down the hall then looked round. The ward was filled with other old people, dying, alone. Terror gripped her.

Leticia sat down and took his hand again.

His eyes flicked open.

'Emily Ann!'

She squeezed his fingertips.

'Here I am.'

'Emily!'

'It's all right, I'm right here.'

His voice was hoarse. 'I . . . I must tell you something . . .'

'Yes?' she leant in.

'That look doesn't suit you, darling.'

He smiled.

She kissed his fingertips. 'Neither does yours.'

He closed his eyes again. 'It seems we've let ourselves go.'

He slipped back into the thick fog of sleep.

His hand went limp in hers.

She was alone.

The C Word

'I can't. Not today, Simon.'

Olivia was sitting on her bed, still in her dressing gown, dark circles under her eyes. Somewhere around four thirty in the morning she finally nodded off, only to wake again in tears. She must've been crying in her sleep. Once they started, she couldn't stem the flow. Sobbing, moaning, practically barking with grief and despair, she worked her way through an entire box of tissues. There was nothing to live for. She was old and childless and alone.

Then, at some ungodly hour, Simon rang.

'You can!'

'No,' she cleared her throat, 'really, I can't!'

'I'm telling you, Olivia, you can!'

'But you don't understand! I've never hung a show before! And I'm . . . I'm,' she struggled to find a delicate way to put it, 'I'm not at my best today, Simon.'

'Olivia,' his voice was firm, 'I need you. Ralph's pulled his back out and it's not finished! And we can't afford to get this

211

show wrong. Besides, you're the only person I know who has the vision I need. It's non-negotiable; I'm calling in all my favours. I need you now!'

Olivia sank to the floor, into the pile of used tissues that had accumulated in a snowy heap around the bed. She couldn't fathom how she was going to get dressed let alone down to the gallery.

'Olivia?' He wouldn't give up.

'OK,' she rasped.

'Great. I'll see you in an hour.'

He hung up.

Olivia blew her nose for the seven thousandth time. She badly needed a cigarette.

Sitting in her dressing gown on the back steps, Olivia fumbled with a box of kitchen matches, trying to light an ancient, stale Gauloise she'd found in an old handbag.

She wasn't a real smoker. There was no style to the way she jammed the cigarette between her lips or struck the match so hard that it snapped in two. The Gauloise was a serious cigarette – thick, acrid. There was smoking and then there was napalming your lungs. But she needed napalm; her mind twisted wildly, to and fro, trying to justify the evidence, while her heart cracked with the same agonizing resistance of an old tree being felled, its trunk snapping painfully, slowly in two.

It was gone. Her world. The entire answer she'd formulated to the question of how to live life.

How could he do that to her? What made her so . . . so disposable?

Taking a deep drag, she choked and spluttered.

When she was done, she'd go back in and ring Simon. He'd have to get someone else. Today was a day for taking tranquillizers washed down by vodka, not for striking out in new directions.

In front of her, the newly erected fountain made a relentless dribbling noise like a leaky faucet. It was a horrific Baroque-inspired confection; a gold-encrusted seashell bowl surrounded by piles of fat, frolicking cherubs and dolphins spitting water. Expensive, ugly, derivative.

She thought about the shiny aluminium gulley cutting, as Ricki put it, like a blade through a bright square of green glass. If only she'd had the courage to listen to her. Taking another drag, she coughed and, pulling her dressing gown tighter, shivered in the brisk morning air.

'Here.'

It was Ricki, holding open a box of Marlboro Lights.

Olivia's face went red.

Before she could say anything, Ricki knelt down, taking the Gauloise from her fingers.

'Let's get rid of that, shall we?' She tossed it into the fountain, where it fizzled out, bobbing up and down in the golden bowl. 'What are you trying to do – kill yourself?'

Not a bad idea, Olivia reflected.

Then Ricki shook out a couple of cigarettes, popped both

into her mouth and lit them with a battered black Zippo. She passed one back to Olivia.

It was all done so smoothly, so confidently. With what her mother would've called 'élan'.

'Thank you.'

Ricki nodded, settled down next to her, stretching out her long legs.

They sat, smoking in silence.

After a while, Ricki nodded to the fountain. 'So, do you like it?'

Olivia struggled to find something nice to say. 'You did a good job.'

'Yeah,' Ricki laughed, 'but do you like it?'

'It's ghastly,' she admitted, too exhausted to be polite.

'Yes. Yes, it is.'

They stared at it.

'It's not too late. We could still get rid of it.'

'But it's what I asked for.' Olivia looked miserably at the pudgy gold putti. 'You gave me exactly what I said I wanted.'

'So what?' Ricki shrugged. 'You're allowed to change your mind.'

What a dangerous concept.

'Am I?'

'Sure. Any time.'

They finished their cigarettes.

Ricki stood up. Holding out her hand, she pulled Olivia to her feet.

'Thanks.'

'And you're . . . you know . . . OK?' Ricki's dark eyes were full of concern. 'You seem a bit stressed.'

It surprised Olivia. No one really asked her how she was. Arnaud certainly didn't, the staff wouldn't dare.

'I'm OK.'

Ricki nodded. 'Good.'

'Thanks for the cigarette.'

'No problem.'

Olivia was about to go in when suddenly she stopped, turned. 'Actually, my husband moved out of the house yesterday.'

It wasn't the sort of thing one said to the gardener. She hadn't intended mentioning it to anyone yet, not even Mimsy.

'Really?' She was refreshingly undramatic. 'What happened?'

'I don't know. We don't seem to get on.'

There was a pause.

'The truth is, he's cheating on me.'

What was the sudden spate of honesty?

Ricki shook her head. 'Cunt!'

'I'm sorry?'

'What a cunt!' she elaborated.

Olivia had never used that word before; she'd never even thought it. In her family, it was considered cutting someone to the very quick to call them 'a bit of an ass'.

'Yes,' she realized, slowly, 'what a cunt!'

It was surprisingly satisfying to say – full of sharp, unapologetic sounds.

215

She said it again.

'An absolute cunt!'

'There we have it. Men! What a fucking fool!'

'Do you think?'

Ricki was emphatic. 'Biggest fool I know!'

It had seemed complicated before; now it was painful but simple. 'Yes. Yes, I suppose so.'

'So what are you going to do?' Ricki wanted to know.

'Me?' The question was almost offensive.

'Yeah.' Ricki leant against the wall, folded her arms in front of her chest. 'What are your plans?'

No one had expected Olivia to do anything before, least of all herself. Action, accomplishments were optional. Surely her dreadful situation gave her immunity from such practicalities.

'I don't know.'

Ricki pulled a tiny weed growing between the paving stones. 'I'd hire a fuck-off lawyer.'

'A lawyer? You mean, you think the marriage is over?'

Ricki looked up. 'Didn't you just say he was sleeping with someone else?'

'Yes, but . . .' her voice trailed off.

In Olivia's family marriages limped under the burden of far greater betrayals than just infidelity. She could practically hear her father's voice, 'When a Van der Lyden makes their bed, they lie in it!' Lord knows how many women he'd had over the years.

'How could you ever trust him again?' Ricki pointed out.

Did I ever trust him? Olivia wondered.

Ricki began unpacking her tools. 'Well, at least you have your job. That's a real solace in a time like this.'

Olivia had never thought of the gallery as an actual job. She'd treated it more as a dalliance. 'Something to keep me off the streets,' was how she put it to Mimsy.

'Get on with your own life,' Ricki selected a narrow trowel, 'that's the best revenge.'

'Yes, you're right,' Olivia agreed, not entirely sure it was true.

Ricki set about weeding in earnest.

Get on with your own life.

The words hung in the air, like a gauntlet thrown. What would her life be like without Arnaud to hide behind? Suddenly the prospect was intriguing as well as daunting.

Olivia watched as Ricki crouched low, weeding the flower beds in the pale sunlight. She was so strong, so sure of herself. Just being near her shored Olivia up; gave her clarity.

She'd needed to talk to someone, someone she could trust. How odd that it should be her.

Olivia wandered back into the house.

Something had shifted. The thick, cold, suffocating weight she'd known most of her life, dampening her spirit, was gone. In its place, something new, dangerous stirred. It fluttered, dark, uncontrollable, in the pit of her stomach.

'Cunt,' she muttered under her breath, climbing the stairs. The word resonated, clean, tough, full of unfamiliar power. She chanted it like a mantra. 'Cunt, cunt, cunt, cunt, cunt, cunt!'

Gaunt passed her on the way down. 'Good morning, madam.'

'Good morning. Cunt, cunt, cunt!' She rounded the landing. 'Oh, and Gaunt, put the coffee on, will you? I need it strong today.'

'Very good, madam.'

Simon was waiting for her; she had a job to do.

Breakfast at Graff

They glittered in the window of Graff: a pair of tiny, delicate, wholly unexpected heart-shaped diamond earrings.

And they were perfect. So perfect that Hughie was arrested as he walked down Bond Street the next morning; quite literally prevented from moving another inch as soon as his eye caught sight of them.

Diamonds! That's what girls loved! They wanted diamonds and men who could afford to buy them.

He stopped, pressed his nose up against the window and examined them as closely as he could.

And now that he had a job he could be one of those men!

The debilitating malaise he'd woken with was replaced by the giddy thrill of anticipation. They'd look wonderful on Leticia! She'd be so impressed! So grateful! How could she fail to love him if he gave her diamonds?

He checked his watch.

He was due to meet Marco in a few minutes.

Marco specialized in a series of flirts known as 'Sexy

Foreigner'. Among his trademark personas were Racing Driver, Lost Architect, and his favourite, Roaming Photographer. Camera clicking, he had descended upon many an unsuspecting mark, transforming their entire outlook with a few shots and the promise of slipping their photo into the next issue of Italian *Vogue*. Flick and Valentine agreed that Hughie was more *Room with a View* than *La Dolce Vita* but Marco was still drafted to teach Hughie the rudiments of his smouldering eye contact.

Still, how long could it take to enquire about the price of a pair of earrings?

Hughie rang the bell and the impeccably dressed middle-aged gentleman inside buzzed him in. The interior of the shop was furnished with all the opulence of a grand hotel lobby, only in miniature.

'Sir!' the man exclaimed, grasping Hughie's hand and pumping it up and down. 'What a pleasure, sir, to see you! Percival Bryce, at your service! What can I do for you?'

Hughie wasn't used to being greeted with such enthusiasm. It must be the suit. 'Well, I couldn't help but notice the heart earrings in the window . . .'

Mr Bryce practically exploded with glee. 'An excellent choice! Tasteful! Discreet! And so reasonable! Would you like to see them, sir?'

'Yes,' Hughie decided. 'Why not?'

Mr Bryce took a formidable collection of keys from the drawer of a gold–and–mahogany Empire desk and unlocked the window.

'So when we say reasonable,' Hughie ventured, 'we're talking how much?'

Mr Bryce placed the earrings at artful angles on a black velvet cloth. 'Five thousand pounds!' The words rolled off his tongue, as if it were the most delightful sum in the world. 'Come! Sit near them! Touch them if you like!' He pulled out a chair, patted the seat invitingly. 'Is this your first diamond purchase?'

'As a matter of fact, it is. Or rather, it could be,' Hughie corrected himself, reeling from the price. 'Actually, I was just curious.'

'Excellent! Curiosity is the most delightful of all human characteristics. We never know where it may lead us. Ah!' he sighed dreamily. 'There's nothing like your first diamond purchase! Nothing quite like it in the world! May I get you a glass of champagne? Deirdre! Deirdre, a glass of champagne, please!'

A pretty blonde girl appeared with a champagne glass balanced on a silver tray.

'Thank you.' Hughie took it.

'Shall we see them on? What do you think? Yes, why not!' Mr Bryce answered his own question. 'Deirdre, will you do the honours?'

Deirdre put the earrings on.

'Look at the way the light catches them!' Mr Bryce lifted her hair up. 'Amazing! And the hearts! So romantic!'

'Yes. Quite.' Hughie sipped his champagne.

Mr Bryce stood back, radiating pleasure. 'Is there anything more beautiful than a woman wearing diamonds? I ask you, sir! Isn't she a vision?'

'Very nice, no doubt about it,' Hughie agreed.

'Now,' Mr Bryce's brow furrowed, 'I must ask you, please don't think I'm being impertinent, but have you had anything to eat? It's so difficult to make any big decisions on an empty stomach. Impossible, I'd say! Deirdre will gladly rustle you up something if you like. A croissant perhaps? Or a bit of toast?'

Hughie settled back into his chair. 'I don't suppose you've got a *pain au chocolat* knocking about?'

'A *pain au chocolat*!' He clapped his hands. 'An excellent choice! We have here a man of taste, Deirdre!'

She smiled.

'As it comes or slightly warmed?'

'Oh, slightly warmed, I think.'

'Yes, yes, of course! A slightly warmed *pain au chocolat* at once, Deirdre!'

She picked up her tray and headed for the back room.

'Deirdre!' Mr Bryce's tone sharpened, as if recalling an errant dog. 'The earrings, please!'

Reddening, she took them off.

'Now, Mr . . . ?'

'Mr Venables-Smythe.'

All the colour drained from Mr Percival Bryce's unseasonably tanned face, yet his smile remained intact.

'Venables-Smythe?' he repeated.

'Yes, that's right.'

'As in, Rowena Venables-Smythe, formerly Rowena Compton Jakes?'

'That's my mother! Hey, that's amazing! How do you know her?'

'I don't. I mean, I used to see her . . . mind you, this was many years ago. She used to work at Tiffany's, across the street.' He fussed with velvet. 'She wouldn't remember me, I'm sure. Please don't mention it. No need to bring up that you saw me or popped in . . . Oh, look! Your *pain au chocolat*! Thank you, Deirdre. Is she well? Happy? Your mother, I mean. I imagine she is. Why wouldn't she be? After all,' he concluded grimly, 'your father is a very dashing, very well-to-do man!'

'Dad died years ago. A fishing accident off the coast of Malta. They never found him.'

Mr Bryce's spirits seemed to lift. 'Really? I'm so sorry! How awful for you! Really? Is he quite dead?'

Hughie bit into the *pain au chocolat*; a river of warm dark chocolate filled his mouth. 'Mmmm,' he nodded. 'Quite. She's never really recovered.'

'I see,' Mr Bryce murmured to himself. 'No men in her life, then?'

'Not unless you count Jack Daniels and Johnny Walker.'

Mr Bryce drifted over to the window, looking out across the street at the grand façade of Tiffany's. 'I suspect she's suffered from inconsolable grief. Some wounds never really heal.' He sighed. 'She used to ride a bicycle to work. It was blue.'

The idea of his mother maintaining her balance on anything, let alone a moving vehicle, was shocking.

Mr Bryce stood there for quite a while, long enough for Hughie to finish the *pain au chocolat* and drain his champagne glass. The glamour of the situation was just beginning to pall when he finally turned round.

'Perhaps, Mr Venables-Smythe,' he sniffed, dabbing his eyes discreetly with a silk hanky, 'we might be able to come to some arrangement about the earrings.'

'Really? That's good of you! What sort of arrangement?'

'Well, diamonds are quite an investment, aren't they? Not something one does lightly.'

'Not at five grand a pop!'

'Sometimes people like a second opinion. A female perspective, so to speak.' He traced his fingers casually along the edge of the desk. 'A mother's opinion is often invaluable in a case like this one. If I remember correctly, your mother always possessed impeccable taste.'

'Yes, well . . .' Hughie hadn't intended even to tell his mother let alone ask her opinion. She'd undoubtedly object on the grounds that he should be doing something more constructive with his money, like paying his sister rent or buying food.

'If you were to bring her in, perhaps?'

Hughie frowned.

'Two thousand five hundred!' Mr Bryce blurted out suddenly. 'You can have the earrings for half their normal price, contingent, of course, on the circumstances I've just mentioned!'

'You mean, my mother . . .'

'Yes, yes, yes!' He waved his hand in front of his face, as if it pained him to hear the details repeated again. 'I think we understand each other, Mr Venables-Smythe, do we not?'

'Yes, of course.'

He really was incredibly highly strung. Hughie felt for him. Reverting to a bit of Old Harrovian charm, he inclined his head politely and extended his hand. 'And I'm very sensible, Mr Bryce, of the generosity of your extremely kind offer.'

It seemed to calm him down.

Mr Bryce shook it gratefully. 'Excellent! Excellent indeed! I will put the earrings to one side, shall I? And I look forward to seeing you in the next few days. Here,' he produced a card from his inside pocket, 'take my number. I'm always available, always available!' He patted Hughie on the back, opened the door, shook his hand another three times before ejecting him from the shop.

Back on the street, Hughie imagined Leticia's expression as she opened the dark navy box; the gasp of joy as she discovered the beautiful diamond earrings glittering inside. He could see them, framing her face, lost temporarily in the tangle of her dark hair and then emerging again, dazzling as they caught the light. And then he imagined the look in her eyes.

That was what it was all about.

Then he bumped smack into Marco, striding up Bond Street, furious.

'Hey! You're late!' Marco shouted. 'I said ten o'clock! In the morning, right! I can't work this way, understand? Ten o'clock is ten o'clock! Not eleven, not two!' He stopped quite suddenly. 'Wait a minute! You,' he waggled a finger in Hughie's face, 'you've been looking at jewellery! I can tell!'

Hughie started. 'No, no, you've got it all wrong!'

Was he psychic?

'I've got it all wrong, eh? Look, what's that?' He brushed a few crumbs from Hughie's lapel. 'And this?' He jabbed at a bit of chocolate on Hughie's chin. 'And is that champagne I smell? You don't get that at McDonald's, do you? You've got a woman, Smith! I know it!'

'Smythe! Venables-Smythe!'

'Smith, Smythe, whatever you're called, you're in big trouble!'

'I was just looking! Browsing, that's all.'

Marco snorted. 'Men don't browse for jewellery!'

'Whatever you're thinking, you're wrong! I've just been dumped. Ask Henry if you don't believe me. I'm a dedicated flirt. One hundred per cent.'

Marco looked unconvinced.

'It's for my sister,' Hughie lied.

'You're lying!'

'Maybe.'

'You're playing with fire. Love is not a toy!'

'Oh, please! All of you go on about it as if it were the Plague! So, I was looking at earrings. So what? You act as if I were mainlining heroin!'

'Ahhh! Now I see! You've never been in love. That's why you're so cock-like!'

'Cocky.'

'Whatever! You have no experience of the madness; no respect for the danger! You, Smith,' he poked Hughie firmly in the chest, 'are arrogant!'

Hughie took exception. 'Well, you, sir,' he poked Marco back, 'are obviously frigid!'

'Frigid!' A wild look flared in Marco's eyes. 'You accuse me, Marco Michelangelo Dante Spangol – the King of Love – of being frigid?'

'Yes.'

'You are mad! Insane! I am a master flirt! The finest in London!'

'Ah, yes! But for all your flirting, Marco, have you ever once dared to fall in love?'

'Love?' Marco snorted. 'Love!'

'Yes, love!'

Marco hesitated and in that moment, his Italian bravado deflated before Hughie's eyes. His shoulders fell forward beneath his impeccable black wool Prada suit; his eyes dimmed by melancholy. Even his lustrous dark curls sagged around his face.

'No,' he answered quietly.

This wasn't quite what Hughie was expecting. 'Really?'

'Ah, Smith! I have never known the joy of love.' And he sighed, staring dejectedly at the ground.

'I see.'

Somehow their argument had derailed, plunging into dark, unexpected and intimate waters. The Marco he knew – the bold, flamboyant master of both Lost Architect and Racing Driver, disappeared. In his place a rather lonely, tired-looking man remained.

A hot cup of tea was probably in order.

'Listen,' Hughie gestured to a small outdoor café, 'how about I buy you a drink?'

Soon they were sitting at a table and the sad, ironic history of Marco Michelangelo Dante Spangol came to light.

'You see, Smith, the difficulty is I am so handsome,' Marco explained sadly. 'It's a curse really. From the moment I was born, I've always been irresistible to women. When I was a baby, my mother had to push me with a blanket over the carriage . . . what is it?'

'Pram?'

'Yes, pram! Even in the height of summer so that I was hidden from strangers trying to kiss me. And when I was a little boy, at school, I had to sit next to a different little girl every day of the week so that they wouldn't fight with one another.'

'Good God!'

Marco sighed heavily. 'All my life I could have any woman I wanted. And I have. But it's so empty, Smith! You see, the world has no meaning for me. I've known beautiful women, successful women, talented women, models, actresses, athletes but I've never known a woman who was my match. All the time, I hear, "I love you, Marco!" but I can never really say, "I love you," in return.'

'But what are you looking for?'

'Fire! Passion!' He banged his fist on the table. 'Resistance, Smith! What I want is a woman who doesn't want me! But look at me: I'm thirty-four now and more handsome than ever! I'm starting to think maybe the woman of my dreams doesn't exist.'

They sat a while.

For the first time, Hughie concentrated on the admiring glances of the women who walked by. He liked to think that some of them were for him, but he had to concede that Marco got more than his fair share.

'This is the only job I can do,' Marco continued, downing his coffee in one go. 'In and out; no contact. If I work in a normal profession, I leave a trail of broken hearts. Here, at least I do the world a little bit of good. Waitress! Another espresso, please.'

The girl fluttered her lashes. 'It's on the house!'

'See?' Marco groaned miserably. 'It's hopeless!' He held up a teaspoon, examining his reflection. 'If only my nose were larger or my jaw weaker . . .'

For a moment, he looked as though he might cry.

Hughie was relieved when Henry ambled up, on his way to the office.

'Hughie! Just the man I need to see! I've got a job for you.' He paused. 'Everything OK?'

Hughie leapt to his feet. 'Never been better!'

Marco just blinked.

'OK, well, we'd better get a move on. We've got a lot on today,' Henry said, checking his watch. 'See you later, Marco! Marco?'

But Marco was in another world. When they left he was turning his espresso cup around and around on its tiny little saucer, staring into space.

'Let me guess,' Henry steered Hughie towards a white van parked across the street, 'he got started on his hopeless quest for love.'

'How did you know?'

'We've all been there.' Henry shook his head. 'Poor Marco! But more importantly, how you doing, old boy? Feeling better? I was really worried when I left you.'

'Humm . . .' Hughie couldn't decide if playing the wounded lover gave him a certain tragic depth. It certainly required a lot of effort. He changed the subject instead. 'I'm ready for my first real day. Where do we begin?'

'At the beginning, with flower delivery.' Henry opened the back of the van and chucked him a T-shirt and hat. 'Put these on. Once we're on the road, I'll brief you. This job's a good example of a classic mark; married a while, three kids, another one on the way . . . virtually drowning in domesticity. You'll see.' He smiled. 'The married women of this world need us, Hughie; need us more than even they know.'

230

Professional Massagers of the Female Ego at Large
(Part One)

Meanwhile, in the less fashionable districts of South London, Amy Mortimer opened her wardrobe door. Two flights below, she could hear the dull, siren roar of her children wailing. She wavered, fighting the desire to waddle downstairs and sort everything out.

No. The nanny was there. The whole point of the nanny was so Amy could be free to bathe and dress and even sometimes leave the house. That's what they paid her for.

Only nothing in her closet fitted any more. She stared at the clothes in front of her, half of them still wrapped in dry-cleaning plastic; the only remaining evidence of her once, well-groomed, size-ten former life. It had been years since she'd been able to fit into them. They were a shrine to a self that had been completely obliterated.

Amy sighed.

'Mummy! Mummy! Muuuuuuuummmmmmyyyyyy!' Angus was screaming. She could hear him flinging his little body up the stairs and then the sound of the nanny intercepting; struggling to prise his fingers off the hall banister.

'Noooooooooooooooooooo! Mummy! Noooooooooooooooo!' He was like some tiny extra in *Schindler's List* being dragged off by the Nazis.

Amy made herself close the bedroom door. Why had nature designed small children's cries to tear a mother's heart in two? In fact, the whole business of being a mother was just one long exercise in guilt and compromise. Sitting on the edge of the unmade bed, she began to cry. The harder she cried, the more the baby inside her kicked.

With her luck, it was probably another boy.

Kick, kick, kick.

I'm hormonal, she told herself. This is normal. These are just buckets of hormones racing around my veins. Pull yourself together.

Exhaustion dragged at her. She wanted to lie down but that was a whole half-hour performance: the placement of pillows under the bump, between the legs, something to wrap her arm around . . . she hadn't slept in years. Why start now?

So she forced herself up again, and looked around.

The windows needed to be washed. She had the vague recollection of thinking the same thing the last time she was pregnant. Nothing had been done about it then and things were probably going to go the same way now.

Opening Jonathan's wardrobe, she selected one of his best, handmade shirts. Thank God he had a paunch. And retrieving her elastic-panelled maternity jeans from where they were crumpled on the floor, she struggled into them. There were some shoes somewhere . . . wait, what was this? A pair of bright orange beach flip-flops? Perfect. At least she didn't have to bend down.

Then she picked up a small notepad she kept by her bedside table and referred to a list she'd made last night.

Amy was fond of making lists. In her heyday as an events organizer, she'd been able to plough through them, ticking off each entry with remarkable speed. Even when she was a little girl, her world had been clean and tidy, its parameters neatly marked by lists of accomplishments. She prided herself on being able to get things done, to face the mundane tasks of everyday life head on and emerge triumphant. But lately her lists had failed to deliver the same satisfaction. Instead of getting shorter, they only seemed to grow. And their contents overwhelmed her.

This one began brightly enough. '*Shoes for Angus, haircuts for all the boys, Dylan's dental appointment, water filters, new nursing bras, nightgowns, and knickers . . .*' But then came, '*Ring garden maintenance company, ask about infestation of big, black bugs (possible health hazards of small children eating fertilizer).*' Followed by, '*Ask doctor about ADD link to fish fingers, vacuum sand from downstairs sofa, order extra-long rubber sheets for Felix and Angus, apologize to new neighbour about noise, flying dirt and Dylan kicking down lattice fence, DO LAUNDRY, DO LAUNDRY, DO LAUNDRY! Boys to clean their rooms* [was she deluded?] *and not to leave wet swimming trunks under beds!!!'*

And then, at the bottom of the page, just before she'd gone to bed, she'd written, *'Must see latest show at the Royal Academy.'*

The Royal Academy?

Leaning over, she grabbed her reading glasses from the bedside table.

'Must see latest show at the Royal Academy.'

It didn't even look like her handwriting.

The phrase struck her as so blatantly out of step with the reality of her day-to-day life as to be psychotic. It smacked of the kind of fatuous promise she sometimes made to her single friends: 'Oh, yes! We must see the latest show at the Royal Academy! Shall I give you a ring next week?' Of course, they both knew she was lying. But here it was, popping up, entirely independent of social artifice; the strange, forlorn desire to attend a cultural event.

She sat down again on the edge of the bed and stared at the paper in her hand. It was the only thing on the list that was even remotely appealing.

And for a moment she imagined herself, dressed in something other than maternity jeans and orange flip-flops, walking slowly through the grand rooms.

Her breath slowed.

The baby stopped kicking.

Here was the catalogue in her hands; the satisfying weight of thick, glossy paper and years of scholarship. The smell of wooden floors and leather banquettes enveloped her, and there was space – space above and around; space between objects and people, between information and images; a luxurious sense of perspective that was so lacking in daily life. She was taking her time, moving slowly, forming opinions and feeling the gentle surge of energy as her mind contemplated something new; something beyond her narrow sphere of experience. She was peaceful, exhilarated; anonymous.

And there was something else, another quality that evaded her . . .

Then it came.

In her vision, she was single.

Not just single, but childless; wandering free, with no lists, no mobile phone; no presence pressing, jostling for position in her mind.

Her heart beat faster; guilt seeped through her. But her imagination bounded forward anyway.

She left the gallery, this new single self and, sitting happily by herself, took the bus home.

Now she could see the darling little one-bedroom flat she lived in, somewhere near the canal in Little Venice. Here was the tiny, bright kitchen, just right for one, always clean . . . the living room with a cat, curled into the seat cushion of an old armchair, basking in a square of sunshine . . . an unashamedly romantic bedroom adorned with floral prints and mounds of soft pillows . . . A whole life unfolded before her; a peaceful, quiet, unhurried existence.

Suddenly she was frightened.

Did she really want a cat and a clean kitchen? She'd fought so hard, so long for her filthy South London home, bad-tempered husband and brood of children.

Passing a hand over her face, she rubbed her eyes.

Hormones. It was all hormones.

She stood up. If she wanted to go so badly, she could ask Jonathan to go with her. They could easily book a babysitter and have lunch.

And then she sat down again, quickly. Her heart contracted. She felt sick.

That was exactly what she didn't want.

Quite unwillingly, she unearthed a nugget of truth she wished she'd left buried.

It wasn't just that Jonathan didn't do visual art. Or that free time was at such a premium, he'd consider it a waste. But the thought of trying to jolly him along, of having to be extra bright and effervescent to weather another one of his inevitable bad moods, force-feeding him art, was unbearable. The dream had been about wandering around alone and free. And Jonathan, this man she'd pursued, won and married with the single-minded passion of a zealot, would ruin the day.

In that moment, the full horror of her situation dawned on her.

She was married to a man she couldn't take to the Royal Academy.

Then another unwanted truth emerged; pressing into her

consciousness with such violence she thought it would suffo-
cate her.

She was lonely.

Incredibly, indescribably lonely.

Lying down on the bed, not quite sure how she would ever
get up again, Amy Mortimer listened to the sound of her children being rounded up and trotted off to the park. Already she
was redundant. Some day soon they would leave her. They
would go to school and grow up and get girlfriends she would
hate. And she would be left alone with Jonathan. She'd made
a mistake; a terrible mistake! Pressing her face into the pillow,
she wept, astounded by her own stupidity. How could she have
been so naive; so deluded and misinformed? What on earth
had given her the idea that forcing this irritable, overweight
man to marry her and produce child after child in this cramped,
disgusting house would ever make her happy?

All this time, she wanted a cat and a clean kitchen and she
never even knew it!

The doorbell rang.

'Oh, fuck off!' she growled.

But as it sounded again she hauled herself upright and
grabbed a tissue, blowing her nose.

Then she began the long descent to the front door, leaning
heavily on the banister, her orange flips-flops sucking and flap-
ping against the soles of her swollen feet.

'Yes?' she barked, swinging the door wide.

A young man was standing there holding a bunch of flowers.

He smiled. He was so good-looking. She wished she were wearing something more attractive.

'Hello,' he said, 'I'm sorry if I've disturbed you.'

Amy smiled back. 'Oh, no!' she lied.

'Good. I wonder if I could ask you for a favour.'

'Certainly.'

'You see, these are for next door. No one's home and I wondered if I could leave them with you.'

'Oh.' She had thought they were for her. But of course, that was stupid; her birthday wasn't for ages yet, her anniversary had just gone, and Jonathan wasn't the type of man to send flowers for no reason. 'Of course.' She took the flowers from him. 'They're beautiful.'

'Yes,' he looked at her thoughtfully, 'though to be honest, they're kind of ordinary, don't you think?'

'Ordinary?'

'Yeah,' he leant against the door frame. 'Dull.'

'Really? So what would you send,' she challenged, 'or perhaps you wouldn't send anything at all?'

'Me? I'm a less-is-more kind of man.'

'Obviously you and my husband think alike, only he's more of a "none is enough" kind of guy.'

'I'm not that bad! It's just I like smaller, more intimate gestures. Personally, I'm a fan of the single white rose.'

She laughed; it was such an odd thing for a young man to say. 'Why is that?'

He shrugged his shoulders; looked at her with the most

238

remarkable blue eyes. 'It's more romantic,' he admitted softly. 'Sexier, don't you think?' He grinned again; a cheeky, slightly naughty grin. Her heart leapt.

'Well, I wouldn't know.' She could feel her face flushing. (Was he flirting with her? Right here on her own doorstep?) Her eyes met his. 'No one's ever done that sort of thing for me.'

'No!' He seemed genuinely shocked to hear it. 'That's criminal!'

'Criminal, maybe, but also true.'

He paused, looking at her.

She shifted, suddenly self-conscious. 'Well, anyway . . .'

'But don't you agree? I mean, not that I've ever done it myself.' His voice faded and to her surprise, he coloured slightly. 'I guess I've never been inspired by anyone. It's a more personal gesture, though . . . don't you think?'

'It sounds lovely,' she conceded.

They stood a moment.

'I'm keeping you.'

'No, no, it's all right.'

'Well,' he backed slowly down the steps, 'thanks very much. I really appreciate you looking after those.'

'My pleasure.'

He tipped his cap at her and headed to his van.

Amy closed the door. She couldn't remember the last time someone had spoken to her in that way. It stirred up a nostalgic longing tinged by a surge of almost adolescent excitement. Putting the flowers on the hall table, she gazed at her reflection in the mirror. Maybe her old self hadn't disappeared entirely; maybe somewhere below the surface she was still visible: a naughty, sexy, hopeful woman, still capable of inspiring desire.

'Or not,' she thought, sighing heavily.

Who was she kidding? How could she inspire anyone?

She was about to climb upstairs and retreat again to her bedroom, when the doorbell rang a second time.

She opened it and there was the young flower-delivery man again.

He was smiling shyly, holding the most perfect single white long-stemmed rose she'd ever seen.

'Oh!'

'I think you're right,' he blushed, handing it to her. 'One isn't enough – you deserve a whole armful of white roses!'

Then he bounded off the front step.

As he headed back to the van he turned.

'I hope your baby is as beautiful as you are!' he called.

For the first time in her life, Amy Mortimer was speechless.

Hughie climbed into the front seat of the van next to Henry, breathless with exhilaration.

'I think that went rather well!' he beamed.

'Yeeeeessss,' Henry was looking in the rear-view mirror.

Something wasn't quite right.

The woman was still standing in the doorway.

There was something odd about the way she was holding on to the door frame.

Suddenly she doubled over, clutching her stomach.

The white rose fell to the ground.

'Oh, dear,' Henry sighed, 'I think we have a problem.'

Leticia lay in her bed, immobile, the curtains of her bedroom drawn against the late-morning light. Her limbs felt like cement; thick, inflated like a Henry Moore sculpture. She moved her head to one side; it throbbed.

Outside, London had roused itself; bathed, dressed, breakfasted and thrust itself forward once more unto the breach. But inside her narrow bedroom, Leticia dreamed of night. It wasn't that she longed for more sleep. Sleep didn't matter. But she pined for the hours of darkness when finally the world outside matched her interior landscape.

It was time to go to work. Time to get up.

But what was the point?

More rich women, more designs, more work, more gowns, more money, more women . . . on and on and on it went without purpose or meaning. All the things she'd believed in so passionately, suddenly lost their sweetness, leaving only the dry dust of habit and duty behind.

She turned on her back.

What if Leo died? What would she have in her life that was lasting and important?

Nothing.

What was worse is that she worked very long and hard at having nothing. She took a great deal of care to have sex with men she didn't love. She spent all her time making a shop which catered to women she didn't rate. Even her name was false.

When Leo did die, which would happen some day, she would be alone.

Leticia closed her eyes.

And then there was Hughie. The whole scene had been so messy. Instead of walking away feeling free, she'd run away, exposed and unravelled. Did she love him? He was just a kid. Or was it that any tenderness was unfamiliar to her now?

It wasn't a comforting train of thought. In fact, it was so discomfiting that Leticia dragged herself out of bed, got dressed and went to the shop, just to get away from her own morbid reflections.

Only when she arrived, the electricity wasn't working.

She rang the company. Some nonsense about her not paying the bill. She tried to give them a debit card over the phone. The payment was denied.

She rang the bank. A man in deepest India explained that even her overdraft was overdrawn. She argued and swore. He remained irritatingly calm.

It was only when she hung up and sat down, in the dark, fuming, that she noticed something else.

The dripping noise was back.

Professional Massagers of the Female Ego at Large
(Part Two)

Henry took Hughie to an elegant café in Sloane Square. They sat down and ordered a couple of coffees.

'That was unusual,' Hughie said after a while.

'Hummm.'

They both sipped their coffee.

'A bit of a hose-out and I expect that van will be good as new.'

'Yes, yes,' Henry agreed. 'I imagine it will.'

The memory of Amy Mortimer, howling and prostrate in the back of the van, was difficult to erase.

'Has that ever happened to you before?'

'No,' Henry frowned, 'no, it hasn't. Well, I suppose,' he said, brightening, 'that we can only regard it as some kind of omen – a good one, I hope!'

Hughie raised his cup. 'New life and all that!'

'Exactly! Onwards and upwards!'

They both stared into space.

It had all been so graphic; the language alone left scars only time could heal.

Henry rallied first. 'Yes, well, be that as it may.'

'Exactly.'

'Now, you've read about this one? She's only young. You need to be careful, Smythe. Mind you don't leer at her.'

'Leer! I'm a little young for leering!'

'Well, mind you don't. OK. This one is easy,' Henry said. 'All you need is a copy of *The Times* and a good-quality pen. The pen is very important,' he added, giving Hughie a stern look. 'An ordinary pen won't do at all. It needs to be an expensive, good-quality pen. Like this.' He took out a thick black Mont Blanc pen. 'Nothing too garish, mind you. No diamonds or God forbid, semi-precious stones . . . just a well-made, handsome pen that demonstrates you have both taste and means. Got it?'

'Got it.'

'The right props, young Smythe, sorts the men from the boys. You can use this one today. Now, the premise is simple, all that's required is that you look like a genius . . .'

Poor Amber Marks left the house at the same time every day.

She told her mother she was studying at the library but in reality she spent most of the time wandering up and down the King's Road or drinking cups of tea and reading Zola in the original French at Oriel, the café on the corner of Sloane Square. It wasn't that she liked Zola so much as she thought it made her look smart, complicated and interesting. And Poor Amber Marks was desperate to be all of these things.

The truth was, she didn't know who or what she should be any more. Not since 'the Incident' over three months ago. It happened in her first year of reading languages at Oxford. To start with, she seemed to be doing all right. Making friends proved tricky and the course work was definitely challenging, but she seemed to be holding her own. However, slowly, things grew worse. Expectation rose. The competition increased. Amber couldn't sleep for worry. More and more she spent time on her own. Then the full-blown panic attacks started and the tears, non-stop crying jags, day and night. Finally the college rang her parents.

Her mother referred to it as a 'bit of a wobble'; her father liked to call it an 'academic break'. But they all knew that it was bigger than that. Amber couldn't cope with the rigorous demands of Oxford, only no one liked to say it out loud. It had meant so much to her parents that she got in. They had such plans for her – medicine, law, publishing; apparently there was nothing she couldn't do.

Except survive her education.

'Poor Amber,' her mother sighed, loudly and often when they were alone. 'She's lost her confidence.'

'Yes, poor Amber,' her father agreed. 'But what's to be done?'

Taking a seat by the window, looking out onto Sloane Square, Amber ordered a cup of tea. Stirring in a packet of sugar, she stared out at the passing pedestrians. They all looked so capable. How many of them had graduated with first-class degrees?

A young man walked in and sat down at the table next to her. Amber couldn't help but notice how handsome he was, tall with wild blond hair, dimples and a pair of striking blue eyes. He couldn't be much older than she was. She hid behind her book. He ordered a coffee and took out a pen and a copy of *The Times* crossword. She watched as he filled it in with remarkable speed.

She was fascinated. He must be so bright!

Then he frowned. As he pushed his hair back impatiently from his face, the pen fell to the floor at her feet.

'Oh! I'm so sorry!' he said.

She bent to pick it up. It wasn't an ordinary pen, but heavy, smooth, elegant; nicely weighted in her hand. It was the pen of someone who'd made it in this world but didn't need to shout about it or hide it.

She passed it back. 'There you go.'

'Thank you!' he smiled.

'It's nothing,' she said quietly, taking up her book.

'Look, I know it's cheeky but there's one clue I just can't get. Would you mind having a look? I hate to leave a crossword unfinished.' He tilted his head slightly and smiled at her in such a way that she found herself smiling back.

'OK, but I can't make any guarantees,' she warned.

'You star! It's this one,' he leant in close, pointing to the clue. 'French for . . .'

It had been a long time since Amber had allowed anyone, let alone a handsome man, so close to her. The stranger's shoulder rubbed against hers as she examined the paper. The air around him was charged with a subtle sexual energy and he smelt so lovely, warm and fresh.

It was an easy clue; she could see he'd got most of the really tricky ones straight off. But even though she knew the answer instantly, she lingered, enjoying the proximity of him.

'Hummm . . .' she pretended to think. 'It might be . . . un coup de foudre'

'But of course! You clever girl! That's er . . . isn't it?'

'*RE*,' she corrected him.

'Of course!' He nodded, filling it in. 'I should've asked you straight away; here you are reading, what is it?' He peered at her book. 'Zola! Genius girl! Might have saved myself half the morning!'

'I'm hardly a genius!' She could feel her face growing warm. 'Just good at French, that's all.'

'Well,' he settled back, 'it's more than I could do.'

'But you got all the rest,' she reminded him. 'And so quickly!'

He made a face. 'What's left of my education . . . such as it was.'

'Such as it was?' She was intrigued.

'It's nothing.'

'No, I'm curious. What do you mean?'

'Well, I never graduated,' he confessed, taking a sip of his coffee. 'You're talking to a drop-out. I went to Cambridge to study English but it just wasn't for me. I know it's meant to be a big deal and my parents were upset but it doesn't suit everyone. Maybe you think that's stupid,' he added quickly. 'But I wanted to travel, work, find my own feet.'

Amber stared at him. 'You just left?' The idea hadn't occurred to her. She'd imagined having another breakdown, being sent away or having to leave (probably in an ambulance) but she never thought of just walking away and doing something different.

'Yeah. I thought, so what if everyone else thinks this is the be all and end all – I just felt like I was suffocating.'

She couldn't quite believe it. 'And what do you do now?'

He laughed. 'You'll never believe it – I've got an interview in ten minutes next door at the Royal Court!'

'Oh, you're an actor.' No wonder he was talking to her; they were all such extroverts.

'A director,' he said. 'We're going to discuss a new play I'd like to do. But listen, I'm prattling. That's the trouble with pretty girls, I babble like an idiot when I'm around them!'

She giggled.

'Hey,' he leant in again, 'I don't suppose you're an actress, are you? Looking for some young director to cast you in a hot new play?'

'Me! Never!'

'But you'd be perfect!'

'Really? For what part?' she asked eagerly.

'Any part! Look at you – bright, beautiful!' He shrugged his shoulders. 'You'd just be perfect, full stop! Damn!' He looked at his watch. 'I'm on the verge of losing this job before I've even got it.'

He stood, leaving a five-pound note on the table, and Amber felt a sudden wave of panic. Normally she hated talking to strangers but now she didn't want him to leave. On an impulse, she stood too.

'It was lovely to meet you. It's weird, I can't explain how much it's helped me to talk to you . . . I mean . . . oh, I don't know how to put it . . .' I'm gushing, she thought. I have to stop gushing! 'Anyway, I hope it all works out well for you. I'm sure it will.' She thrust her hand out awkwardly. 'Good luck!'

He was looking at her, smiling, the most beautiful man she'd ever seen.

Then he shook his head slowly. 'No, no, this won't do at all,' he said softly.

Hughie gazed down at Amber, at her open face and large brown eyes.

He'd never been responsible for anything or anyone before and now here he was, holding, for one brief moment, this girl in the palm of his hand. She was so fragile. He felt powerful;

more masculine than he'd ever felt in his life. Already she was changed, lively, more confident. But he wanted to do more; he wanted to transform her, to crack her wide open. It wouldn't take much. She was so malleable, staring into his eyes, lips parted, body tilting forward . . .

Hughie pulled her to him. She melted beneath him, her mouth warm and soft against his, her whole frame sighing with the release of . . .

Something hard sent him reeling into the sweet trolley.

'Hey!' Amber cried.

When he looked up, Henry was pulling him off the floor. 'Excuse me, Mr Jones,' he growled, 'you're late!'

Before Hughie could say anything, Henry pushed him out the door and dragged him another hundred yards into an alleyway behind the café.

'What were you thinking of!' He cuffed Hughie around the ear.

'Ow!'

'Weren't you listening at all? No physical contact!'

'I'm sorry.' Hughie rubbed the side of his head. 'I don't know what came over me!'

'You were blinded! Blinded by power. It happens to all of us at one time or the other but I've never seen it quite so badly or quite so soon!' He shook his head.

'I've never felt so . . . so,' Hughie wanted to giggle, 'you know . . .'

'Yes, excited,' Henry sighed, pressing his hand across his eyes.

250

'Flirting can be very erotic, very intense. But you've got to learn to control yourself! Now, we've got to get out of here!' Henry hailed a cab. 'Bond Street,' he shouted to the driver. And he climbed in, pulling Hughie after him.

No Ordinary Mark

Flick sat alone in her office, cutting out yet another photo of Olivia Bourgalt du Coudray for her file. This was no ordinary mark. Here was one case where preparation was crucial.

Flick's particular talent, groomed by Valentine, was to read between the lines of women's lives, to excavate with all the instinctive wisdom of a white witch, what would touch them, stir them most.

Only Olivia Bourgalt du Coudray was proving difficult.

It should've been easy. Her life was extremely well documented. Although she didn't appear to seek out media attention, she naturally attracted it. And miraculously, it was mostly confined to her public appearances. Either she did nothing to excite speculation in her private life or she'd managed that almost impossible task of taming the British press.

However, there was an impenetrable quality about her; as if she were protected by a haze of steely perfection.

What was this woman lacking?

Flick snipped the last bit of paper away and added the photo to the already bulging brief.

She wasn't making much progress.

Yawning, she leant back in her chair. The flat was quiet. Late-afternoon sun filtered in through the window behind her desk, warming her back.

Valentine was out. All the boys busy; even young Hughie.

She smiled. He was a strange, rare talent; a bit like a child behind the wheel of a Ferrari; he'd be either brilliant or a disaster. Careful cultivation was needed. But he couldn't be in better hands than Henry's.

How many young men had she auditioned, trained, watched as they struggled to find their feet in this strange half-world of flirting? Few had the necessary ability or self-control. If truth be known, it took a young man with a tragic history to be successful in this game. To flirt with the intention of seduction, intimacy, romance was one thing. But to flirt and leave, again and again and again, six, seven times a day, required an altogether different sensibility.

Sometimes Flick wondered who was lonelier – the women they flirted with or the flirts themselves?

And where did that put her, at the centre of this web of fragile human transactions? Were they really helping to heal the rifts which separated couples or were they, in fact, simply distracting them, dangling a shiny object in front of crying children to stem their tears?

She looked around her office – at the wooden filing cabinets, the crowded bookcases, her desk piled high with client files and finally, at the backs of her hands, holding the newspaper clippings.

There was no denying it: they were old-lady hands, wrinkled and worn. No amount of hand cream would hold back time.

'You're getting cynical, old girl,' she said out loud. 'Remember, it's just a job.'

Then something caught her attention. Picking up another photo, she looked hard.

No, she wasn't just imagining it: there was an unmistakable sadness in Olivia's eyes; a kind of helpless resignation.

Sadness?

Flick pulled out a few more recent clippings and lined them up one next to the other.

There it was – the same forlorn quality, which had eluded her at first, was now instantly apparent in each one of them.

What did Olivia Bourgalt du Coudray have to be unhappy about? Her life was charmed! Flick concentrated harder.

Again she looked at Olivia's clean, coiffed, blonde hair, trim neat figure, elegant, impeccable clothes. Then she spotted her smile; the gritted teeth, tension running along the whole length of the jawline, grinding the back molars together. She could practically feel the strength of will that kept Olivia together; a thick, cold terror of exposing herself in any way, shape or form.

Sitting back in her chair, Flick pressed her hands together under her chin.

What was she so afraid of?

Suddenly it came. 'She has a secret!'

But what?

A lover?

An addiction?

A child?

Again, she examined Olivia's face for clues.

Then, looking into the frightened eyes of one of the richest women in the world, Flick recognized something from her own modest childhood: Olivia was ashamed.

As a good Irish Catholic, Flick had been raised with shame, like a cucumber pickled in vinegar and spice. She knew what it was like to be saturated by it so completely that it was almost impossible to tell where you ended and guilt began. In fact, her childhood had been filled with large, powerful, creative women, all pretending to be small, cheerful and uncomplicated – frightened of what might happen if they let themselves go. And it was shame that had accomplished this feat so effectively – binding them like corsets. Shame for being strong, shame for being interesting, shame for being human. It had baffled and frustrated her as a little girl but it infuriated her now.

Then Flick thought over the long, painful years she'd spent posing as a likely, sanitized version of herself and of how lonely and empty it had been – even, or perhaps especially, during her marriage. She'd always told herself that one day soon, when she felt better about herself, more comfortable, she'd be a bit freer with her husband, a bit more willing to show him who she really was. But he'd died before she ever dared to try. In fact, it was only in her solitude and through her strange association with Valentine that she came to know herself at all.

Such a waste!

Flick had never been particularly ambitious, never had any grand dreams of conquering the world. But here, in the quiet of 111 Half Moon Street, she saw an opportunity to accomplish something of real and lasting importance. Perhaps there was a way of liberating this woman from herself. Of freeing her from whatever secret it was that held her so tightly in its grasp.

Was it possible that something as slight as a flirt could succeed in so great a task? Could a woman be seduced into a freer, more daring version of herself?

She wasn't sure. And it wouldn't be easy: she'd need help, inspiration.

One thing was certain: the fragile future of Olivia Bourgalt du Coudray now rested firmly in her old-lady hands.

Drip, Drip, Drip

'Well?' Leticia peered over Sam's shoulder as he examined the pipes underneath the bathroom floorboards with a torch. 'What is it?'

'A leak.'

'What do you mean?'

'Well,' he looked up at her, 'funnily enough it's the same leak I looked at before only now it's worse.' Sitting back on his heels, he wiped his hands with a rag. Two days' stubble darkened his jaw; his hair, badly in need of a trim, curling almost to his shoulders. He'd been doubling up, working for private clients during the day while spending nights installing bathrooms and kitchens in a new luxury development in Willesden. All he wanted right now was a strong cup of tea. Not that he was likely to get one from her. 'What did you think would happen? That it would just repair itself?'

'There's no need to be rude.'

'I'm not being rude, just realistic.' He rummaged around in

257

his bag, straining to see. 'Look, any chance of turning the lights on?'

'Not today.' She concentrated on the floor. 'No electricity.'

'If you need a good electrician . . .'

'No, I don't need a good electrician!' This was all so humiliating. 'It has to do . . . to do with the bill.'

'Miscalculated?'

'Unpaid,' she mumbled.

'Ah,' he made a face. 'I don't mind telling you that's not the sort of information a tradesman likes to hear.' He got out his torch again. 'The best thing for me to do right now is turn the water off at the mains. I don't suppose you know where the stopcock is?'

She stared blankly at him.

'Nah, didn't think so.'

His back smarted as he got up. Too much time curled into cramped spaces. He headed for the workroom.

Leticia trailed after him.

'So what are you going to do?' She sounded like a child.

'Fix it.' He looked under the sink.

'But . . . you see,' how could she put this? 'I'm having something of a cash-flow crisis. Just a temporary one, but all the same . . .'

'Sell some more knickers.'

'It isn't that easy.'

He scanned the room. 'Why not?'

'Well, for starters,' she informed him haughtily, 'they're tailor made. Depending on the design they take days to produce.'

'That's not very savvy, is it?'

Her eyes widened. Who was this person?

'Savvy isn't the point!'

He located the stopcock in the boiler cupboard. 'In business, savvy is the whole point. You should get a commission. Flog your stuff to one of the big chain stores.'

'I'm a designer not a businesswoman,' she corrected him.

'And it shows. Look, how you make your money or don't make it is none of my concern. But you've got to do something about this leak whether you like it or not. Now I can do it, or someone else can do it; doesn't bother me either way. But it needs to be done. And I like to be paid for my work. I'm funny like that. So,' he twisted it to the off position, 'what I propose is you make up your mind and let me know.' He turned round, twirling his wrench from finger to finger. 'But as of right now, you have no water.'

'You're blackmailing me!'

He raised an eyebrow. 'Blackmailing you? Lady, I'm saving you a fortune in more damage! But fine!' He turned back to the valve. 'If you want to come back tomorrow into a shop entirely flooded, be my guest.'

Leticia imagined all her beautiful French silks completely destroyed; her wonderful furniture drowning in filthy London water. 'No! No! Listen, I'll sort the finances. When can you start?'

He smiled, pushed a dark curl out of his eyes. 'It just so happens I've begun. Now, any chance of a cup of tea?'

Professional Massagers of the Female Ego at Large
(Part Three)

The cab pulled up in front of Hermès. Henry had made them drive with both windows down to give Hughie a blast of fresh air and by the time they got out, he was feeling a bit more clear-headed. Henry was right: he'd been temporarily intoxicated and now regretted groping the girl. She was just a kid, after all. From now on he was going to do only what he was told, no more and no less.

'Right,' Henry stopped before they went in, 'I'm going to show you the way it's done. This is the classic shopping flirt, a speciality of mine. And all you have to do is watch, understood?'

Hughie nodded obediently.

'Good.' He smoothed down his hair with his hands. 'This one couldn't be simpler, Smythe. Each mark will have a particular weakness – jewellery, shoes, handbags . . . Let's do scarves today. Anyway, all you have to do is pretend to be shopping for someone else, someone neutral – in my case it's always a niece or a goddaughter but for you, I should think a sister would do nicely.' They made their way through the front door, weaving past the crowds of Japanese tourists.

'Not under any circumstances use a girlfriend, for obvious reasons. Once you spot your mark, all you have to do is go directly to the sales assistant – try to choose a man if you can, other women can throw off a good flirt – and ask, quite loudly, to see all the most expensive, exclusive items. Remember, all we're doing here is giving a little light lift to the ego; we're observing, making contact and re-framing.' He scanned the room. 'Here's a likely candidate,' he nodded in the direction of a woman in the corner. 'Wouldn't say boo to a goose. We'll be in and out of here in no time. Now,' he fixed Hughie with a look, 'observe my detachment. The skill of a physician, remember?'

'Right.'

'Browse a little. Stand near enough to hear but try not to be too obvious. You might want to make notes.'

Hughie watched as Henry ambled casually over to a long glass case filled with exquisite silk scarves. There, he parked himself next to a tall bony woman in her late fifties with limp brown hair, sensible lace-up shoes and an ancient Burberry mac belted around her narrow waist.

Henry smiled.

She stared back.

Clearing his throat, he caught the eye of the nearest sales assistant and signalled to him.

'I'd like to see some scarves, please!' He turned to the woman. 'I hope I'm not cutting in. Were you waiting to be served?'

'No, no!' she said, her face flushing a violent shade of red. 'I was just . . . just looking.'

The assistant proceeded to unfold a selection of scarves across the counter. 'This is the new season's line,' he informed Henry.

Henry tilted his head thoughtfully to one side. 'Hummm. It's difficult,' he sighed. 'You see, it's for my goddaughter. The truth is, I feel a bit out of touch. Pardon me,' he flashed the woman another smile, worthy of Cary Grant himself. 'Would you be so kind as to give me your opinion? I couldn't help but notice that you seem to know a thing or two about fashion,' he nodded to her miserable apparel, 'and I'd be so grateful for a woman's insight.'

'Me? Oh, I'm not sure . . . they're all so lovely!'

'Well, do you think you might be willing to try one on for me?' Henry turned to the assistant. 'Would you mind?'

'Feel free,' he said.

'You see, she's awfully young, only twenty-two – about your age, really.' Henry gazed into the woman's sad grey eyes. 'Her colouring's not as delicate as yours; she's pretty, of course, just not as soignée as you are. Do you mind?'

'Oh, no! If you think I'll do. No, not at all!'

Henry draped the luxurious, cool silk scarf artfully around her shoulders then stood back.

She flushed again. 'Well, what do you think?'

Henry regarded her as if she were nothing less than Botticelli's Venus. 'If only Poppy had your style!' he said at last. 'Such a neck! Like a swan! And the shape of your chin!'

'My chin?' She turned to examine herself in the mirror, tilting her head. 'You, you think I look nice?'

'You are nothing less than a vision!'

The assistant snorted.

Henry ignored him. 'The only difficulty now is: you've ruined it for me. It would be a sacrilege to buy another woman that scarf after I've finally seen what it really should look like.'

'I don't believe it!' she giggled, girlishly.

'It's true.' Henry shook his head, smiling sadly. 'I'm sensitive to these matters. Once I've seen perfection, I find it impossible to accept anything less. Poor old Poppy will have to make do with something else.'

The woman stood mesmerized by her own reflection.

'I suppose I'll just put these away then,' the assistant snapped, bending down to reopen the case.

'It's been an unexpected pleasure.' Henry bowed again then moved away, nodding to Hughie, who was lurking behind the umbrella display.

That's when Hughie saw the woman shove one of the scarves into her pocket with lightning speed.

He tried to signal to Henry but Henry just glared at him.

'Oh, dear, is that the time!' She sprinted for the door.

'Allow me!' Henry, ever the gentleman, rushed to open it for her, watching as she scampered down the street.

The assistant looked up. 'Oh, my God! Thief!'

There was a collective gasp.

'Where?' Henry looked round.

'There!' The assistant pointed to him. 'Thief!'

Henry blinked. 'I'm afraid there's been a misunderstanding!'

'Thief! Thief!' The assistant shrieked.

Half a dozen black-suited security guards appeared, each the size of a small car.

Hughie lurched into action, bundling Henry out the door, onto Bond Street. 'Run!' he shouted, grabbing him by the tie, yanking him along. 'Come on, old man! Keep up!'

'Oh, bugger it to hell!' Henry cried, sprinting after him.

To the Lighthouse

If you've ever held your own newborn child, you will know exactly what Jonathan Mortimer felt like, holding the tiny little girl, curled, fast asleep, in the crook of his arm. I won't attempt to describe it, but suffice to say, it's one of the great moments that life has to offer – a brief reprieve when all is well with the world, when mother and baby are safe, when relief and triumph mingle in a way that occurs all too rarely.

The curtains were drawn around the bed but they didn't block out the noise of the other women and babies on the ward or the smell of the curry that the Indian woman's mother had brought to her exhausted daughter in the bed next to Amy's.

Still, Jonathan was oblivious. In fact it wasn't until he looked up, beaming with ridiculous paternal pride at his 'achievement', that he noticed Amy was unusually subdued. She was still in a way that was entirely separate from the Hallmark moment he was experiencing, and it frightened him. So he said what he always said when he didn't know what to say.

'I love you, darling.'

'Is that so, Johnny?'

She hardly ever called him Johnny. It was a term of endearment that harked back to another life they'd shared, before the division of domestic labour forced them onto more formal terms.

He laughed like a bad actor playing the Ghost of Christmas Present. 'What's all this? Of course I do! I think someone's got a touch of the baby blues!'

She turned away. 'Maybe.'

This was not his Amy; resilient, strident, list-making Amy.

This was another version, but a version he recognized all the same. Again, it echoed back to the young woman he'd wooed and won, who used to lie next to him at night, trying on various future visions of happiness like a child trying on dressing-up clothes.

The little girl turned fretfully in her sleep, clenching and unclenching her tiny red hand. Jonathan slipped his little finger into her palm and she settled again, holding on with all her might.

And suddenly Jonathan saw what had been lost on him for many years.

It was all so fragile.

Only it wasn't just the baby that seemed small and delicate. It was Amy and him, their whole life together.

The thread that bound them was frayed and taut, stretched to the very point of snapping.

He felt lost.

He wanted her back; the Amy who knew what to do in every situation, who refused to be bowed by the grinding unrelenting business of everyday life, whose vision of their home and family usually blinded him with the same certain, unswerving power of a lighthouse beam. And it struck him that perhaps he'd been childish in his expectations of her, that maybe he'd taken her strength for granted.

'I love you, darling,' he said again, because, of course, he didn't know what else to say.

But also because, for the first time in a very long time, he actually meant it.

The Savoy

Valentine sat across from Hughie and Henry with his hands pressed against his forehead. 'Never, ever, in my entire life—' He stopped himself, unable to continue, shaking his head. 'It's been a disaster, gentlemen! A farce!'

'The thing is—' Henry began.

'No!' Valentine raised his hand to stop him. 'I don't want to hear it! I am stunned, Mr Venables-Smythe! Completely at a loss for words!'

(This didn't stop him from elaborating further.)

'What could've possessed you?' He stood up, pacing the room. 'After everything we told you about the dangers of touching the mark!'

'I think you're being a bit hard on him,' Henry mumbled.

Valentine swirled round. 'Do you?' His tone was lethal. 'Do you really?'

Henry straightened. 'Actually, I do. If it was anyone's fault it was mine. He was shadowing me. And he did save me from being arrested.'

Hughie looked across. 'Thank you, Henry.'

'Don't mention it.'

'The two of you are equally irresponsible!' Valentine despaired. 'I have half a mind to fire you both!'

'Please don't.' Flick was standing in the doorway. 'At least, not until you've heard my idea.'

Valentine glowered. This was clearly his show; he didn't like being upstaged.

'I need some help,' she continued. 'Maybe Hughie could take a break from the streets and give me a hand instead. It would allow him to take stock; get a feel for the tone of what we do.'

'Perhaps,' Valentine conceded. 'But that's an important job, for a big client. It needs a delicate touch.'

'He'll be under my jurisdiction,' Flick promised, looking across to Hughie. 'I'll take you on but only on the understanding that you'll follow my instructions to the letter.'

'Oh, absolutely!' Hughie agreed. 'I'm at your command.'

'Yes, well,' Valentine straightened his cuffs, 'I would be lying if I said I didn't have serious reservations about your ability to be reformed into a useful member of this organization, Hughie. But I will give you one more chance to redeem yourself. This is an extremely important assignment. If you prove trustworthy, I will review your situation.'

He crossed to the door.

Henry and Hughie stood up, awkward as two cadets in the presence of a senior officer. 'But needless to say, I'm not just disappointed, gentlemen.' He paused, looking from one to the other. 'I'm disgusted!'

And then he left.

(In fact, as it was his flat, he didn't have anywhere to go, so he just stood in the bedroom for a few minutes.)

Flick flashed Hughie a look. 'Make no mistake, I've just saved your arse,' she assured him, walking back to her office.

'Well,' Hughie slapped Henry on the back, 'that went pretty well, don't you think?'

'Oh, dear.' Henry mopped his brow with a handkerchief. Hughie had never seen him so tired or drained.

'Are you all right?'

'Oh, dear,' Henry said again. 'I think we'd better go home now.'

'Come on, old chap.'

And Hughie took him back to the Savoy.

What Henry referred to as keeping a room at the Savoy, was in fact an entire suite. Along with a generous bedroom, bathroom and dressing room, there was also a living room with a fireplace, dining table and even a baby grand piano near the window overlooking the Thames and the Embankment, massed with some of London's most memorable landmarks – the London Eye, Cleopatra's Needle; the dome of St Paul's was just visible and Big Ben sounded clearly when the wind was right.

Hughie rang down for some tea while Henry listlessly checked through his messages, returning phone calls while

Hughie wandered from room to room, absorbing the glamour of Henry's existence. Rows of tailor-made suits lined his wardrobes, piles of history books and biographies were neatly stacked along the windowsills of his bedroom. It was all exquisite but also strangely anonymous. Hughie tried to put his finger on what was missing. Then he realized there were no photographs anywhere; nothing from that former life Henry must've had. It was as if he had no origins, existing only in the present.

'Oh, dear,' Henry sighed, closing the door after the waiter had delivered their tea.

They sat across from one another on the matching silver-grey sofas.

Hughie passed him a cup. 'Come on now, it wasn't that bad!'

'Wasn't that bad!' Henry blinked at him incredulously. 'Do you realize that she never even looked at me? She was nothing! Little more than an outline of a woman! Still, she didn't even notice me!'

Hughie wasn't sure he followed. He'd imagined Henry was upset about the near arrest. But apparently it was something altogether more awful.

Henry put the tea down and crossed to the mirror hanging above the mantelpiece. 'I'm getting old!' Standing sideways, he scrutinized his chin. 'Look! Sagging! Oh, God, it's begun! I'm falling apart!'

Hughie didn't have the heart to tell him that actually, it must have begun some time ago. Instead he tried to focus on the positive.

'You're still a very attractive man.'

Henry turned. 'Really? Then why did she do it? Why? It's never happened before. Shopping is my speciality; I created it! Nine times out of ten a woman will leave without even buying anything – that's how good I am! Or rather, how good I used to be. But this one . . . she's so unaffected she had the presence of mind to plan and execute a robbery right under my nose!'

'You make it sound like *The Thomas Crown Affair*! It's hardly a robbery, Henry! The old bird nicked a scarf.'

He wasn't taking this well.

'The point is, Smythe, it's never happened before! Never!' He turned back to his reflection. 'Look at this! Do you see this? That isn't just a line, it's a furrow! I have a furrow the size of the M25 between my eyes!'

'It makes you look distinguished.'

'Ha!' Henry made the same sort of sarcastic laugh Hughie was used to hearing his mother make after a couple of drinks. 'Don't try to handle me, Hughie!'

'I'm not!'

(He was.)

'Really, Henry, no one would ever know you were, what . . . fifty?'

Hughie had never been good at guessing people's ages. Then again, he'd also never been very good at remembering that he wasn't very good at guessing people's ages, until, of course, it was too late.

Henry blanched and stood there, opening and closing his mouth like a fish. 'You think I'm fifty?'

'No . . . not really . . . did I say that?'

'You did! You said fifty! Fifty fucking years of age!'

'I'm teasing! Come on! Lighten up, Henry! Look at this,' he groped around on the tea tray, 'a shortbread finger! Mmmm! Want one?'

'No, I do not! I can't believe you think I'm that old! I'm shattered! Really shattered!'

'Well, I'm fairly shit at that sort of thing anyway. So tell me, how old are you really?'

Henry stiffened. 'Well, fifty, if you must know.'

Hughie stared at him a moment, then put his tea down. 'OK, now this is stupid. I can handle a world where I have to walk on eggshells around women who are terminally insecure for no particular reason no matter what their age, weight, height, hair colour – you name it! But to live in a world where men are just the same, just as ridiculous?' He stood up emphatically. 'No, I say! Absolutely not! Where is the silent heroism of the lonely male? Where are the Clint Eastwoods, the Steve McQueens, the Robert Mitchums of this world? Where are the men whose whole grooming regime consisted of nothing more than a shit and shave? Who spat in the face of time and wore their wrinkles with pride? I ask you, would Bogart give a toss about plastic surgery? Would John Wayne worry about sunscreen? Would Sean Connery think twice about a double chin? Never! I shudder to think what sort of pale, insipid existence we have to look forward to if we enter into that singular, unfortunately female state of mind that depends wholly on the approval of others before we can ever begin to see ourselves. In short, Henry, you are acting like a girl!'

He sat down again and finished his tea.

Finally Henry spoke.

'I'm . . . I'm so ashamed! My only excuse is that I've been in this profession far too long. It's everything to me – my whole life! And I suppose I've gone a bit . . . a bit mad,' he conceded.

Hughie raised an eyebrow. 'You never had another job?'

Henry said nothing.

'You couldn't have lived all your life in hotels! Why don't you have any photos? What happened to your family?'

Henry closed his eyes. 'I have no family. You see, I'm a fraud, Hughie. A terrible old fraud. I should retire; give it all up. I'm done with this game. Finished!'

Crossing, he opened the cabinet that housed a bar.

'Let's have a real drink,' he said, taking out a bottle of Scotch. He poured out two glasses, handed one to Hughie then sat down again. 'I'll tell you why I have no photos, no family.' He paused, as if he were gathering the strength to go on, then smiled wryly. 'Life is odd, young Smythe.'

'That's a fair assessment.'

'It happened like this,' Henry began. 'When I was very new to the game, some twenty-odd years ago, I was hired to flirt with a young wife. Her husband arranged it; he was a bit of a cad, always getting caught with his pants down, and wanted to cheer her up. And in those days, it was all a bit more rough and ready. Flick didn't prepare reports – she wasn't even with us then. Valentine just used to give us a photo and an intercept point and you had to wing it.' He took a slug of Scotch. 'Well, I was a bit cocky – young, good-looking, money in my pocket. I thought I'd seen it, done it all! The intercept point was Peter Jones and there was my mark, looking at towels.' He paused. A dreamy look filled his eyes. 'The photo didn't do her justice. I'm telling you, from the moment I laid eyes on her, I was smitten! And when I went to speak to her, I was completely tongue-tied. I can't tell you what an ass I made out of myself!' He looked across at Hughie. 'She never bought the towels, young Smythe.'

'What happened?'

'I spent the entire day with her. I took her to lunch, we walked through the park. Valentine went mad. I'd missed so many appointments. I lied – told him I was ill. And the next day we met again. Only we spent it in a hotel.'

'Henry!'

'I know!' He leant forward. 'You see, I loved her! I'd never really been in love before, but I loved her.'

'And did she love you?'

'Yes, I think she did. But nothing came of it.'

'Why not?'

'I'm almost too embarrassed to tell you.'

'Go on!'

276

'I never knew her name! She wouldn't tell me; terribly worried about getting found out. And in those days Valentine thought we didn't need to know things like that. Better for client confidentiality. I couldn't very well ask him without arousing his suspicions. We saw each other a few more times; the last rendezvous we spent here, in this very room. And I told her that if she ever wanted to find me, I'd be here, at the Savoy. It was a bit over the top – I was trying to impress her. But, you see, I like it here. It reminds me of the happiest hours of my life.'

'And you've been waiting for her to contact you ever since?'

Henry sat back. 'I know it seems silly. I should really be looking for some old rich widow so I can retire in peace. But I can't help myself. A man can dream, can't he?'

'She's bound to be a bit rough now,' Hughie warned.

Henry just smiled. 'I'm sorry I made you break up with Leticia. I'm not much of an example to you.'

'Oh, I don't know. It wasn't your idea, was it?' Hughie felt relaxed and peaceful; it was nice to share confidences with Henry. He kicked his shoes off, stretching out on the sofa. 'You're only human, Henry. Hey, do you mind if I kip here for the night? It's a lot more comfortable than at my sister's.'

'Be my guest,' Henry said, finishing off his Scotch.

He got him a spare pillow and a blanket.

'She might still come,' Hughie said.

'She might.'

'And you'll be here.'

'Yes.' Henry paused by the door. 'Oh, she was lovely, Smythe! Blue, sort of greenish eyes . . . actually, maybe they were brown . . . hard to remember now. They were pretty, whatever colour they were.'

Hughie rolled over onto his side. 'So you believe in true love?'

'Absolutely! Without a doubt. Don't you?'

'Utterly.'

Pause.

'So . . . why do you think, I mean, if true love exists, why are we so busy?'

Jamming his hands into his pockets, Henry concentrated. 'Well,' he decided, 'I think it's that they, you know, the rest of them, don't try hard enough.'

'That must be it.'

'Lazy.'

'Unlucky?'

'Much lower standards.'

'Exactly!'

'It's all about staying true to the dream, my boy.'

'Never letting go!'

'Precisely.' Henry turned off the light. 'Goodnight.'

Hughie snuggled down. 'Goodnight.'

Outside, the view of the Embankment and South Bank dazzled. The Millennium Wheel turned almost imperceptibly, Big Ben chimed, the inky black waters of the Thames curved into the distance, reflecting every glowing detail in duplicate.

'She'll be back,' Hughie whispered.

Henry wavered, a dark silhouette by the door. 'Of course she will.'

But for a man who'd waited so long, he sounded oddly unconvinced.

All Hail Athena

Standing alone in the middle of the gallery, Olivia took a deep breath. She'd made it. She wasn't sure how but somehow she'd got through the hours, minute by minute, until now, here she was, at the end of the day.

At last the show was ready.

And what's more, it worked; there was a clear flow from one piece to another, a subtle dynamic of unexpected juxta-positions and parallels. She hadn't believed it was possible; until the last piece was in place it had seemed nothing more than an incoherent jumble. But slowly, surely, she and Simon had worked it through.

'You never know just how they're going to play off one another,' he assured her, as they wrestled a giant canvas of an erect penis into position. 'That's the fun of the thing!'

Olivia had had her doubts, in fact it terrified her, but he was right. What was more, she was good at it; her instinct to move the giant teddy to the foyer, for example. 'Inspired!' Simon congratulated her, delighted. Now it stood like a bold, cartoon Colossus ushering the viewer into another world.

She walked on.

Here were the dustbin photographs, the human-hair tepee, the Myra Hindley Jubilee teaset, and then on into the next room: Red Moriarty's 'What's the Point in Carrying On?'

Olivia stopped.

Here was her life: her velvet sofa, her books, her Holbein drawings . . . Soon people would wander in, stare at it; reach profound conclusions as to its meaning.

She had lived it; was still living it. Did she dare to read the reviews and subject herself to social dissection? Or did she already know everything she needed to know; in short that it had failed to relieve her of the terrible sense of internal weight-lessness?

Only, strangely, she realized, that feeling wasn't here now.

The room and its objects receded from her identity, ebbing away like a bad dream. Her drawing room was empty now, she reminded herself. A vacuum waiting to be filled.

So much of the house was empty now.

Walking on, she came to the last room.

There was nothing in it except for Mrs Henderson's brown velour chair.

'Mrs Henderson Died in this Chair.'

Ugly, common, powerful; it refused to be anything other than what it was.

At first it had revolted her. But the more time she spent

around it, the more she appreciated its uncompromising bland-
ness. It would never be beautiful yet it possessed a horrible
integrity all its own.

That in itself made it rare.

Then she noticed a pair of legs sticking out of it.

She walked round. There was Red Moriarty, asleep in Mrs
Henderson's chair.

'Red!' She gave her shoulder a shake. 'Red! Wake up!'

Her eyes fluttered open. 'Oh! Oh, God, what time is it?'

'Late.' Olivia pulled her up.

'I'm sorry. I guess I feel asleep.' She stretched out like a cat.
'I've got a lot on my mind and Rory's not sleeping at the
moment. It's doing my nut in.'

They walked back through the gallery together.

'How old is Rory?' Olivia asked. 'I'd like to meet him. It
must be a challenge being a single parent.'

'He's three. Yeah,' Red yawned again. 'Challenge is a nice
way to put it. Though to be honest, sometimes I think I have
it easier. I've got friends who are always bitching about how
their partner won't help out, blah, blah, blah, or when they do
do something, it's wrong. They spend the whole time arguing.
For me, the buck stops here,' she pointed to her chest. 'If you
don't expect anything from anyone else, it's simpler. Na, looking
after Rory's not bad. But I do get lonely.' She thought about
Hughie Armstrong Venables-Smythe, the guy who never showed
up again at the café. 'You know, it would be nice to have a
little attention. Someone who noticed you.'

282

'That would be nice,' Olivia agreed wistfully.

'I feel invisible. It's like, ever since Rory was born, I was just the person pushing the pram.'

Olivia wanted to say the right thing; encourage her. 'But you're a beautiful young woman, with a wonderful new career!'

Red looked doubtful. 'Yeah, well . . .'

'I think you're brave. I don't think I could do it,' she admitted.

'You could if you had to. You can do anything you have to, especially for your kid.'

Olivia made no answer. Unlocking the front door, she asked, 'Are you all right to get home? Do you want me to call you a cab?'

'A cab?'

She made it sound as if Olivia were suggesting she be airlifted home.

'Na, I'll take the train. Actually,' Red lingered, pulling at a stray strand of hair, 'I wanted to talk to you about something.'

Olivia turned, interested. 'Of course.' She closed the door. Pulling up a couple of chairs, she patted a seat invitingly. 'Come on. Tell me how I can help.'

'Well, it's just that . . . you see,' Red stared at her hands, 'the thing is, look, I'm just going to say it: I don't know anything about art.'

'Oh!' Olivia laughed with relief. 'You had me worried there for a minute! Red, you know everything there is to know about art! You've created two of the most accomplished pieces I've ever had the privilege to represent!'

'Yes, but . . .' Gathering her courage, she looked Olivia in the eye. 'I need to come clean. I didn't mean to. It was an accident.'

'Oh, yes!' Olivia nodded. 'I've heard that thousands of times. Real art has a life of its own. It's like the universe is co-creating the piece with you and you're just a witness.'

'Well . . . sort of. See, it's not like I went to art school or anything.'

'Vincent van Gogh didn't go to art school.'

'You don't understand . . .'

Olivia smiled. 'I think I do. Look, it's your first show and you're worried about what to say to the press and critics.'

'But I'm a fraud!'

'Red, I won't hear you talk that way! That's just nerves! You're under a great deal of pressure. But look,' she took hold of her hands, 'I'm here to help you. We're going to do this together. You know what? This is my first show too!'

'Really?'

'I've never hung a show before or helped select the artists or overseen the guest list. You and I are in the same boat!'

'Do you think?'

'Absolutely! But that's no reason for us to give up, is it?'

'I guess not.'

Olivia stood, paced the floor. 'So you've never been to art school. Well, why should we hide it? It's actually a selling point. "Red Moriarty: an utterly raw, natural British talent!" The media hate anyone who's accomplished. But they love the Athena myth – the idea that people simply emerge, fully formed, without any effort. You'll fit in perfectly! As a matter of fact, I'm going to send out a press release!' She was becoming really excited. 'What's art got to do with it? For the past century we've been asking the question, "What is art?" And the answer has always been, "Whatever the artist says is art." Now we've pushed it even further. We're asking, "What is an artist?" Can't you see, Red? It's revolutionary!'

Red seemed unconvinced. 'Well, if you think it will work.'

'It will. I promise.' Olivia gave her shoulder a squeeze. 'Now, it's time for you to go home and get a good night's sleep. Big things are about to happen to you and I want you at your best.'

Rose walked along the underground platform, staring at her shoes.

It was like being the only one at the party who didn't get the joke. That wouldn't be so bad, except that it was on her.

Rose looked up. The train pulled into the station.

But she didn't get on.

The doors opened, closed. Off it sped, into the dusty warm darkness of the tunnel.

In front of her, across from the platform, ten feet high, was a giant poster of Mrs Henderson's chair.

'*Don't Miss the Next Generation Show at the Mount Street Gallery!*'

Rose stared at it for a long time.

'Fuck it,' she concluded, turning round.

Out of the tube station she headed, onto Regent Street, sticking her hand out.

The cab pulled up, rolled down his window. 'Where to, darling?'

'Kilburn, please.'

She climbed in, settled back into the seat, looking at the shop windows full of the latest fashions. Maybe this year she could afford some of them.

'You're working late,' the cabby said, catching her reflection in the rear-view mirror.

'Yeah,' she smiled to herself. 'We artist types keep strange hours.'

Love According to Flick

Flick was waiting for Hughie the next day when he arrived at 111 Half Moon Street. No sooner had he walked in the door, than she took his arm, wheeling him out again.

'Come with me,' she commanded.

Once outside, she marched him across the road to a small Italian café, where they ordered coffee and Hughie took advantage of the opportunity to down a second breakfast.

'You're in the doghouse,' Flick announced, watching as he polished off two fried eggs, sausage, bacon, tomato, mushrooms and four slices of toast slathered in butter and marmalade in the same amount of time it would take most people to break open and butter a croissant.

'Yep,' Hughie nodded unperturbed. 'Never had a job yet where the doghouse didn't have my name on it.'

Flick took a dainty sip of latte. 'Well, let's see what we can do to get you out. I've never asked any of the other boys to help me with a project like this one, Hughie, for the simple reason that it requires a certain lightness of touch; an almost magical belief in the power of romance. Flirting is one thing, but this is quite another. I think you have that unique sensibility so I'm giving you a chance to prove yourself – to me, to Valentine, but also to yourself.' She placed her cup back on its saucer. 'Now, let's start with the basics. What do you think the most potent, erotic part of a woman is?'

Hughie concentrated. 'It's a toughie,' he conceded, 'but I'm going to have to say the tits.'

'You're wrong.'

'Damn! Well, it was between the two—'

'It's the imagination,' Flick quickly cut in, 'the imagination, Hughie. If you can capture a woman's imagination, then you will have her. But imagination is a strange creature. It needs time and distance to function properly.'

Hughie nodded.

'Do you understand what that means?'

He shook his head.

'It means that a seduction that takes place slowly, with only the most exquisite images and experiences for the imagination to work on and grab hold of, will yield powerful results. This is our challenge: to stimulate the senses, evoke love and inspire lust without ever being seen.'

'Tricky.'

She considered. 'Not as tricky as one might think. In any good seduction, the person being seduced does most of the work anyway. And remember, I use the words "love" and "lust" but what I'm really referring to is romance.'

'What's the difference?'

'Oh, there's a huge difference!' she laughed. 'Romantic love is an illusion, Hughie. It can be manipulated, twisted, piled up like a bunch of fun-house mirrors. The very nature of it is deceptive. It promises closeness but the only thing it ever really reveals is the dreams and fears of the person with the obsession. That's why it's so easy to control.'

'Hey, that's a bit harsh! You don't really believe that, do you?' he laughed nervously. She painted an altogether darker picture of his noble new profession. 'I mean, what about love at first sight? Romeo and Juliet and all that?'

'This is why I chose you, Hughie,' she winked. 'Because you're young and fresh and still believe Santa Claus is going to shimmy down your chimney come Christmas Eve. That's going to come in handy.' She signalled for the bill. 'This is a business. We provide a service. And like most service-orientated professions, we exploit a basic human need. In our case that need is the desire to be loved. Most people want to be adored but they don't want to do anything to get it. They simply want some attractive stranger to come along out of the blue and find them irresistible. If it were any more complicated than that, we'd be out of a job.'

It sounded a bit too familiar; Leticia was a beautiful stranger who'd seduced him on a bus. One minute he was single, lonely; the next head over heels. But was all the intensity love or something else entirely?

The question frightened him. He pushed it out of his mind.

'Now,' she continued briskly, 'we've received a commission for a woman in Chester Square – a wealthy, elegant, sophisticated and very well-known woman named Olivia Bourgalt du Coudray.'

'Married to that tennis-ball chap, right?'

'Exactly.' She took out her wallet.

'Oh, please! Allow me!'

Flick looked at him. 'Do you actually have any money, Hughie?'

'Well, not as such. But I've got an Amex card.'

'Why don't I take a rain check?' She took a tenner from her wallet, handed it to the waiter. 'Come on.'

They strolled out into the sun.

She slipped her arm through his. 'You see, the truth is no one ever really falls in love with anyone but themselves. Love is a mirror; a reflective surface projecting who we wish we were. What we're all waiting for is someone to come along who will show us something new about ourselves that we can adore. And then, because someone loves us, in turn, we love ourselves. Does that make sense?'

Hughie grunted. It was all getting a bit philosophical. Besides, some lucky sod had just driven by in a new TVR.

Flick took his grunt as a sign of admiration for her powers of perception. 'Now, a good Cyrano,' she continued, 'is a combination of boldness and unavailability. But the beginning is always simple.' She linked her arm through his. 'And so our first stop is Smythson's.'

'What's a Cyrano?'

'Ah,' she smiled, 'I thought you'd never ask!'

The History of the Cyrano
(Another Digression)

During the dark days of the Second World War, when London was a smouldering shadow of its former imperious self, the Charleses' shop in St James's was badly bombed. Celia and the Baron were older now; frailer, living off rations, renting rooms above a bookshop in Curzon Street. Their staff of flirts had all been drafted, some wounded, some killed, serving in Europe, Africa, even Japan. For a while a very handsome Polish refugee named Milos filled in. He had a limp and his English was confusing. But eventually even he was rounded up and sent to work in a munitions factory in Yorkshire. Of course the hairdressing side of the business failed completely; not many women had the money or need for elaborate hairstyles and for those who could afford it, sitting in a front room above a bookshop wouldn't do. Besides, times moved on. Permanent waves were all the rage.

In short, the world was ending. Hitler was invading; London destroyed. And all that was beautiful, was gone.

The Baron took it badly. He'd once pulled himself up by his bootstraps, known greatness; inspired love. Now he was left to sort through dusty second-hand books all day in the shop below while his wife Celia, a woman of property and social standing, scoured the streets for anything of value left in the bomb wreckage.

But life wants love. It demands it.

And so it came to pass that on a dark moonless evening, during the bitterest of winter months, in the middle of a blackout with sirens wailing, a young man rang the bell in Curzon Street.

Cursing, the Baron stumbled down the narrow stairs and opened the door.

It was a soldier, a young captain, beside himself with anxiety, clutching a photograph of the girl he loved. You see, he explained, breathless, his father had told him about the Baron, recommended he find him; said, in fact, that he was the only man in England who could possibly help.

As you can imagine, this bolstered the Baron's ego no end. In a flash the young man was upstairs, drinking a hot cup of tea, explaining to both Celia and the Baron his terrible predicament. He loved this girl. And he was quite sure she loved him, only she had a rather fickle nature. The thing was, he just didn't think he could bear to go off to war, to possible death, without knowing for certain that she would remain faithful.

They nodded.

It was an unusual commission, still, something might be done.

And where could they find her?

'Well,' he smiled nervously, 'only in the most beautiful village in Wales!'

Ah.

Wales.

How could they influence a girl so far away?

Celia looked at the Baron. And he at her.

Then they both looked at the fresh face of the man before them, twenty-one if he was a day, eyes wide with terror. He was to set sail for Normandy in the morning. The photo he was holding, its edges worn from too much tender handling, trembled in his hands.

'She will wait for you.' The Baron clasped his shoulder. 'I promise.'

'But how will you manage it?' he wanted to know.

'Well . . .'

'We have our methods,' Celia assured him, tucking the last bit of not-too-stale bread into his rucksack. 'Trust us.'

Off the young man went, swallowed up into the cold waiting darkness; brave, hopeful again.

And thus began a long series of sleepless nights while the Charleses racked their brains; what could they possibly do to help him?

Not long afterwards, picking through a bombed-out house in Lisson Grove, Celia happened across a slip of paper; nothing more than a single line, written across the back of a calling card.

If I tried to kiss you, would you let me?

The sentiment thrilled of illicit love; just reading it made Celia's heart race. Tucking it into her pocket, her mind tangled with it; stories, images unfolding. There was a play somewhere, in French . . . a man who seduces a woman through letters . . . sexy . . . teasing . . . charming.

Somewhere between Marylebone station and Grosvenor Square it came to her – distance was no obstacle if you never saw the lover! What if they seduced the girl through a series of anonymous notes? If they could focus her romantic imagination on a mysterious stranger, perhaps she'd be too distracted to take up a real lover.

The very next day, an assault was launched on the fickle young woman in Wales. She couldn't imagine who in London was so besotted with her, but the sparse, bold, often poetic sentiments fluttering in her letter box kept her intrigued; too consumed, in fact, to be interested in anyone else.

She had quite a collection by the time the war was over.

And I'm pleased to say that, despite a heady influx of American soldiers, she remained faithful to her noble captain, whose own letters had abruptly stopped after three weeks.

Who never returned.

Who died, in a frozen marsh, under a sky black with the wings of enemy planes, dreaming of a future happiness.

Certain that someone loved him.

The Perfect Plan

At Smythson's stationery shop, Flick purchased several dozen excruciatingly expensive thick, cream-coloured cards and envelopes.

'Note the quality of the paper,' she pointed out to Hughie. 'Everything you use must be of the best possible pedigree, do you understand? Remember, these notes will be the only tangible evidence the subject will have. They'll be read over and over again, shown to close confidantes, discussed, debated. In short, Hughie, they must be perfect. Always choose cream. Other colours look pedestrian. Never choose distinctive designs. They should be anonymous, so while she should be able to trace the fact that they come from Smythson's – which, in itself, is always reassuring – she shouldn't be able to discern anything further.'

They walked back to the office, where Flick referred to a small Rolodex full of cards, each filled with a few lines of text gleaned from poems, lyrics, even fragments overheard in conversation. Here she'd stored hundreds of clues for future use. Finally, she paused and smiled.

'Perfect!'

Then, unpacking the cards, she slipped on a pair of thin white cotton gloves before taking up a fountain pen.

'Gosh!' Hughie observed.

'You may think I'm being paranoid,' she said, 'but you'd be surprised at how many times a woman has resorted to having these notes dusted for fingerprints! Gloves are essential.'

Then in a large, firm hand, not too flowery, not too plain, she wrote across the middle of a blank card.

Blowing on it, she waited for it to dry before slipping it into an envelope and sealing it. Then she addressed it to 'Olivia'.

'Just Olivia?' Hughie asked.

Flick paused thoughtfully. 'The truth is, you could easily go either way. But I have a feeling that most people are quite deferential to her; that everyone calls her by her full title. I'm chancing that not many strangers would call her by her first name only. She might find that a bit provocative. Now, can you ride a bike?'

Hughie hadn't been on a bike for quite some time – not since he was a child. So cycling across town had been a harrowing experience. By the time he finally pulled up in front of 45 Chester Square, he was little more than a collection of raw nerves, and sweating profusely, having spent the last quarter of a mile with a growling black Jaguar firmly up his backside.

On shaky legs, he climbed down, leaning the bike against the metal railings and doubling over to catch his breath. He tried to block out the all-too-vivid memory of Hyde Park Corner; pedalling for all he was worth only to find himself sandwiched in by huge, red buses, leaning on their horns, veering across lanes, sweeping him into fresh flows of speeding cars. Hughie had an epiphany: he might easily die at the hands of this woman in the Range Rover on her way to nothing more pressing than a hair appointment and, as long as he didn't stop the flow of traffic, no one would care or, in fact, blame her.

The door of the house opened.

'You may not leave that here,' a haughty voice informed him. 'Please remove it at once!'

Hughie looked up.

The butler had the knack shared by good domestic staff and public-school masters of instantly rendering those around them inadequate, before they've done or said a thing.

Of course, being a public-school boy, this made Hughie feel right at home.

'Hello!' He bounded up the steps. 'Special delivery. By hand, as they say.'

The butler took the envelope, shuddering as he read it out loud. 'For "Olivia". Indeed. And who are you?'

'Just a courier,' Hughie said. 'I mean, if anyone asks.'

'I see. You're not dressed like a typical courier.'

Hughie looked down at his jeans. 'All my spandex is in the wash.'

The man sniffed. 'Yes, spandex can be difficult.'

'A devil!'

'Best to air-dry it, don't you find?'

'Absolutely.'

'It's the same with all the synthetics. And lurex especially. Plastics are the worst.'

Hughie blinked. 'Definitely.' He backed down the steps. 'Well, OK. Thanks.'

Gaunt watched in satisfaction as Hughie quickly wheeled the bike around the corner and out of sight.

Young people were so easily disturbed. It was as if God had created them for his amusement alone.

The Perfect Plan

(Hughie's Version)

On the other side of Chester Square, on Lyall Street, Hughie parked his bike once more in front of the Chocolate Society, which had a couple of outdoor tables set up under a neat little brown-and-gold-striped awning. There he unearthed a second Smythson's card and envelope he'd lifted from Flick's desk. And, while enjoying a thick cup of dark hot chocolate, he set about writing his own note to Leticia.

He hadn't forgotten about her. Since they'd broken up he had thought about little else. Now, Flick had given him a solution. He would seduce Leticia as a mysterious stranger. Before she knew it, she would be hopelessly in love; unable to resist the skills of the professionals. All he needed to do was duplicate exactly whatever Flick prescribed for Olivia.

Not a bad plan, he congratulated himself.

Unfortunately, he'd forgotten a pen and so had to borrow one from the man behind the counter. It was red. And his own handwriting wasn't nearly as stylish as Flick's; he had a bad habit of writing all in capital letters which gave the note a slightly sinister air − just one step up from cutting and pasting letters out of newspapers. It was only after he'd inadvertently smeared a bit of Belgium's best across one corner that he remembered the importance of the gloves and what a fuss Flick had made over them. But then again, Flick was a woman. They were apt to be a bit over the top about details. So, having only bothered to steal one spare card, he wiped it off as best he could and popped it into the envelope.

And then, because he wasn't quite paying attention and because the bill had just arrived (who would've imagined a cup of hot cocoa could be so much?), he scribbled 'OLIVIA' across the front.

'Damn!' He scratched it out and wrote, 'LETICIA,' under-neath and then, just in case it wasn't convincing enough, he added, 'NOT OLIVIA − I DON'T EVEN KNOW HER,' in the same wooden capitals.

There.

Perhaps not quite as impressive as Flick's but certainly more deeply and genuinely felt.

But time was ticking on. Flick would expect him back at the office soon. So Hughie hopped back on his bike, speed-ing away from the chocolate shop as quickly as he could (he had enough change to leave a generous tip yet not quite enough to actually pay the bill), and headed across the bridge to Pimlico, to drop his love missive through Leticia's door.

That evening two very different women, separated by little more than a few city blocks and several billion pounds, sat alone in their bedrooms, contemplating a strange correspondence that had shattered the seemingly hopeless landscape of their lives. Outside, dusk divided the sky into shades of pink, mauve and darkest purple, and autumn turned the air sharper; quickening with the season's change. Inside, the acceleration continued in the imaginations of Olivia and Leticia, as they stared in wonder at the letters that had arrived by hand that day.

In both cases, the women had been baffled, confused; one, a little alarmed, the other, intrigued.

In both cases, the women spent several long minutes staring out of their bedroom windows, wondering if, somewhere in the gathering twilight, the author of this letter was waiting, maybe even watching from the dimly lit street below.

And in both cases the letter contained only a single line:

I have always known that one day I would find you.

'Now what do we do?'

'Nothing,' Flick smiled. 'Oh, we have research for our next clues, but for now, we just let them wait. Remember what I said, Hughie – it's all about boldness and inaccessibility. We've made a statement. Now we just let it hang there a while,

302

gathering strength in their imaginations. Then when we make even the smallest gesture, it will have increased power because they will have endowed meaning to it that you and I can only guess at.'

'Oh.'

Hughie couldn't pretend he wasn't disappointed. If anything, he wanted to leave more clues, as quickly as possible, just to make sure Leticia was well and truly hooked.

He missed her.

Or at least, he was pretty sure he missed her.

The conversation with Flick seeded uncomfortable doubts. Should it really be this difficult? Did he have to work this hard? Then again, the harder he worked, the more it proved he must love her.

His feelings were his compass. And he had plenty of those; some delicious, some painful; all punctuated by an intense physical longing. It was heroic to suffer for love, sublime.

Besides, with Flick's expertise, he could make Leticia love him . . . whether she wanted to or not.

Venus Blinks

When Hughie got home that night, he found his sister Clara drunk. She'd swigged the best part of a bottle of Tesco's finest Chablis on her own, shoving everything that Malcolm had given her, or, indeed, ever touched into a giant black bin bag in the front room. As this was Hughie's temporary bedroom, he was obliged to sit with her while she told him how she'd discovered Malcolm engaged in an extremely compromising embrace with a male member of staff in the catalogue room of Sotheby's.

'It was that . . . that *creature* from the Small Decorative Objects department!' She had a meat mallet which she now used to whack the eighteenth-century planter Malcolm had given her to pieces. 'The one with the goatee! He told me he was working late on a rush evaluation so I thought, "I'll surprise him. Drop off a sandwich for his supper!" Smoked fucking salmon!' Whack! 'On brown fucking bread!' Whack! 'With lemon and cracked fucking pepper!' She kicked the bag hard. It split open, its contents tumbling onto the floor.

Clara stared at it. Then crumpled, sobbing, onto the sofa.

Hughie opened another bin bag and scooped the remains of the old one inside. Then he got her a roll of toilet tissue from the bathroom.

She blew her nose loudly and refilled her glass.

It was awful to see her like this. Clara wasn't the kind of person who cried; even when she was little. She'd always been tough, never got ill, never let you down; didn't waste time with make-up or clothes or fits of temperament. Hard-working, punctual and resourceful, she was just the sort of person you'd want by your side if there was ever a war. But Clara's considerable self-discipline was useless in matters of the heart and it disturbed Hughie to see her at such a loss.

'But you must've known . . . I mean, everyone knew he was . . .' Hughie paused. He'd never said it out loud. 'You know . . . gay.'

For a moment he thought she might get angry. But instead she tossed back another glug of wine. For a long time she just stared at the floor.

'I knew he had certain . . . inclinations.'

'Then why didn't you . . .'

'Look at me! Go on!' she challenged. 'What do you see? Hardly a "Page 3 Stunna", am I? I'm not like you, Hughie! I'm not beautiful.'

'That's not impor—'

'Just stop!' she cut him off. 'I've always known, Hughie, since I was very young, that I'd have to make do. Always.'

'Clara—'

'Enough.' She stood up, swaying dangerously. 'Enough of this whole damn thing! I'm going to be sick now,' she announced, 'and then I'm going to sleep. Do something useful for once and take out the rubbish, will you? And don't forget your damn keys. There's a good boy.'

She tumbled down the hall and into the bathroom.

Hughie dragged the rubbish down the stairs to the bins outside then sat on the front steps of the house, smoking a final cigarette.

It was late.

Tomorrow Clara would wake up, hungover. She'd put on her navy-blue suit, brush her teeth and get on the tube. He knew Clara. By the end of the day she'd be making a joke of the whole thing, laughing at her own expense; getting on with it, the way she always did.

He took another drag.

Low on the horizon, Venus blinked forlornly in the night sky.

The Invitation

Olivia took the Symthson's card out of her robe pocket. She had spent half the night staring at it, and now here she was, sitting out on the garden steps, looking at it again.

I have always known that one day I would find you.

Such a simple statement. Assertive, absolute. Someone had been looking for her, thinking of her.

But who? And when had he found her?

Did she know him?

It couldn't have come from Arnaud, of that she felt certain. Such a selfless gesture would be impossible for him now.

It had been so long since she'd had any attention, that the thought of someone noticing her was almost unbearable. A whole ocean of longing flooded out; vast and uncontrollable.

I don't know how to behave, she thought. Or what to do. Still another, much younger, more enthusiastic part of her leapt into life. 'I've been noticed!' it squeaked eagerly. 'I'm here! I exist!'

She wanted to toss the card aside; ignore it.

Instead she put it back in her pocket.

Then took it out.

Put it back again.

Finally Ricki arrived.

'Hey,' she looked at Olivia in surprise, flinging a bag of plant food down on the patio. 'What are you doing out here?'

'Just thinking.' Olivia stood up, pulling her dressing gown around her.

'This is getting to be a habit, you waking up at dawn, isn't it?' She dug out her cigarettes. 'Fancy a fag?'

'Yes, please!'

Ricki passed her one and they both lit up.

'Actually, I wanted to show you something.' Olivia handed the card to Ricki. 'What do you make of this?'

'"I have always known that one day I would find you,"' Ricki read out loud, frowning. 'Do you owe someone money?'

'No! It arrived by hand yesterday afternoon. Gaunt said it was delivered by a young man.'

'Hum.'

'Well, what do you think?'

'I don't know.' She gave it back. 'Maybe somebody likes you.'

'But I don't want to be liked!' Olivia blurted out.

'Yeah?' Ricki leant against the wall, blowing a smoke ring into the clear morning air. 'Why not?'

308

Everything she did was so cool.

'Because,' Olivia paced the narrow confines of the grass, 'it means . . . I don't know, losing yourself – getting dragged under. Someone liking you is just the beginning; it always starts nicely but before you know it it's like Persephone being dragged into the Underworld.'

Ricki exhaled. 'You're a control freak, aren't you?'

'What?'

'You have to be in control all the time.' She tucked her cigarette into the side of her mouth and sliced open the bag of plant food with a penknife she kept in her back pocket. 'Do you want my advice? I mean, are you asking for it?'

Olivia wasn't sure. 'OK,' she said half-heartedly.

'Let go. See what happens. It's only a note. Might all turn out to be nothing.'

Olivia hadn't considered that. Suddenly it turning out to be nothing didn't seem like so much fun either.

'Turn on the hose, will you?' Ricki ordered – she was hauling out the sack of plant food which she mixed with the water in a large green plastic watering can. 'It's like an invitation, isn't it?' she continued, pouring the mixture onto a row of white roses.

'To what?'

'To something unknown. Something you hadn't considered.'

'And I'm meant to like that?'

Ricki turned. Olivia couldn't quite read the expression on her face; was it amusement?

'No. Maybe.' She shrugged her shoulders. 'Does it matter?'

'Of course it matters!' Was she being deliberately provocative? 'Would you like to be dragged into the unknown by some
stranger?'

'Ah, but you make it sound so sexy!' Taking a final drag,
Ricki ground her cigarette out under the heel of her boot.
'What's known becomes unknown, what's familiar gets lost,
what's dead springs back to life. That,' she nodded to the card,
'is an invite. You don't have to accept it; you can throw it away
if you like. But really, what have you got to lose? Your life is
changing whether you want it to or not.'

She's quite intelligent, Olivia thought. And wise.

'How do you know all this?'

'I don't; I'm making it up. Actually,' Ricki laughed wryly, 'I
got dragged into the unknown by some stranger.'

'What happened?'

She looked past Olivia, into the distance. 'My world fell
apart. Then it came together again in a completely different
way. And then, of course,' she added softly, 'that fell apart too.'
She shrugged her shoulders. 'So it goes.'

'I'm frightened.' It came out of Olivia's mouth before she
could stop it: small, childish. Here she was, a forty-year-old
woman, standing in her dressing gown, telling the gardener her
innermost fears. It was insane.

But Ricki took it in her stride.

'Yeah,' she nodded. 'That's normal. You'd have to be crazy
not to be scared.'

'But what do I do?' Again, the words spilled out before she could stop them.

'Here.' Ricki handed her the watering can. 'Do the back row. Make sure you really douse them.'

Had she heard correctly?

'You want me to water flowers?'

'Yeah.' Ricki bent down. 'I'm going to tackle these weeds.'

Olivia wasn't used to taking orders from her staff or, for that matter, engaging in manual labour. But she was so stunned that she did as she was told.

The sun was warm, the earth smelt cool and black and rich.

Olivia watered.

Ricki weeded.

Time passed.

And gradually, Olivia forgot to be frightened.

Gradually, it started to dawn on her that this really was quite a nice little garden after all.

On the House

'Hey, Smith! What's the matter? You look like someone killed your dog!' Marco sat down next to Hughie at a table outside the Italian café the next morning.

Hughie explained about Clara and Malcolm. 'It just makes me sad. I mean, sure, she's no oil painting but she's a great girl. I hate to see her so upset.'

Marco nodded.

Then he had an idea.

'You know what? You know what I'm going to do for you?' He took out his phone, checked through his diary. 'Where did you say she worked? The City? I've got a three o'clock and a four fifteen in the City tomorrow afternoon, Smith! I can easily fit her in, if you like!'

'Really?' Hughie was touched. 'You'd do that for me? You know I can't pay your normal rate . . .'

Marco gave him a shove. 'What are you talking about? It's on the house! For you, absolutely free of charge! Now,' he took out a pen and paper, 'tell me again what the company's called.

312

And her name.' He clapped Hughie on the back. 'I'm telling you, by five o'clock tomorrow, she'll be a different girl! I might try International Polo Player on her; I haven't done that one in a while. Do you think I look tanned enough?'

'Definitely.'

Hughie scribbled down Clara's details and passed them back.

'*Grazie!*' Marco said, slipping the paper into his breast pocket as he got up.

'Marco, I can't thank you enough . . .'

'Think nothing of it. Now, are you ready for tonight? It's a big operation; biggest I've even been in on.'

'I think so. It's all a bit complicated.'

'You'll be great!' Marco squeezed his shoulder. 'Now, don't give your sister another thought, Smith! I guarantee tomorrow will be the most exciting afternoon of her life!'

He set off, swaggering with bonhomie, and Hughie relaxed. He felt considerably better. So much better, that he ordered an early lunch to celebrate.

It's Me ... Emily

Leticia sat next to Leo, holding his hand. 'How are you, darling?' She stroked his cheek softly. 'It's me . . . Emily.'

His skin was cool. She folded another blanket out over him.

'Shall I show you something? It might interest you. It came yesterday.' Leticia pulled the card out of her handbag. '"I have always known that one day I would find you." Strange, don't you think? I mean, it just arrived, out of the blue. But before you get carried away by how romantic it is, look, there's the stain in one corner. Now smell – it's chocolate! And please cast your eye over the handwriting. Scary, huh? I'm sure I've seen it somewhere before.' She turned the card over. 'Of course, you know who it reminds me of.' Her face clouded. 'Just the sort of thing he used to do.'

They sat a while.

'I suppose it could be Hughie,' she considered, brightening. 'Though it seems a bit creative for a public-school boy, don't you agree? I told you I let him go. What a disaster that was!

You were right of course. I should never have started the whole thing. And now I've got this plumber banging around the shop and trouble with the bank . . .' She pressed his palm more tightly. 'I don't know what's happened to me lately. I seem to have lost my way, a bit. For a while I felt like I knew what I was doing but now . . .'

'Ms Vane?'

She looked up.

It was the ward nurse. 'Visiting hours are over now.'

'Yes. OK.' She stood, pulled her coat on. 'What do you say? Tomorrow, same time, same place, Your Lordship?'

The nurse tucked the blanket in, carefully placing Leo's hands at his side.

'I'll take that as a yes.' Leticia crossed to the door.

She paused, signalled. The nurse came over.

'When do you think he'll come out of it?' she whispered.

'It's hard to say. He's stable.'

'How long do they . . . I mean, you think he will come out, don't you?'

She looked at Leticia kindly. 'It's hard to say,' she said again.

'Do you think he can hear me?'

'Yes.' Her voice was firm, reassuring. 'I think he can.'

'Oh! I almost forgot.' Rummaging in her handbag, Leticia pulled out a faded picture: a serious, plain young girl and dashing silver-haired man. Propping it up on his bedside table, she leant over and kissed Leo's forehead. 'I thought that might give you a smile when you wake up.'

'Do you want this?' The nurse held up the anonymous note.

Leticia looked at it; at the nurse, the bed, Leo, far away; unreachable. Enveloped in a permanent sleep; a mass of machines beeping behind him, keeping him alive.

'No, thank you. It's not important.'

Walk with Me

It had just gone seven and Olivia was locking up the gallery. Her footsteps echoed as she walked through the cool, white rooms, switching off lights and checking doors. It was an hour of the day that affected her a great deal – a time when she imagined most people would either be going home to their families or heading out for an evening on the town. When she left the gallery, she was all too aware that she'd return home to find Chester Square conspicuously empty. And even though piles of invitations came every week, she wasn't fond of going out. Loneliness isn't relieved in a crowd.

So she lingered, drawing out the last few tasks – washing up the tea mugs and tidying the leaflets on the front desk until finally there was nothing left to do. Retrieving her handbag from the office, she flicked off the final set of lights and was about to open the front door when she spotted something on the floor.

As she picked it up, her heart leapt in her chest. It was the same Smythson's cream-coloured notepaper as last time! Someone must have only just dropped it in.

She tore open the envelope. Inside another card in the same hand read:

Walk with me.

She turned the card over.

It was blank.

But where? she wondered. Walk where?

Closing the front door, she locked it then turned around, half-expecting to see someone waiting for her outside.

But there was no one.

The early-evening air was cool, pleasant; the golden sky splashed with red and orange. Rush hour had been and gone, the street was quiet and empty.

Then she noticed, on the ground at her feet, an arrow pointing towards the large iron gate of Mount Street Gardens. It was made of three long calla lilies.

Her favourite flowers!

They couldn't have been there long; they were still fresh and cool to the touch.

How had this person known?

Gathering the flowers up, she crossed and headed into the garden. It was all but abandoned. Tall plane trees lined the walk, and the fountain in the centre burbled softly. Elegant red-brick Edwardian mansion blocks bordered each edge and the pathways were lined with wooden benches.

Olivia found herself drawn to the fountain. There around the edge, spelt out in shiny, new pennies, was written, '*Make a wish.*'

She laughed in delight. It seemed bad form to ruin the message, so she fished one out of her bag and closed her eyes.

'To the unknown,' she whispered, throwing it in.

Then she noticed that one of the wooden benches had a small bottle of champagne and a glass on it. Around the top of the bottle was a luggage tag. '*May I buy you a drink?*' it said.

Again, Olivia couldn't help but laugh out loud with pleasure.

She sat down and popped open the champagne. The glass was long, of heavy crystal that sent the light dancing in rainbows. Whoever was seducing her had imagination, taste and, she thought, watching the champagne bubble into the glass, money.

She leant back. A breeze sent a handful of dry leaves waltzing down the path. Somewhere, from one of the top-corner flats, a piano began to play, something soft, effortless, jazzy and nostalgic.

Then a bum ambled in through the far gate.

Oh no, she thought. Just when everything was so lovely.

Sure enough, he spotted her with the champagne and made a beeline for her.

She tried to avert her eyes, but he stopped right in front of her and thrust out his hand. He held open a slim box of black Sobranie cigarettes.

'May I offer you a fag?' His voice was surprisingly posh.

Olivia stared. How had he known her guilty secret?

'Yes, thank you,' she flushed, taking one.

The bum produced a rather nice silver lighter. 'Enjoy!' And he lit it, before moving on.

Olivia leant back, sipping the champagne and smoking her

cigarette. She felt like Beauty in the Cocteau film of *La Belle et La Bête*. All around her unseen hands were busy, anticipating her every desire – even the ones that no one knew about, like a longed-for cigarette. It was both unreal and enchanting suddenly to have the city she knew so well transformed from an indifferent, occasionally hostile one, to a poetic symphony of carefully orchestrated pleasures.

Someone had gone to an enormous amount of trouble. But would he appear? She looked from one entrance to the other. Would he be tall, short, young, old? Was it the mysterious young man on the bike?

The light began to fade.

No one, not even the cigarette bum, came in.

Olivia finished the champagne and waited a few more minutes, just in case another extraordinary event occurred. Then she wrapped the beautiful crystal glass in a tissue and slipped it in her handbag, heading out of the opposite gate.

A black cab pulled up. 'Olivia?'

'Yes?'

The driver opened the door. 'Chester Square, right?'

'Yes. But how do you know?'

'It's too far to walk,' he smiled. 'No need to worry. I'm fully licensed. And the fare's already paid.'

'By whom?'

'No idea. Radio cab, see?' he pointed to a sign on his door. 'It came through the central office. Now, shall we?'

She climbed in and shut the door.

London sped past, cool air against her skin. The champagne left her exhilarated yet languid; it was a delicious, dangerous feeling.

The cab pulled up at Chester Square. Olivia stepped out and it drove away.

Fishing for her keys, she realized that once she stepped over the threshold, her adventure would be over. She would be engulfed again in the Bourgalt du Coudray world where nothing enchanting or magical would or could ever happen.

Turning, she took one last look round. If only her secret admirer would reveal himself!

But the streets were empty.

She pushed open the door.

Suddenly the sky lit up behind her, as a flurry of fireworks exploded above her head. Twisting and turning, they shone bright red, green, blue and searing white against the black night. Olivia gasped. Running into the street she searched to see where they'd come from. But they were over almost as quickly as they had begun. Apart from a few of the neighbours peering out of their windows, the street was abandoned.

Heart pounding, she climbed up the steps and closed the door behind her. Another envelope was waiting on the hall table:

Sweet dreams.

It was hard work arranging the evening-walk scenario. Hughie found himself running all over town with shopping lists from

Flick, who was nothing if not demanding. Twice she sent him back to Asprey because the crystal champagne glass wasn't quite right, and she interrogated the firework man on the length, height, sound and colour of the display with all the intensity of a general planning a military attack.

'I want a bouquet of fireworks,' she instructed him. 'A spray of light and colour!'

He just nodded and said over and over, 'Well, it'll be loud.'

Jez was roped in to make the calla-lily arrow and set out the champagne while Marco cleared the park by pretending to be a mime artist. (He was suspiciously good at it.) Then Flick laid out the coins and Hughie dived into a local pub toilet to don his street-vagrant costume, complete with black wig and beard. Texts buzzed back and forth as they tracked Olivia's progress via the satellite navigation on their phones to ensure precision timing.

In the end they all agreed it had been a triumph.

But, as the others headed off to celebrate in the pub, Hughie felt uneasy. He hadn't realized just how many people were needed to pull off an operation like this one. It occurred to him that maybe the clues he'd left for Leticia were perhaps a little less well planned and executed than they needed to be to guarantee success.

Leticia forced her way through the large flap of clear plastic sheeting Sam had put over the bathroom door to keep the dust out of the main shop. Her beautiful bathroom was unrecognizable: all the floorboards around the bath were torn up; tiles were missing; copper pipes gleamed in a stack near the door. Sam was welding a couple together, sparks dancing in a haze of dust and early-evening light.

'Stand back!' he ordered.

She froze in the doorway.

'I didn't want you to catch fire,' he explained, turning off the blowtorch and pushing the goggles off his face. He grinned up at her. 'Tell me you're here to offer me a cup of tea.'

Leticia was not amused. 'I'm here to ask how long this is going to take. I can't go on rescheduling appointments indefinitely and the dirt is ruining my fabric!'

'I'm doing it as quickly as I can, Your Ladyship. And if you hadn't noticed, this is the second evening running I'm working late.'

She hated the way he spoke to her. She wanted to say something smart and caustic to put him in his place, but sleepless nights meant her wit was shot. 'Yes, well . . . fine!' she snapped and turning on her heel, marched back into the workroom.

'I can't wait till that fucking thing is done!' she fumed, checking her phone messages.

Nothing.

Still no news from the hospital.

Of course, she'd only checked five minutes ago.

Wearily, she eyed the mounting stack of post on the counter, running her fingers over the dozens of envelopes. She couldn't bring herself to face it. Rummaging through she found another postcard from her parents, this time from the sunny beaches of Eilat.

Dear Emily Ann,

Hope all is well with you. Too hot here but enjoying every minute with the grandchildren. We are all hoping maybe you will join us next year . . . what are the chances of you designing yourself a bikini!

They didn't know about Leo; she hadn't told them. Perhaps if she kept it a secret, waited one more day, things would change, for the better.

Just seeing her mother's handwriting touched a raw nerve. She slipped the card back under the bottom of the pile.

Everything was falling apart; unravelling like a badly made jumper. Her business, her shop, Leo . . . Fear threatened to drown out everything else. Enough! Tossing her phone into her handbag, she flung it over her shoulder decisively. Time to get some air.

'I'm off!' she called. 'Just pull the door shut when you go!'

The door slammed.

Sam emerged, covered in dust, empty tea mug in hand.

The least she could do was put the bloody kettle on!

He searched around for the tea bags. All he could find were little pale green tins of loose tea from Fortnum and Mason – Lapsang Souchong, Earl Grey, Green Tea with Mint.

He opened one and smelt it. 'Jesus!'

That's when he spotted she'd left her keys on the counter.

Grabbing them, he rushed to the front door. 'Hey!' he called out after her. 'Hey, Your Ladyship!'

But Leticia was nowhere to be seen.

The truth was Hughie didn't have the funds for calla lilies, fireworks or champagne.

When Leticia arrived home, there was another anonymous note and a series of arrows fashioned from melting Smarties on the pavement.

She opened the envelope.

Walk with me.

The arrows were pointing to the garden in the middle of the square. She pushed open the wrought-iron gate. It was all but empty.

The evening air was cool and sharp. A breeze stirred the trees.

She began to walk, taking one of the narrow paths that led around the outside. Eventually she came to a bench. There was a bottle of Babycham on it.

'*Fancy a drink?*' said the Post-it stuck to the front.

She sat down, holding it. It was as if she were floating somewhere outside herself, far away.

Suddenly a couple of little tow-headed girls ran up with sparklers, dancing in front of her, giggling.

'We're going to sing you a song!' they chorused.

'OK.'

They sang 'Hit Me Baby One More Time', waving their sparklers around, before tearing back across the square.

'Who sent you?' she called.

But they had disappeared into the dusk.

Leticia sat very still.

The sky darkened; luminous navy blue.

In the houses across the street, lights glimmered in the windows. They formed glowing backdrops for small domestic scenes – a husband leaning to kiss his wife hello; two women laughing, opening a bottle of wine; a hassled mother chasing a naked toddler.

Life unfolding; warm, vibrant . . . distant.

A cool gust of wind bowed the tall trees.

It was late; the garden empty.

Leticia got up; headed to the far gate.

There, around the edge of a bird bath, was a message spelt out in shiny new pennies along the rim. '*Make a wish*,' it said.

She stared at it.

Turning, she crumpled the note into a tight little ball and threw it into the bin.

Sam pulled up in his van and got out.

He checked the address on the water-bill envelope he had found in her workroom. This was the place; it must be her home.

He rang the bell.

No answer.

'Well, of course, you pillock!' he berated himself. 'She can't be inside – you've got her bloody keys!'

Now what?

Turning, he scanned the empty garden square. Maybe she was headed back to the shop. Had he passed her and not noticed?

'Fuck!' This was all more trouble than it was worth. He was about to climb back in his van when he saw someone in the far corner of the square, running out of the garden.

It was her.

'Leticia!' he shouted.

She turned.

The big black Bentley roared out of nowhere.

It never even stopped; knocking her sideways onto the pavement before speeding away.

Into the Care of Mr Lewis

When Leticia opened her eyes Sam was holding her.

'Take it easy. How many fingers am I holding up?'

'I don't know.' She tried to sit up. 'Ahhh!'

'Concentrate,' he commanded. 'How many?'

She focused. 'Three.'

'Good. Very good. Where does it hurt?'

'Everywhere. My head mostly.'

'Relax.' He cradled her tighter. 'Don't worry, it will be OK. There's an ambulance coming.'

'I don't need an ambulance. I live right across the street.' It was hard to keep her eyes open; she felt so sleepy. 'Please, just take me home.'

'No. And look at me, understand? Look at my eyes.'

She was too tired; too aching to fight. So she looked into Sam's eyes. They were green, flecked with gold; steady.

'How are you doing?' His voice sounded far away.

Everything hurt; every bit was in pain. 'He's not coming back. He's gone.'

'Who?'

The ambulance arrived. Sam lifted her up, placed her down somewhere, yes; she was on a bed. Yes, in an ambulance.

'Are you coming?' the driver asked.

'Yes.'

There was Sam, sitting next to her, holding her hand tight.

'You don't need to do that,' Leticia murmured, closing her eyes.

'Shhhh. Don't try to talk.'

All she remembered for a few moments was the sound of sirens. But they were her sirens.

'We're here,' Sam said.

'Where?'

'Accident and Emergency.'

Leticia tried again to force herself upright. Swinging her legs out, she stood up; felt dangerously dizzy. She gripped the door handle hard.

'Steady on!' Sam grabbed her about the waist and flung her arm around his shoulder. 'Lean on me.'

'I don't need any help.' The ground spun under her feet. 'I'm going to be sick.'

Sam and another medic veered her towards a row of low shrubs just in time. When she was done, they piled her into Accident and Emergency, where she passed out.

When she came to, she was on a trolley. Someone was holding her hand. It was a warm, solid hand. She flicked her eyes open.

It was Sam's hand.

He smiled.

'She's awake,' he called, searching for a doctor.

Leticia tried to turn her head but it felt as though it was made of marble. Her neck was sore and unbearably stiff. A young doctor came over.

'Well, looks like you've got a nasty concussion. No broken bones or internal injuries so far as we can tell. We'll do some more tests all the same. Is there someone at home we can contact?'

'I live alone.'

'I see.' He sighed the sigh of a man fighting a losing battle. 'I don't think it's serious but even after we release you, it's not safe for you to be on your own. You'll need plenty of bed rest and you're going to have one hell of a headache. Someone needs to look after you.'

Leticia thought of Leo in St Thomas's hospital on the other side of town and of her parents, finally living their dream of a homecoming to Israel. Then she thought of Hughie.

'There is no one.' And, much to her shame, she began to cry.

'I'll look after her,' Sam said quietly.

'No!' She tried to shake her head. 'Oooww!'

'Excellent.' The doctor made a note on the chart. 'To be released into the care of Mr . . . ?'

'Lewis.'

'Mr Lewis,' the physician wrote, 'for at least forty-eight hours.'

'Forty-eight hours! You want me to spend forty-eight hours

with . . . with . . . a stranger! You don't understand; I've only just met this man!'

'I'm not offering for my own amusement,' Sam pointed out. 'It's not like I haven't got better things to do with my time.'

'So do them!' she snapped. 'I'm not some invalid!'

'Actually,' the doctor interrupted, 'that's exactly what you are.' He rubbed his eyes wearily. 'Look, unless the CAT scan shows significant damage, we don't have enough beds to keep you. So I suggest you accept this gentleman's kind offer and work something out.'

'If I was really going to do you harm would I have bothered to ring an ambulance?' Sam asked.

'Exactly.' The doctor tossed her medical chart on top of her stomach. 'Now, if you'll excuse me, I have a stabbing, a mugging, a couple of overdoses and at least four alcohol poisonings to attend to. DJ! Take this woman up to imaging, please!'

Sam sat down again, crossed his arms in front of his chest. 'I'll be right here when you get back.'

'Great,' she muttered, as the porter, a kid with an iPod tucked into his ear, loped over and gave the trolley a shove that sent her flying halfway down the hall.

'Hey! Easy does it!' Sam shouted.

The kid reached out a long arm, stopping a head-on collision between her and a wheelchair-bound pensioner just in the nick of time before expertly wheeling her around the corner, all to the throbbing bassline of 50 Cent.

* * *

It did not suit Leticia to be handed over to the care of Sam Lewis, registered plumber.

Sullen and silent, she stared out of the window of his white Transit van. Dawn was breaking, the streets empty, cold. They pulled up in front of her flat in Pimlico.

'I've got it.' Sam walked round, opened her door and held out his arm. 'Here.'

'No. I'm fine.' She struggled to climb out but she was so tired; the ground seemed miles away. Reluctantly, she took his arm. 'Thank you.'

Opening her bag, she rummaged around. 'Damn! I've lost my keys!'

Sam took them out of his pocket. 'You left them in the shop. I was looking for you, trying to give them back, when you had the accident.'

'You were?' she asked awkwardly.

'Let me get that.' He opened the front door and helped her up the stairs.

'Great. OK. Thanks for all your help.' She stopped on the hall landing, held out her hand. 'I can take it from here.'

'Oh, really?' he smiled. 'This from the woman who walked into the dustbins in the hospital car park.' He reached around her and unlocked the door.

'A momentary lapse of direction.'

'You apologized to them. Very polite, you are.' He nudged her inside. 'I don't mind telling you, you could do with a bath. Now, where's the kettle?'

'Oh, please!' she snapped. 'Make yourself at home, why don't you?'

He looked around the living room with its marble fireplace, polished parquet floor and dainty matching cornflower-blue Empire chairs. 'Thanks, Marie Antoinette. I'll do my best.'

'Look, I'm not having you staying here, do you understand?'

'You haven't even got a sofa. What am I meant to do? Curl up like a cat in one of those chairs? This may come as a surprise to you but I actually own a home of my own.'

'I just want to be clear about what I won't accept.'

'Oh, yeah?' He looked amused. Leaning against the mantelpiece, he folded his arms across his chest. 'Let's have it then. What are your requirements for someone who's willing to help you?'

He was wrong-footing her deliberately.

'Look, there's no need to be like that! I'm just trying to set some boundaries.'

'How about this: you rest and recover and I'll look in on you, make sure you have food to eat, that you're doing OK; not passed out on the living-room floor, etc.' He frowned, suddenly subdued. 'Is that clear enough?'

She couldn't make him out. He seemed genuinely concerned. For some reason that frightened her.

She tried to put her hands on her hips, set him on guard, but it required more energy than she had. In fact, she needed to sit down. 'See, that's what I don't get! What's in it for you?'

'Nothing.'

'So why do it?'

'You need help.'

This was not a logical response. It infuriated her. Or rather, confused her.

'But why you? You're not related or married to me; it's not your job.'

He shrugged his shoulders. 'Life isn't all about jobs.' He surprised himself. 'I mean, there's more to it. Maybe.'

Her eyes narrowed. 'You fancy your chances, do you?'

He seemed to think this was hilarious. 'For your information, you have vomit on your collar, your hair looks like the wrong end of a broom, and just for the record you're one of the most bad-tempered people I've ever met in my life! Hate to break the news, but you're hardly the woman of my dreams.'

'Oh, really?' This was the last straw.

'Really. Now, shall I run that bath or will you?'

'I will,' she mumbled, making her way into the bathroom, slamming the door behind her. Turning on the taps, she looked in the mirror. He was right; she had sick down her front, two great mascara-panda eyes and a full-blown scarecrow head.

Fuck.

How had her life come to this?

A little while later, there was a knock. 'You decent?'

Cracking open the door, he passed her a steaming mug of tea. 'First thing I'm buying is tea bags. Tins of loose tea

in a bloody tea ball! You don't half make life hard for yourself.'

The door shut.

Leticia sat, clutching the mug of tea.

Maybe he had a point.

International Polo Player

Marco was so impressed and, quite frankly, surprised by his generous offer that he decided to make Clara Venables-Smythe the first hit of the day. The sooner he did her, the sooner he could regale everyone with tales of his munificence.

So, armed with nothing but her work address and a brief description, he pitched up at Blare and Boom Public Relations Company in the City and proceeded to flirt with the receptionist. He convinced her to point Clara out under the pretence of having a blind date with her that evening and as lunch-time rolled around, the receptionist slyly indicated a tall, hearty-looking girl with a sandy-coloured bob, dressed like a 1970s airline hostess in a navy suit and pumps.

Marco followed her out of the building and around the corner, where she stopped to buy a bacon sandwich and a cup of tea and then on to the newsagent's for a copy of the *Evening Standard*. After that, she crossed over and down the block, moving at really quite a lick, before locating a secluded bench in the garden of Finsbury Circus to eat her lunch.

That's when Marco made his move.

'*Scusi*?' he grinned, flicking his wonderful black curls out of his eyes. 'I wonder if you could help me.'

Clara looked up.

Marco gazed longingly at her.

Time itself seemed to stand still.

That is, until Clara rolled her eyes. 'Yes, what do you want?'

Marco smiled even harder. 'You see, *bella*, I'm a little bit lost. I'm looking for Roehampton Street. I have a very important appointment . . .'

'It's over there,' she said, pointing to the left.

'Ah! *Bravo!* I knew you'd be the right person to ask!' he laughed. 'You are like my guardian angel!'

She winced.

This shook Marco. No woman had ever winced at him before.

'You see,' he tossed his hair again and thrust his handsome chin into the air, 'I'm an . . . an international polo player and . . .'

'What are you doing here?'

'*Scusi*?'

'If you're a polo player, what are you doing in the middle of the City?'

Marco hadn't thought of this. It had been a while since he'd done Polo Player. Its success in the past had depended largely on the fact that most marks would've been thrilled to meet a real live polo player anywhere.

337

'I have a very important appointment,' he asserted.

'I see.'

'With a potential sponsor,' he added, proud of his ingenuity.

Her eyes narrowed.

'Which one?'

Like many beautiful people, Marco was used to getting by on his looks. He hadn't bothered to keep up with the polo scene at all. One of the big champagne names would have been perfect but, desperate for inspiration, he said the first name he saw, on a billboard across the street.

'Potato Poppers.'

'Potato Poppers?' Her expression was deadpan. 'As in "Potato Poppers, the crisp in a can"?'

'Yes, exactly!' He straightened. 'We're trying to bring polo to the masses!'

'How noble.' She bent over her paper again. 'Well, then. You'd better get going, hadn't you?'

'*Grazie.*'

He wandered off for a few yards then stopped.

Never had he suffered such a total lack of response. No woman had ever survived the devastating double whammy of his riveting smile and molten, lingering eye contact! How could she fail to be impressed by an international polo player? Could it be that he'd failed?

What madness! He'd never failed!

She obviously hadn't understood him.

He went back.

'Sorry, *bella* . . .'

'It's you again.'

'Yes, it's me.'

'Well?'

Marco laughed. 'You know, I like your style! You're very direct! It's really very charming!'

She stared at him.

'OK, so what I was going to say is, I'm here from Rome and I'm not familiar with London and I wonder if you, being a gorgeous, accomplished young woman,' he paused to give her another patented Marco look, 'could recommend some places to visit while I'm here.'

'You need a guide book. The newsagent will have one.'

He laughed again, more desperate this time. 'Ah, but that's not the same, is it?'

'No, it isn't.'

She took another bite of her sandwich.

A sick feeling took root in the pit of Marco's stomach. How could this be so difficult? What was wrong with this woman?

'I'm only asking because—'

'Look, I don't want to recommend places for you to see. I don't want to chat. I just want to read my paper and eat my lunch, OK?'

Marco couldn't believe it. 'But . . . but why?'

'Why what?'

'Why don't you want to talk to me? Is there something wrong with me?'

'Yes.'

How offensive! 'What?'

She put down her paper. 'You're lying, for starters. You're not a polo player and you don't have an appointment.'

'How do you know?'

'I know because your hands are completely uncallused and there is no Roehampton Street.'

'But you said it was to the left!'

She unwrapped the other half of her bacon sandwich. 'I lied too. Now bugger off.'

'But . . .'

She waggled her mobile phone in the air. 'I'm calling the police now.'

Marco stormed across the park.

This was outrageous! A complete and utter fiasco! Not only that, Smith was expecting him to charm her; he couldn't possibly go back with his tail between his legs and admit that he'd failed.

When he reached the other side of the park, he realized his hands were shaking. How was he going to manage his three o'clock or four fifteen in this state! No, this girl had to be sorted out, here and now! His honour depended on it.

He went back again.

'Hello.'

'You're mentally ill, aren't you?'

'Why would you say such a thing? That's just rude! I say hello and you say, "You're mentally ill"! Really, you're not even giving me a chance!'

'You are, aren't you?'

Marco tried a different tack. 'I came back to say I was sorry. You're right, I'm not a polo player.'

'I knew that already.'

'The truth is, I'm an architect. I'm here working on a big project for the City of London.'

'What project?'

He wasn't going to fall for that one again. 'It's top secret.'

'I see,' she smiled.

'You don't believe me.'

'No.'

This was too infuriating!

'All right,' he flicked back his hair again (he had a habit of flicking his hair when he was nervous), 'well, I'll tell you but you must promise to keep it a secret. We're building a huge . . . a huge . . .' Marco's mind raced. Dome? Wheel? 'Actually, we're building an enormous pyramid!'

'Really?' At last she seemed impressed.

'Yes, that's right.' He leant casually against the bench. 'In the centre of Hyde Park. I'm using only glass and aluminium. Daring but effective. It's going to be magnificent!'

She nodded. 'I'm only asking because I'm in public relations and handle media enquiries for the Royal Parks Press Office from time to time. I'm sure someone would've mentioned to me if they were building an enormous pyramid in Hyde Park.' She stood up, folded the paper under her arm and threw away the rest of her lunch. 'It's been fascinating meeting you, Mentally Ill Italian Man. Now might be a good time to take your meds. Ciao!'

She loped off with long, heavy strides.

Never, in his entire career, had he met with such defiance, such stubbornness, such ridicule! It was unheard of! Impossible!

Could it be that this perfectly ordinary creature was immune to his charms?

Suddenly a painful, burning sensation radiated out from his ribcage.

Marco collapsed onto the bench, clutching his chest.

Was he having a heart attack?

No – the sensation deepened, filling his whole body with the delicious pain of pure animal longing.

Here was the feeling he'd dreamt of all his life – the thrill of the chase; the elusive ache of unrequited love! At last, a woman he could pursue!

'My God!' he gasped, euphoric with long-lost hope. 'She does exist! Here she is! My perfect woman lives!'

If only she wasn't convinced he was insane.

Leticia Eats

After her bath Leticia had a long nap. Sometime in the early afternoon, she woke up to the smell of frying bacon and sausages.

Cooking?

In her house?

Throwing a dressing gown on, she staggered into the kitchen. 'What are you doing?'

'Making breakfast.' Sam turned over the sausages. 'Do you want beans as well? I'm having them.'

She watched in horror as he opened a tin of baked beans.

Leticia's kitchen had never been used for the preparation of food; in the three years she'd lived there she'd never even turned on the oven. Her one-meal-a-day rule meant that cooking was a distant memory. In time, she'd come to regard the kitchen as a kind of quaint period feature maintained out of affection rather than necessity. It was disorientating, even disturbing, to see it in use. The hob was covered in pots and pans, bubbling and sizzling, surfaces were crowded with wrappers and soiled

343

cutlery. My God! Even the grill was on! And food trailed across the counter: white bread, a thick slab of butter, chipolatas, mushrooms, tomatoes . . .

'Where did you get all this?'

He gave the pan a good shake. 'From a shop, darling. A grocery store. You had bugger all in your fridge. Half a lemon and a bottle of vodka.' He took a couple of plates out of the cupboard. 'Now, scrambled or fried?'

'What?'

'Eggs? How do you like them?'

There was a sharp intake of breath.

'OK, scrambled,' he guessed. 'Sit down.' He popped a couple of slices of bread in the toaster.

Leticia sat down. Was it her imagination or did Sam look different? He seemed cleaner, less plumber-ish. If she didn't know any better, she might almost have considered him handsome.

He put a plate piled high with sausages, bacon, eggs, beans, grilled tomato and buttered toast right in front of her.

No one had ever made her breakfast before. She felt giddy just looking at it.

'You don't honestly expect me to eat all this!'

'God forbid.' He sat down next to her with an equally full plate and began to tuck in with relish. 'So how's that head of yours?'

'Rotten. But better.'

'Do you need anything? Paracetamol? A cold compress?'

'No. Do you know how to make a cold compress?'

He shook his head. 'I'm thinking wet rag on forehead. Does that sound right to you?'

'Maybe but I'll pass.' She picked gingerly at a bit of bacon. 'So, have you always been a plumber?'

He looked at her sideways. 'That's right. I was born with a plunger in my hand.'

'You take everything I say the wrong way; it's like you're determined to think the worst of me.'

'I'm sorry. No, I haven't always been a plumber. I had a dazzling career as a builder before that and when I came out of school I enjoyed six months' serving the Great British Public at Curry's Electrical Appliances.'

She sampled the eggs. 'I see.'

'What?' His eyes met hers.

'Nothing, I was just wondering.' She bit daintily into a slice of toast.

'And while we're interviewing each other, what about you, Miss Vane?' He held an invisible microphone under her chin. 'Have you always designed knickers for a living?' And he started to laugh, nearly choking on his beans.

'What's so funny?'

'I don't know, it just suits you, you know? Lingerie! Bespoke lingerie at that!'

'What do you mean, it suits me?'

'Well, no offence, but clearly you're a bit . . . how shall we put it? Rarefied, to say the least.'

'Rarefied! And what's wrong with that?'

'Nothing. If you like your tea in a silver tea ball and your knickers tailor made.'

'So I like pretty things; quality things. Is that a crime?'

'Not at all. But you haven't got any food in the fridge. Or a sofa you can sit on. Or,' he added, 'anyone to look after you.'

'I don't need anyone to look after me,' she snapped. 'And don't call me Miss Vane!'

'What am I meant to call you?'

'Ms not Miss.'

'Ms . . . Miss . . . what's the difference?'

'One is the mark of independence, the other a sign of failure.'

'No one can call you a failure.' He finished off his eggs.

'Exactly.'

'Are you going to eat your mushrooms?'

'No.' She pushed her plate away. He took not only the mushrooms but two sausages, the rest of the bacon, and the grilled tomato as well.

She toyed with the teaspoon in the sugar bowl. Rarefied indeed!

She led a wonderful, exotic life anyone would be envious of. Why was he so difficult to impress?

'Actually,' she heard herself saying, 'I have a mysterious admirer.' As soon as she'd said it, she wished she'd kept her mouth shut.

'Oh, really?' Up went an eyebrow. 'And what does that entail?'

346

'Well, he leaves me notes and strange, magical clues . . .'

'Like what?'

'Like champagne in the garden . . .'

'Champagne. Really?'

She re-crossed her legs. 'Yes. Well, sort of. And little messages all over town.'

He snorted.

'What's wrong with that?'

'Well, you're a bit old for a treasure hunt, don't you think? And besides, have you ever seen this guy? Do you have any idea who he is?'

'No. But that's the whole point; it's part of the adventure.'

'Yeah, well.' He mopped his plate with a piece of toast and popped it in his mouth.

'Some people would think that's romantic.' She shouldn't have told him; now she felt stupid.

'To each his own.' He stood up, clearing the plates away.

'I think it's charming.'

He shrugged. 'Some guy wants to woo you with a bunch of, I don't know, what is it? Little messages and party games? That's great. No doubt it's a real laugh. It just strikes me as kind of sad that he'd need to, that's all. You must know him from somewhere – he can't be a complete stranger. So why can't he just ask you out on a date?'

She'd never thought of that. 'I don't know.'

'There we go.' He piled the plates in the sink, turned on the taps.

Why couldn't he ask her out? Was she so unapproachable? Come to think of it, she'd seduced every man she'd been with in her adult life. Had anyone ever asked her out?

Leticia sat, drinking her tea-bag tea, disturbed by the vision of herself that Sam had painted. Was she really so shallow? So . . . prissy?

He finished the washing up. 'There, all done.' He collected his coat and a worn-out black duffle bag by the door.

'You're going?' Somehow she'd decided he was completely at her disposal. If there was one thing more irritating than having a stranger foisted upon you, it was having him leave promptly.

'I've got your bathroom to repair and an exhibition to go to.'

'An exhibition?'

'Yeah, a friend of mine has become an artist. I promised I'd pitch up and support her. But if you like, I'll stop by later and see how you're getting on.'

'Sure. Well, I mean, only if you want to.'

'Might as well. Who knows,' he grinned, opening the door, 'you might have another message from your secret admirer by then!'

'Maybe I will!' she said, too loud, too fast.

The door closed.

An exhibition! The thought of him wandering around a gallery, making small talk, felt like a kind of betrayal.

Her flat was silent in a new way. Strange how quickly she'd

got used to the long lope of his footsteps on her polished wood floors. The clearing of his throat. The smell of him . . . what was it? She sniffed. This morning it was bacon.

Leticia set off to her linen cupboard to find a scented candle at once.

Heather and Lemon Thyme. Perfect.

It reminded her of the North; of wide open spaces. Of the kind of place a man like Sam might like.

Not her world at all.

The Last Resort

After organizing some more clues with Flick, Hughie met up with Henry late in the afternoon for a couple of quick hits, just to keep his hand in.

The first one was a classic Parking Meter job. The mark was doing some shopping in Notting Hill. Hughie and Henry waited by the car for the money to run out on her meter. Then, just as the woman came into view, flushed and out of breath, rushing back to save her car from the ticket warden, Hughie popped a few extra coins in.

'I hope you don't mind,' he smiled as she ran up. 'I know it's a liberty but I saw you earlier and I didn't want you to get a ticket.'

The woman, clutching a collection of bags, gaped at him. 'You . . . you saw me earlier?'

'Yes, I was waiting for my friend. Of course, I couldn't help but notice you.'

'Really? Me?'

Hughie laughed. 'What's so strange about that? Anyway,'

he nodded, indicating her wedding band, 'I can see now you've already been scooped up. To be honest, I feel a bit of a fool!' His cheeks glowed with his now famous blush. 'I'm sure you think I'm ridiculous, stalking strangers. But there you go. Sometimes you have to take a chance, right?'

The woman was entranced. 'Yes! Yes, of course!'

And Hughie strolled away, leaving her in a delightful state of shock.

The second hit was equally straightforward, known in the trade as 'Café Regrets'.

This time Hughie waited outside a crowded bistro while Henry followed the mark in and ordered a coffee. She was sitting alone, reading the paper. After a few minutes, he made eye contact. She smiled and pretended to be deeply absorbed in the verities of the Dow Jones Index. Then he followed up by asking for a light. They chatted briefly, he finished his coffee and then signalled to the waiter for the bill.

Hughie saw her look up, watching a little sadly as Henry walked away.

Then, on cue, the waiter appeared with a tall glass of champagne.

'But I didn't order this,' she frowned.

The waiter smiled. 'From the gentleman,' he said, placing it gently in front of her along with a single line, written across a cocktail napkin.

'*If only you weren't wearing a ring,*' it said.

'Oh!' she giggled in surprise, pressing her fingers over her mouth.

'Oh, indeed!' grinned the waiter.

After that, Henry and Hughie walked towards Portobello Road, stopping for a drink in a dingy pub aptly named the Last Resort.

After they'd downed a few, Henry became serious.

'Young Smythe,' Henry said, leaning forward, 'I want you to be the first to know. I'm retiring.'

'Retiring! But why?'

Henry sighed. 'I've been thinking a lot about the conversation we had the other day. And it's time I faced up to facts. I'm not getting any younger and this is a young man's game. Not only that, but the thing is, Hughie, I'd never told anyone what I told you about my Peter Jones lover. I don't even know her name!' He took another gulp of his pint. 'It's time I gave up on these ridiculous notions of finding the perfect woman. I've got a mark tomorrow evening who's rich as Croesus and recently widowed. I've made up my mind. I'm going to bite the bullet and as long as she doesn't have two heads, I'm going to do my best to marry her. I wanted you to be the first to know.'

'Do you really need an old widow?'

'Well, I'm quite expensive to keep. The truth is, I've become used to a particular lifestyle. And I can't flirt for ever.'

'I see.' Hughie felt that bleak, cold, wet-flannel feeling that signals the end of an era coming on. 'I suppose congratulations are in order. Though I wish you wouldn't. I'm awfully fond of you.'

'And I'm fond of you, young Smythe.'

They looked at each other, got a bit sentimental and didn't know what to say. So they ordered a round of shots and embarked on a series of toasts.

'Here's to you and your new life!'

'Here's to rich widows!'

'Here's to Peter Jones and its excellent linen department!'

Henry began to cry.

'OK, forget about Peter Jones. Here's to John Lewis instead!'

By now they'd had quite a lot to drink. Gravity tugged like a terrier and consonants were hard work.

Henry wrapped an arm around Hughie's shoulders. 'Promise me, young Smythe, that you won't give up that girl you love. That's the best advice I can give you. Woo her while you have the chance and get out of this game!'

Hughie let his head rest on Henry's shoulder. 'Actually, I have a confession. You see, I haven't quite given her up after all.'

And he told Henry about the Cyrano and the earrings.

'Excellent plan! Buy her love!'

'There's this chap at Graff,' Hughie explained, 'he's going to give me a deal. Wants to meet my mother for some reason.'

'When are you due to see him again?'

'On Friday, late afternoon.'

'I'll tell you what,' Henry offered, 'let me come with you.

You leave him to me! We'll have those earrings for a song, my son! No one can bargain like I can! This calls for a drink!'

'A drink!' Hughie chimed, pounding on the bar.

'To love!' they toasted.

'And never giving up!'

Henry became weepy again and eventually the landlord turned them out.

The Next Generation

'What's the Point in Carrying On?' and 'Mrs Henderson Died in this Chair' were the triumphs of the Next Generation Show.

The better papers were awash with reviews heralding the dawn of a new era, accompanied by large colour photos of Red Moriarty, the Fresh Face of British Art, wearing a white T-shirt and tiny shorts. ('Don't look like you've made an effort,' Simon instructed. 'That would be uncool. Julian Schnabel wore a sarong and sandals under his tux jacket when he won his Oscar.' 'Who?' Rose asked. 'Never mind,' said Simon. 'You can overdress to minor events once you're famous, but a key to becoming famous in the first place is to underdress for anything of significance.') And so, provided it was skimpy, Rose was allowed to wear whatever she'd pop on to do the cleaning in, disappointing her, thrilling everyone else.

Mick, Rose's dad, was the hit of the party. Clean-shaven and out of his boiler suit, he cut something of a dash in an unstructured dark linen suit Rose had never seen before.

'Where'd you get that?' she wanted to know.

'Picked it up on Marylebone High Street. Paul Smith. Nice, huh? Got it at Cancer Research,' he winked. 'Nice bits and pieces over there.'

After an evening of conquests, Rose saw him leave with a tall blonde on his arm who had a passion for property development and, Mick confided later, 'certain very useful fantasies involving a bit of rough'.

Ricki put in a brief appearance, clutching an untouched glass of champagne, looking uncharacteristically nervous. 'Not quite my scene,' she apologized, leaning in to kiss Rose on the cheek before she left.

Even Sam showed.

He'd come straight from work and didn't stay long. Apparently he needed to look in on a client on his way home.

'Hey, I recognize that chair from somewhere!' He concentrated. 'Didn't that belong to that old lady . . . you know, what's her name?'

'Mrs Henderson,' Rose filled in the blank.

'Yeah! My dad used to have to repair her boiler about five times each winter. She was damned if she was going to replace it. Wow.' He took another sip of his champagne. 'So that's her chair, huh?'

'Yeah.'

She could feel him searching for something enthusiastic to say.

'Hey.' He nodded up and down like one of those plastic dogs people put in the backs of their cars. 'Well done you!'

'So they tell me.'

The rest of the night Rose was ferried around by Simon, being introduced to dozens of much older people, who spoke to her about her work at length in terms she couldn't follow. It was shocking to hear how much they read into it.

'The faded doily! So moving!'

'And the smell of the piece! How did you manage that?'

'The cards – are they a specific size for a reason?'

She found that if she paused long enough, they answered their own questions.

All in all, the less she did, the more successful she became.

By the end of the week, a positive frenzy had built up around her. Almost anything she touched was regarded not only as a work of art but also as a searing social commentary. Two days after the opening, she put a tea mug down on the reception desk, only to discover that it appeared on eBay and was snapped up by an American collector for six hundred pounds that same evening.

Apparently the title of the work was 'My Mug is Empty'.

From then on she drank from disposable cups.

Also, there were rumours that her opening-night shorts were being copied and knocked off for Topshop, the highest honour the British public have to offer. The fact that they came from there originally made the whole chain of events surreal.

Invitations began flooding in. She was asked to design a range of jewellery for Garrard's. Elton John begged her to stay in his large pink villa near Monte Carlo. And it was soon rumoured that she had a coke habit and was engaging in lesbian sex with Kate Moss in front of their children. Bizarrely, she was also asked to front a campaign for single mothers.

'Don't read the press,' Simon warned her, 'just inspire them.'

'But how?'

'Ignore them.'

It was excellent advice.

By doing absolutely nothing at all, Rose, aka Red Moriarty, had all the makings of a phenomenon.

Waiting

Leticia looked at the kitchen clock, furious.

Then she walked over to the window and checked again. Outside, a thin drizzle muted the evening sky, forcing the heads of passers-by downward; quickening their pace. In one corner, black clouds gathered ominously. Staring out onto the street, she tried to discern the identities of people who were little more than outlines, hurrying towards her.

Nothing.

He wasn't coming. Sam said he would but clearly he wasn't.

She paced the floor. Her rage intensified. What was she doing sitting around here like an idiot, for some man she hardly knew?

It was pathetic!

She couldn't remember the last time she'd mooned about like this. It had been years since she'd waited for anyone.

Not since . . .

She stopped.

Rain thudded dully against the window.

Leticia sat down hard in one of the blue chairs. The room

was suddenly cold, dark; the interior tired, even vulgar in the half-light.

After a while, she got up and put on her coat.

The wind had risen. It struck her face like a hand when she opened the front door; bitter, sobering. Figures scuttled past her, ducking towards the nearest shelter as lightning seared across the sky. Halfway down the street, the heavens erupted. She didn't care. Head bowed, she walked on towards St George's Square. Huge raindrops pelted the pavement. Thunder growled. Gutters filled and in minutes overflowed.

Wet hair clinging to her head, Leticia trudged on, past the square, to the abandoned shores of the Embankment. There she sat down on one of the uncomfortable Victorian benches that lined its borders, staring out at the slate-grey waters of the Thames.

The first time she had seen him, was at university. She was twenty and he was twenty-one, studying mathematics. Pale, tall and very slender, he had a mass of wild, thick brown hair that defied gravity, radiating out from his head in all directions, like a child's drawing of the sun. It looked as if he dressed in the dark, from his father's wardrobe rather than his own, in shirts that hung off his shoulders and trousers that bagged and threatened to slide down his hips, despite the belt he wore. But he had a face like a Victorian postcard of an angel with fine, delicate features, large grey eyes and a high forehead. His lips were curved into a permanent half-smile; like a saint in ecstasy.

She'd never seen anyone so beautiful; never known anyone so clever.

All the signs were there, right from the beginning, if she'd only known to look for them. The way he spoke, as if it were a race to articulate one thought before another one overtook; the fact that he never remembered to eat or sleep or pay his rent.

The way he declared his love for her on their third date.

No one had ever loved her before.

They were inseparable for seven years.

Leticia took a packet of cigarettes from her coat pocket, doubled over, cupping her hand around the flame of her lighter, and lit one, inhaling deeply.

She would've done anything to protect him. She just never imagined he'd need protection from himself.

The worst of the storm was over. Pulling her coat more tightly, she got up and leant out over the edge of the railing, staring down into the murky, black water of the Thames.

For months afterwards, she'd looked out of windows, scanned streets, listened for the sound of his car or his footsteps.

For months afterwards, she'd waited.

As she approached, crossing the square in the gathering darkness, she hardly recognized Sam. He was standing in the portico of her building, leaning against the door frame, holding a blue plastic bag. Washed and freshly shaven, he had on black leather jacket, clean jeans. The long dark hair didn't seem as unruly as usual. It curled gently around his face, framing his eyes. Then he saw her. His face hardened. 'Where have you been?' He walked down the steps, into the soft rain, stopping under the pale ring of light from the street lamp in front of the house.

She stopped too. 'You came.'

'Yeah. Where have you been?'

He was angry.

He'd been waiting.

'Jesus, look at the state of you! What have you been doing?' He took her arm. 'You're drenched!'

She pulled away. 'You're shouting at me!'

'Yes, I'm shouting at you!' His eyes flashed. 'I've been here, standing around like a fool for an hour, ringing your bloody bell! I didn't know what had happened to you! You could be passed out upstairs for all I know!'

'Would it matter?'

'Oh, for fuck's sake!' He shook his head. 'Here.' He thrust the blue plastic bag at her.

'What's that?'

'Supper. Cold fish and chips.'

He walked away, took out his keys.

She turned: 'Where are you going?'

'Home. You're obviously fine, obviously you can look after yourself. And I think,' he opened the door of his van, 'that my services here are no longer required.'

'So I'm fixed, am I?' She hurled the question out, surprised by her own bitterness.

'Fixed?' He slammed the door shut so hard the whole van shuddered. 'Lady, you're broken in ways that I couldn't even begin to repair!'

'How dare you!' She threw the blue plastic bag at him but he dodged it, its contents exploding onto the wet pavement. 'Who the fuck are you to tell me I'm broken? I'm not some household project for you to tinker with! Why don't you get your own life instead of trying to insinuate yourself into mine!'

'Are you mad? Do you think I want anything to do with your life?'

'At least I have one! I haven't got to wait for someone else's to fall apart just so I can have a purpose!'

He grabbed her arm. 'You spoilt brat!'

'You're hurting me!' She twisted away but he held fast.

He pulled her close, his face inches from hers. 'I only helped you because there was no one else to do it!'

'I know. Let go.'

He didn't let go. Instead he held her tighter. 'I wanted to help you. Do you understand? I wanted to!' The expression in his wild, celadon eyes had an intensity she couldn't read, had never seen.

She shook her head, numbly; anger draining away. 'No.' Her head fell forward, resting on his shoulder; it smelt of leather, rain, the warmth of his skin. 'I don't understand anything.'

Leticia lay on her bed staring at the ceiling rose, at the slow ebb of light as night closed in.

Sam sat on the floor next to her.

They'd been there some time.

'You don't have to stay.'

'I know.'

A few more minutes passed; the room got darker.

'Where did you go?'

She blinked; above, the ceiling rose blurred, melted.

'To the river.'

Tears ran down her face, into her ear, cold and wet. 'I was engaged once.' She turned her face away. 'But he was unwell.'

'He died,' he concluded softly.

A silvery shadow cut across the floor; the outline of the tree outside the window.

'He killed himself.'

'Jesus.'

Night had fallen. The room was bathed in cold blue moonlight.

'I hate love,' she whispered. 'I wish I'd never known it; that it didn't exist.'

Outside, the storm was over, the streets deserted; puddles sparkling in the moonlight.

No one noticed the rattle of something coming through the letter box downstairs.

Or the telltale squeak of a rusty wheel as a shadowy figure cycled unsteadily across the empty square.

Meant for Better Things

Gaunt delivered the cream-coloured envelope to Olivia first thing in the morning.

'For you, madame. By hand.'

'Thank you. And these,' she indicated a round vase brimming with fragrant, delicately coloured sweet peas. 'Who sent these?'

'The gardener brought them.'

'How beautiful!' Her fingers brushed the thin, papery petals. How had she managed to get them at this time of year? What good taste she had!

'Thank you, Gaunt.'

Gaunt left.

Olivia sat down and opened the card.

'*Dream with me,*' it read.

She turned it over. On the back there was an address.

The Royal Opera House, Covent Garden,
eight o'clock tonight.

Smiling, she pressed the card to her lips.

Someone in this vast, unknowable city was seducing her.

Leticia was soaking in a hot bath when Juan's call came through.

'Hello?'

'He's awake.'

Standing up, she grabbed a towel. 'I'm on my way.'

She was in such a rush that she didn't even open the card she found on the mat, but stuffed it straight into her coat pocket on her way to the hospital.

Leo was sitting up in bed when Leticia arrived, propped up on pillows. Juan was there, they were laughing about something. There was a palpable look of relief in Juan's eyes. She paused a moment, before they caught sight of her, to watch them together. There was an unmistakable warmth and ease between them.

Then Leo saw her, waved. She came over and began unpacking the goodies she'd brought from her local deli.

'Here we go! Fresh fruit salad, sesame chicken with stir-fried vegetables and noodles, a generous slice of double chocolate cake. Nothing grey or lumpy or in the least bit puréed.'

Leo clapped his hands in glee. 'At last! A reason to live! Cake first, I think.'

She passed it to him with a plastic fork. He was frail but the old glint was back in his eye.

'I can't tell you how good it is to see you looking so well,' she smiled. It was a lie; he looked pale and wan and dreadfully thin. But he was awake and moving and that's what mattered.

'I second that!' Juan leant over and kissed Leo on the forehead. 'Off to work. All I do is go from one hospital to the other these days. See you later.'

As he passed, he clasped Leticia's shoulder and gave it a squeeze. 'You OK?'

He was so thoughtful; she regretted all the times she'd dismissed him as some Brazilian toyboy.

'I'm fine,' she nodded. 'Just a bit of a headache.'

'OK.' He seemed unconvinced. 'But look after yourself, right?'

He headed off.

Leticia turned back to Leo, who was slowly but steadily making his way through the chocolate cake. She was so relieved to see him sitting up, alive and safe, she could cry. At the same time she wanted to hit him.

'I love you.'

He smiled. 'I love you too.'

'I missed you.'

'I was in a coma but I'm sure I missed you too.'

She cut to the chase.

'Why didn't you tell me you were so sick?'

'I didn't want to frighten you,' he said, matter-of-factly.

'You make it sound as if I were a child; someone to be protected from the rude facts of life. I could have helped you; looked after you.'

He looked at her. 'You weren't even looking after yourself.'

'Yes, but . . .'

'Darling,' he put his fork down, 'reality hasn't been your strong point recently.'

This was unusually blunt; not like Leo at all. 'What do you mean?'

'I've watched you, over the past few years, build this life, this persona, your wonderful business, which I'm so proud of . . .' He stopped, searching for the words. 'I know it's strange coming from me, and I don't mean it as a criticism but I could only guess at how much pain you had to be in to create such a fantastical existence.'

It was as if a bucket of iced water had been thrown over her head.

'Fantastical?'

'It's like you've being playing a part; a bit of every diva we've ever dressed. You never eat, you smoke all day, you work yourself stupid and then have these unsuitable young lovers. I didn't tell you because I didn't think you could cope,' he continued. 'The last blow life dealt you seemed to wound you too deeply.' His expression was so sad she thought he might cry. 'And I've been frightened for you, Emily Ann.'

'Frightened?' How could her actions have so much impact? 'But I don't understand! What have I done wrong?'

'Oh, angel! You haven't done anything wrong – please don't misunderstand me. I haven't got a lot of reprieves in me, so forgive me. But this matters; it matters to me very much. It's like you've been frozen in a world of make-believe, where real life can't touch you, ever since Michael died.'

'Why do we always say he died?' she asked bitterly. 'He killed himself! It was a choice!'

'He was ill.'

'What does that mean? Ill. What is that supposed to mean?' She wiped the tears away; furious to be crying again. 'He left me! But you know what's worse than that? I believed, Leo, I really believed that when I found someone I loved and when he loved me, then I'd be safe.' She wanted to laugh with the stupidity of it. 'I thought love was supposed to conquer all!'

But she wasn't laughing; she was sobbing now. It was more than she could take: the relief of Leo being safe; the pain of hearing his disappointment in her.

'Come here.' He held out a thin arm and she tucked herself underneath it, into the warm hollow of his chest. His heart beat reassuringly against her ear. 'You've lost your innocence, that's all.' He stroked her hair gently. 'It's agony, I know. But it's a good thing. Innocence is attractive in children but it makes brittle, disappointed adults.'

She closed her eyes, and clung to him.

'There are all sorts of things that love can't conquer,' he went on. 'Natural disasters, for example, and illness; cruel twists of fate; even simple human nature can very easily trump it every time. It wasn't meant to provide immunity from fate or grief or pain. In fact, so often it's the cause, isn't it?'

She nodded.

'But what it does is throw us into the midst of life with the best intentions possible; give us courage, passion, hope; make wonderful fools of us — always pushing us to be more than we would normally be. More than any other experience love carves away at us, like great lumps of marble sculpted into works of art. That, I think, is what they mean by "love conquers all". It doesn't transcend life. But it gives it integrity, a noble aim, no matter what the result.'

Leticia sat up and blew her nose. 'You . . . you think I'm fantastical?'

'I think you've suffered a great loss and, in your grief, you've tried to control what is beyond your control.'

He was talking in riddles.

'Which is?'

'Your heart, your nature, the very person you are. It's as if you've created a great big cardboard cut-out to hide behind.'

His words sliced through her.

She stared at the floor, at the ugly blue-laminate speckled tiles. 'I was just trying . . . trying to . . . I don't know.'

'Look at me,' he commanded.

She didn't want to but she forced her gaze upwards.

'You were meant for better things, Emily Ann Fink. For much better things than one-night stands and knickers. And I've got news for you: there's more love where that came from.'

'Yeah, but what kind of idiot signs up to be annihilated all over again?'

Leo grinned and put his hand up. 'Clap if you believe in fairies!'

She shook her head. 'No. I don't. I don't want to!'

'It's the way of the world; the nature of the thing. To sit out on love because you've been devastated is just bad manners. It's like refusing to play any party games because it's not your birthday and you don't get to keep the presents. And I know for a fact, young lady, that you've got more courage than that.'

A Suitable Client

It was early afternoon when Leticia left the hospital. She wandered, directionless, along the South Bank, not wanting to go home. Leo's words had pierced the fragile balloon of her pride and ego.

Then she remembered the card in her pocket. Taking it out, she opened it.

Dream with me. The Royal Opera House, Covent Garden,
eight o'clock tonight.

Her heart contracted. If only she could show it to someone; someone who understood her.

She would go to the shop. Sam would know what to do. Besides, she could check on his progress.

When she got there the shop was empty.

He must be on his lunch break, she thought, closing the door behind her.

Walking through to the back, she went into the bathroom. To her surprise, it was done. The plastic sheeting had been taken down, the floorboards replaced, the slipper bath was clean, taps polished, even the piles of grey dust had been vacuumed away. It looked as if nothing had ever happened.

She turned on the tap. Out came the water, clear and strong, no more groaning or shuddering.

It was finished.

Leticia sat down on top of the toilet seat.

Everything was in perfect working order. All the tools had been cleared away, even the dreaded tea mug. Sam was gone.

Of course, she berated herself. What had she imagined? He was there to do a job. Like he said, anything else was just him being kind.

She wandered back into the main shop. There were messages to listen to, appointments to reschedule, orders to check. Instead, she looked round at the beautiful furnishings, the cobalt-blue chandelier, the thousands of pounds' worth of exquisite fabrics.

Rarefied.

Fantastical.

This was her world, the one she'd created; a stage set upon which she performed like a magician, dazzling with a bit of silk and lace.

But who was her real audience?

She'd gone to all this trouble just to fool herself.

The door opened. A flustered woman backed a baby buggy laboriously up the steps.

She must have the wrong shop. Nevertheless Leticia held

the door open. It seemed cruel to send her straight back down again after such an effort.

'Thanks.' The woman was wearing a pair of orange flip-flops, milk-stained maternity jeans and a man's button-down shirt. In the buggy, a pink newborn slept soundly.

'Can I help you?'

'Bordello, right? You do lingerie?'

'Yes, but by appointment only. Actually, the shop isn't even open right now.'

The woman yanked her shirt closed where the buttons strained over her bosom. It gaped back open. 'I couldn't get through on the phone so I came down especially . . .'

Leticia hesitated, irritated. She didn't deal with maternity gowns; there was no point making something for a woman who was most likely going to shrink three sizes before the garment was done. It was a waste of time and effort.

She decided to get rid of her as quickly as possible. 'I couldn't help noticing you've just had a baby.'

'Yes?'

'Well, it's probably best to wait a few months. I'm only suggesting because the whole process is expensive and your body is bound to change.'

'Bound to change?' the woman laughed. 'I've been waiting to lose the baby weight for about seven years!'

Leticia smiled.

'I'm serious.'

Leticia stopped smiling. 'I wouldn't want us to embark upon

a long, costly process that doesn't really meet your needs. You're breastfeeding, right? See, I don't do anything for breastfeeding mothers.'

'Why not?'

Leticia wasn't in the mood for confrontation. This woman wasn't even a suitable client. 'It's just,' she sighed, 'it's just that the pieces I make are less practical and more along the lines of fantasy.' She reached across her desk to a small silver box. 'But, if you'd like to contact me again in a few months, here's my card.'

The woman took the card, and stared at it, frowning. There was apparently something baffling in what she heard.

Some people were so determined, Leticia thought, crossing to open the door. It was tedious but inevitable.

The woman looked up. 'What makes you think domestic life isn't a fantasy?'

'I'm sorry?'

The woman took a deep breath and in that breath gained about two inches in height.

'What makes you think it isn't the biggest fantasy going? Look, I realize that you're fobbing me off; I'm probably not rich enough or chic enough for you. But I spend all of my time in my nightdress whether I like it or not. And I'd like it if it looked nice. Actually, more than nice – fucking fantastic.'

'Look, I'm not implying—'

'Are you married?'

'No.'

'Have you got kids?'

Leticia shook her head.

'I'm going to tell you something that no magazine or novel or television show will ever let on. Love wears you down. We think of it as hearts and flowers and happily ever after but in real life, the things you have to do in the name of love kill you. I don't know what it's like for men, but that's what it does to women. You end up doing a thousand things a day in the name of love that you wouldn't ask a dog to do. And you never question it – not once. Why would you? It's love, isn't it? Then you wonder why you don't feel romantic. Why, in fact, you don't feel anything at all. I've been waiting for things to change, putting off my life till the kids are older or they sleep through the night or until my figure comes back, or my husband notices me . . . you name it, I've been waiting for it. And that's not who I am.' She gestured to her body. 'See this? I'm fed up with waiting. And I'm going to dress myself in the best bloody nightdress I can buy. So my question to you is: Are you going to make it? Or,' her eyes flashed, 'are you going to write me off as another fat middle-aged middle-class woman who will just have to mend and make do?'

Leticia stared at the woman in shock. Her first instinct was to be offended. But instead she found herself admiring the woman's frankness. It had been a long time since anyone had spoken to her so passionately. Plenty of women wanted a Leticia Vane original, but this woman *needed* a nightdress. And it had also been a long time since Leticia had produced something new or really useful.

'What's your name?'

'Amy. Amy Mortimer.'

Leticia picked up a notebook and gestured to one of the chairs. 'Would you like to sit down, Mrs Mortimer? Now,' she selected a fresh pencil, 'I want you to tell me exactly what your requirements are and how I can help you.'

Unusual

Rose felt unusual. She spent the afternoon playing trains with Rory, setting up track and, more importantly, building blocks the engines could smash into. It was reassuringly repetitive, like all games with small children. Yet she didn't feel comforted. She tried to cuddle him, but he wriggled away. All she wanted was to hold him; to be quiet, warm and safe. But he was intent on racing around the flat, ploughing into pillows on the bed. She was out of step, off kilter, even with him.

After a while, she pulled out the buggy.

'Come on. Let's go for a walk.'

She found herself strolling towards Jack's Café without even realizing what she was doing. Part of her wanted to go back in time, to the old and familiar. Or at least to have a good look at it again.

Pushing open the door with Rory's buggy, she was accosted by familiar smells – the warm fug of a hundred slices of toast, the enticing saltiness of piles of fried bacon and the extra-strong lemon-scented bleach they used to clean the tables and floors.

(She'd insisted on lemon; it was the only thing that seemed to cut through the smell of chip fat. How touching. They hadn't bothered to change it when she'd gone.)

All in all, the café seemed smaller but cleaner than she remembered. There was Bert, scrubbing the grill in the back, and another young girl, a replacement Rose, with black hair, too much eyeliner and a tight T-shirt that read, 'I'm no angel,' leaning on the counter by the cash register, ignoring Rose as she chatted away on her mobile phone. Here were the landmarks of her past; all safe, all intact. Relief swept over her. It meant a great deal that it was still here; something solid and unchanging from the life she'd cast off so freely.

Then she saw a familiar figure. It was Sam, staring into space at one of the far tables.

Rory squirmed in his pushchair and held out his arms. 'Down!' he shouted. 'I want to get down!'

Out he came, barrelling happily between the empty tables, collecting all the salt and pepper shakers and forming them into opposing battle lines. The dark-haired girl glowered at him, but was too busy planning the details of her Saturday night to do anything more.

Rose slid into the booth across from Sam. He looked up.

'Hey, kid,' he smiled. He seemed distracted. 'How's it going?' he asked, taking a sip of cold tea. Beside him, a pile of invoices and catalogues lay untouched.

'Great!' she nodded. 'Really great.'

'How do you like being an artist?'

'Oh, you know!' she laughed. Suddenly it was there again: the feeling of falling, spinning out of control. Turning, she looked out of the window for something to focus on. But everything out there was shifting too.

'No,' Sam said. 'I don't know. Why don't you tell me?'

Rose looked up. His eyes were kind, waiting. She never could hide anything from him.

'It's not like I thought it would be,' she confessed. Her throat tightened, as though she might cry. What did she have to cry about?

'It's . . . I'm . . . really, really . . . confused.'

'Well,' he concentrated on his teacup, turning it round and round in its saucer. 'That'll make two of us.'

'Why are you confused?'

Rory pushed a garrison of salt shakers to the floor. They rolled in all directions. 'Kabam!' he shouted gleefully, preparing to do the same to the pepper shakers.

'Stop it!' Rose rushed to pick them up. The dark-haired girl rolled her eyes but did nothing to help. Eventually Rose managed to slide an angry, wriggling Rory next to her in the seat across from Sam, placating him with an improvised game of building up packets of sugar for his toy train to run into.

'You were saying?' he prompted.

'I don't know what I was saying. What were you saying?'

'Nothing.'

They both watched Rory ram the sugar packets with a battered Thomas the Tank Engine.

'I want something,' Sam said at last.

'What?'

His fingers drummed the table, agitated. 'Something I can't have.'

'What makes you think you can't have it?'

'Because,' he forced his hands through his hair, exasperated, groping for words, 'because it involves . . . I don't know . . . making a complete, total arse of myself for something that most likely won't come off anyway.'

Rose thought a moment. 'Yeah. I get that.'

Sam was like solid ground for her; real. He always hit the nail on the head.

They both stared out of the window.

'I want something too,' she confessed.

'What?'

'I want to be a real artist, Sam.' She looked up. 'How crazy is that?'

The café was getting ready to close. The dark-haired girl was cashing up the till, Bert was mopping the floor. Outside, colour drained away from the sky and a cool grey mist rose from the ground. Street lamps glowed dimly in the dusk.

He shook his head. 'So, what are we going to do?'

Rory climbed on top of Rose, nestling into her lap; suddenly still. She stroked his head, inhaling the warm clean smell of his hair.

'Make arses out of ourselves, I suppose.'

The Opera

Dressed in a clingy black jersey sheath with a plunging neck-line, piles of black pearls wound round her neck, Leticia sat at her kitchen table, holding the anonymous card.

The performance was at eight.

It was seven fifteen.

If she was going to go, she should go now.

Still, she sat, turning the card over, slowly, again and again.

There's more love where that came from.

Great.

But did she want more?

When Olivia arrived at the Opera House that evening, it was closed. There was no performance. She'd gone to a great deal of trouble getting dressed, finally choosing a flowing dress of icy blue-grey silk, draped over her slender figure like water around a reed. She felt foolish, standing in front of the locked building, clearly dressed for an evening out, clutching a silver evening bag and cashmere cardigan. Passers-by seemed to be smirking at her.

Just as she was about to give up and hail a taxi home, a young man appeared in an usher's uniform.

'I'm sorry to keep you waiting,' he smiled. 'This way, please.'

Olivia followed him around the corner. The door to the balcony was open.

He stopped. 'Straight up,' he said. 'Sit anywhere you like.'

Olivia climbed the stairs. They were steep. Her high heels echoed on the concrete floor. When she reached the top, it widened into the balcony. The lights were on, the curtain down; she was alone. The young man had told her to sit anywhere, so, moving carefully on the steep rake, she walked down the centre aisle to the middle seat in the front row. There was a small box of Godiva chocolates on the seat next to her. The note on top read: '*Enjoy the show.*'

Almost immediately the orchestra filed in to the pit. They were dressed in street clothes. It must be a dress rehearsal. Moments later the lights dimmed, the conductor appeared at the rostrum, and the music began. Great waves of sound flooded the empty theatre.

The curtain rose. She was being treated to her own private performance!

Settling back, she opened the box of chocolates and bit into one. Dark and slightly bitter, its thin outer coating gave way; her mouth was filled with the perfumed sweetness of vanilla and violets. All around her the music swelled and grew, voices plummeting and rising, twining in and around each other in unrestrained passion.

Olivia was breathless from the beauty of it, from the blackness that surrounded her; the soft silk against her bare skin. Yet a single thought plagued her: if only I weren't alone.

Then suddenly she wasn't.

Someone slipped into the back row.

It must be her admirer!

Turning, she strained to see in the darkness.

Leticia was late.

She followed the usher, climbed the dark, narrow stairs, far below her the opera was already in full flight. *La Bohème*. Artists, poets, dying seamstresses . . .

There was someone in the front row, a blonde woman. She turned, nodded.

Leticia nodded back.

What was this? Two for the price of one?

Settling into the back row, she felt old, overdressed, irritable. Slipping off her shoes, she stretched out her toes. Her feet hurt.

Apparently this was the nature of the beast, the party game in full swing. A card, a date, the chance to meet some mysterious stranger . . .

The tenor launched into his aria.

And suddenly, very clearly, Leticia knew she'd had enough.

She didn't know what would happen if she went home, took off the dress and the pearls, closed the door. Maybe she'd start crying and never stop; maybe she'd never be able to pull herself together and no one would ever want to be near her again.

But she'd had enough.

No more strangers; no more pursuits or intrigues. No more clues, scrambling in the dark with fragments of the truth, filling the spaces in between with fantasy.

There might be more love where that came from, but she didn't want it on the same terms any more.

Far below her, on stage, Mimi and Alfredo clutched desperately at one another, voices reaching unreal heights of beauty and passion. That can't be love, Leticia determined. They've only just met; they don't even know one another.

Real love couldn't possibly be so shallow.

Hughie stood outside, tucked into a doorway across the street from the Opera House.

She was in there; his love!

And he wondered if his plan was working, if Leticia were delighted by the performance, intrigued by the clever notes, softening under the weight of his devotion.

Leaning against the door frame, he lit a cigarette, enjoying the torment of being separated from her, yet so close. This was what love was about: the pain of desire and longing; the exquisite mixture of agony and hope before the loved one appeared.

Then suddenly she did appear.

The balcony door swung open across the street and out came Leticia.

She was walking towards him.

Hughie froze. What to do? Hide? Run away?

As it was, he just stood there.

She looked up.

For a moment she said nothing. Then, a long sigh, a shake of the head. 'Oh, Hughie!'

Just by the way she said his name, he knew the gig was up.

'Hey!' he grinned sheepishly. 'By the way,' he quickly stubbed out his cigarette, 'may I just say how beautiful you're looking tonight?'

His compliment didn't seem to penetrate.

'Oh, Hughie!' she sighed again, a heavy, leaden sigh. 'Oh, God, Hughie!'

The gig wasn't just up; apparently it was over.

'You didn't like it?' he deduced.

Leticia sat down on the doorstep. It was dirty, dusty; smelling of Special Brew.

He settled gingerly next to her. 'My darling?'

'Fuck, Hughie!' She looked at him, her brown eyes sad. For the first time, she looked older; tired; properly in her thirties. 'Fuck!' she said again, shaking her head.

And then, to his horror, she began to cry.

'Fuck, Hughie! Fuck!'

Hughie sat next to her, rubbing her back; completely out

of his depth. He was frightened, disappointed, confused. What had happened? How could it have gone so wrong? He'd done everything Flick said.

And it had failed; spectacularly.

A couple of guys lurched out of the pub across the road, laughing too loudly. He wished they were somewhere more private.

Black tears rolled down Leticia's face. 'Oh, God, Hughie! What a cunt I am!'

'No, no, of course not!'

'Yes.' She looked up at him; her nose was running. He wanted her to do something about it but he wasn't sure how to weave it into the conversation. Was a gesture too obvious?

As it happened, she took a tissue out of her evening bag and blew hard. She made a kind of trumpeting noise; one that wasn't entirely consistent with his image of her.

'Fuck!' she said again, closing her eyes.

This seemed to be the crux of the conversation.

'But what's wrong?'

She rubbed her eyes with her fists, two grey mascara smears across her cheeks.

'This . . . the notes . . .' She shook her head. 'What were you doing?'

Suddenly he felt as if he were three years old. Even his voice was small. 'Making you love me.'

She sighed again; again her eyes filled with tears. Taking his hand, she squeezed it hard. 'Fuck, Hughie. Fuck!'

And this time he got it; it hit him forcibly, like a kick in the chest.

They sat, holding hands on the filthy doorstep in Covent Garden.

It was over.

Well and truly done.

Liberty

Olivia climbed up the stairs. It was late; the house empty and quiet.

Without turning on the lights, she opened her wardrobe, began to undress. Light streamed in from the street lamps in the square outside her bedroom window. And watching herself in the mirror, she unzipped the dress, slipping it down, slowly over her hips. She felt languid, warm. It crumpled in a silken heap at her feet. She stepped out of her panties. Then she was naked, skin luminous in cool, blue light.

It was odd to think of her body as hers. For so long, she'd considered it only in terms of what might please her husband. But now it belonged to her again. She ran her fingers over her breasts. They stiffened at the touch.

There was her vagina: pubic hair closely, neatly cropped, the lips visible, glistening. Ever since the performance began, she'd been aroused. It wasn't like her. She was normally so contained. But something, maybe the music, maybe the heady experience of being seduced by a stranger, had excited her and now, at last, she was alone.

Arnaud had bought her a vibrator; something pink, made of plastic. He was fond of props; fond of anything that made him seem sophisticated and sexually adventuresome. They'd never used it. He'd shown it to her, winked and leered a bit and then popped it, along with some other 'toys', into a drawer in his bedside table, where it remained untouched. She'd been horrified at the time.

But a week ago, she'd bought herself another one, from Liberty's of all places.

She'd been staring at it in the lingerie department for about two minutes before she worked out what it was. Handmade from clear, flawless glass, the thick, long shaft curved gently, with a dazzling crown of Swarovski crystals around the top. It cost nearly a thousand pounds. And try as she might to concentrate on floral cotton pyjamas, Olivia's attention kept wandering back to the display case where it sat in full view.

This fascinated her. Here she was in Liberty's, home of the Arts and Crafts movement and universally acknowledged as the perfect place to buy your mother a scarf, staring at a diamante dildo. The expense of it made her giddy; the idea of spending so much money on her private, sexual pleasure was wildly decadent in an age when decadence at all was difficult to achieve.

Blushing, she asked to see it. The sales assistant, brisk and businesslike, focused demurely on the middle distance as Olivia ran her fingers along its cool, smooth surface. 'I'll take it,' she said, surprised by her own certainty. And, as the assistant wrapped it up, she realized she hadn't been that exposed in front of anyone before.

Now she pulled the box out from its hiding place under the bed and unwrapped it from the tissue paper. And, retrieving the Philippe Starck Ghost chair, she positioned it in front of the full-length mirror, sat down, and spread her legs.

Here were her breasts, her thighs, the round slope of her tummy and her vagina, open wide for all to see. For a moment her mother's voice sounded in her head. 'A lady always sits with her legs together! What if someone should see your panties?' Implicit in her mother's tone was the assumption that they would be dirty.

What if someone did see?

Olivia thought of the sales assistant. She'd known exactly what Olivia would use it for.

She spread her legs wider.

What if everyone could see?

The cool crystal slid inside.

She had pornographic longings. She'd had them for ages. Unbecoming, unladylike, animalistic. Desires she'd never shown anyone.

And now she was acting on them, fucking herself in full view.

Was she disgusting?

Or was she sexy, real, alive?

She threw her head back. Her mouth was dry; beads of

sweat formed on the backs of her thighs and between her shoulder blades. Her mind was besieged with images.

She was surrounded. There was a crowd of men, dressed in suits, watching her, their breaths shallow with desire. Then they disappeared, melting away.

And now they were women – two beautiful, naked brunettes with soft, round breasts. They were touching her skin . . . peeling away the layers of her clothes. Moving slowly, languidly, their warm, wet tongues licking her . . .

She stiffened.

No.

Stop.

Olivia tried to morph them back into men. Young men, dancers perhaps, lean and muscular, arms encircling her, rigid, rubbing against her. Now their fingers were working their way under her skirt . . . large, male hands, thick, strong fingers . . . but the image wouldn't stick.

The women were back again.

They were dressed in tight black YSL skirts and expensive high-heeled shoes, leaning back into a gold damask sofa. Only now they had shiny black bobs, like the mysterious girl in the back of the theatre. The buttons of their silk blouses were undone. They were playing coyly, rubbing each other's nipples until they were stiff.

Her desire grew.

Smiling, they pulled up their skirts. The tops of their white thighs gave way to dark curls of hair.

She bit into her lower lip with a groan.

'Can you see?' they teased, fingers straying into the swollen pink flesh. 'Arnaud might be anywhere and here we are, begging you!'

The overwhelming tide of orgasm threatened.

OK. Stop!

Stop!

Men!

Sex is about MEN! Olivia reminded herself.

And once more, she tried to force a male presence back into her fantasy. A man on the sofa, trousers open, enormous, red cock ... OK, huge, unreal cock ... maybe he's masturbating ... what about a dog? Another man? Three?

'Can you see our pussies?' They were back again.

The big-cocked men vanished.

'Yes,' she whispered to her imaginary temptresses. 'Yes, yes!'

One after the other, she kissed them. She was the dominant one, the one forcing their legs apart, burying her face between their perfumed thighs. They arched their backs and sighed. And Olivia Elizabeth Annabelle Bourgalt du Coudray, possessed with lust, dripping with sweat, and thrusting a thousand-pound dildo, devoured her fantasy lovers with a hunger she could no longer control.

She came.

It was all over. She was back; breathless; a little cold; alone. She pushed her hair off her face.

Her first impulse was to feel silly or ashamed. But to her surprise, the biggest sensation was one of relief.

Perhaps it was all for the best, she thought, unsticking herself from the plastic chair, if Arnaud and she no longer shared a room.

She stood up.

And taking the crystal dildo and her imaginary lovers with her, she climbed beneath the covers of her enormous, empty marital bed.

Meanwhile, back in the less fashionable districts of South London, Jonathan Mortimer was having a dream. There were approximately ten minutes between the time when either the baby, the three-year-old or the six-year-old would wake in the night and want to be held, fed, changed or comforted. And in this time, Jonathan had a vision of a life, different from the Victorian fantasy that both he and Amy had originally imagined, but satisfying nevertheless.

In this dream, he saw himself in the kitchen, with an apron on. Normally this would've disturbed him, but this was no girlie number, but a clean solid masculine strip of white cloth, knotted roughly around his waist, Gordon Ramsay style.

And Jonathan was making something.

With his hands.

Anyone who has spent their days in front of a computer or with their ear attached to a phone will be familiar with the novelty of using one's hands in a constructive way. Jonathan felt useful and industrious. And the kitchen was filled with warmth and peace; sunlight filtered in through windows high above; counter tops were clean and orderly. Jonathan knew exactly why he was here and what he was doing – a feeling that he hadn't had in his waking life for years.

Amy walked in, with a bag in her hand. He knew she was leaving. But it wasn't a bad thing. No distress. She even kissed him goodbye. Then something truly wonderful happened. The most amazing smell filled the house. Even in his sleep, his mouth watered and Jonathan realized he was baking bread. He opened the oven, but instead of hot loaves, out popped his children, one after the other, laughing and merry, like characters out of a Grimm fairy tale.

Then the baby cried and he woke up.

But even as he sat in the dark, cradling his tiny daughter, a feeling of profound contentment persisted.

If only he could hold on to that feeling – that sense of usefulness, of being present.

Pressing his lips to his now sleeping daughter's head, he wondered how difficult it was to make bread.

Professional

Flick was having a cup of tea when Hughie arrived at the flat the next morning.

'Oh, good!' She put her cup down, referring to a list on her desk. 'I've got some errands for you to run. Our mark is bubbling along nicely. And I'm very pleased with you, Hughie,' she smiled. 'You're coming along nicely too.'

'Hum.'

'Now, there's a specialist bookshop in Curzon Street. I've asked them to set something aside for me and I want you to collect it, please.' She looked up, frowned. 'Hughie, you haven't shaved!'

Skulking around the edge of the room, staring at his shoes, Hughie dug his hands even further into his pockets. 'I forgot. What do you want me to get?'

'A book.' Flick took off her reading glasses. 'What's got into you today?'

'Nothing.'

'Bollocks. I'm not blind. Sit down, Hughie.'

Sighing listlessly, he dragged himself over to a chair.

Flick folded her hands in front of her on the desk. 'What's going on?'

'It's just . . .' he shrugged his shoulders, crossed his legs, jogged his foot up and down in frustration, 'I don't get this.'

'Get what?'

'What we do – what this is all about! I mean, it's not like it actually works or anything!'

She looked at him, hard. 'How would you know?'

Eyes back on the floor, he nibbled his nails. 'I don't know,' he mumbled.

'Hughie?'

He crossed his arms defensively.

'Hughie, have you been practising our methods on an un-authorized mark, by any chance?'

'So what if I have?' he challenged. Bouncing up, he paced the floor. 'It doesn't work! What's the whole point of this stupid, useless profession if it doesn't even work!'

She took a deep breath. He was always going to be a bit of a wild card.

'It depends on what you mean by work,' she said after a moment.

Suddenly his defences crumbled. He looked crushed, all puppy-dog eyes. 'She doesn't love me.'

Flick crossed, shut the door then perched on the corner of her desk, trying to decide if she should lecture him or not and, more importantly, if it would penetrate.

'It didn't work,' he muttered again, sinking back into his chair, deflated and despondent.

Flick was silent. There were platitudes, promises, dozens of clichés . . . none of these would ease his pain.

'No, it doesn't do that, Hughie. In the same way that a wedding ring is not a marriage, a Cyrano is not a relationship. So you're right, it doesn't work.'

'So why do we even bother?'

'For the same reason that Tiffany's still sell rings: because people want them. People want romance. It's not love but it's a light glimmering in the darkness when love feels forgotten. Besides,' her face softened, 'where would any of us be without it?'

'I thought if I could do it properly, do all the right things, prove to her that I cared . . .' His voice trailed off.

'Well,' her tone was almost brisk, 'you gave it a shot.'

'What does that mean?' He was offended.

'It means you're the kind of guy who gives life a try. That's going to stand you in good stead.'

'Great.' He kicked the side of the chair petulantly.

'Do you know where our real strength lies?' she continued. 'I mean, as professionals?'

He shook his head.

'We're not in love, Hughie. That makes it a hell of a lot easier.'

'Not today,' he admitted.

'No, maybe not today. But soon it will fade. And in its place, hope will return.'

He looked unconvinced.

'I promise,' she added, with a wry smile.

Flick's smiles were infectious. 'Thanks for not telling me off.'

'You're welcome.'

'So,' he sighed, pulling himself up, 'what was the name of the bookshop?'

Slipping on her glasses, Flick moved round to the other side of her desk. 'Heywood Hill,' she said, jotting it down on a piece of paper and passing it to him. 'They're holding a first-edition Pablo Neruda under my name. Oh, and Hughie?'

'Yeah?'

She flashed him a look. 'Buy a razor. After all, you're a professional now.'

Perspective

Rose walked up the front steps of the National Gallery in Trafalgar Square. The very magnitude of the place filled her with dread. But Olivia had insisted that this was the place to start. It was shocking how busy it was; full of children, young people, tourists. Were they really all enjoying themselves?

Olivia was waiting in the main foyer. Spotting Rose, she waved eagerly.

'Are you excited?' she asked, coming over, planting a kiss on her cheek.

'Yeah, well . . .' It had seemed like a good idea at the time, asking Olivia to teach her something about art. But now fear supplanted enthusiasm.

Luckily, Olivia had enough for both of them. Linking her arm through Rose's, she gave it a squeeze. 'Well, shall we?'

Together, they made their way up the grand marble staircase. This was what art was about: vast, imposing buildings filled with large paintings of haughty women in white wigs staring out of huge gold frames.

This was the art that Rose knew. She also knew that she couldn't do it. Even before she got to the top of the stairs, she wanted to turn round and run home. Still, desperation and good manners forced her on.

'I think it's so brilliant that you're expanding your influences!' Olivia dodged a long line of German schoolchildren.

'Well, it's a little more basic than that.'

'I have to say, this has got to be one of my favourite places in the whole world!'

It would be, Rose thought. Olivia was probably a direct descendant of the women in the white wigs.

'Let's start with late Gothic, Pre-Renaissance.'

'Sure. Great.' Here was a whole new language barring her way. Already, she was defeated.

They turned into one of the side galleries.

Rose stopped.

This wasn't what she was expecting at all.

Wall after wall of the most intensely coloured canvases; the paint jewel-like, clear, vibrant, ornamented with gold leaf. These were all the colours she'd loved so much as a child – crimson, scarlet, sapphire blue, bright emerald green . . . colours she'd imagined you were meant to grow out of. But they were all here, glorious and bold, lining the walls of the National Gallery.

And the figures weren't daunting either. They were lively; comical even. It wasn't a glossy display of perfection at all, but something altogether more compelling.

Olivia stopped in front of a Duccio painting of Jesus raising

Lazarus. 'Here's a great example of both the strengths and problems of Early Renaissance painting.' She waved Rose over. 'Have a look.'

In one corner of the painting Lazarus was dead, then Jesus was arriving, then he was bringing him back to life with everyone rejoicing. Rose was relieved. At least she knew the story.

'The thing about these paintings is the strong narrative quality, which is all religious in nature. Remember, most people would only ever encounter art in a church. And of course, no one could read. So these paintings were vital. Look at how the whole story is all on top of one another, everything happening at the same time.'

'That wall's all wonky,' Rose pointed out.

'Yes, they didn't understand about perspective in the late Middle Ages. Wonderful use of colour, terrific movement created by the folds of the drapery, but sadly, it wasn't until much later, when Brunelleschi made his famous scientific discovery about perspective and the idea of the vanishing point, that artists were able to use it properly.'

Rose stared at the painting.

'Vanishing point?'

'Yes. Now, if you compare it to this one . . .'

But Rose didn't move.

'Are you sure?' What Olivia was saying didn't make sense.

'Sure about what?'

'Well,' Rose concentrated, 'if he can't paint perspective, how come he can paint the wall from all those different angles? I mean, he can do it, right?'

Olivia tilted her head to one side. 'Well . . .'

'Maybe he just doesn't want to.'

'What do you mean?'

'I don't know.' Rose shrugged her shoulders. 'It's just, maybe it's sort of like a comic book.'

'A comic book.' Olivia was clearly not impressed.

'Yeah. You know how in a comic book they divide the page up into blocks so that the whole story can be on one page? Well, this looks the same. What if they're not trying to make you think about what great artists they are but about the story? Which, you have to admit, is pretty cool – guy raises the dead and all.'

Olivia tried to explain it more clearly this time. 'It's a well-known fact, Red, that Brunelleschi's system of linear perspective altered the entire course of art and architecture—'

'Yes, I'm sure,' Rose cut her off, 'I'm not saying it didn't. But couldn't it also be true that there's something else going on too?'

Olivia sighed. (She was meant to be the authority here.) 'I suppose so.'

'I mean, in a weird way, there's something completely real about it, isn't there? After all, people think these stories are true, right? And when I remember things, I don't remember it all in chronological order. I remember it all at once, jumbled, as if it were happening all at the same time.'

'Yes . . .'

It had been a long time, maybe years, since Olivia had really looked at the Duccio. She remembered seeing it for the first time on a slide in an art-history lecture, absorbing the opinions of her tutor unquestioningly; the same ones she was offering up to Red now.

She turned back to the painting.

'Well, I guess that's a valid way of looking at it,' she admitted slowly.

'It's really cool,' Rose decided.

She wandered into the next room and Olivia trailed in after her.

There was a Piero Della Francesca 'Madonna and Child' on the wall opposite.

Rose sat down on the wooden bench in front of it.

She'd always imagined real art to be lofty and difficult; that you needed to be an intellectual to grasp its meaning. But here was a scene she understood perfectly.

The Madonna was as young as she'd been when she had Rory. She glowed with quiet self-containment, a quality Rose recognized instantly; she and the baby were in a world all their own. That first year with Rory, they had been so connected, communicating with the slightest shift or sound. The baby Jesus was wriggling about, the way that all babies do when they're about ready to walk; Mary was having difficulty keeping him on her lap. And Rose identified the ready index fingers of all would-be toddlers, forever pointing, poised to poke at anything and everything around them.

Olivia sat next to her. 'It's beautiful.'

'Yeah,' Rose agreed. 'Which is weird, because she's really just a teenage single mother, isn't she?'

Olivia looked at her in surprise. She'd never imagined the age of the Madonna or her circumstances. She hadn't bothered to translate them into present-tense reality. The image had always been distant, twee even; the stuff of Christian chocolate-box sentiment.

But Rose couldn't take her eyes off it. Peace pervaded. The Madonna was beautiful, the baby Jesus was beautiful, the folds of her dress and the neat countryside behind them were all beautiful; composed. For a moment, Rose felt part of the same vision, as if something of the same thread of beauty ran through her own life, if only she could see it.

'She's not ashamed.'

Olivia looked closely at her. 'No. Not at all.'

'That's how I feel. All the time.'

The sudden intimacy startled Olivia. Here was a young woman whose circumstances couldn't be more different from her own – with youth, talent, a blossoming career and a beautiful child – but wasn't that the way she felt too?

A great feeling of protectiveness and closeness welled up inside her.

Tour groups came and went, streams of people drifting along.

'Do you think the painter used models?' Rose asked after a while.

'Most certainly.'

'I wonder if that was her baby. What do you think?'

'Oh, yes,' Olivia decided, a whole story unfolding in her head of the painter's secret muse and their illegitimate child.

She wondered how many Madonnas in history were modelled on the features of wayward young women?

It made her smile.

How could she have missed the fact that the most painted motif of all time was of a teenage single parent? A woman whose life had undoubtedly strayed a long way from her childhood hopes and dreams. Yet here she was, offered as a radiant symbol of eternal serenity.

Maybe you don't get to be loving, accepting and calm until you've understood what it is to lose your childhood dreams.

They sat a while.

Rose turned to the painting opposite.

It was the 'Martyrdom of St Sebastian'.

'Look!'

'What?'

'God, that's so weird! I mean, how can a young man, hands and feet all tied up and with arrows sticking out of him, be beautiful? But look!'

'I don't know,' Olivia admitted.

And she experienced something she hadn't felt in a long time: wonder.

The gallery she knew so well was suddenly fresh and new. She didn't have the answers; they weren't to be found in a stack of art-history books. That filled her with hope. Life had expanded; she was no longer so frightened that everything had to be nailed down, explained away.

And wasn't that perspective too?

Different from Brunelleschi and his mathematical formulations, a great deal more comic book and wonky, but also somehow more real.

Two for the Price of One

Henry was waiting outside Graff when Hughie arrived.

'I'd nearly given up on you!' Henry said, slapping him on the back. 'Where have you been?'

Hughie sighed. 'To be honest, there's no point even going in. I'm not going to buy the earrings now.'

'Why? What's happened?'

'She doesn't love me,' he confessed, miserably.

'Nonsense! You've had a tiff, that's all. Nothing an expensive gift can't fix.' He steered Hughie towards the door. 'Besides, we're here now and I suppose I'd better price a few engagement rings myself.'

'Really?' Had it gone that far, that quickly? 'How is the widow Finegold?'

(Henry had recently been assigned to flirt with a ridiculously wealthy, hopelessly frail older widow, Eleanor Finegold of Kensington Park West, who fulfilled all his requirements for a future wife, i.e. that she should be rich and on her deathbed. He was pursuing the matter with a great deal of diligence, if not gusto.)

'Oh, she's all right, I suppose.' He stared bleakly into the middle distance. 'If only she weren't so fond of chopped-egg-and-onion sandwiches.'

Hughie knew it pained Henry to do what he was doing. But at least Eleanor Finegold existed and had enough money to keep Henry outfitted in expensive face creams, Savile Row suits and non-surgical procedures.

'Shall we?' asked Henry, rallying. He pushed the door open.

There was Percy's assistant, Deirdre, poised with champagne glasses on a tray.

She smiled her ingenuous smile. 'Good afternoon, gentlemen.'

Percival Bryce bounced into the room, dressed in a particularly dashing ensemble of a dark grey suit, blue shirt and raspberry-coloured tie. A diamond tie pin sparkled in its silk folds, gold cufflinks gleamed at his wrists. He'd had his hair cut and smelt of lemons and lavender – a combination that reminded Hughie of lavatory-cleaning fluid but which was in fact a very expensive purchase from Penhaligon's the day before.

'Mr Venables-Smythe!' he beamed, pumping Hughie's hand vigorously. 'The day has come! The day has come! I'm thrilled! I hope you are too! Everything is ready for your mother's arrival. I hope she's still imminent?' he asked eagerly.

Hughie nodded. 'On her way this very minute. Thing is—'

'Splendid! Splendid! A toast!' he cried, taking a glass from Deirdre's tray. 'To love, gentlemen!'

'To love!' Henry took a large gulp.

'Yes,' Hughie hesitated, 'speaking of which—'

'Nice place you have here.' Henry stepped forward. 'Please, allow me to introduce myself. Henry Montifore. My young friend's asked me to help him choose a gift for his girlfriend and I assured him that, being men of the world, we could work out a deal.' A golden shaft of sunlight sliced through the window, bathing Henry and his smile of newly whitened teeth in its warm glow.

'Mr Venables-Smythe and I have already come to an arrangement,' Mr Bryce informed him, straightening his pink tie.

'Yes, about that,' Hughie began, 'see the thing is—'

'Ah, but there are arrangements and then there are deals!' Henry persisted. 'See, I myself am in the market for an engagement ring. A ring of considerable size, I might add.'

'I see . . .'

'When diamonds are purchased en masse, so to speak, surely prices become a bit more flexible. Now,' Henry strolled casually in front of the display case, 'my only question is, if I should need to return the ring for any reason, for example, sudden death, is there a policy regarding that?'

The shop bell rang.

Percy stiffened.

'It's your mother!' he hissed, to no one in particular. 'How do I look?' he demanded.

'You look fine! What's all this? A bit of a soft spot for someone?' Henry winked at Percy, who came over quite flustered. And, sensing the chance to build what is known in the business as a 'rapport' with the man in charge of the diamonds, Henry strutted over to the door. 'Wait there,' he advised. 'Allow me!' He pulled the door open, froze. 'Good God!'

He and Hughie's mother both just stood there.

Percival Bryce frowned. He pushed past Henry and smiled at Rowena.

'Mrs Venables-Smythe! Come in! Please!' He pulled her in from the street. 'No need to linger on the doorstep!'

'Hey, Mum!' Hughie nodded.

Physically, his mother looked the way she always did: dark, shoulder-length hair swept back by a thick black velvet hairband, surrounding an elfin face with rather sad brown eyes; a longish grey wool skirt, red cashmere jumper, the dreaded driving shoes and a very old Chanel quilted bag, kept because it was only just recognizably a Chanel handbag. But there was something terribly wrong about her; as though she'd been dismantled from the inside. She walked in, staring at Henry.

He, in turn, gaped in a manner Hughie wasn't entirely sure was polite.

All this was lost on Percy Bryce. 'You and I haven't met in a long time,' he gushed. 'I don't expect you'd remember me. My name is—'

'You're Hughie's mother?' Henry cut in.

For the first time in many years, Hughie saw his mother blush. Her face went not just red, but deep violet. She fiddled nervously with the frayed strap of her handbag.

'Hughie . . . how . . . how do you know this man?' Her voice was accusatory.

'We work together. Henry's my, well, sort of like a boss.'

'You're Hughie's mother!' Henry repeated.

'You knew,' she said quietly, 'about the children.'

'I knew about the girl.'

'Have you met before?' Hughie asked.

They both turned to him with stricken looks.

'Is that a yes?' he ventured.

It was an awkward moment.

And a long one at that.

'Yes, well, be that as it may! How about a glass of champagne?' Percy offered, nudging Deirdre forward.

Rowena took a glass, downed it in one. Her hands were shaking.

Aspects of Percy's romantic projection were definitely being challenged. Still, he forged on. 'Yes, as I was saying, my name is Percival Bryce and believe it or not, Rowena, I remember you from when you used to cycle into Tiffany's across the street!'

'Rowena!' Henry echoed, in heart-wrenching tones.

She looked at him with terrible sadness. 'Yes.'

'Yes, Rowena!' Percival broke in, ushering her towards a seat in front of his desk. 'You've come all this way. I expect you want to see these diamond earrings. If I remember correctly, you always had such exquisite taste and your son has apparently inherited it from you!'

He took out the black velvet cloth. The diamond heart earrings sparkled and flashed.

Hughie sighed. They were just as perfect as he remembered them.

Rowena Venables-Smythe sat in front of the diamonds. But her eyes were unseeing. The shapes and colours blurred, melting and separating as she blinked back the tears. The terrible tension that had kept her buoyed, bouncing bravely on the choppy sea of life, was suddenly dispelled. She was visibly sinking, right before their eyes.

'Henry,' she whispered, reaching out a small hand.

Henry grasped it and fell, quite dramatically, to his knees. 'My darling!' He pressed her fingers to his lips. 'My darling, darling girl!'

This was shocking.

Hughie was stunned, Percy was appalled. Even Deirdre was vaguely amused.

'Rowena! How many years have I waited to know your name! I could never have guessed it would be so beautiful!'

And it dawned, very slowly on Hughie, as all things must, that there was only one woman whose name interested Henry.

'Good God, Henry! You've been doing my mum!'

'What?' Percy shrieked, hitting a note not many grown men could reach.

'Hughie!' his mother reprimanded.

But Hughie was beyond recall. An unholy rage exploded from him. He grabbed Henry by the collar, dragged him to his feet.

'I thought you were my friend! But all the while you were deceiving me!'

It was a betrayal that hurt more than he could have anticipated. In truth, Henry had been so much more to him. And for this reason, Hughie punched him extra hard.

'Oh, my goodness!' Percy Bryce squealed. 'Fisiticuffs in Graff! This will never do! Stop it now!' He pressed a buzzer.

Henry put up no resistance and rolled, like a well-heeled rugby ball, into the feet of the security men who had vaulted up to the showroom floor.

'Stop it, Hughie!' his mother screamed. 'Stop it right now! I won't have you hitting your father!'

Everyone stopped, jaws dangling wide.

'My . . . my . . . my father?'

Even Henry looked surprised. He sat, rubbing his chin, gawping at both of them.

Rowena straightened defiantly. Years of anxious guilt and worry fell away from her as she spoke. 'Yes, Hughie, your father. The truth is, Henry and I met one fateful summer's day in the linen department of Peter Jones.' She gazed at Henry adoringly. 'Our love was like a lightning bolt: instant and uncontrollable. Despite all efforts to restrain ourselves, we succumbed.'

'Quite a few times, as I recall,' Henry mumbled.

Hughie shot him a look.

'And, although I did my best to forget Henry and return to your father as a faithful wife, you were already conceived. You see, my dear Hughie, you are the son of Henry Montifore, the only man I ever really loved.'

'But . . . but what about Dad?'

'I have every reason to believe that the man whom you think of as your father, who is, in fact, only Clara's father, is not dead at all but ran off with that cheap-looking secretary of his and is living a bigamous life in Australia. I'm sorry to break the news to you like this, darling. I had intended to lie to you for the rest of my life. I must say, the strain on my nerves over the years has been tremendous. Actually,' she looked up at Deirdre, 'I wouldn't mind another glass of that champagne.'

Hughie slumped against a marble pillar.

Henry was his father! And his father was not his father at all but just some man in Australia. Clara had been right all these years; they weren't from the same gene pool at all. The faded photo he'd carried with him most of his life, poring over, dreaming on, mourning, was of little more than a stranger.

Henry looked across at him. 'I'm sorry, Hughie. You must believe me when I say, I had no idea.'

Hughie tried to swallow, but his mouth was dry. He tried to speak, no words came out.

Henry crawled over to him.

Suddenly Hughie could see a thousand likenesses: the same blue eyes, the same dimpled cheeks, the rich abundant hair . . .

They stared at one another in wonder.

'Forgive me.' Henry touched Hughie's cheek tenderly, his voice rough with feeling, 'But all my life I've wanted a son.'

Hughie closed his eyes, feeling for the first time the warm hollow of his father's hand.

'Forget about it, Dad.'

After quite a few manly embraces and tears, and much to Percival Bryce's extreme horror, Henry chose to cement his utter happiness and the future of his new family by crawling over to where Rowena sat and taking her hand in his.

'Now that I've found you again, we must never be parted. Rowena Venables-Smythe, will you marry me?'

She sighed wearily. 'Oh, all right.'

'Percy, my dear man! I need to buy an engagement ring!' Henry beamed, rising from the floor. 'Show us something vulgar! And Hughie,' he offered Hughie a hand, pulling him up to his feet, 'now, I need your advice!'

And so it happened that Hughie found a father, Henry a son and wife, Rowena a husband and a very good-quality ring, while Percival Bryce found himself selling diamonds to the one man in London who had robbed him of the great love of his life, giving him a fifteen per cent discount to boot.

Domestic Harmony

'Be careful!' Arnaud snapped to his valet, Kipps. 'Not too short! I want body and movement, do you understand? Body and movement!'

Kipps nodded.

He'd heard the body-and-movement speech before – many times before. It was a great challenge to work for a man who wanted you to cut his hair every day; a challenge that Kipps didn't have the energy or desire to meet. Most of the time all he did was pull the hair a bit at the back, jostle the scissors around and pretend he was cutting it. (Pulling Mr Bourgalt du Coudray's hair was the only perk of the job.) So he frowned as if he were engaged in a bit of precision styling and gave Mr Bourgalt du Coudray's hair a good yank.

'Ow!'

'You need to be still, sir,' Kipps instructed, holding the razor-sharp blades dangerously close to his ear. 'I don't want my hand to slip,' he added smoothly.

Arnaud froze, a victim of his own vanity, while Kipps yanked away.

It was important that he looked good today. Hundreds of reporters would be gathered for the launch of the Nemesis All-Pro Sport 2000 tennis shoe this afternoon. The presence of Men's Top Seed Ivaldos Ivaldovaldovich meant that they were already foaming at the mouth for the Hyde Park event. And Svetlana had prepared a special treat for him afterwards, involving herself and two girlfriends.

But even more importantly, today was the day he would put Olivia back in her proper place and domestic peace would be restored. Jonathan Mortimer had provided him with all the information he needed to shame her into compliance. And even though the Dorchester was reasonably comfortable, he was looking forward to spending the night in his own home; firmly king of his castle once more. After all, it was the principle of the thing.

Finally Kipps stopped pulling his hair. He got up, flicking the flowing mane he imagined from side to side.

'Body and movement,' Kipps observed.

Arnaud couldn't see any difference, but he was damned if his valet was going to get the better of him. 'Yes, much better. Well done.' And he gave Kipps a fifty-pound note, just to show him who was boss, which Kipps acknowledged with a slight pursing of the lips.

It was important that he looked good today; in so many ways, it was bound to be memorable.

★ ★ ★

Jonathan Mortimer was slacking. He was meant to be wrestling the older boys into their school uniforms, and force feeding them cornflakes, but instead he sneaked into his study, looking up an online property service instead.

Increasingly this was his overriding obsession. How far out of London would they have to move if he wanted to leave his job and start again, some place new?

The answer wasn't promising. Would Amy and the boys be happy in Surbiton?

Was anyone happy in Surbiton?

And yet the fantasy persisted. Again and again he played out the scenario in his head – striding up to Arnaud Bourgalt du Coudray, quitting his job and then indulging in a detailed catalogue of Arnaud's failings as a human being. By now he could practically do the speech in iambic pentameter. But the painful truth was, he was trapped. Trapped into doing all sorts of unpalatable things for a man he abhorred, day after day, week after week, month after month – for as long as it would take him to pay off the mortgage, send the children to school, pay for their holidays . . .

He ran his fingers through his thinning hair. Maybe if he played the lottery.

'Surbiton, eh? I hear it's nice this time of year.'

He looked up.

Amy was in the doorway, wearing a fitted blue nightdress, arms crossed. She looked fresh and pretty. Somewhere at the top of the house, the boys could be heard causing untold damage to themselves and their surroundings.

'Sorry. I'm on my way.' He stood up, closing the laptop guiltily. 'On my way.'

But Amy stepped inside, closed the door and sat down. She looked at him; her eyes were very clear, still.

'This isn't working, is it?'

Jonathan sat down again. 'We're tired. This is a bad time. We should have this conversation when we're rested.'

'There's never a good time. We have years before we'll be rested.'

'The boys . . .'

'Yes, they can wait. They can be late to school. Believe me, their teachers will be delighted. And we need to talk.'

All she was doing was stating a fact; a simple, self-evident fact. It wasn't working. It hadn't worked in a while. A long while. They both knew that. But it was her demeanour that unnerved him. No tears, no shouting; she was calm, undramatic.

'It isn't working,' she said again, folding her hands into her lap. 'Is it?'

And in that moment, everything Jonathan had ever loved about Amy came into sharp focus. Her courage, her clarity, her resourcefulness. The way her hands were so small, and her smile lopsided.

He reached out, touched her arm.

'Don't leave me. I don't want you to leave me.'

This didn't have quite the effect he expected. Not that it was calculated; it was immediate and sincere. But whenever he'd come clean like that in the past, something had changed, shifted. Normally that something was Amy.

Instead she tilted her head to one side.

'We are neither of us happy, Jonathan. That's no big deal. But we don't even have the hope of future happiness. And that matters a lot.'

It was a wrecking ball, swinging out of control. The fragile balance of their life was being levelled by his wife's ruthless, accurate assessment. Jonathan floundered, grasping for a rebuttal of equal impact to stem the devastation.

'But I love you,' he pleaded.

It had once been the answer to all their problems, packing equal if not more weight against any unpleasant truth. Now it floated, irrelevant, a footnote buried at the end of a long, complicated passage.

By the way, they loved each other.

The plot lurched on regardless.

'Something has to change. And the answer isn't Surbiton,' she said.

'OK, great.' He was sweating. He always sweated when he was nervous. 'We can go anywhere you want.'

This had no effect either.

'Or nowhere. We can stay here. I can take on more hours.'

She shook her head. There was something of the Sphinx about her today; about her self-possession and containment. He was guessing at riddles when she already knew the answers.

'Do you like my nightdress?'

He blinked. 'Pardon me?'

'This nightdress, do you like it?'

'Yes. Yes, it's very pretty.'

'Good. Because I've been offered some work, helping to market these new designs. And my question to you is this: Would you be willing to cut down your hours and spend more time with the boys?'

Faux Pas

Checking the address Mimsy had given her one more time, Olivia pushed open the door of the tiny shop and walked inside. It swung shut and the noise from the street outside receded.

It was empty.

She waited a few moments then called out.

'Hello? Hello? Anyone there?'

No answer.

'Hello?'

Nothing.

She looked round. It didn't feel like a shop at all; she couldn't see any stock anywhere. It was more like a small, intimate turn-of-the-century drawing room. In fact, it looked very much like its name – Bordello. A little camp, slightly louche but intriguing all the same.

She sat down in one of the salon chairs.

Mimsy had insisted she book the appointment months ago when her whole focus had been on saving her marriage. 'Sex is the most powerful weapon in your arsenal,' she'd instructed. 'Get the wrapping right and who cares about the present inside!'

Who cares? She certainly didn't.

'Hello?' she called out again, irritated.

What a waste of time! Why am I even bothering to go through all this anyway?

She was about to leave when she heard something.

Walking over to the back door, she called out again. 'Hello!'

Then, her eye rested on something familiar.

A Smythson's cream-coloured card on the desk.

> '*Walk with me,*'

She picked it up.

There, underneath it, another one.

> *Dream with me.*

Then something truly bizarre happened.

Out of the back room came the girl with the black bob – the one who'd been at the Opera House.

'I'm sorry I kept you waiting,' she smiled. 'I'm Leticia.'

Olivia's mind reeled. What was she doing here? How did she get those cards?

'Why don't you sit down and relax while I get you a drink? You look like you could use one.' She disappeared into the back room.

Olivia moved numbly to a chair.

Suddenly all the pieces came together.

That girl is my admirer; she's in love with me!

Leticia returned with a tall glass of champagne.

'Here,' she handed it to Olivia and perched on the arm of the chair opposite. Olivia watched as she crossed her long legs. She was very attractive. Quite girlie. Leticia gave her a wink. 'Bottoms up! Well, have you had a chance to think about it? Do you know what you want?'

My God, she was direct!

Still, it was refreshing.

Swallowing hard, Olivia found herself nodding.

'Good!' Leticia had a low, naughty laugh. 'That's the way I like it! No beating around the bush!' She shimmied over to the window. 'Well then, we might as well get straight to business in hand. Have a good glug of that and then let's get you undressed.' She pulled the curtains shut at the front of the shop. 'If you're feeling shy we can use the bathroom. I've had it redone.'

Olivia just stared.

'I'll tell you a secret,' Leticia leant in. 'I've wanted to do you for years!'

It was difficult to speak. 'Really?'

'You've got a wonderful figure! I can't wait to get my hands on it. Now, what did I do with my measuring tape?'

She ducked into the back room again.

Olivia tried to unbutton her blouse but her hands were shaking. Try to be cool, she told herself. Act like you've done this before.

Leticia came back.

'Don't be nervous,' her voice was like velvet. 'Here, let me help you.' She began to unbutton Olivia's blouse.

The shop was dark and warm, sweetly scented of fig. She was so close, so beautiful.

'Do you mind,' Olivia's voice was hoarse, 'if we . . . if we start off slowly? It's just . . . I've never . . .'

Leticia's face was only a few inches from her own; warm breath, mouth soft.

'Anything you like.' She looked up coyly. 'I'll be very gentle.'

Olivia gazed into Leticia's deep brown eyes.

If ever she was going to do it, now was the moment.

And pulling Leticia closer, she kissed her.

It wasn't the first time Leticia had been kissed by a woman. Any girl with as much sexual experience as Leticia was bound to have a few female entanglements in her past.

It's just she hadn't been expecting to be kissed by the prim wife of a world-famous billionaire in the middle of the morning.

It wasn't unpleasant but it was surprising. For a moment, she even found herself kissing back. But when Olivia's hands began to stray, she'd had enough.

'Look,' she pushed Olivia away, 'I'm not gay.'

Olivia turned bright red. 'You're not?'

'No.'

'But . . . I mean . . . neither am I! Of course I'm not! I just thought . . . you see, I've seen you before and with the cards and seeing you at the Royal Opera House and . . . what I mean is, I thought that you . . . that is to say, I gathered that . . .'

The woman was babbling.

(I'm babbling, thought Olivia.)

The next thing Leticia knew she was buttoning her blouse, gathering her things together.

'I'm so sorry!' She was clearly mortified. 'I beg your pardon! I most sincerely apologize! I certainly didn't mean to . . . to . . . grab at you. I'm really terribly, terribly sorry!'

And with that, she bolted, leaving the door ajar and bumping into a lamppost as she hurried down the street.

Leticia sat down on the chaise longue.

It wasn't the first time one of her clients had got out of hand. The intimate nature of the fittings meant stiff nipples and damp knickers were all part of a day's work. And naturally, every once in a while, someone made a lunge for her.

Who would've guessed it of Little Miss Blonde Bob, though?

Olivia sat in her car, crying.

She'd sexually assaulted a shop girl!

What if Arnaud found out?

What if her mother found out?

How humiliating! Grabbing at the poor girl like that!

What was the social remedy of a situation like this? Send flowers? Write a note of apology? '*I deeply regret molesting you last Thursday* . . .' Were there any rules of etiquette for such a disastrous faux pas?

She stopped.

Faux pas? What a tiny, mewing little word!

If only it were a faux pas!

But it wasn't anything so trivial. Whether she liked it or not, it was a life-defining moment. The truth was, for a few brief seconds, she'd been whole; connected to a part of her that had always been free floating and unsatisfied. That was the real torment: not that she'd wanted it, but that she still wanted it. The encounter had only whetted her appetite. Visions of kissing, sucking, licking, biting filled her brain.

I'm a lesbian, she thought.

I'm just a great big, pussy-loving dyke!

And she cried even harder.

Speed

It was the end of the day when the bell sounded.

Leticia was in the workroom, making some final adjustments to the nightdress she was working on: another maternity model with a unique adjustable bra. If she could only work out a way to make the cups more comfortable without adding extra padding— extra padding being the one thing nursing mothers really didn't need. Then she might be able to send it over to Amy this evening, for a trial run.

Folding it away carefully, she paused to admire the crisp periwinkle-blue cotton again. Her regular French supplier had been only too thrilled to create a non-iron fabric in fresh colour ways. She'd imagined he'd be disdainful but his enthusiasm surprised her. It seemed she wasn't the only one who'd needed a challenge.

Turning out the light, she walked through the shop, opened the door.

It was Sam, leaning against a big black Ducati motorcycle. She almost didn't recognize him. Dressed in jeans and a black

429

T-shirt, his hair swept off his face, neatly trimmed, there was a different energy about him; a gleam in his eye.

'Hello,' he grinned, flashing a pair of dimples she hadn't noticed before. 'I was working in the neighbourhood. Thought I'd stop by.'

The door slammed shut behind her. She hardly noticed. 'Where did you get that bike?'

'I bought it. Business is good.' His gaze was unexpectedly bold; direct. 'Do you like it?'

What was he doing here, showered, shaven? Where were his tools?

She walked down the steps slowly.

'Seems a bit . . . what's the word I'm looking for? Not extravagant . . .' she caught his eye. 'Could it be rarefied?'

'Right!' he laughed, nodding. 'I see! You're not going to let me forget that one.'

She shook her head. 'Nope.'

He folded his arms across his chest. (He has muscles, she thought, suddenly disorientated to be so physically aware of him.) 'So,' he was all swagger and confidence, 'seeing as I'm here, do you want a ride?'

Leticia had never been on a bike before. She was wary of anything fast that wasn't under her complete control. Her face must've given her away.

'You're not scared, are you?' He sounded incredulous, as if she couldn't possibly be scared of anything.

'No. Of course not!' He wasn't going to get the better of her.

Strolling over, she moved a little slower, a deliberate sway to her hips.

'Sure,' she shrugged lightly, as if it were so much a part of the daily grind as to be boring.

He handed her a helmet. 'Have you ever been on a bike before? You'll have to hang on tight.'

'I think I can do that,' she said, fastening it under her chin.

He got on and she climbed up behind him, hiking her dress up around her legs. Then she wrapped her arms around his waist. It had been a while since she'd been that close to a man. The muscles of his back were strong, taut, and there was a delicious, mesmerizing smell.

'What are you wearing?'

'Something new.' He revved the motor; the engine growled into life. 'Narcissus. Do you like it?'

She breathed in deeply. 'Ummm.'

'If I'm going too fast, just squeeze, OK?' he called.

'OK!'

He accelerated and her stomach lurched.

They drove off. Leticia pressed against him, thighs against his. They sped, ducking through traffic, with terrifying speed.

'Are you OK?'

She swallowed hard. 'Fine!' she shouted back.

Then they hit the Embankment and Sam really opened it up. The Houses of Parliament, Westminster Bridge, Downing Street, flashed past, the roar of the motor stopping people in their tracks.

She gripped tighter and closed her eyes. Suddenly they were flying, slicing through the wind; euphoria replaced fear. She was laughing, with a freedom she hadn't felt since she was a child. It was dangerous. But she was safe. Sam wouldn't let her fall.

All too soon they pulled back up in front of the shop, the ride was over.

He turned off the engine.

'You can let go now,' he reminded her softly.

'Oh, sure.'

She climbed down, legs surprisingly shaky.

'Here!' He reached out an arm to steady her. 'So, what do you think?'

It was a ridiculous feeling: physical, light-headed, like a fairground ride. 'Worth every penny!' She laughed again, pulling off the helmet. 'Oh, God!' She fussed with her hair. 'Do I look a wreck?'

'No,' his eyes fixed on hers. 'You're beautiful.'

A Deadly Virus

Valentine sat on the other side from Hughie of the vast mahogany desk in his office, hands gripped in front of him. Flick hovered nervously behind him, arms folded across her chest, lips pursed tightly together. It was an all-too-familiar scenario in Hughie's life. He'd sat across from countless glowering headmasters and employers over the years; each major chapter in his life had drawn to a close with a variation on the scene they were about to play out now. And, a little like falling down the stairs, the trick was, he'd found, to give way and relax; the floppier and more compliant, the less bruising afterwards.

Valentine exhaled through his nose like a bull. 'Hughie, is it true that Henry has just become engaged to your mother?'

'Yes, sir.'

'And that Marco has been pursuing your sister?'

'Well . . .'

'Do you realize he's resigned? Says he's in love with her?'

'My sister?' He shook his head. 'That's not possible, sir.'

'Can you spot a trend, Hughie? A common thread? Or is it necessary for me to spell it out to you?'

'Well,' Hughie was still struggling with the idea of Marco and Clara, 'there's a lot going on there.'

'No, Hughie, there's a lot of *you* going on there. Out of four employees, two have been completely corrupted by your presence. Two solid, dependable, extremely talented men have been, in only a few short weeks, altered beyond all recognition just by your proximity.'

'Thank you, sir.'

Valentine banged his fist on the table. 'It is not a compliment, Hughie! It is a very serious charge!'

Flick touched his arm. 'Valentine . . .'

His eyes flashed, nostrils flared.

She let go.

'You blame me for them falling in love?' Hughie asked.

'I blame you, Hughie, for introducing chaos into this organization! And love is chaos of the highest order. We do not do love. We don't engage in it, we don't even pretend it. We flirt. That is all. We titillate and leave. Somehow you have contrived to add, I cannot even believe I'm saying this, an unwanted depth to an industry that depends on skimming the surface of human encounters. Before you came, my men were perfectly happy. But now they all want relationships! Intimacy! Love!'

Hughie sat forward. 'You think I have depth?'

Valentine stood up. 'Hughie, I have come to the conclusion that you are a romantic. And romance is a deadly virus to us.

Therefore, despite the initial talent you demonstrated, I find that you are constitutionally incapable of performing your duties. You are relieved of your position at once.'

Flick leant forward. 'Valentine . . .'

He glared at her. 'Please allow me to continue, Ms Flickering. I will require your watch and your phone immediately. You may keep the suits. However, in light of the considerable expense of outfitting you, I will deduct the costs from your pay packet.'

'Oh. And what will that leave me with?'

Valentine consulted a paper in front of him. 'Very roughly, you owe us £227.50.'

'I see.'

'Of course, I'm willing to write that amount off,' Valentine added graciously.

'Thank you.'

Hughie took off the watch and passed both it and the PDA across the desk. Then he stood up. 'I'd just like to say, Mr Charles, that in spite of my deficiencies, I've had a cracking time as a member of your employ and feel I've learnt a great deal. I'm sorry I led the boys astray. It wasn't my intention. And I suppose you're right; I am a romantic. The truth is, I believe in love. I like being around it, I like being in it.' He dug his hands into his pockets. 'Maybe I am a virus. Then again, maybe, some diseases are worth catching.' He held out his hand. 'No hard feelings, I hope.'

Valentine shook it. 'Good luck, Mr Venables-Smythe, in whatever it is that you end up doing.'

Hughie looked across at Flick. 'See you at the races?'

She nodded sadly. 'Or cricket, perhaps.'

He smiled.

She looked down at the floor.

Then reluctantly, he left.

'Valentine . . .'

'Not now, Flick!' Valentine sank back into his desk chair, head in hands. 'My business is in utter turmoil!'

'But it wasn't the boy's fault.'

'Please!' he snapped. 'I cannot abide any more discussion on this subject!'

'You're making a mistake,' she persisted.

'What I am doing is running a business which has been in my family for decades! I'm perfectly aware of what is right and wrong and the last thing I require is advice from you!'

'Yes. Of course.' She turned on her heel.

Walking back into her office, she turned off her computer, switched on the answerphone and collected her coat and bag.

Then Flick walked out of 111 Half Moon Street for the last time, closing the door firmly behind her.

The Good Wife

Olivia stood miserably backstage in the Nemisis 2000 pyramid, watching as minions wearing headsets and talking on mobile phones rushed back and forth in a state of organized hysteria.

Arnaud had sent a car. No message; no reference to anything that had happened between them. She was expected to be there, that was all. It was her duty.

So here she was, squeezed into the Chanel suit Arnaud had biked round for the occasion. She wondered if he'd chosen it himself. More likely one of his PAs had done it. There were shoes and a bag, coordinated but not matching. Beautifully tailored, outrageously coloured, it was the uniform of her class; just the right combination of fashionable and traditional. Blonde hair, smooth and shiny, neat figure, manicured hands, tasteful jewellery – no one would ever imagine she was anything other than the perfect corporate wife. All topped off with the tense little smile; back molars grinding together behind a quick flash of white teeth.

Ivaldos Ivaldovaldovich had arrived with his entourage, looking very tanned and handsome in his white tennis outfit.

Some marketing men were trying to show him the shoe with its exceptionally springy sole but he was in the middle of trading some shares over the phone and waved them away.

Olivia couldn't concentrate. I'm a lesbian, she thought over and over. I have to stop being a lesbian. What could she do? Cold showers? Maybe she could just go back; think herself straight again. Did it show? Could people tell?

Across the room Ivaldos Ivaldovaldovich paced back and forth. He was considered a great heart-throb in the tennis world. Nearly six foot seven, he was a giant of a man, and yet he moved with the natural physical assurance and economy of a great athlete. He radiated a magnetic, larger-than-life presence that was difficult to take your eyes off. And he was incredibly successful, reputed to be as ruthless off the court as on, in matters of both the heart and business.

'*Da. Da. Da.*' He paused to take in his reflection and adjust himself in his shorts. '*Da.*'

He turned, spotted Olivia and flashed her a wide Wimbledon Win smile.

She smiled back weakly.

Nothing, she despaired. Here is one of the most famous playboys of the age and I feel nothing!

Then the hairs prickled on the back of her neck. All the hysterical people on headsets paused mid-sentence.

Arnaud had arrived.

Strutting towards her purposefully, he looked older than she remembered and shorter.

She stood up, dutifully.

'Olivia!'

Why was he shouting? 'Yes?'

He grabbed her arm, practically dragging her around the corner, into a small office filled with spare sound equipment. He slammed the door.

'My God, Arnaud! What are you doing?' Struggling not to trip over a pile of extension leads, she shook him off. 'Stop manhandling me!'

He turned, hands in pockets. 'You look so nice, darling. Do you like your gift?'

Had he gone completely insane?

'It's fine,' she said, tugging the jacket straight again. 'Though it isn't really a gift, is it, if I have to wear it.'

He laughed, circling in front of her. 'You don't have to wear it. You don't have to do anything you don't want to do. But life is expensive, don't you find? Too expensive to navigate alone.' He was taking something out of his breast pocket. 'Especially if one has seen better days,' he added, handing it to her.

Her heart seized.

They were the Smythson's cards; her cards!

'Where did you get these?' she asked, suddenly terrified.

'What does it matter where I got them?' he shrugged. 'The important thing is that I do have them. And it looks to me, my dear, as if you've been having some sort of pathetic, middle-aged affair.'

Olivia stared at the cards, mind reeling. Was it Leticia, the girl in the lingerie shop? Had she gone to Arnaud with the threat of selling her story to the papers and he bought her off? Or had Gaunt been spying on her?

'You're wrong,' she murmured.

'Am I?' He tossed his hair back. 'My lawyers seem to think otherwise.'

'Lawyers?'

He came up behind her, traced his fingers lightly along her shoulder. 'Yes, you remember: lawyers. Men who take money away from unfaithful, ungrateful people and keep it for them-selves. Unless, of course, no action is taken. In which case, they're despondent. But marriage isn't to be taken for granted, is it? I don't know about you, but I have no desire to simply throw away the past. However, I think you'll agree, things cannot go on as they were.'

It was hard for her to think; even to see.

'Maybe we could have some sort of life together. Though to be quite honest, this is enough to have you out on your ear without a penny. Do you understand that? That is a point I wish to make perfectly clear: no court in the land would do anything else.'

She felt faint; sick. 'Yes, Arnaud.'

'Good.' He squeezed her arm affectionately. 'I think it's time you gave up the gallery, started taking your position as a wife seriously.'

She stared at him in horror. 'But . . . but . . .'

'Are you defying me?' His voice was low, disturbingly calm. 'Remember, life is expensive, Olivia. And you're a little old, don't you think, to be starting again. What are you fit for? Making coffees at Starbucks?' he chuckled. 'I'm being mean, aren't I? Forgive me. You could always go back home, work in the jewellery department of Saks Fifth Avenue. Now,' he swung the door wide, standing beside it like someone letting out a dog, 'go out front and take your seat like a good girl. As far as I'm concerned, this discussion is over.'

Moving numbly, Olivia wandered out of the office, through the clusters of people, all staring at her, towards the auditorium.

Arnaud watched with satisfaction as she nearly collided with one of the catering staff, serving drinks.

It had been worth it, every penny.

She was back. Frail, distraught; eager to please.

Of course, the timing was everything. His mother had taught him that. If you're going to humiliate someone, there's nothing quite like a public event.

The makeshift auditorium was full; everyone who was anyone in the London sporting scene was milling about, drinking champagne, eating canapés, working the press. A band played upbeat Latino dance rhythms while beautiful young women in spandex shorts refilled glasses.

Olivia entered unnoticed, stumbling over to the far corner and sitting down heavily in one of the folding chairs.

Betrayal burned across her chest; so much so that she had to resist the desire to double over. Her mind whirred. She was trapped. What else did Arnaud know about her? What were her options?

She gripped the cards tightly.

They had been magical; a passport into a parallel universe where she was beloved, valued, free.

Now they seemed tawdry, pathetic.

She pressed her fingertips to her forehead. She had to think; come up with a plan.

Suddenly the gleaming diamonds of her eternity ring caught her eye.

She remembered the day he'd given it to her, after the miscarriage.

It was late in the afternoon when he finally returned from his business trip. Lying on the bed, hollow with grief, she turned. He was standing in the doorway. And before she could even open her mouth, he'd produced the ring box from his coat pocket.

All the words, the tears, pushed aside to make room for a pantomime of delight and gratitude. He would've paid any price to keep her quiet that day.

It was always like that; would always be like that. The life her parents led unfolded before her, at her feet. The way was familiar, well worn; full of lies and deceptions; thousands of compromises all for a scrap of security; a band of hard, shiny stones.

Stillness descended; her head stopped whirring.

All around her, people were laughing, drinking; joking.

So what if she walked away with nothing?

Was she really about to sell herself so short?

Standing, Olivia looked around for the exit.

That's when she saw her.

Moving languidly, with a self-possession only the most beautiful people have, her sexual energy was enough to part the people around her as she slipped out from backstage.

He'd invited her. Right under her nose.

Olivia didn't need to be told – the dark-haired girl with the round face and the Gucci dress was his mistress.

But there was something more; she radiated a certain glow.

Opportunity comes in strange guises.

Slipping the cards into her purse, Olivia straightened her Chanel skirt.

And timing was everything.

Arnaud gave a signal and the presentation began. Throbbing futuristic music blared from the enormous loudspeakers. Lights flashed. Two dozen half-naked dancers gyrated out onstage and the disembodied voice of a famous actor boomed, 'In all the world only one can be the best. And only once in a generation does the best reveal itself.' The music surged and dancers flapped about in a frenzy of mildly pornographic poses. A huge projection of a tennis shoe appeared on the screen, revolving slowly through space. 'Today Bourgalt du Coudray Industries

offers you the rare chance to witness the birth of a legend –
the Nemesis All-Pro Sport 2000 Tennis Shoe. Not just a shoe,
but a whole new way of sporting life for only £299 suggested
retail price. And here to introduce this amazing new product
is the Men's Top Seed, Ivaldos Ivaldovaldovich, and the man
with the vision himself, Arnaud Bourgalt du Coudray!'

Arnaud and Ivaldos Ivaldovaldovich strutted onstage.
Instantly the press surged to their feet and they were engulfed
in a flurry of flashing bulbs.

Arnaud looked out into the audience of press and industry
dignitaries. There were so many more here than even he'd
anticipated. Beaming, he grabbed Ivaldos Ivaldovaldovich's hand
and held it high. The photographers went wild. He was at the
very centre of the universe; the all-seeing eye of the world's
press confirmed that he had made it once and for all. Never
again could anyone claim he lived off the money and reputation of his family. He was his own man at last!

'I love this shoe!' Ivaldos proclaimed, as was specified in his
contract. 'I will win Wimbledon again next year wearing this
remarkable piece of footwear genius!'

A roar of applause!

More photos!

Arnaud beamed down at the adoring crowd.

What was that?

His wife, waving?

He smiled and waved back.

Then, almost as if it were happening in slow motion, he

watched as she made her way through the crowd, through the sea of flashbulbs, towards Svetlana.

What was she doing?

Then something truly awful happened; the press turned the wonderful warmth of their gaze away from Arnaud.

Instead, the heated conversation between Olivia and Svetlana became their focus. And above all the noise of the crowd and cameras, the words 'mistress' and 'pregnant' hit him.

Ivaldos Ivaldovaldovich let go of his hand.

Once again he was caught in a flurry of flashbulbs but this time it was neither warm nor approving. A barrage of questions hit him.

'Is it true?'

'Is this woman your mistress?'

'Is she really pregnant with your love child?'

'How long have you been unfaithful to your wife?'

'Are you going to have it DNA tested?'

'£299 is a bit much for a tennis shoe, don't you think?'

'He promised me a life together!' Svetlana seized her opportunity, tossing her head back and pouting provocatively. 'I love him and he loves me! We're going to be happy!'

'That's a lie!' Arnaud protested.

'It's all true! I swear!'

Ivaldos Ivaldovaldovich stormed off the stage.

The cameras went wild.

'These are utterly false allegations!' Arnaud protested, grabbing the microphone. 'I would never be unfaithful to my wife.

We have a wonderful, solid marriage built on trust and shared values. This girl is nothing more than an opportunist! Let her say what she likes! My wife is as devoted to me as I am to her. Our marriage will weather this storm!'

He searched everywhere for Olivia's face in the crowd and he wasn't the only one. Reporters clambered over one another like insects, trying to find the elegant, betrayed wife in the hottest love triangle of the year.

But she had disappeared.

Olivia lifted the sledgehammer above her head.

'Cunt!' Down it came. Whack!

A fat-faced cupid sailed across the garden.

'Fucking cunting cunt!' She took another swing.

Crash! A dolphin split in two. Water shot out everywhere, spraying her in the eye, soaking the Chanel suit. And a crack formed in the gold bowl of the fountain.

'Cunt, cunt, cunt, cunt, cunt!'

Smash! Bang! Crash! Pieces of stone flew into the air, landing in the flower beds. She didn't care. He was a cunt of the highest order! Pregnant! There, right in front of her while he paraded his dumb blonde wife for the world's press!

She swung the sledgehammer hard, smashing the face off another ugly cherub.

'You fucking cunt!' she screamed, her shoulder smarting from the impact.

Then what was left of the fountain spluttered out and died.

Drenched and struggling for breath, Olivia looked up.

Ricki was standing near the far wall; she'd turned off the water. Olivia leant against the hammer, staring at her.

'Thanks,' she said at last, recovering herself.

'Are you all right?'

'No.'

They surveyed the damage. This was nothing compared to what she was going to do to his bank account, she thought bitterly.

Ricki walked over. 'Does it help?'

Olivia shook her head. 'Not really. But at least the garden looks better.' She was suddenly exhausted. Sinking down on the steps, she pushed wet hair off her face.

The suit was ruined.

Good.

Ricki sat down next to her. 'I'm afraid it's already hit the tabloids. There's a crowd of paparazzi outside. I'm really sorry.'

'Pass me that, will you?' Olivia nodded in the direction of the little clutch bag lying on the steps.

Ricki handed it to her and Olivia pulled out a packet of Marlboros. Shaking a couple out, she lit them, gave one to Ricki.

'Thanks.' Ricki took a deep drag, leant back on her elbows. 'How can I help?'

Olivia said nothing.

'It must be hell,' Ricki added, after a moment

'It is hell.'

'Heartbreak is the worst.'

'Heartbreak?' Olivia looked across. 'I'm not heartbroken. No, my pride is broken. My faith in humanity is broken. But my heart? Actually,' she paused, feeling the swell of something else beneath the pain and rage, 'my heart is free.'

They sat a minute, smoking in the last of the late-afternoon sun. It was quiet; peaceful; no more dribbling of the ugly fountain.

Then something occurred to Olivia. 'You usually come in the morning, don't you? What are you doing here so late?'

For a while, Ricki didn't answer, but concentrated, carefully flicking the ash from the end of her cigarette. Then she took something out of her pocket, passed it over.

Olivia's heart leapt.

It was a cream-coloured card.

'*Fancy dinner?*' it read.

She looked at Ricki in amazement. 'Was it you?'

Dark eyes sparkling, Ricki exhaled slowly.

'Would you like it to be?'

A Cold November Evening

Leticia stepped over the piles of paper spread out on the floor of her shop. Some of it was from Amy, who was busy filing through years of Leticia's accounts, but quite a lot was from her boys who were colouring in pictures, using Leticia's old scrap paper and best drawing pencils. They were good boys really, and they knew the drill now. Every Wednesday afternoon she would close early, Amy would bring them from school and, while she waded through the paperwork, they played. Then they all went out for pizza and ice cream.

Amy's organizational skills were nothing less than miraculous. Her involvement had transformed the business, in more ways than one. Of course, normally Jonathan had the boys when she was working but at the moment he had a big case on. And to her surprise, Leticia enjoyed having them around; enjoyed the fact that after years of believing there couldn't possibly be a maternal bone in her body, she looked forward to seeing them. And they wanted to be with her too; they trusted her.

Leticia passed Amy a hot mug of tea. 'So, is it a disaster?'

449

'No,' she took a sip, 'not a disaster. In fact, you have more money than you realize. You just have to stop spending it like water.'

'Ah. I knew there was a rub.'

Amy smiled up at her. 'We'll get there in the end. The new M & S range will set you back on track. You just have to be careful now. A few more beans on toast and a little less sushi.'

'Point taken.'

It was strange doing the new Vane Mummies maternity range for a chain like M & S; completely against her ethos. But after struggling to create a workable piece for Amy, she'd discovered she enjoyed the challenge. And she'd fought too hard to figure out the solutions of an elegant maternity nightdress (which were considerable), not to capitalize on them. It was refreshing too, to work with a team of people; others who were enthusiastic. After years of being entirely self-propelled, the support felt luxurious; she hadn't realized how lonely and exhausted she was.

Even Leo was impressed.

'I told you you were meant for better things!' he gloated, sitting up in bed, paging through the glossy new season's catalogue.

'Yes, but nursing bras?' She adjusted his pillows.

'That's how it goes, sunshine!' He peered over the top of his glasses. 'One minute designing them, the next, wearing them!'

She just laughed, shook her head.

He was ever the optimist.

Pausing to look over Angus's shoulder, Leticia tried her luck again. 'Is that Thomas the Tank Engine? Or Percy?'

Angus gazed up sadly. She was hopeless. 'James, of course!'

The door swung open.

'Hey, Johnny!' Amy climbed off the floor to kiss her husband hello. The boys clambered around his trouser legs. 'What are you doing here?'

Jonathan enveloped them in a universal bear hug. 'Got off early.' He smiled at Leticia. 'Hope you don't mind. I just thought maybe we could all go over to that new hamburger joint for an early supper.' He kissed Amy's forehead. 'I feel like I haven't seen you all week.'

Amy looked to Leticia eagerly. 'Is that OK with you?'

'You're welcome to join us,' Jonathan added. 'Goes without saying.'

'Perhaps another time,' Leticia smiled. 'I've still got plenty of work here. And this is a real treat – you don't normally get off early, do you?'

'Ever since the du Coudray divorce proceedings began, life has got a lot easier for me. I'll tell you, it's a hell of a lot easier working for the wife than the husband. Now, grab your stuff, guys. Who's this?' He picked up Angus's drawing. 'That looks like James, the red engine! Am I right?'

Angus beamed. 'It is!'

Jonathan rubbed his head. 'Brilliant stuff, mate!'

Leticia watched as they gathered everyone and all their stuff together and headed out to the car.

Closing the door, she locked it, pausing to pick up a few stray pencils from the floor.

Everything was different now, and yet, still so much of her outward life was the same. A familiar wave of grief washed over her. Taking a deep breath, she arranged the pencils back in their box.

She was unexpectedly tired.

Maybe she wouldn't work tonight. Maybe she would walk home instead.

Or maybe, she thought, pausing to turn off the lights in the main shop, she might visit her parents in Hampstead Garden Suburb. A bowl of hot chicken soup, crammed with matzo balls, and plenty of gossip was just what she needed on a cold November night.

She picked up Amy's mug and headed back into the workroom. Staring out of the window at the tiny garden in the back, already bathed in the darkness, she washed up the cups in hot soapy water.

I'll pick up some bread on the way, she decided. Now, to cab or not to cab? Instantly she thought of Amy's expression when she handed her the receipt and laughed out loud. OK, OK! The bus then.

Moving automatically, she wiped the counter clean, arranging the boxes of sugar, biscuits, tea . . . There alongside the expensive tins of Darjeeling and Earl Grey stood a great big box of PG Tips.

452

Life Jogs On

The ad appeared in the back of *The Times* just before Christmas.
It read:

> *Handsome, well-educated, outgoing young men required for*
> *daring new business opportunity. Please send CV and photo to:*
> M. M. Flickering
> 12 Summerhouse Drive
> London, NW3 2EZ

Hughie was sitting at his usual table, the one next to the
window in Jack's Café, armed with a pen he'd nicked from
Clara, his mobile phone which was running out of credit, and
enjoying a strong cup of builder's tea and a full English breakfast. It had been a while, months actually. But nothing had
changed; the food was as deliciously greasy as ever.

Spotting the ad, he circled it, and leaning back, lit a fresh
cigarette to celebrate.

A daring new business opportunity; just the ticket! And
M. M. Flickering . . . could that be who he thought it was?

A little red-haired waitress came over, handed him the bill.

'I say,' he smiled up at her, flashing his wonderful dimples. 'You don't by any chance take Amex, do you?'

'Sure.'

He blinked in surprise. 'Really?'

'Is that a problem?' There was something in the way she was looking at him that made him wonder if by any chance he'd rubbed her up the wrong way. She stared at him, hands on hips. 'I mean, you had intended to pay, right?'

Just then his phone rang. 'Pardon me,' he apologized, grateful to take the call. 'Hello?'

'Hughie, where are you?'

'Dad? I'm having breakfast. Where are you?'

'I'm at the church, Hughie.'

'Really? What time is it?'

'It's almost twelve. The rehearsal's in ten minutes, and your mother and I are expecting you to be on time. Are you wearing a suit?'

Hughie was not wearing a suit.

'The Goring requires a suit and tie for the rehearsal lunch. And I know for a fact that you own one. By the way, Jez is still knitting the wedding dress. Clara's put on a few pounds – too much pasta, I suspect – and he's had to expand it. Your mother is extremely distressed. It's all I can do to keep her away from the brandy. Are you smoking?'

'No.' Hughie stubbed it out. 'I'm on my way, Dad. May be slightly late.'

'You're the best man, Hughie! Really, the sooner you learn to grow up and act like an adult—'

'Dad?'

'Yes?'

'Nothing,' Hughie smiled, 'just like calling you Dad.'

Then his phone ran out of credit.

Two tables over, Sam was reading an email on his laptop from Ricki. She was in Boston with her girlfriend, meeting the family. He chuckled. They sounded a nightmare! Ricki was more than a match for any stuck-up American socialites but he missed her.

'Hey, that's a nice bit of kit!' Rose said, delivering his beans on toast.

'Yeah,' he folded the lid down proudly. 'Thought I'd splash out. Great for all my accounts and invoices. So,' he stirred some sugar in his tea, 'how's the course?'

'Great! I've got this fantastic idea for my end-of-term project. I'm going to make one of those blue plaques like they have on houses where famous people lived except it will say, "Red Moriarty works here," and I'm going to stick it on the front of the café. And then people will be able to come in and watch me work!' She looked thrilled. 'Don't you see? It's a living installation!'

'Or just another London café.'

'Oh, Sam!' She rolled her eyes. 'You're not even trying to understand! See, it's all about who we think we are; identity and the value of work; fame and our obsession with status . . .' She stopped. 'I'm wasting my time with you, aren't I?'

'Yup,' he nodded. 'I'll never get it. Let me know when you make something I can hang on my wall. Hey,' he laughed. 'I should've bought that fucking chair while Mrs Henderson was still alive!'

She swatted him with her tea towel. 'You couldn't afford it now! It went to a Japanese collector. It's covered all my fees at the Slade.' She stuck her tongue out at him. 'So there!'

'Order up!' Bert called.

Hughie counted out the change in his pocket, pulled on his coat.

'Leaving so soon?' The red-haired waitress was back; she plopped an order of toast down at the table opposite.

Hughie nodded to the pile of coins on the table. 'Seems I didn't have to resort to the plastic after all.'

'Humm,' she poked through, adding it up.

There was something about her, he decided. The colour of her hair, her delicate porcelain features; she looked like the heroine of a pre-Raphaelite painting. He wondered why he hadn't noticed it before.

He leant back casually against the counter. 'Would you like to have a drink sometime?'

She stared up at him. 'Are you serious?'

'Here.' He jotted down his number on the back of his bill and handed it to her. 'Give me a call. The name's Hughie. I haven't got any phone credit at the moment.' He crossed, swung the door wide. Cold wind rushed in, rustling the papers of the regulars. 'But I will have,' he assured her, turning to regale her with one last radiant smile. 'Soon!'

The door closed.

'Order up!'

Shaking her head, Rose slipped the number into her apron pocket, headed back to the kitchen.

Out on the streets of Kilburn, Hughie tucked the paper with its promise of daring future employment under his arm, scanning the horizon for a bus or a cab or maybe even a stray tie that he could wear to the rehearsal lunch.

The sun sparkled, clear and bright. The day beckoned, full of potential greatness and unknown adversity.

Anything might happen, he reflected with satisfaction, stepping over some squashed plums by the fruit seller's on the corner. Anything at all.

Meanwhile, in a comfortable corner of Mayfair, Valentine Charles was reading the classified pages of *The Times* with serious concern. Across the Channel, in the South of France, Arnaud Bourgalt du Coudray dozed in a bath chair in the grounds of an expensive rest home where he'd retreated after discovering his wife in bed with the gardener. While still closer to home, on the streets of Belgravia, Emily Ann Fink sauntered to her shop, the drawings for her new range of silk bespoke boxer shorts tucked under her arm, to discover that someone had left her an anonymous note.

So life jogs on, as surely it must.

But that is another story.

Win gorgeous lingerie
from
DAMARiS
'sine qua non'

'The fashion pack and celebrities are going mad for Damaris' latest collection' *Vogue*

One lucky winner will win luxurious lingerie from Damaris' couture collection, up to the value of £1,000. Five runners-up will receive high-fashion pieces from the Mimi Holliday range, up to the value of £85.

To enter, simply log onto
www.damaris.co.uk/flirt

Terms and conditions apply: see www.harpercollins.co.uk for full details.

DAMARIS

The ubiquitous trademark Bow knicker, with its sexy bottom cleavage and flowing silk tails, sums up the image of Damaris: cheeky and seductive but not gratuitously sexy. The customer is getting a piece of avant-garde, luxury underwear in the finest silks, satins, chiffons and even snakeskin adorned with gold lame, pom-poms, feathers and Swarovski Crystals.

MIMI HOLLIDAY

The diffusion line is a more wearable version of Damaris, using some subtle mainline twists but at more affordable prices. The twice annual collections are epitomised by Bardoesque structured Balcony bras and skimming hipster knickers. The designs, which flatter all figures, transcend all age groups, and come in silk satin and French silk chiffon.

Such beautiful lingerie deserves to come gorgeously wrapped and the packaging is as exquisite as the items inside.

Both Damaris and Mimi Holliday are both available online at www.damaris-london.co.uk

'Grown women have fought at tills for Damaris' divine lingerie' *Elle*